Five Seasons of Charlie Francis

ADVANCE PRAISE FOR FIVE SEASONS OF CHARLIE FRANCIS

"In *Five Seasons of Charlie Francis,* Danica Roache expertly navigates the complexities of existing as an Indigenous mother and scholar. Roache tackles complex issues of motherhood, racism, Indigenous representation, and life in rural Nova Scotia with incredible prose and exceptional wit. A remarkable story that I had a hard time putting down. A definite must-read!"

AMANDA PETERS

author of *The Berry Pickers,* winner of the 2024 Carnegie Medal of Excellence in Fiction

"Danica Roache's debut is a beautiful exploration of being a young Indigenous woman in Canada at the turn of the millennium. Roache tactfully portrays the prejudices and racism Indigenous people experience in health care and academia while also delivering a heartwarming and often darkly funny romance in the midst of tragic grief. Charlie Francis is a young woman who is ambitious, a little misguided, but doing her best as she pursues her dream of a PhD while navigating being a young mother. This novel is nostalgic and so authentic. I felt like I knew every character on a personal level and Charlie's experiences feeling like such a mirror is a testament to Roache's expertise in craft. *Five Seasons of Charlie Francis* is good medicine and Danica Roache is an author to watch."

DANICA NAVA

USA Today bestselling author of *Love is a War Song*

"Danica Roache's debut novel knocked me off my feet, helped me back up again, and sent me on my way enlightened, invigorated, and impatiently awaiting her next one. Heartbreaking yet heartwarming, funny and fearless, her pristine prose weaves the strands of several powerful stories into a beautiful, chaotic, and colourful tapestry. Brilliant. Danica Roache has arrived."

TERRY FALLIS

two-time winner of the Stephen Leacock Medal for Humour

"In this stunning fiction debut, Danica Roache has created a beautiful, intimate portrait of an L'nu'skw entering adulthood and the heartache and hilarity that ensues. Filled with humour and heart, *Five Seasons of Charlie Francis* explores how identity converges in personal and public history, in family and ceremony, and the sometimes surprising ways that we build a sense of home."

TIFFANY MORRIS

author of the Shirley Jackson– and Aurora award–nominated *Green Fuse Burning*

"A charming, witty coming-of-age story about a young, type-A Mi'kmaq woman making one of the biggest decisions of her life. Heartbreaking as it is humorous, the story pulls you in and does not let you go."

DAWN DUMONT

author of the Leacock-shortlisted *The Prairie Chicken Dance Tour*

Five Seasons of Charlie Francis

Danica Roache

Vagrant Press

Vagrant Press is an imprint of
Nimbus Publishing Limited
3660 Strawberry Hill Street, Halifax, NS, B3K 5A9
(902) 455-4286 nimbus.ca

Nimbus Publishing is based in Kjipuktuk, Mi'kma'ki, the traditional territory of the Mi'kmaq People.

Printed and bound in Canada

NB1786

Editing & Cover Design: Whitney Moran
Interior Design & Typesetting: Bee Stanton

Library and Archives Canada Cataloguing in Publication

Title: Five seasons of Charlie Francis / Danica Roache.

Names: Roache, Danica, author. Identifiers: Canadiana (print) 20250197650 | Canadiana (ebook) 20250197669 | ISBN 9781774714645 (softcover) | ISBN 9781774714652 (EPUB)
Subjects: LCGFT: Novels.
Classification: LCC PS8635.O1217 F58 2025 | DDC C813/.6—dc23

Canada Council for the Arts | Conseil des arts du Canada

Nimbus Publishing acknowledges the financial support for its publishing activities from the Government of Canada, the Canada Council for the Arts, and from the Province of Nova Scotia. We are pleased to work in partnership with the Province of Nova Scotia to develop and promote our creative industries for the benefit of all Nova Scotians.

For my papa,
I wish I could talk to you about all this.

Year One

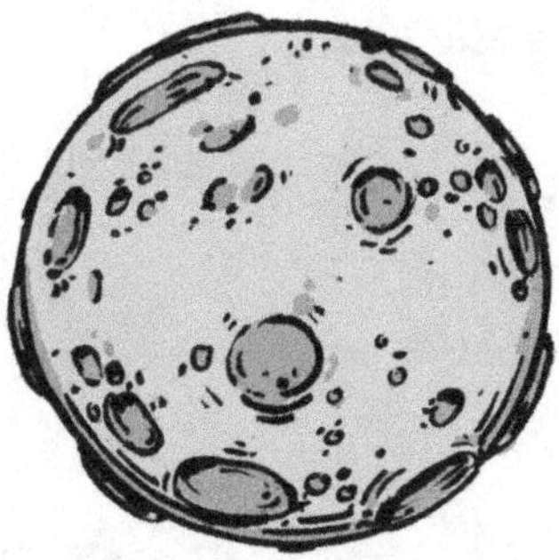

Wikewiku's

(Wig-gay-wee-goos)

Animal Fattening Time

one

"HE WAS THIIIIS BIG." DAD STRETCHED HIS HANDS OUT TO EITHER side of his body. "And the antlers. Biggest I've ever seen."

I laughed. "Bullshit. I'll believe it when I see it." A few years ago, Dad caught a bass he claimed was twenty-four pounds. When he weighed the fish, it barely made it past eight.

"It's all in tiny pieces now. Frank said he gave me a third, but I'm not so sure."

Every time Dad and his cousins killed a moose, he claimed it was the biggest one he'd ever seen. At this rate, next year's moose would be bigger than a school bus.

"Take a picture next time, yeah?" The wind bit at my cheeks and made the tips of my ears burn. I wish I'd worn a hat. It felt too cold for November. It made me nervous for the rest of the winter.

"Take a picture," Dad scoffed as Mom bounded out the back door. She took the steps two at a time and made her way across the lawn. Dad clicked his tongue and waved me off.

The pig Dad and I had just slaughtered was strung up in the barn, blood dripping into a basin below. My hands had shaken as I'd lifted the rifle. I'd known, with upsetting clarity, everything that came after. The startled squeal the pig would make before it met the Creator. The sound of it hitting the ground: a sickening thud, then total silence. Before the pig was even dead, I'd known the weight of its body and how it would feel to drag it across the cold dirt. I'd known the exact amount of pressure needed to puncture the skin; how it would feel to slit the throat and sever the head; how the warmth of its gushing blood would feel on my hands.

Despite knowing all of this, or maybe because I knew of all this, it never got easier. I'd stared down the rifle at the pig, trying to focus on the sound of Dad's cough and my own unsteady breath. Anything to distract myself. But the noises had reverberated in my ears long after the pig stopped moving.

The paddock gate slammed closed, and I turned away from the dangling pig.

"You guys see Billy lately?" Mom yelled, her voice barely louder than the wind.

Dad shook his head. "Nah, not since Friday."

It wasn't unusual for Billy to take off for a weekend, but he'd always come back by Sunday morning at the latest. He'd make some joke about being home for church and then disappear upstairs to sleep the day away. Billy had now missed whatever unspoken marker we all had, one that drew the line between normality and cause for concern.

"Damn it." Mom zipped up her jacket. She yanked her hood up; the matted faux fur framed her face and did a half-ass job of sheltering it from the November chill. She sighed. "I'll go check the usual spots then."

"I'll come with ya." Dad slapped the haunch of the pig. "This guy's gotta drain anyways. You all good, Charlie?"

"Yeah. I'm just gonna clean up."

Dad looked out the barn doors, then back toward the pig; he liked to joke that the government had tried to turn the Mi'kmaq into farmers and it hadn't worked.

"Not one farmer," he'd say. "Until I met your mother."

They'd been halfway to a homestead by the time he and Mom were twenty-one.

Dad pulled off his bloody gloves and tossed them onto an overturned bucket. He brushed his black chin-length hair out of his eyes, revealing streaks of grey near his temples. He was growing it out and it had looked ridiculous for months. Despite all our poking fun, he was determined to have it long enough to braid.

"Later, kid." Dad ruffled my hair, then tucked his hands in his pockets and followed Mom to the truck.

I was alone with the dead animal beside me; the dried blood made my cold hands feel heavy and unclean. I'd thrown up the first time I killed a pig. My brother howled with laughter until Dad called him over to slit the throat. Then Johnny had joined me, heaving over the paddock fence. He'd looked just as ill as I'd felt.

I grinned. It was a good memory, a funny one we fondly recalled. Was that psychotic? Probably a little.

The countryside was still and quiet. I could easily pretend there was no one else in the world but me, with my warm memories and serial-killer hands. Just a butcher on a backroad off the Cobequid

Bay. My grin faded as I held my hands out in front of me, unsure what to do with the blood and dirt. I hesitated before wiping my hands on the jacket Dad had given me to wear—my jeans were new, and I wasn't ready to cover them in pig's blood quite yet. Each year I told Dad it was the last year I'd help him kill the family pig, and each year I found myself back in this damn field with blood on my hands. I walked towards the back door of the house and wondered how many pig-killing seasons a person could endure before they went mad.

Sixteen years ago our next-door neighbour, Mr. Mackay, casually mentioned that raising and butchering your own animals was way cheaper than buying meat from the store. Dad had never looked back. He also insisted we use every part of the pig we could. I appreciated Dad's desire to not be wasteful, until we got to the point in the year where we had to eat the organs.

Johnny and I regularly cursed Mr. Mackay's name—that is, up until his death seven years ago. It wasn't that we were opposed to cussing out a ghost, but Johnny had said something spiteful after helping to kill the pig and the next day Mr. Mackay dropped dead. Johnny freaked out, convinced he had magic powers.

I kicked off my boots and left them outside. The bell above the back door tinkled as I stepped into the kitchen. I carefully peeled off my jacket and tossed it into the washing machine.

A large pot simmered on the stovetop, the smell of tomato and basil a welcome change from the metallic tang of blood. *The Vinyl Cafe* was on the radio. The kitchen counters were crowded with jars: spices, sugars, dried beans, mismatched buttons and bolts. There were three junk drawers and a cupboard filled to the brim with odds and ends that no one knew what to do with. Herbs hung above the sink, a braid of sweetgrass in the centre; the cupboards were stockpiled with canned goods, most of which had probably expired. The kitchen was chaotic and, if you didn't know its ins and outs, claustrophobic. But coming in from the cold, I found it warm and comforting.

I jogged up the stairs and paused in front of the bathroom door. At the end of the short hallway, Billy's door was shut. As a kid, I'd always thought Uncle Billy was so free and fun; I never seemed to remember the dark days or slurred speech. It's funny how the Billy of my childhood and the Billy of now were so hard for me to reconcile. Yet Billy hadn't changed. He was constant in his ups and downs, predictable in his inconsistencies. My uncle had these amazing highs that enthralled me as a child, but he also had lows that sucked the joy out of everyone. One day he'd be running around the house singing "Dancing Queen" at the top of his lungs, and the next he'd do something drastic like shave his head and disappear into his bedroom for days. His absence and isolation cast a larger pall than any fit of screaming and cursing he ever had. When Billy's bedroom door was shut, you knew to stay away.

Even as I stood there with my bloody hands, knowing his room was empty, the silence in the hallway felt loud. I pushed open the bathroom door with my foot, then used it to turn on the shower. Scalding water filled the bathroom with steam. I shimmied out of my clothing and flinched as the hot water hit my skin. The water at my feet mixed with dirt and blood as it swirled down the drain. I popped open the top of my mom's shampoo. It was different from the last time I'd been here. It smelled like old ladies, roses and musk. I scrunched up my nose and stuck out my tongue, gagging. She just bought whatever was on sale, with no regard for scent memory.

By the end of the shower, my skin had turned a bright pink and the grime underneath my fingernails had been washed away. My skin looked clean, even though what Johnny called "the death-bringer heebie-jeebies" still hung on.

I wiped away the condensation from the mirror, then bent over and shook out my hair, the ends touching the floor. I stood back up and brushed the hair out of my face, studying my reflection. Last week, Fiona dragged me to a party and some drunk girl had looked at me and asked, "What are you?"

What are you?

I knew what the girl was getting at, but I'd stared at her, hoping she'd realize her mistake. After a few beats of silence, she'd clarified:

"Are you French? Asian?"

When I explained I was part Mi'kmaw she'd asked if that was in Europe. When I said it meant I was Native, she'd looked disappointed.

"You don't look like an Indian." She took a sip of her beer. "Maybe wear your hair in braids?" she offered, like I'd asked her for tips on how to look more like myself.

One time on the playground in elementary school, just after summer break—my skin darker, my hair in braids—another kid's mom had told me I looked like an Indian princess, and then told her kid to go play with someone else.

I always seemed to be disappointing someone. I either looked too Native or not Native enough, though I didn't really know what that meant. My cousin Andrew was on band council and had blond hair and blue eyes. Did that make him less Native? The obvious answer was no. But apparently that answer wasn't obvious to everyone.

My hair, a few shades lighter than my dad's, was long, almost to my waist. Dark smudges underneath my eyes only seemed to get darker every year. I had my nan's high cheekbones. My dad's nose. I had my mom's hazel eyes and Irish Catholic propensity for guilt and self-loathing.

I scrubbed the towel over my face, harder than necessary. My body was soft. Rounder in places than it had been the year before. *This is fine. I don't hate it. It's okay,* I chanted in my head as I ran the towel over my stomach and breasts. *I'm not sixteen anymore. Bodies can change.* I ran the towel down my legs as I completed my mantra, then slipped into an oversized shirt and sweatpants. I hesitated at the top of the stairs and looked back at Billy's closed door. *I should check his room, right? I'm not being nosy.* Nan would tell me I was being totally nele'k, but Nan wasn't here right now.

The hinges on the door creaked as I opened it. The room was dark, the air stale. I threw open the blinds and cracked the window, careful not to disturb the rock collection on the sill. The light caught on dust motes in the air. Every surface was piled high with crap no one else would ever keep. Wrappers, manuals for appliances we no longer had, half-empty mugs of coffee filmy with congealed milk. The walls were plastered with posters from the late eighties and early nineties, relics of Billy's grunge-era youth. The bedsheets were discoloured and wrinkled, the duvet twisted at the foot of the bed. I drummed my fingers on the bedside table.

"Christ, Billy."

I tore the sheets off the bed and threw them into the hallway, along with his stained pillow. I quickly remade the bed with fresh sheets and one of the pillows from my own bedroom.

It still looked like shit, but I hoped it was enough to make him come home.

Fiona had crammed a stack of magazines in my backpack before I left for the weekend. Most of them were obsessed with Y2K. So far, I had studiously avoided reading about it; I didn't need another thing to get worked up about. We'd all either die or we wouldn't, or whatever it was people thought was going to happen.

"Read them," she said as I ran out the door. "I have many things I want to discuss when you get back."

"Yeah, yeah." I waved her off while I searched for my car keys.

"Pay particular attention to the article on orgasms," she yelled out the second-floor window of our building as I crossed the street. I turned around and saluted her.

I sat down on my bed now and pulled out the crumpled stack. The first cover featured an up-and-coming popstar I hadn't heard of. In big pink letters under her face were the words *What A Girl Wants*; off to the side in tinier black print it said, *how to have it all*, followed by *flat abs—fast!*

I rolled my eyes. What a girl wants is to not be bombarded with this shit daily. But who was I kidding, I'd read the article on orgasms first. I flipped to the table of contents.

The front door slammed and footsteps sounded down the hall. It seemed too early for my parents to be home from checking Billy's haunts. They must've found him—probably hungover and bitter, or maybe still drunk. Maybe he'd be happy drunk. Mom would still be pissed at him, but he'd be charming enough—crack enough jokes, say enough nice things—she'd eventually forgive him. He'd say "I can't help it, I'm Irish," and laugh it off like it was a genetic predisposition inherited from his ancestors and not rampant alcoholism borne from teenage substance abuse.

I heard Adam yell my name. Not my parents then. I didn't answer. He called my name again, more of a question this time. His clunky steps filled the silence as he walked into the kitchen. I placed the magazine on the bed and quietly made my way downstairs.

Adam was hunched over the pot of spaghetti sauce simmering on the stove, broad shoulders stretching his worn flannel and wild auburn hair sticking out from his backwards baseball cap. He hadn't noticed me come into the kitchen. I tiptoed across the room, reached up, and wrenched the hat off his head.

"Adam MacDonald, you get away from that sauce!"

He whipped around, one hand clutching his chest, the other holding a wooden spoon dripping the incriminating sauce. He leaned against the stove and panted. There was a bit of tomato sauce in his beard.

"Jesus Christ, Charlie, I almost pissed myself right here in this kitchen. On this floor." He motioned with the wooden spoon and splattered red across the hardwood. He put the spoon on the counter.

"Serves you right. Eating food before it's done."

"Charlie." Adam spread his arms out defensively, hands in the air. "You know I'm helpless when it comes to your cooking. I smelled it all the way from my house and I hopped right in my car."

I cocked my hip, his hat still in my hand. "Bullshit."

He laughed. "Yeah, you're right. Your mom called me," he said, leaning in to give me a hug. "I'm glad you're home."

Adam wrapped his arms around my shoulders and squeezed so hard I involuntarily grunted. "I mean I figured you'd be home soon, it being the killing season and all." He took his hat from me.

"Ugh," I groaned. "Those pigs are going to be the death of me."

"No, Charlie, I think you are quite *literally* going to be the death of them." He placed his baseball cap snugly on my head and smiled, his face filled with warmth. "Charlie, when're you gonna come home for good and marry me? You could make your spaghetti sauce every Sunday. Our kids would love it."

"Oh, I could, could I?" I tried to ignore the tiny ache in my sternum. Adam's words were kindle to a tiny, unspoken, unacknowledged fire that flared in my chest whenever the idea of motherhood was brought up. But kids weren't in my five-year plan. And the five-year plan was everything.

Adam's smile grew. "Yes, as the man of the house I would allow it." He crouched down and wiped the splattered sauce off the floor, then leaned against the counter again.

I smirked back. "Well then."

"Well then, let's pick a wedding date?"

"Adam, as domestic and quaint as that sounds, I will never marry you because it's an outdated institution and I'm not a piece of property."

He scratched his jawline, still grinning. "Didn't say no to kids and cooking though, did ya?"

"Are you gonna ask me this every time I come home?"

"Only until you give in to my redneck charm and rugged good looks."

"Okay, so every time." I took off the cap and handed it back to him. "You haven't seen Billy, have you?" Adam shook his head. "Mom and Dad are out looking for him." I worried my bottom lip.

"It seems like they're always out looking for him." Adam's gaze darted between my eyes and my lips.

"Yeah, well. He's her brother, what's she gonna do?"

"I know, I know. I'm just sayin.'"

I leaned against the counter next to him. "You staying for supper?"

"Why the hell else do you think I'm here?"

"To help scald and gut the pig?"

Adam made a face. "Charlie, you know I can't…I eat the meat, I don't kill it."

I was about to remind Adam that the pig was already dead when he sniffed, his brow furrowing. "What's that smell?" he asked.

I shrugged. Maybe if I feigned ignorance, he wouldn't realize the stench was me. I should've used my dad's three-in-one body wash instead.

He sniffed again. "It's like an old lady smell."

"Oh, fuck off. It's my mom's shampoo."

Adam grimaced. "It's revolting."

"Thanks for keeping me humble." I reached over and put the top back on the pot. "Now come on, you can hold the bucket."

The flow of blood had slowed to a trickle when Adam and I went to check on the pig. By the time we finished scalding and cleaning it, the sun had sunk below the tops of the trees, swathes of pink, orange, and purple smeared across the sky.

"God, I miss these sunsets." I took in the sky and the quiet and breathed deeply. Somewhere not so far off, the scent of burning wood from a neighbour's wood stove wove together with the cool freshness of the evening. Adam stood beside me, a large white bucket in his arms, and looked like he was going to be sick. I'd been butchering pigs every autumn since I was fifteen. Billy used to help my dad, but then he started drinking more and his hands got too shaky and he wasn't much use, so Johnny and I stepped in. Adam usually made himself scarce during what he'd dubbed "the killing season," saying he didn't want to know all the gory details of where his meat came from.

"So, this guy asked me on a date. He wanted to go out this weekend." I looked at Adam, who scowled while I tossed unwanted pig parts into the bucket in his arms. "I told him I couldn't because I had to go home and help my dad kill a pig." A lung thudded in the bucket and Adam's furrowed brow deepened as his cheeks puffed out, like he was trying to hold in the contents of his stomach. I laughed. "Turns out he was a vegetarian, so I don't think I'm going to hear from him any time soon." I turned back to Adam and held the heart between us. Blood oozed between my fingers.

Adam watched me with a look of confusion, maybe even horror. "You always look like you're a step away from death yourself after the killing, but you're like a kid in a candy shop come butchering time."

I smiled but it didn't reach my eyes. "What's dead is dead is dead. It's the actual making the pig dead that gets to me." I placed the heart a little more gently in the bucket and then carefully rooted around inside the carcass. "It's like some fucked-up second nature now." I pulled out the other lung and placed it in the bucket. "I wish it wasn't." Adam breathed through his nose and looked up at the ceiling.

"Guess who I saw at a party a few weeks ago," I asked, attempting to distract him.

"Who?"

"No, guess."

Adam sighed. "I don't know. Fiona?"

"Okay, yeah, obviously. But that's not who I'm talking about."

"Who?"

"Gina."

"Gina Smith?" His voice was filled with disdain.

I nodded and tried not to smile. "Are you ever going to forgive her?"

"No."

"It was the tiniest ding I've ever seen. Her car basically kissed your car."

"It's not that she hit my car. It's that she hit my car and then left. She fled the scene of a crime." I doubled over. He sounded so disgruntled. "Stop laughing. She's a felon." Adam shifted the bucket in his hands.

I caught my breath. He was dead serious. "It was just so long ago."

"I don't care. I will never forget, and I will never forgive."

"Oh, Jesus."

"She's clearly an awful person. Who would do that?" Adam went on as I turned back to the pig one last time.

"Do you think it's healthy for you to hold all these grudges against people?"

He shrugged, unintentionally sloshing around the bucket's contents. "It gives me something to do during the winter months."

"Maybe let some of them go, yeah? Like, how many are truly unforgiveable?"

"All of them."

I rolled my eyes and stuck my hand in the pig one more time, feeling around for any forgotten organs. I thought about asking Adam to check but decided not to be mean.

"Okay, we're done."

"Thank god." Adam's shoulders sagged in relief.

It was cold enough that we'd be able to leave the pig hanging in the barn until the next day, when we'd carve up the meat. As we raised the pig higher, headlights lit up the backyard. Doors slammed and my parents muttered to one another as they crossed through the paddock.

"Mom?" I called out.

She appeared at the barn door, hair falling out of a hastily tied ponytail, mascara smudged. She looked tired and worn. I didn't need to ask to know they hadn't found Billy.

"He'll turn up," Adam offered.

She sighed, looked up at the ceiling, and blinked rapidly. "He's such an asshole." Her voice was tight.

Dad appeared behind her and leaned against the doorframe. "We're gonna call the station tomorrow."

"Probably a good idea." Adam placed the bucket in the deep freeze, happy to get rid of it.

"I'll get the pasta started," I muttered as I trudged out of the barn. I didn't know what to say. How to make things better. But food, especially pasta, made everything better—at least for a minute. Adam followed.

"It's going to be all right, June," I heard Dad say.

"You don't know that," Mom replied.

two

"HOW MANY TIMES HAVE YOU MICROWAVED THAT COFFEE today?" I asked.

Mom paused, holding the cup in front of her. The mug was old, the words *Crystal Palace* starting to fade. She shrugged. "I don't know. A few?"

"Is that healthy?"

"Is what healthy?" She put the mug in the microwave and started pressing buttons.

"Drinking something that's spent that much time in the microwave?"

"Do you know how much coffee we'd go through if she got a fresh mug every time she forgot about her last one?" Dad shuddered at the thought of excess spending. "Drink the toxic sludge, I say!"

Mom shrugged again, her tiny shoulders small peaks in my dad's high school sweater. At least, I assumed it was his. He dropped out in grade eleven and I'd never actually seen him wear it. "I can't help it," she said. "I get distracted. I've got shit to do." Mom was a prime candidate for an ADHD diagnosis.

When Dad and Adam started talking about last night's hockey game, I grabbed a book out of my backpack.

"What's that for?" Dad asked, interrupting Adam's play-by-play.

"My thesis," I said, handing the book to him for inspection.

Adam stretched his arm along the back of my chair and squeezed my shoulder.

Dad thumbed through the book quickly then handed it back to me. "Know what you're writing about yet?"

"I'm still narrowing it down, but I think I want to talk about The Song Fishermen and the curation of a folk identity in Nova Scotia." My explanation was met with a blank stare. "The Song Fishermen was a group of poets in the late 1920s. There's a really clever poem about Spotted Dick. Like, the dessert. It's funny." Another blank stare. "Never mind."

Dad shook his head. "What does that have to do with anything? Did you know when your Nan was little, the government forced her and her family to move into an unfinished house on the rez? You should write about that."

I put the book back in my backpack, unsure how to respond. Mi'kmaw history was always a passing mention in the history classes I took. It hadn't occurred to me to write about it for my thesis. But I wasn't about to admit that to him.

"How're the scholarship applications going? Have you sent any off?" Mom sat back down at the table, toxic coffee in hand.

"Not yet," I replied, grateful to not have to answer Dad. "I thought this weekend might be a good break before I look over them one more time. I'll send them off once I get back to the city."

Adam dropped his arm from the back of my chair and went to get another beer.

As the porch door creaked open, Mom hastily stubbed her half-smoked cigarette onto the step and smiled sheepishly. "Bad habit," she muttered, then mimed zipping her lips.

"Bad habit? Yes. Secret habit? No." I smiled and sat down, gently leaning into her.

She laughed without actual mirth while staring out across the front lawn. "Adam gone home?"

I nodded and flicked the cigarette butt farther away from me.

"What's with you and him?"

"Nothing." I shrugged. "He's just a friend."

Mom quirked her eyebrow.

"He is!" People always read too much into my relationship with Adam. For years, my grampa called him my boyfriend. Whether he was genuinely confused or just taking the piss, I wasn't sure.

"If you say so."

We sat that way for a few minutes. The quiet was absolute. Even the birds had paused their evening song. We were blanketed by a lack of noise, and to speak felt sacrilegious, like the entirety of our problems might come crashing down if we uttered a single word. Then Dad turned on TSN and the moment passed.

"You know he wasn't taking his meds, eh?"

"Billy?"

Mom nodded. "Found the bottle in his drawer, basically full. When I tried to ask him about it, he got so friggin' owly. Told me to piss off and stop treating him like a child. Said it's no wonder Johnny buggered off out west and you moved to the city."

Not so far off a crow cawed in the growing dark, the cheers of the TV crowd just a tiny bit softer. "Mom, you know it's not like that, right?" I angled away to look at her. "Johnny needed a job and there sure as hell aren't a lot around here. And yeah, maybe I needed to get away, but not from you. Never from you. This place, these people. I like going to the store and not knowing every single person and their entire life story."

My mom felt bad enough about Billy right now I couldn't bring myself to explain that every time a store closed, a doctor moved away, or a house fell into irreparable ruin, it was like the town I grew up in was one step closer to no longer existing. Like the community I felt on the outskirts of was on a slow march toward death and I didn't want to stand there and witness it. There were other reasons, things my mom couldn't understand in the same ways my dad and brother could, like the sometimes subtle, often overt, racism.

"I know, I know." Mom patted my leg. "Billy was just spouting shit. Although I do wonder if either of you will ever move back."

I let the unintelligible noise of TSN fill the space between us.

When I was fifteen, I found a suicide note Billy had written. I had been looking for the copy of *Howl's Moving Castle* I'd lent him. Instead I found this tiny note laid flat on his desk, his chicken scratch just legible enough for me to make out the gist. In a panic I'd run downstairs and tried to find someone to help. Nobody was home. I'd burst through the front door, ready to search the property, only to narrowly avoid running straight into Billy, who sat on the front step with his head in his hands.

I sat down beside him, my back ramrod straight.

Billy looked over at me. Looked down at the crumpled note in my hand.

The silence dragged between the two of us. Eventually, he said, "You don't have to worry. That's a few days old. I've decided not to do it."

My heart was still in my throat. "Why would you even want to?"

"Do you really want to know?"

I nodded.

Billy sighed. "I feel useless. Stagnant. Like, what the fuck am I doing here in this godforsaken town? What have I even done with my life? Shit all. It's hard not to feel worthless. Like the rest of my life isn't worth living." He sighed. "Thinking about all the years I've got left to live makes me tired."

Billy scratched his chin. "Don't stay here, okay? You're too smart. And the people here can be so cruel. I don't have to tell you that."

The week before, someone at school had called me the S-word and Johnny had gone ballistic. He got suspended for starting a fight while the racist guy got off scot-free.

"Go somewhere else," Billy eventually said. He thought for a minute. "God, I was your age yesterday," he added, as if taken by surprise. "And then I—what? Took a nap? And now I'm almost thirty and I'm just...here? What kind of life is that?" He mumbled the last part. "Just find something you're good at and run with it because anything would be better than being here. Don't get stuck."

"Do you think you would ever move back?" Mom asked, pulling me back to the present; the front step creaked as she shifted her weight. The cheers from the television seemed louder.

I sighed. "I don't know, Mom."

She reached over and patted my thigh. "I get it. Grad school. Academic superstardom. The five-year plan." She said the last bit with exaggerated grandiosity.

I snorted.

"I'm not trying to make you feel bad, I just miss having you down the hall."

"I know."

Mom chewed at the corner of her thumbnail. "We checked everywhere. Where do you think he is?"

"Hell if I know."

three

I FOLLOWED THE SMELL OF COFFEE DOWN THE HALLWAY. Still half asleep, I clotheslined myself on the telephone cord stretched across the entryway. Mom was curled up in a chair, phone in hand. I ducked under the cord, mouthed *sorry*, and headed towards the coffee pot.

"Yeah, Barb, I know." Mom ground her teeth. "He's a bipolar alcoholic, not a fucking madman. Can you just file the report. Please?"

Mom had a foul mouth—she'd cussed like a sailor all my life—but her hostility towards Barb, the town's resident gossip, who also happened to be the receptionist at the police station, was shocking. She usually saved her wrath for later in the day.

"Mm-hmm. Okay. Sure." Mom ran a hand down her face. "No, I don't think it has anything to do with the Y2K, Barb." Mom rolled her eyes. "Yes, I'm worried about it too." She looked at me, her eyes wide with exasperation. "I'm sure your TV shows will still be on in January. Okay, bye Barb."

I stifled a laugh while she handed me the phone to hang up on the wall.

"Report's filed," she announced with an air of crazed cheerfulness.

"So I heard." I took a sip of coffee.

Mom moved past me, refilled her mug, then headed out the back door, the back pocket of her pants shaped like a cigarette pack.

I sat down in the chair and reached for the phone on the wall. I dialled a familiar number.

The greeting I received could only be deciphered by someone who'd spent years forced to talk to my brother before he was fully awake.

"Morning, Johnny."

"Hey, Charlie." Fondness found its way into his groggy tone. "How's home?"

"Billy's missing, Mom's a mess, Dad won't stop talking about hockey, and Adam is, well, Adam. On top of that I had to kill Henry yesterday."

Johnny grunted sympathetically.

"Billy's missing-missing, Johnny. No one's seen him since Friday."

I heard the sound of him rolling over. "It's only Monday."

"Yeah, but when has Billy ever been gone this long before?"

There was a beat of silence.

"Him and Mom got into it right before he went MIA," I whispered into the phone. "I can tell she thinks it was the reason."

"Do you think it was?"

I took a breath. "No, I don't. You should see his room. It's a mess. I changed the sheets but it's still disgusting. It's going to be a shit show when he finally comes home."

"For once I'm glad I'm five provinces over. Have fun dealing with that."

"I won't be here for it. As soon as he's home, I'm heading back into the city."

"Sucks to be Mom and Dad."

"No kidding."

After we hung up, I sat at the kitchen table and drummed my fingers against the scarred wood. Billy had made the table for my parents as a wedding present. My uncle's lingering presence was scattered all around the house: the myriad woodworking projects he'd fiddled with throughout the years, the bright yellow living room he'd painted when the rest of us had gone away for the weekend, his movie collection, alphabetically categorized in the living room. It stung to be able to see and touch all of these things he'd owned and made and done and yet feel so disconnected from him. I could see all these pieces of himself that he'd left behind. But I had no idea where he was.

"What's up?" Fiona answered on the first ring. This had been a morning of phone calls. Dad had called his parents earlier. Nan was probably calling everyone in her phonebook as I sat here. Was it necessary to activate the family phone tree? Probably not. But it was comforting to hear familiar voices.

"I'm gonna be home longer than I thought. Billy's missing..."

"Oh shit."

"It's probably nothing. I'm sure he's fine." I thought I was telling the truth, but it felt like a lie.

"Do you need me to do anything?"

"No. I'm just gonna hang around here until he shows up."

"Okay. I will hold the fort down in your absence." Fiona took a sip of something. "Did you send off your applications?"

"Not yet. I was going to do it once I got back."

"Do you want me to mail them for you?"

Mom walked into the kitchen and put her coffee in the microwave.

"No, I want to look over them again. There's still time. Thanks though."

"I'm so excited for Toronto. It's going to be amazing." Fiona sung the last word. "You have no idea. There are so many good restaurants. And so many cute guys. I know you've got your weird little thing with Adam—"

"I don't have a weird little thing..."

"Okay, I mean you do, but that's not the point. Toronto is going to be da bomb."

"Yeah, I'm excited." I watched Mom's back as she stared out the window above the kitchen sink.

"You don't sound excited—oh, are your parents in the room? Remind me why you haven't told them?"

I lowered my voice. "There's no point unless it actually happens."

"Charlie, you have a super-nerd-level GPA. It's obviously happening. You and me, grad school, Tdot."

The microwave beeped. Mom grabbed her mug and went back into the living room.

"Fine. *When* it happens, I will tell them." I checked the clock. It was almost ten. "Don't you have class in twenty minutes?"

"Oh shit! Love you, bye!" Fiona yelled.

She hung up before I could tell her I loved her too.

four

THE END OF THE JOINT SMOULDERED IN THE GROWING DARK. The embers flared as Adam inhaled. From the rooftop outside my window, I watched his lips as smoke funnelled out into the night.

I'd done nothing all day. After Dad and I cut up the pig, I'd paced the house, bounced on our rusted trampoline out back, and read the article on orgasms. I should've done homework but I could barely get my brain to settle enough to read the *five steps to securing your pleasure*, let alone read about anti-modernism and cultural selection in Nova Scotia.

Adam offered the joint to me; our fingers brushed as I took it.

I tried not to cough as the smoke burned my throat, but I couldn't help it.

Adam laughed and patted my back. "You can never handle it."

"It's not like I'm a seasoned pot smoker," I said between coughs. "I only smoke with you because you're a bad influence."

"I'm a wonderful influence."

I laughed and handed the joint back to him.

"Why don't you come home as much?" he asked.

"I come home. I'm home right now." My shoulders tensed. I didn't want to fight.

Adam raised an eyebrow. "For birthdays and to kill a pig. You used to come back, like, every weekend."

I shrugged. "There's more to do in the city."

"No. It's just easier to entertain yourself. You don't have to be creative."

"I disagree, wholeheartedly. But let's say you're right, which you're not—"

"I am."

I rolled my eyes. "Maybe I don't want to be creative."

"Lazy."

I shoved his shoulder.

Adam handed the joint back and I inhaled.

We passed it back and forth in silence for a while, Adam staring straight ahead while I looked up at the sky and tried to find the Big Dipper. The stars seemed closer. They always did, like they wanted to come say hello as soon as I got stoned. I liked when they did. I liked sitting next to Adam on this roof with the stars right in front of our faces.

"Is that it?" I pointed to a spot in the sky that looked the same as all the others.

"No." He didn't have to ask what I was looking for. "That's Cassiopeia."

"Really?" I couldn't hide my excitement.

"No."

I punched his shoulder. "You suck."

Adam laughed. "Christ, it's cold out." He pulled his hat down.

I could feel the tension seep out of my body, the weed making my limbs loose and my thoughts soft. "Will you stay the night?"

Surprise flickered across Adam's face. "Now who's the bad influence? I'm an innocent and you're corrupting me." He held his hands to his chest in mock indignation, then stubbed the roach out and turned to climb back through my window. I followed behind, toppled through the open window, and fell, headfirst, onto my bed. I scrambled upright and brushed the hair out of my face. Adam was smiling at me.

I pushed down hard on the window frame, but it wouldn't budge. "Can you..."

Adam closed the window effortlessly. He took off his socks, sweater, and pants before he climbed into my bed and pulled the comforter up to his chin. I slipped my socks off and got in beside him. Aside from camping trips, with too many people crammed into a too-small tent, Adam and I had never slept beside each other. In the dark, my thoughts hazy, I craved the solidity of him.

I curled my body around his and tried to soak up his warmth while I told myself it didn't have to mean anything.

five

"SORRY FOR CALLING SO EARLY, I JUST FIGURED YOU GUYS would want to know as soon as we found anything." An RCMP officer leaned against the counter, his back to me as he talked to my parents. I walked into the kitchen, Adam behind me. The officer turned around and I recognized his blond hair and kind eyes.

"Oh. Hi, Eddie."

Eddie gave me a small nod while I shuffled towards the coffee pot, now wholly aware of my slovenly and braless state. I tried to smell myself without anyone noticing, worried I reeked of pot from the night before. Eddie Riggins was two years ahead of Adam and Johnny in high school; he'd gone off to join the RCMP as soon as he could and was lucky enough to be stationed back home, although I was sure this posting was considered undesirable by most.

Adam gave Eddie a pat on the shoulder and then took the coffee I held out for him. Mom sat at the kitchen table, legs curled beneath her, while Dad stood behind her, his forearms on the back of her chair.

"What's the news?" Adam asked.

Eddie cleared his throat. "We found Billy's car this morning. Up by the old MacGilvray place."

The abandoned pig farm was about a twenty-minute drive from our house, down a long dirt road that cut through blueberry fields and forest.

"So, what does that mean?" I asked.

Eddie turned to me. "It means we're going to do a search of the woods and surrounding fields."

"For what? A body?" Mom's voice was higher than normal. Already angry.

"Just for anything that might be helpful."

Dad began to rub Mom's shoulders while she gripped her mug, her knuckles white. I was worried she might break it. Adam inched closer to me, his body pressed against mine.

"Is that something we can help with?" Dad asked. "Doing something useful sounds a hell of a lot better than sitting around."

Eddie's tone was careful. "At this point we're sending a few officers to do a preliminary search of the area surrounding the vehicle before we figure out our next move. Right now, you folks should just sit tight and wait."

Adam showed Eddie out while Mom bit her tongue.

"Sit tight and wait?" she burst out as soon as the front door slammed. "Wait for what? A body to show up?"

"Maybe he's just out wandering around. Maybe he's lost?" I offered, desperate to make the situation seem less dire.

"He did get that book recently—that one about wilderness survival," Dad said.

I nodded. "He wanted to try living on the land. Remember how adamant he was about survival skills after watching *Waterworld*?" Every time Billy watched a post-apocalyptic movie, he'd spiral because of his inability to survive without a microwave and instant noodles.

"Maybe he got inspired," Dad added.

Mom shook her head and sighed; the three of us were pulling at straws and we all knew it.

The house entered a state of uncertainty. We became muted versions of ourselves; we didn't know what to do while we waited for news. Dad still watched TV, but kept the volume low; Mom, who normally sounded like a freight train barrelling around the house, walked with light feet, opening doors and moving objects with a slow and careful deliberateness. It was like we all thought that if we moved too fast or made too much noise, we would somehow affect the narrative playing out. Like one forcefully shut door would put Billy on our porch in a body bag.

Eventually, Adam left for work and Mom disappeared upstairs. I sat next to Dad and watched hockey highlights. I went to the kitchen to make a pie with freezer-burnt blueberries saved from the summer, but we were out of butter. I tried to read the article on how to have it all, because it seemed impossible. I read the first paragraph twice and then gave up.

I grabbed my keys, Dad's flannel, and a cigarette from Mom's stash and hopped in my car.

The beach was a ten-minute drive from my parents' house. It was the only other part of this place that felt like home to me. I parked at the end of a potholed dirt road beside a run-down pickup truck. In the distance a handful of people lined the edge of the cliff, waiting for the tide to come in; their silhouettes moved against the grey afternoon sky, opening folding chairs and preparing their fishing lines.

The shoreline was half rust-coloured clay, half rock. The water, a choppy mess of brown, ebbed closer. As kids, Adam, Johnny, and I would pretend it was chocolate milk.

I kicked my shoes off, rolled up my pants, and stepped into the waves. It was ice cold. My jaw clenched as I willed myself to adjust to the temperature. I moved farther into the water until it lapped at the hem of my pants. I stood there until my feet went numb and the water had almost reached my shoes on the beach behind me.

I felt the cigarette in my pocket, but I was unsure of what to do. I didn't grow up with traditional teachings. My dad was just reclaiming those ways now. Like most Mi'kmaq of his generation, he grew up Catholic. I wished Aunt Darlene were here. She would tell me what to do.

I took out the cigarette and snapped it in half. Putting one half back in my pocket, I shook the contents of the other onto my palm. Did offering tobacco to the Creator feel awkward because it was unfamiliar? Or because I wasn't sure whether I actually believed, and just felt like I should? Maybe it was that I only thought to do this when shit went sideways.

I knew that the water was real. That mud and dirt and rock existed.

But did Creator exist? And if they did, would they care what I had to ask of them?

What was a tiny pile of cigarette guts going to do?

I tipped my palm; the tobacco fell into the water and dissipated with the tide.

"Keep him safe," I mumbled.

On the way back to my car I picked up a flat oval rock. On one side was a tiny fossil of a stick, about a centimetre long. I ran my thumb along the bumpy ridge of the indent while I made my way back along the beach toward the dirt road. When I climbed into the driver's seat, I dumped the rock in the cupholder and drove home.

six

I STOOD ON THE TOP STEP OF THE FRONT PORCH AS THE RCMP vehicle slowly made its way up my parents' driveway. Mom and Dad stood at the base of the stairs. Adam leaned on the porch railing beside me. The sun hung low over the trees, tendrils of pink, purple, and orange spread out across the sky. The last bright swatches of light were quickly disappearing, shrinking back across the lawn towards the treeline. Somewhere close by, a crow cawed. Supper had been eaten and the dishes had been done. We'd all gathered in the living room afterwards to listen to the news, the television quiet enough to hear the crunch of gravel when the cruiser turned into the driveway.

I pulled my sweater tighter around my body as Eddie Riggins climbed out. He ran a hand through his hair before making his way across the lawn. He stopped short of coming up the porch steps. He opened his mouth, then closed it. The furrow in his brow and the rigid line of his shoulders told us everything.

"I'm so sorry." Eddie shifted his weight from one leg to the other. "We found Billy. He, ah." He looked past us, as if the words he needed were written on our front door. "He hung himself in the woods, a few kilometres from where we found his car." The blunt nature of his words was jarring. Everything hung in suspension for a brief moment. My body stilled, my vision clouded. Eddie's words didn't make sense. I felt Adam's arm tighten around my shoulders, and I watched as my mother collapsed on the bottom porch step. Eddie reached out, placed a hand on my father's shoulder, kept talking softly, then turned and walked away.

I shrugged off Adam's arm and went inside. He caught the door before it slammed shut, followed me into the kitchen, and hovered in the doorway while I stomped about. I practically threw a kettle filled with water onto the stove, then turned the burner on high. I crossed my arms and watched, waiting for it to boil. My fingernails dug into the flesh of my arm.

I was angry, which surprised me, and made me even angrier because I should have been sad. I should've been sobbing. My uncle Billy, who could be a volatile alcoholic, but so kind and so good, was dead. In that moment, I didn't want to cry. I wanted to scream and throw things and I wanted to throttle Billy for doing something that made my family hurt so much.

He'd told me almost a decade ago that I didn't need to worry. Now, here I was, standing in my parents' kitchen, my body short-circuiting with every negative emotion I could name. It didn't feel real. Billy. My body. My hands tingled. My insides hummed. My mind was a cacophony of sounds.

I flinched as Adam placed a tentative hand on my shoulder.

I couldn't look at him. "I made his bed, Adam."

Adam stood right behind me, close enough that if I leaned back, I would be pressed against him. Steam was rising from the kettle now, filling the space between us.

"I made his bed like he was still alive." A shriek, the screaming whine of the kettle. "I fluffed his fucking pillow."

Adam reached over and turned off the burner.

"It's okay." He pulled me into him briefly. "It's okay," he said again, guiding me down the hallway and up the stairs into my bedroom. He turned off the overhead light and sat down on the bed. I sat beside him and clutched his hand like a lifeline, my fingernails digging into his skin.

"Don't leave." I still couldn't make eye contact.

"Don't worry, I won't," Adam whispered back.

I don't know how long we sat like that.

At some point Adam moved in front of me. He crouched on the floor and slipped my socks off because he knew I didn't like to sleep with them on. Then he lay down behind me, pulled me closer, and brought his arm around my middle. He anchored me. My hand tangled with his. On the top of his hand were four red indents like crescent moons; they mirrored the moon in the sky. Wikewiku's was waning. Soon a new moon cycle would begin. Keptekewiku's, Rivers Freezing Over Time, would start and Billy wouldn't be here for it.

I traced the curved lines with my finger, regretting that I had hurt him in any way.

My mother's sobs shot up from the porch, each guttural heave shattering the silence that filled my room.

seven

I WOKE UP JUST PAST DAWN. ADAM WAS CURLED AROUND ME, his arm still draped across my waist. For a moment, in that blurry haze between sleep and waking, everything seemed all right. Then a rooster crowed and I remembered that Billy was dead and my mom was devastated and there was a giant hole in our family, and I wasn't sure how we would ever fill it or if we were even supposed to.

I looked up at the ceiling and breathed out. I waited to see how long I could stay like that, lungs empty, body sunk into the mattress. Whatever anger I'd felt the night before had fizzled out, leaving me drained and empty in the cold light of day.

The twin bed creaked as Adam stretched. He groaned softly and I turned toward him. We were so close our noses almost touched. His face was soft with sleep, dried drool stuck in the corner of his beard. I wet my thumb and rubbed the spit away. His eyes were filled with tenderness; I focused on the corner of his mouth as he spoke.

"How're you feeling?"

I shrugged, my eyes trained on his chin. Maybe if I stayed like this forever, tracing the lines of his face, every barely there wrinkle on his skin, I wouldn't have to confront the sadness pooling in my chest. "Thanks for staying last night."

"Of course."

We lay in silence as the sun slowly crept higher in the sky.

"What do I do, Adam?"

"First," he brushed loose hairs out of my face, "we call Johnny, then we make breakfast, then we plan a funeral."

I worried if I tried to talk, I might start to cry. So I nodded, my hair rubbing against the pillow.

I went to brush my teeth. It seemed the most normal thing to do in a day that had no hope of normalcy. I closed the bathroom door quietly and climbed into the bathtub, pulled the shower curtain closed, and sat very still for a moment. Billy's body wash sat on the lower ledge, some generic brand he'd been buying forever. I flipped the top and breathed in the familiar scent: it was Sunday afternoon drives and midnight dance-off challenges I'd refused to accept.

My shoulders shook as I absorbed the sound of each sob. I would dance every time he asked if I could just have him back. I pushed my palms into my eyelids and pressed so hard white light flashed across the black.

The doorknob rattled.

"Just a second." My voice was strained. I put Billy's body wash back in its place and opened the shower curtain. I turned on the tap, tightened my ponytail, and splashed water on my face.

When I opened the door, Dad was on the other side.

"Okay?" he asked.

I'm sure I didn't look it. I shrugged and smiled weakly, closed-lipped.

"Not okay." Dad pulled me into a hug so tight there was no room for anything else. He pressed his lips to the top of my head. "This is the pits, Tu's," he murmured.

Cocooned in my father's arms, sunlight stretching down the hallway, I didn't want to exist beyond this moment. Outside this hug were a lot of hard things I didn't want to face. But I also didn't want to cry again and my chest was starting to fill with emotions heavy and viscous. I stepped back and looked over my dad's shoulders. An *Employees Only* sticker was stuck on Johnny's door, the corner finally starting to peel after a decade.

"Has anyone called Johnny?" I asked.

"Not yet."

"I will," I offered, desperate for something to do.

Dad glanced at my brother's closed bedroom door. "That'd be really helpful." He gave me one last hug before going into the bathroom.

I made my way downstairs and outside. I slipped on muddy boots and trudged across the backyard towards the barn. Frost clung to the blades of grass that crunched under my feet, my breath like small clouds. I rubbed the sleep from my eyes and tried to gather the parts of me that felt flattened and stretched out. I grabbed the chicken feed and slipped through the paddock gate. I sprinkled it on the ground for the chickens who clucked around my feet. Maudie, the family cat, slunk out of some unseen corner and wound her way through my legs. I scooped her up and dropped the empty bucket by the paddock gate.

Back in the kitchen, Adam had started a pot of coffee. I placed Maudie on the counter and accepted the mug he held out for me. The coffee was a little too hot and the mug burned my palm as I held it.

Adam started to make breakfast. A dozen eggs. An inordinate number of potatoes. I couldn't help but admire how he did it, just seemed to carry on. But then, he'd had more practice than I had.

"How did you…when your mom died, how did you deal with it?"

Adam held the bowl of eggs against his stomach as he whisked. "Honestly, I don't really remember. I was so young. My dad let me get Pop-Tarts and we watched a lot of *Mr. Dressup.*" He shrugged. "I know that's not super helpful."

"No, it's…I mean. You're right. It isn't helpful. I'm not sure how much power Pop-Tarts hold in this house. *Mr. Dressup* obviously holds a lot of sway." The joke slipped out before I could consider what I was saying. It left a bad feeling in my mouth.

Adam smiled like he pitied me. "Probably not enough."

"Yeah." I took a sip of coffee and let the warmth spread throughout my body. "What was the first thing on the list, again?"

He poured the eggs into a pan. "Call Johnny."

"Right." I didn't want to do it. Even though I'd just told my dad I would. I wasn't sure I could say it out loud. I didn't want Billy's death to exist outside this house. Right now, I could pretend this was all a fucked-up fever dream. But I knew the longer I waited, the worse it would be.

I ran the spiralled phone cord through my fingers as I curled up on a kitchen chair and waited for Johnny to pick up.

"Got the machine," I said to Adam, waiting for his permission to give up. He looked at me with a sad smile and I knew I had to keep trying. But Johnny was impossible to wake up at the best of times; add the time difference to the equation and he was probably still drooling on his pillow. I hung up and called again. It rang and rang. I was about to hang up when Johnny answered.

"What's up, chicken butt?" he asked, his voice groggy.

"Uh…" I paused, could hear my voice threatening to crack. My eyes burned and I blinked back tears. I made a sound, but no words came out.

"Christ. He's dead, isn't he?"

"Mhm." I nodded unnecessarily.

Johnny swore on the other end of the line. "I can't believe I answered the phone like that. I was half asleep, I wasn't thinking straight. I'm sorry. How are you?"

How was I? My throat constricted, words stuck somewhere between my heart and my mouth. My mind blanked.

"When's the funeral?" Johnny asked, unperturbed by my lack of response.

"We haven't…figured that out yet."

"I doubt I can get home for it." Johnny swore again.

"It's okay. I'm sure—" I tried to placate Johnny, but he was absorbed in a one-sided conversation with himself about logistics and flights. It was comforting trying to keep up with his rapid-fire train of thought. It felt normal.

"How's Mom?" Johnny asked.

I squeezed the bridge of my nose. "Last night when she was crying…I've never heard her make a noise like that. I'm not sure I've ever heard anybody make a noise like that. I haven't seen her this morning."

"And Dad?"

"I think he's too busy holding Mom up to feel much of anything right now."

"Have you told Nan and Grampa yet?"

"No."

"Are you going to do a salite?" Johnny asked.

"What?" I asked, watching Adam move about my parents' kitchen. He was so at ease here.

"You know, the auction after the funeral. To raise money for the family."

"Oh. Right. Uh, I don't know." I scrubbed my face. "Billy's not even Mi'kmaw."

"Mindy's friend's brother from Millbrook did it for his girlfriend. She was white. Plus, they'd only been dating for, like, six months. I spent fifty bucks on a Pink Floyd album."

"I don't know how. Like, what do I even say? 'Hey, my white uncle died, give us your stuff to auction off'?" The idea of asking for help overwhelmed me. I didn't know how to coordinate a salite. What if people only agreed to help because they felt like they had to?

"I mean, there's probably a better way to ask. Ask Nan, she'll tell you."

"Here." Adam placed a plate of food in front of me.

Thanks, I mouthed.

Johnny stopped mid-word: "Is that Adam? Put him on, would you?"

Adam took the phone and stepped into the hallway.

I pushed the food around on my plate and listened to Adam's half of the conversation. Johnny had a tendency to be bossy, and from Adam's responses, he was on a bit of a rampage. I rested my head in my hands and tried to think of all the things Johnny was telling Adam to do while Adam responded with a series of clipped yeses, uh-huhs, of courses, no problems, and finally, "obviously, dipshit."

Adam handed the phone back to me and grimaced.

"I've got to get ready for work," came my brother's voice, followed by a yawn.

"Johnny it's like 4:00 A.M. there."

"Right. Well, I guess I'll just stare at the wall for the next hour and a half and then get ready for work. But let me know if you need anything, okay?" He sounded tired.

"Okay," I replied, not sure what Johnny could achieve from Fort Mac.

"I love you, Charlie."

"Love you too."

I ate a mouthful of egg and listened to the dial tone.

eight

BILLY'S ROOM WAS EXACTLY HOW I'D LEFT IT. MOM SAT ON THE edge of the bed, wrinkling the fresh sheets.

"Hey Mom, I called Johnny and told him. I also called Nan and Grampa, so they're going to come by. I was just—"

"Have you even cried yet?" Mom stared out the window. The back of her hair was matted and fuzzy; the cold sunlight shone through the wisps, my mom's hair like a bleached-blond halo.

"I…what? Yes." I stalled in the doorway, mid-step, unsure where to go both conversationally and physically.

"Sorry, Charlie. I didn't mean for it to come out like that."

"It's fine." I walked over and sat beside her.

"Thank you. For doing all that." She patted my leg.

"Yeah, no problem."

The bookshelves across from the bed were crammed with old paperbacks. A good third of them were ones I thought I'd lost, and Billy had sworn he hadn't seen.

"Did Billy want to be cremated or…" I trailed off.

Mom worried her bottom lip. "I actually don't know."

"Me neither. Dad called the…I don't know, whoever you're supposed to call, and they asked. Apparently, it was cold enough that he didn't, um, you know…they said an open casket would be fine for the wake."

My mom turned to me. "Do we need a wake? I don't even know if Billy wanted one."

I shrugged. I wanted to ask if it really mattered what he wanted. He was dead. Was anything that came next really for Billy? Or was it to make us feel better? Maybe he was somewhere above or below or beside me screaming that he wanted the full package, wake and all. Maybe he was yelling that he wanted us to leave him in a field and let the earth have him. How could I know him and love him and not know what he wanted?

"I don't know that we can afford one. Why is death so expensive?" Mom asked.

"I don't think there are rules, really. We can do whatever we want, can't we? We could nix the wake, have an open casket at the service?" I suggested.

"An open casket." Mom considered it. "He might've been weirded out at the idea of people staring at him."

"True. He might have also loved the idea of forcing everyone to look at him."

Mom's smile was sad. "I think he'd like that best of all."

"All right, open casket it is." I stood up. "So, we need clothes then." I started to rifle through Billy's closet. "He always wore this." I pulled out a blue and burgundy plaid flannel.

"Put it with the grey cardigan." Mom went to Billy's dresser, pulling open one drawer, then another. "And these pants." She handed me a pair of beige khakis. "And this shirt." It was a vintage *Big Trouble in Little China* shirt Johnny had given Billy a couple Christmases ago. Kurt Russell was front and centre in a tank top, baring his arms and his gun, while Kim Cattrall lounged in the bottom right corner, wearing a pout and baring what Johnny claimed was "a tasteful amount of cleavage."

I smiled, seeing all the items together. "Billy would've loved this outfit."

Mom's eyes dimmed. "Yeah, he would have."

I looked back at the closet. In the middle of the chaos of mixed prints and beloved knits was a bright, mustard yellow cardigan. I ran the worn yarn through my fingers.

"You should take that," Mom said softly.

I thumbed the ribbed yarn at the end of the sleeve. It was soft from years of wear. There was a hole where Billy's thumb had worn through the stitches, stretching them apart until it could easily fit.

"Maybe." I let the sleeve fall back into place and closed the closet. "How are you doing? Can I get you anything?"

Mom didn't answer right away.

"I'm all alone now." She was looking out the window again.

"You've got us." I sat back down beside her.

"I've got all these memories of people—" She paused. "How many people are left that remember my parents?"

My grandparents on my mom's side had died within a year of one another when I was three.

"There's no one else in the world who knows how my mom sounded when she sang in the kitchen. How it felt to be hugged by my father." She wet her lips. "And now Billy." Her face crumpled.

I sat in the dusty afternoon light and rubbed my mother's back while she cried.

nine

THE FUNERAL WAS HELD AT THE ROADSIDE CHURCH BY DOUG'S General Store. On one side was a graveyard, on the other, a bright pink-and-blue ice cream stand boarded up for the winter. The parking lot steadily filled as people arrived, piling out of their cars dressed in black. I knew every single person, and I couldn't help but wonder why most of them had come.

Adam appeared at my side. "You're glaring."

I pulled Billy's mustard yellow cardigan tighter around my shoulders. It was a bright burst of sun amidst a sea of black. "I just wonder why they're all here."

Adam shrugged. "To pay their respects."

I didn't really buy that. I looked at Adam and told him so without words.

"Because it's a small town and people will notice if they don't come," Adam amended.

"That seems more like it."

Dad's family gathered in the corner of the parking lot, a huddle of brown faces and black hair. He liked to call them the Indian contingent. Nan was there with my aunt Darlene, my dad's cousins, and a handful of kids. My grampa got out of his car and joined the group, his face the only white one in the crowd.

The church was dark compared to the cold brightness of the parking lot. It was small, with old wooden pews and stained-glass windows depicting biblical characters and events I should've known, having done the whole Sunday school thing, but didn't. The casket was front and centre, directly under a crucified Jesus who hung from the ceiling, bouquets of blue hydrangeas, forget-me-nots, and morning glories on either side. They were beautiful. I wondered if Billy would feel better knowing my parents had agreed to spend an absurd amount on flowers. I glanced at Billy's casket and then looked back at the flowers. The lid of the casket had been lifted up.

I hadn't seen him until today. It seemed like he no longer belonged to us.

I took a deep breath and went to stand in front of Billy. A small part of me hoped it was all a mistake. That the RCMP had been confused. That I'd look down and realize it wasn't him.

I looked down.

That small, unspoken hope died.

Billy's face was a bit puffy, the skin around his neck bruised. He could've just been sleeping. With a lot of makeup on. The embalmer had tried their hardest to hide the fact that Billy had hung himself, but not even the thickest drugstore concealer could change that fact.

He seemed peaceful, which didn't seem right; Billy was always exploding with something—happiness, bitterness, disappointment—you name it, and Billy felt it in spades. His arms were crossed over his stomach and his cardigan and plaid shirt were placed in such a way that you couldn't see the T-shirt underneath. I hesitated, unsure if it was okay to touch him, whether death made his body inaccessible to me. Would Father Andrew jump out from behind the overpriced floral arrangement and slap my hand away?

I gently unbuttoned the top of the plaid shirt. My fingers shook, which made the task hard. I pulled the plaid and cardigan back just enough so that the top of the T-shirt was visible, Patrick Swayze's voluminous hair peeking out. I stepped back, giving both Billy and myself a little space. My throat was tight and my eyes stung.

"I don't really know what to say," I whispered. "If you were right about everything then you're just gone and you can't hear me and nothing I say matters. I don't know if that's more or less comforting than you listening to everything I say." I looked around the room, a blurring of green banners, gold accents, and marble floors, as tears pooled in my eyes.

"I wish you hadn't done it. But I know you felt like you had to, even if I don't really understand and think you're kind of stupid." I drew in a shaky breath. "This is a terrible goodbye. But this is kind of a terrible day, so..." I used the sleeve of the cardigan to wipe my tears. "I love you, Billy. I miss you. And I wish I never had to say goodbye." I took in his face one more time. Then I turned my back on the casket and sat down next to Adam in the first row of pews.

The funeral started out poorly when the organist, Phyllis, who was pushing ninety and partially deaf, played the opening hymn so atrociously I genuinely worried she was stroking out in the midst of the service. But she looked quite content banging away at the keys and I had to wonder if she just didn't know how to play the organ.

"Jesus fucking Christ." My dad ran his hands up and down his face.

"Shut the hell up, Nick. You can't take the Lord's name in vain in a goddamn church." My mom wiped the tears from her face, blew her nose in a crumpled tissue, and broke out in a fresh round of sobs. We were barely separated—Dad and Adam sat between us—but even still, Mom's crying was drowned out by the cacophony of random notes swelling to a horrible, chaotic crescendo.

Billy would've been beside himself.

The priest entered from a door to the side of the altar and Phyllis immediately stopped playing. Father Andrew took his sweet time as he ascended the three stairs and four feet of tile that led to the pulpit, his measured steps loud in the now solemn church. He'd also taken his sweet time leading us through the Stations of the Cross when I was seven and riding the emotional roller-coaster that is Jesus's crucifixion.

The priest cleared his throat and adjusted his stole. "We are gathered here today to celebrate the life of William Murphy," he began in a rich and practiced voice.

William Murphy?

Billy had only been *William* when he was pretending to be a pompous asshole to get a laugh out of Johnny and me. I'd figured the organ playing would be the low point, but clearly the sermon was going to give it a run for its money.

I hadn't picked any hymns or prayers because I didn't think Billy would care. But I was beginning to realize I might.

With no other funeral options in our small town, everyone was forced to be Christian, at least in death. The funny thing was, the most religious person in the room was probably my nan; she'd smudge with sage she grew herself and an hour later you'd find her with her rosary mumbling ten Hail Marys. Most Mi'kmaq were faithful Catholics. I'd always thought it weird, given the church had run the residential school in Shubie. While my nan hadn't been sent there, she knew lots of people who had been and the stories were traumatic. And yet, I'd been to mass in the church on the rez and there was always enthusiastic drumming, hymns sung in Mi'kmaw, and a statue of Mary wearing regalia.

The priest called my dad up to the stage.

He lumbered up to the podium and, unfolding a single piece of paper, cleared his throat.

"I'm not—I'm not particularly good at writing things down. Billy was a good man. He was a great person to have on your team because he cared. He cared a lot. He cared so much that sometimes it felt like too much. But now..." Dad cleared his throat again. "Now that he's gone, I know it wasn't too much. What I, what we"—he looked at Mom—"wouldn't give to have him here now.

"Billy used to always come fishing with me. But he couldn't stay still. He was always moving around, scaring the fish away. It annoyed me." Dad looked to the back of the church. He opened his mouth, let out a huff, then looked at his piece of paper again. "I would gladly never catch a fish again if it meant he would still be here. Billy didn't believe in anything. But it's a comfort to think of him being with Kisu'lkw, the Creator."

Father Andrew coughed.

Dad folded up the piece of paper, his hands shaking. "Anyway, that's it. That's all I got to say."

Adam handed me a bunch of squished tissues. I blew my nose loudly.

At the end of the service, Father Andrew told us all to go in peace. The casket was closed. Dad, Adam, a friend of Billy's, and three of Dad's cousins hefted Billy onto their shoulders and made their way down the centre aisle of the church. From her seat next to me, Mom stared at the spot where the casket had been until I gently nudged her.

Our immediate family followed the pallbearers into the stark afternoon light while Phyllis absolutely butchered "The Parting Glass" and everyone else descended to the church basement for squares and weak coffee. Father Andrew had insisted the burial happen after the reception, but Mom wanted it right away. The plot we'd chosen was a few rows down from Mom and Billy's parents; it had been dug out this morning, the fresh earth in a churned-up pile of rock and dirt and grass next to the hole. We stood and watched as the casket sank below the grass.

I didn't listen to what Father Andrew had to say, his voice a droning noise in the background punctuated by my mom's whimpers.

It was over so quickly, but nothing felt final. There was no closure in burying Billy, only a dizzying confusion. I'd come home last Saturday expecting to kill a pig and head back to the city the next day; now, almost a week later, I was standing at the foot of my uncle's grave.

I didn't know how long a person was supposed to stand at a grave after their loved one had been buried, but I might have stood there forever if Adam hadn't taken my hand and led me to the church basement.

The reception hall was filled with faux-wood tables with metal legs. The dirty white walls were covered in crude crayon renderings of Bible stories done by kids in Sunday school. My favourite was the one of Jesus getting ice cream at the stand next to the church, the cross leaning against the bright pink wall of the shack. People talked about Billy, but they also talked about their own goings-on, using the funeral as a way to catch up. A social occasion. When I was in high school a kid in my class had died in a drunk driving accident. That room had felt slick with grief. I didn't know whether to feel relieved or angry that this room didn't.

Church basement halls are weird places. Just last winter, Adam's cousin got married and everyone gathered in the hall to celebrate. Everyone was happy and joyful and laughter reverberated from the corners of the room. For years people have congregated in the basement hall of this middle-of-nowhere church to celebrate. To mourn. To laugh. To gossip. To remember. How many moments could one basement shelter? How could a room contain so many disparate emotions? Did the drywall and laminate floors absorb the happiness and sorrow? Was the brown stain on the ceiling water damage or a muddying of mixed emotions? Was any earthly thing meant to house so many contradictory feelings?

Aunt Darlene pulled me into a hug, yanking me back to the present.

"I'm so sorry, dear," she murmured into my hair.

I hugged her back, squeezing a little too hard.

"You guys doing a salite?" she asked.

"No. We thought about it, but..." I trailed off.

"I could've planned it if you'd wanted." She paused. "I was about to say keep it in mind for next time, but that seems real morbid. Here, I brought you this." She rifled through her purse and handed me a bundle of sage.

"Thanks." I held the bundle in front of me. Even in this room full of weak coffee and body odour, I could smell its strong earthy scent. It reminded me of Nan's house, of family dinners and childhood sleepovers.

Darlene rolled her eyes. I must've looked as awkward as I felt. "Will you promise to smudge? It can help, I swear," she said.

"I don't..." I wasn't brought up smudging. I didn't know how to do it without feeling like a phony. Dad had only started doing it again a few years back. Johnny liked to say Dad was in his *tradish* era.

"Just don't be a dumbass about it, ya know? You gotta go into it with sincerity."

"*Don't be a dumbass*? Is that an Elder teaching?"

Darlene shoved my shoulder. "Don't be a smartass either, eh? Just do it. You'll feel better."

"I will, thanks." I slipped the sage into the pocket of Billy's cardigan.

Darlene hugged me again before going off to find her kids.

My grandparents sat at the table closest to the dessert squares. They were heatedly discussing something. Nan's brow furrowed while she leaned towards Grampa, who was leaned back in his chair; he waved his hands in the air as if trying to shoo away a bad smell.

"Now Agnes, I'm only having five, don't have a cow."

"Lord have mercy, Albert, I'm just looking out for your health, God knows why I want you to live any longer."

"What?" Grampa asked, adjusting the volume on his hearing aid.

"YOUR. HEALTH," Nan all but yelled.

"My health is fine."

"You're a diabetic who's going deaf."

"I'm pre-diabetic and the—Oh, hello Charlotte." Grampa's demeanour changed when he caught sight of me. Only he called me Charlotte. He sat up straight and patted the chair beside him. "Have a seat, have a square." He took a date square off the napkin closest to Nan and handed it to me with a wink. He looked like Dad when he did that. Dad's features were all Nan, but his facial expressions were Grampa. There is more than one family photo where, in the background, they are unintentionally making the exact same face.

"Thanks," I muttered. I shoved the square into my mouth and slouched back in the unforgiving plastic chair. Nan reached over and took my hand in hers, squeezed tightly and then let go. She then pulled my grampa's square-laden napkin toward herself, eating the remaining three desserts quickly while he spoke to an old man wearing an all-denim outfit.

I sat with my grandparents for most of the reception and half listened to their conversations, hearing nothing that sounded like the grief I felt inside.

ten

THE RECEPTION CARRIED OVER TO OUR HOUSE. PEOPLE STOPPED by with casseroles and stayed for coffee, beer, and leftover squares. For the first time since I'd been home, our living room was filled with people and noise and warmth. I listened to snippets of conversation but didn't join in; smiled at the stories people told about Billy, but didn't tell any of my own. None of them involved him getting too drunk, or too angry, or too sad; they were all good stories, happy stories. The best stories.

No one talked about how he died, and I didn't know if that made it better or worse. It felt like both a glaring omission and a subtle reprieve.

"I was so sad when I heard about Billy." A man I vaguely recognized stopped in front of me. "I truly am sorry for your loss."

"Thank you. Thanks for coming." I'd had the same conversation dozens of times today.

I went to the kitchen and moved dishes from one spot on the counter to another. Nan ignored me while she flipped luski. She took one out of the pan and placed it on the Spirit Plate next to some carrots and a pile of banana gummies I'd picked up at the store. I'd thought I might clean, but my attempt was proving ineffective. After playing musical dishes for a few more minutes, I wiped my hands on a dishtowel and went to my room.

I left behind the din of folk music, clanking cups, and quiet chatter. Alone, everything caught up to me. I was exhausted. Drained from the constant condolences and strained conversations; from everybody refusing to say the word *suicide*, like it tarnished Billy's memory. Killing himself was the last thing Billy ever did. We couldn't change how he died, no matter how much we might want to. Not saying the word made it seem odious and suffocating. But mostly, I felt exhausted from the revelation that the people I loved could be so easily taken from me.

I flopped back onto my bed. I wanted to become one with the mattress. The stairs to my bedroom had felt particularly steep and crooked. The stars stuck on my bedroom ceiling were dancing. I'd probably had too much to drink.

"Hey."

I sat up. Judging by how Adam leaned against the doorframe, he'd drunk too much too.

"Can I come in?" he asked.

I nodded.

Adam quietly shut the door then sat next to me on the bed. He reached over and grabbed my hand, held it tightly. How many times had we sat like this in the past week?

"You okay?"

I looked up at the ceiling and let out a shaky breath. "I think I just forgot that people can die, you know? Like, I forgot that people aren't always going to be there. That things won't stay the same forever." I turned to face Adam. "Billy is gone. I'm never going to hear him laugh again, never going to watch *Big Trouble in Little China* with him again."

"You hate that movie." Adam smiled, the creases at the corners of his eyes crinkled.

He'd attempted to tame his wild hair, the unkempt curls tucked behind his ears. The subtle effort was meant to go unnoticed, but it didn't. I noticed everything about Adam, and his tucked curls made my heart ache. His nose, which he'd broken in a game of Red Rover when we were kids, was crooked. I wanted to reach out and touch his face. I wondered how his beard would feel against my palm. Instead, I squeezed his hand a little harder.

"One day I'm going to come home and you won't be in my parents' kitchen, asking me to marry you, talking about what we should name our kids, eating my spaghetti sauce before it's done."

With his free hand Adam reached up and brushed his thumb across my cheek, wiping away a tear. His hand hovered while his eyes traced the curves of my face. There was a hesitancy in how he held his hand, how he looked at me. The world stilled and I thought about how many almost-moments Adam and I had had over the years. Propelled by the notion of loss and the fear that one day Adam might not be there, I leaned in and planted a soft kiss on his lips. His fingers, still beside my face, hesitated briefly before they tangled in my hair. He pulled me closer and deepened the kiss. He smelled like woodsmoke and tasted like cheap beer.

Adam pulled back suddenly and pressed his forehead against mine. "Charlie," he said, a breath of uncertainty.

I took his face in my hands. "Can you please, for once in your life, just not talk?"

I moved to fill the space he had created. As we kissed, our movements became frantic and awkward. Adam's dress shirt, the sleeves rolled up, caught on his elbows as I tried to lift it over his head. His fingers fumbled with the buttons at the back of my dress as I struggled with the buckle of his belt. He stood and took off his pants.

"Socks," I mumbled while I tried to shimmy out of my dress. Adam rolled his eyes, took off his socks, and came back to the bed. It creaked and groaned as we lay down. Adam hovered above me in just his boxers. I was a little breathless as I struggled to take my bra off. Adam moved his hand down the length of my side, and his light touch sent a shiver down my body. He stopped at my underwear; his fingers toyed with the waistband. He pulled back, a pained look on his face. "I don't have a…" he trailed off.

"I'm on the pill." I paused. "I'm also chlamydia free." I smiled, hoping to ease some of the tension.

Adam snorted. "You know, I wasn't sure."

"Are you sure about this?" I ran the palm of my hand along the side of his face and looked into his eyes.

"Charlie, I've—" Adam closed his mouth abruptly, his brow furrowed. "Yes, I'm sure."

I nodded. "Okay then."

He breathed through his nose. "Okay then."

I wanted to ask what it was he had started to say, but all thought was driven from my mind as Adam slid my underwear off my hips and down my legs.

eleven

I WOKE UP AS THE SUN ROSE THE NEXT MORNING, MY MOUTH fuzzy and dry. Adam slept naked beside me, his arm draped protectively across my middle. I'd woken up with him next to me for the past few days. It felt normal now, like we'd done this for years. I wanted to wrap myself in the feeling and tear it to bits at the same time. Regret began to fill my lungs.

When the tides in the Cobequid Bay went out and left stretches of mudflats, I could walk halfway to the other shore. Sometimes the mud engulfed my feet, right up to my ankles, and made it hard to move. The longer you stayed stuck, the harder it was to keep going.

With Adam's legs entangled with mine, his warm breath tickling my shoulder, I couldn't say what was so wrong with getting stuck. In this bed, I'd gladly be swallowed whole.

Which was why I had to get up.

I quietly dressed and made my way downstairs, slipped on muddy rain boots, and trudged outside to feed the chickens. The early morning sun filtered through the trees and as light broke through the cool mist, it caught on the frosted grass. As they always did in the cold months, the chickens huddled in their coop and waited for the noise of rustling feed before making an appearance.

The wooden fence creaked with cold and age as I leaned against it, watching the chickens peck at the frozen earth. One year Billy decided the chickens needed protection against the cold, so he made us knit small capes for them. I made a mental note to ask Billy if we should make new ones for them before I remembered.

In my hazy and half-asleep mind, Billy was inside, asleep, like the rest of my family. But he wasn't. His room was empty and there was no one to concern themselves with the chickens' higher needs anymore.

There is a rickety bridge that crosses over Portapique River. As kids, Johnny and Adam would jump off it into the water below. I was always too scared. One year, after weeks of being teased by them, I finally worked up the courage. I threw myself off the bridge and, barrelling toward the river, realized I'd jumped all wrong. I ended up belly flopping into the frigid water. This felt a lot like that. The slow dawning of a harsh, irrefutable truth, suspended in midair, knowing it was going to hurt but unable to do anything about it. Billy's death was the stinging slap of the water on my stomach, which left me floundering and hoping I didn't drown.

I dropped the empty feed bucket, leaned forward, and rested my forehead on the topmost rung of the paddock fence.

I stared down at my mud-splattered boots. There was still pig blood on the right toe, a persistent reminder of life and death and what gets left behind.

A second pair of boots appeared, the toes almost touching mine. I straightened. Adam was on the other side of the fence. Much like that time at the river, Adam was there to pull me to shore. But this time I couldn't willingly sink into his arms.

I wiped my hands across my cheeks, smearing tears I wished he hadn't seen.

"Let's go inside." Adam held open the gate for me. He offered his hand, but I pretended not to see. I walked past him into the house.

Mom was hunched over the kitchen table, like it wouldn't be possible to remain upright if she didn't have that support. She toyed with the knife beside her breakfast plate.

"Are you heading home today, T'us?" Dad asked.

"Yeah. Probably within the hour." I might as well rip the Band-Aid off and get going. I could feel Adam watching me. I could still feel his hands on my skin, the intoxicating weight of him on top of me.

I had to get out of here soon, or I'd never leave. And that was the last thing Billy would want for me.

"Can't you stay any longer?" Mom asked.

"Not really."

"Why not?" Her voice was sharp.

"I've got classes and homework."

"Whatever. I bet you can't wait to get out of here." She was right. But I wasn't about to tell her that.

"June—" Dad tried to interrupt.

Mom ignored him. "You're running, Charlie."

"I am not." I was.

Mom huffed.

"I'm sorry that my life is in the city."

Mom stabbed her scalloped potatoes so forcefully I wondered if she was pretending they were me.

"I wish I could stay longer." It was only a tiny lie. "But I've already stayed longer than I planned to."

Adam moved away from my side and refilled his coffee mug.

Mom pushed away the plate of uneaten food.

I looked at Dad with wide eyes. He returned my expression and shrugged his shoulders.

I sighed and went upstairs to quickly pack my bags and then came back down to say goodbye. I felt like an asshole for leaving so soon, but I didn't have a choice. My skin was starting to feel too tight, like it didn't fit right. All I wanted to do was hide under my blanket at my apartment and never leave again. My mom called it *turtling*. Fiona called it *avoidance*. Johnny called it *being chickenshit*. Whatever the terminology, I wanted to do it right now.

I stood in the kitchen doorway and waited for someone to acknowledge that I was leaving.

"Okay, bye," I bit out when no one did.

"Have a safe drive." Dad got up and hugged me. "Love you."

"Love you too."

I looked down at Mom.

She looked down at the table.

"I love you, Mom."

"Love you too." She picked up the knife again and tapped the sharp end on the table.

I hovered for a moment and then shot a glance towards Adam, who stood by the door to the kitchen. He let me walk past him before he followed me out the front door.

"Charlie, can we talk?" he asked as the door slammed. He jogged after me.

"Can we give it a few days?" I asked when I reached my car. "I just need time."

For things to settle. To overthink. To figure out how to act like this didn't happen. I kicked at the gravel, scattering tiny rocks.

"Of course you do." There was a hint of laughter in Adam's voice, but something else, too—defeat? Resignation?

I wanted to defend myself. From what, I wasn't entirely sure.

"Bye, Charlie."

"See ya, Adam."

The engine took its time turning over; it was a game we liked to play. A sort of *will I or won't I.* Adam rapped a knuckle on my window. I rolled it down.

"Let me look at your engine next time you're back."

"It's fine."

"Charlie—"

"I swear, it's just a personality quirk. It's fine."

"Are you seriously trying to argue with a mechanic right now?"

I struggled not to roll my eyes. "Fine. I promise."

"Have a safe drive." Adam patted the hood of the car and walked back to my parents' house.

I pressed play on the dash, not knowing what CD was in there. The Tragically Hip burst through the speakers. I turned up the volume and let Gord Downie drown everything else out on my drive back to Halifax.

twelve

"FIONA?" I CALLED, SLIPPING OFF MY SHOES AND STARTING UP the stairwell, my footsteps heavy.

"Charlie?" Fiona stuck her head out the second-floor entryway. She met me halfway down the stairs and enveloped me in a hug.

I wrapped my arms around her and squeezed hard. "Why aren't you wearing any pants?"

Fiona leaned back to look me in the eyes. "How are you?"

I sighed. "I don't know. I just...I still haven't fully wrapped my head around it." I looked down at the mismatched socks on my feet. Fiona's, on the step above mine, were bare, her toenails painted green. When we first moved in, I had thought the stairwell carpet was so ugly it was cute. I stared at it now, brown and stained and picked apart by past tenants' cats. It might just be ugly, I couldn't decide. Fiona said she could tell what mood I was in based on how I felt about the carpet.

"How was the funeral?"

I shrugged. "I don't really want to talk about it."

"How's Adam?" Fiona feigned nonchalance, but there was a reason she'd gotten a C in theatre second year.

I didn't bother to beat around the bush. I knew I'd eventually tell her, so I might as well tell her right away, save us both the trouble.

"We had sex."

"WHAT?" she all but shrieked. "You had SEX? How was it? Was it magical? Did he propose right after? Did he confess his undying love?"

I winced. "Nothing so dramatic, sorry."

"Tell me everything."

How was I supposed to describe what having sex with Adam felt like? How could I put into words the feeling of homecoming? Or the brutal sadness that immediately followed it?

"It was..." I hesitated. "Good? I don't know, Fi, it just—it was nice."

"Nice?" Fiona groaned. "I want penis size. Orgasm quality. I want—"

"Fiona?" A shirtless guy I didn't know stuck his head through our doorway. "Are you coming back?"

"Oh. Hey, Greg." Fiona blinked up at him. "Um, in a second."

Greg disappeared from sight.

"Were you about to…? Is that why you don't have pants on?"

"Maybe…"

"You seemed a little surprised to see him. Did you…forget about him?" I smirked.

Fiona scrunched up her face. "Just for like, a second."

"Oh my god, poor Greg."

"Hey, Greg is fine. Greg already got a very skillful blow job. Greg can wait. You're more important than Greg and his sexual needs."

"Gee, thanks."

"Do you want me to kick him out? We can stuff our faces and watch *She's All That*?"

"No, you finish up." I gestured upstairs. "I'm going to get groceries. We can stuff our faces later."

"Okay." Fiona kissed my forehead then darted back up the stairs. It was only then that I noticed she was wearing a thong.

I hid behind my library book. I was so hungry I thought I might die, but I knew as soon as I got up someone would take my spot. I slouched in my chair and slowly unwrapped my granola bar, flinching every time the wrapper crinkled. This might be the first rule I'd ever broken. I normally ate before coming to the library, but I'd felt nauseous earlier.

Fiona and I had a two-hour gap between classes on Wednesdays. Every week we met here to study. I liked studying in the library because of the forced quiet. I liked the smell of the books. I felt more capable of academic feats in this hallowed space than I did at home, slumped on the couch. Fiona liked to study in the library because during the second week of the semester we stumbled across a couple having sex in the stacks. She kept coming back, hoping it would happen again.

"Where's Jason?" Fiona asked, looking around. "He's usually making moon eyes at you by the time I get here."

"I don't know." I stayed hidden behind my book.

I peeked over just in time to see Fiona slowly turn her head to look at me.

"Tell me." Fiona would ask until I gave in.

"He asked me out." God I was weak.

"And you said?"

I took a bite of granola bar.

Fiona groaned. The person at the table next to us shot her a look.

I didn't want to get kicked out of the library. I just wanted to study. "I said no," I whispered, hoping to end this conversation. "Actually, I said I had to go home to kill a pig."

"We are never going to see Jason again. He was helping me with stats. What am I supposed to do now?" Fiona was aghast.

"So, you're saying I should have said yes to the creepy vegetarian so he would keep doing your homework?"

"Yes." Fiona nodded. "Jason was hot. He was nice."

I leaned back in my seat, arms crossed over my chest. "Yeah but he wasn't—" *Adam*. I'd almost said Adam. Good god, Fiona would've had a field day with that—"my type," I finished. I grabbed another granola bar from my bag and unwrapped it. This time I didn't hesitate when the wrapper crinkled.

"Maybe I can convince Jason to help me study for my exam." Fiona tapped her fingernails on the lacquered table. She paused. "Are you sure you can't stomach one little date?"

"I'm sure he'd help you study regardless. For what it's worth, I don't think you need Jason."

Fiona slumped in her seat. "Now I have to figure out what I need on the exam to pass the course."

"Or, get this, you could just study." I pulled out a book from the pile beside me and put the one I'd hidden behind on top.

"Now's not the time for logic."

"Of course not."

I flipped to the chapter I was supposed to be reading: Pre-1900s Immigration and Industrialization in Canada.

"Can I have a granola bar?" Fiona asked.

I reached into my bag and handed her one.

She took it, then looked down at the paper in front of her. "According to my stellar math, I need to get a 167 percent on my final exam." She paused. "That cannot be right."

"Maybe you do need Jason," I admitted before going back to my work.

thirteen

TODAY WAS THE DAY.

I had outlined the square on my Maud Lewis wall calendar and written in neat capital letters: *MAIL APPLICATIONS*. I could practically recite them from memory. I'd put the completed packages in envelopes the night before and stuffed them in my desk drawer, ready. Even if I wasn't sure I was.

I stood at the graffitied mailbox and clutched the manila envelopes with their oh-so-carefully-printed addresses: a scholarship application and two grad school applications, one to stay at Dalhousie, and the other for the University of Toronto. I felt like I was on the precipice of something. As if just by placing the applications in the mail, my fate was sealed.

I was the first person in my family to go to university. My dad liked to say that my going to grad school was like an athlete breaking their own world record.

I pulled the mailbox open and, after a quick final check of the addresses, let them fall through the slot. They landed at the bottom of the box and that was that. They were out of my control.

I tried to work up some appropriate emotion. Excitement. Happiness. Optimism. Instead, I wanted to puke.

"Charlie!" Fiona yelled from the front stoop. "We need to get to the farmers' market before it closes!"

I walked back towards her. "It's not my fault you refused to get out of bed." The farther I got from the mailboxes, the sicker I felt.

"Come on." Fiona took my hand and pulled me down the street.

"You know you're about to spend, like, fifty bucks for stuff I could get at home by offering the neighbour a loaf of bread." She was shorter than me, but I struggled to keep pace with her.

"Yeah, yeah." She darted across Oxford Street towards the bus stop, dragging me along. A car honked as the driver slammed on their brakes. "Just because you grew up in middle-of-nowhere farm-ville where everyone has a weirdly quaint skill, doesn't mean you can't enjoy a farmers' market with your lovely roommate."

I waved at the driver and mouthed *sorry*. "You know, I'd prefer to die quietly in my bed."

Fiona let go of my hand as she stepped onto the sidewalk. "You're always so dramatic," she huffed.

"Oh, that's rich."

Fiona stuck her mittened hand up in the air. "I'm giving you the finger, just so you know."

"Okay, thanks for keeping me in the loop."

When the bus eventually came, we staggered to two empty seats.

"Guess what my mom told me last night."

I grimaced, scrunching up my nose. She knew I hated guessing.

"Fine. Rachel had another baby. Isn't that crazy?"

"Is it?" Young people having kids didn't seem that wild to me. Fiona's cousin was close to our age, but my mom had been young when she'd had me and Johnny.

"It is. Three years ago I had to, quite literally, slide her drunk ass home on an icy sidewalk. And now she's going to be a mom of two? The times really do be changing. It's kind of sad."

"What is? The fact that she can't get so inebriated you have to roll her home?" I rifled through my bag for a cough drop.

"Wow, you're in a mood today."

Fiona was right. I felt tired. A little under the weather. And, in the twenty minutes since I'd mailed my grad school applications, had convinced myself I'd accidently sent them excerpts from my junior high diary.

The bus pulled up beside the Oxford. It was the only rep cinema left in town. Billy always made me go with him when he came to visit. Even here, I found Billy in everything. The most unexpected things would make me want to cry. Yesterday I'd had to choke back tears when I'd seen a stack of Cherry Blossom candies, their garish yellow boxes an alarming reminder of the grief I wore like a scarf wrapped tightly around my neck.

I apologized.

"Maybe take a nap when we get home."

I never took naps, but that didn't seem like a bad suggestion.

A bunch of students shuffled onto the bus and flashed their passes.

"It's just that Rachel had her whole life ahead of her and now she's just popping out babies." Fiona made a disgruntled face. "She just finished university. I feel like she hasn't even lived."

I laughed. "You're acting like becoming a mother is a death sentence."

"I know it's not. But, like, maybe it is a little bit? What about her career? Even just, like, having fun." Fiona played with her hair. "I still think it's sad."

"Maybe she *wants* to pop out babies."

"Would you?"

"I don't know. Eventually?"

Fiona's gaze widened. "Charlie, she's only a year older than us."

"Yeah, but isn't your family stupidly rich? And isn't her boyfriend older and also stupidly rich? She can afford to have babies. We"—I gestured between the two of us—"cannot. Well, I guess you could." Fiona grimaced. "Sorry, but Rachel can pop out as many kids as she wants."

"Whatever." Fiona rolled her eyes, and looked out the window as the bus turned onto Coburg Road.

The university rolled by my window. Fiona leaned over, putting her head on my shoulder. I closed my eyes and rested my head atop hers.

fourteen

I JOLTED AWAKE AT THE SOUND OF THE PHONE. I'D BEEN READ-ing about the history of Oak Island, all the theories of what treasure its fabled Money Pit contained coalescing into folktale and myth. I'd fallen asleep on the couch wondering how fact gets turned into story over time. I stretched, rubbed my eyes, and hoped Fiona would get it.

"Is someone going to answer that?" Fiona yelled from down the hall.

"Can you?" I asked, pulling the blanket up to my chin.

"I'm pooping!"

"Fine." I tossed the blanket aside and slowly got off the couch. Maybe they'd hang up.

"Okay. Great. If it's for me, tell them I'm doing something else." The bathroom door shut as I picked up the receiver.

"Charlie?" It was Adam.

"Hey." I wrapped the phone cord around my fingers.

"It's Adam."

"I know."

"Oh."

There was a long, awkward pause.

"I hadn't heard from you."

"Sorry." I'd been back in Halifax for less than a week.

"You don't have to apologize. I just wanted to see how you were doing."

Another pause.

"How are you feeling?" he asked.

"Weird." I took a deep breath. I was being a jerk and I needed to stop. Why did my body stiffen at the first sign of tenderness? Why couldn't I just accept his kindness? "I don't know how else to describe it. I'm tired. I'm sad. I feel really rundown. And I just miss him. You probably understand though."

"Not really." Something rustled. A chair scraped across the floor. "I was so young when my mom died. I don't remember her except through stories people tell me, and pictures. If we crossed paths right now, we wouldn't recognize each other. And that's super shitty. I miss her, but not, like, as a person, more as an idea. Which seems super messed up when I say it out loud. I guess I just never had the chance to know her." Adam paused, and this time it didn't feel weird. "I think everything you're feeling is normal."

He cleared his throat. "How are you feeling about the, uh, other thing?"

I'd been stupidly optimistic to think this wouldn't get brought up.

"You mean the fact that we had sex right after my uncle's funeral?"

"Uh...yeah, that. I guess."

Fiona shimmied into the kitchen. She pointed to the phone, then raised her arms in question.

"The timing was not great." I mouthed *Adam*.

"Sorry," Adam breathed out loudly.

"You didn't do anything wrong. It was a mutual undertaking."

"You make it sound like...a business deal or something."

"Sorry." I wanted to bang my head against the wall.

"You don't—" Adam sighed. "Do you want...I called because I was wondering. Would you want to go out sometime, like on a date." He paused. "With me."

My heart thunked. An irregular palpitation. Maybe I was going into cardiac arrest. At least if I had a heart attack, I wouldn't have to answer his question. I untangled my fingers from the cord and let it drop. I rubbed my chest. I wished he'd never asked.

"I don't think that's a good idea."

"Can I ask why?"

Because I want it too badly. Because it would be so easy to fall in love with you. Because Billy told me to run and now I can't not.

"I just don't think it is." Every part of me felt weighed down.

"Okay. Well, uh..." Adam let the unfinished sentence hang in the air. "Since I've just made everything fifty times more awkward, I'm going to go. See you next time you're home."

"Sure. Bye A—"

The dial tone cut me off.

fifteen

THE CEILING OF MY BEDROOM WAS GROSS. THERE WAS A CONcerning stain in the far corner, presumably from water damage, and an equally concerning crack in the plaster running down the middle. I turned off the light when I'd gotten sick of looking at them, but somehow I was more aware of my ceiling's imperfections in the dark. They loomed above me, a testament to poorly maintained apartments across this perpetually damp city.

I rolled onto my side and tried to get comfortable. I fluffed my pillow. Repositioned my legs.

I never thought a twin-sized bed could feel so big.

I wanted Adam's arm around my middle. I wanted our legs entangled. I wanted to be mildly annoyed he was hogging the blankets, only for him to wake up and accuse me of doing the same.

I didn't miss his morning breath, but I would gladly take it if it meant I got everything else.

I was restless. I missed him all the time. It hadn't been like this before. Of course I'd missed him, he was one of my best friends, but not like this. This was a full-body ache. This complicated matters. I had to shut it down, I just didn't know how.

I'd made the right decision. I had to remind myself again and again, because it certainly didn't feel like it. There was no future for me and Adam, no world in which one of us didn't have to give up the plans we'd made for ourselves.

Don't get stuck, I heard Billy remind me.

I reached for the Discman on my bedside table and listened to the entirety of *Fallow* before falling asleep.

sixteen

"HI, SWEET KITTIES," I WHEEZED. I STOPPED TO SMILE AT THE Monastery Lane cats, despite the crushing weight of my groceries.

The cats ignored me. I continued on.

I wasn't made to handle multiple stress points at once. I did not thrive in chaos and uncertainty, which is why I'd reached for a ten-kilogram bag of flour instead of the tiny one I usually bought. I staggered down the street, struggling to hold the flour in my arms while my backpack full of food weighed me down from behind. I thought they would work as a counterbalance system, but it just made it harder to walk. A garbage bag had been torn open on the corner of Allan and Harvard; crows pecked at the plastic and foil, looking for scraps. I imagined them pecking at my body if I were to lose my footing.

I was sweatier than anyone should be by the end of November when I finally made it to our apartment. I dodged the slightly rotten porch step and made it inside. I don't know that I would call him a slumlord, but our landlord definitely walked the line.

Where the walls had been poorly patched, Fiona and I had hung posters. We crammed our clothes and all the things we didn't know what to do with into the apartment's single closet. We did our best, which wasn't that great. Between the two of us we had minimal repair skills, little time outside of school and friends—the latter more Fiona's issue than mine—and barely any money. Though Fiona was well-off, her parents were still pissed at her for coming to school out east and made no effort to help her out. There's no room for a home-décor budget when you're living off no-name instant noodles.

The kitchen was oddly laid out. The stove was right beside the sink, the two separated by a sliver of counter. Clear across the room in a far corner was the fridge. There was also a really low-hanging pendant lamp, slightly too far right to be considered the middle of the room and which we'd both learned to avoid after whacking our heads numerous times. The one saving grace of the apartment was the hardwood floors.

Dad had a mini heart attack when he helped us move in.

"Why the hell would you rent this place?" he asked, totally disgusted by our new home.

"Look at the floors, Nick!" Fiona gestured with a grand sweep of her hand.

"They need to be refinished."

"Do you think they're original?" She'd been hoping for a conversation piece.

Dad cursed and went to get another box.

I dumped the bag of flour and my backpack onto the counter and unloaded everything I'd bought. First, I measured out the yeast and dumped it into a bowl with warm water and a pinch of sugar. In the ten minutes it took the yeast to proof, I tried to put away the rest of the food: a fun challenge. I washed my hands just before the timer dinged, jimmying the faucet in its special way to turn it off. Next, I put the rest of the ingredients in the bowl with the now foamy yeast and mixed it a few times before turning it out on the kitchen table. Then I began to knead the dough, pushing and pulling, flipping and stretching, until it became less sticky, the texture soft and smooth.

"Okay, seriously, you have to stop baking."

I looked up from the dough.

"I'm not kidding," Fiona continued, "when I say that my pants barely fit anymore. One of us needs to have some self-control in this situation and I can tell you it will not be me."

"I don't know if I can. If I stop considering the suppleness of my dough, I may have an honest-to-god breakdown."

I was on the couch, halfway through a book, four thick slices of bread on my stomach, when Fiona stumbled up the stairs.

"Hello, sweet baby!" she slurred as she sidestepped into the living room and kicked off her boots.

I took a huge bite of bread and turned the page.

Fiona undid her pants, let out a long sigh, then took them off completely before sitting next to me. "How're we feeling?"

"Fine." I tried not to sigh. I'd been perfectly content with my bread and my book.

"Do you want a hug?"

"No," I said, taking a bite and placing the slice back on my stomach.

"Yes, you do." Fiona crawled on top of me. She nestled her head by mine, then relaxed completely. Her body weight pushed us farther into the cushion, squishing my book and bread between us. "Why haven't you called Adam back? You clearly want to bone him again."

I grimaced. "Your breath smells like peppermint schnapps and donair."

Fiona held my face in her hands, forcing me to look at her. "Answer the question, biiiiitch."

"He hasn't called me either."

"You broke his sad hillbilly heart, why would he call you back?" Fiona pointed a finger toward the ceiling and crossed her eyes, "Furthermore, that's such a junior-high answer."

"I'm basically fresh out of junior high. Am I not allowed moments of immaturity?"

Fiona shook her head dramatically. "You're not going to call and then Adam is going to go zoom zoom fast bye bye and then you will be a sad burrito." She sat up. "But don't fret—" She placed the back of her hand against my cheek. "I will tend to you. I will make sure you are warm and toasty and your cheese is all melted." She paused. "Do you think that Mexican place is open right now?" She stood up quickly, wavered a bit, then confidently walked towards the kitchen. "I'm going to call them and ask." She burped as she left the room.

I picked up one of my slices of bread, it was sad and squashed.

I missed Adam. I didn't want him to go "zoom zoom fast bye bye." I wanted to sleep in his bed and wake up and kiss him and have him be the person I called whenever I felt sad. It would be so easy to love Adam, to say fuck it to grad school, to move home, get stuck there and be happy about it, at least for a little while. But eventually I would regret it, wouldn't I?

Right now, according to my plan, my life in five years was a PhD program, maybe here, maybe Toronto, maybe somewhere else. What would my life look like in five years if I called Adam right now? Would I be happy? Would I resent him? Would I be sitting on my parents' porch wondering how I'd gotten there?

As much as it hurt, it was easier not to call, to just stay the course.

So, I ate my squished bread, which had become my life force over the last week, and listened to Fiona promise whatever poor soul had answered the phone that she'd be a good girl if they just brought her three burritos.

seventeen

THE GUY NEXT TO ME SMELLED LIKE ONIONS. AND BLEACH. But maybe also compost. If this class didn't end soon I was going to simultaneously throw up and crumple to the floor. Dr. Driscoll droned on about the Halifax Explosion. I wished I would explode. I looked to the clock on the wall. Five minutes to go.

I'd been really interested in the lecture for the first half, when Dr. Driscoll spoke about the wreckage of the sugar refinery on the waterfront. The proposal I'd submitted for my grad school application dealt with the historical and contemporary hierarchy of sugars. This might be important for my thesis. But then the guy next to me leaned over to grab something from his backpack and I'd been undone. I tried to breathe through my mouth, but it didn't help.

I felt a little clammy. The milk I put in my coffee this morning had only been a day past it's best before. Dad loved to remind me those dates were a scam. Maybe he was wrong. Then again, I'd puked a few times this week. Someone had sneezed on me last week on the bus. Maybe I'd caught something.

The professor closed his book. Thank god. I was packed up and ready to leave before he finished dismissing the class. I dashed out. I just needed fresh air, and to never sit next to that guy again, and I'd be fine.

I was about fifteen minutes from my apartment when I gagged. The need to vomit was so strong I couldn't even try to stop it. Thankfully I was on a side street. Small blessings and all. I held on to a telephone pole and dry heaved. Once. Twice. Then nothing. I stood up, brushed my hair away from my face, and kept walking. My stomach felt marginally better, but I wasn't naïve enough to think I was safe. I tried power walking, which wasn't great. So, I tried walking slowly, which felt worse.

I'd almost made it my apartment when I had to retch again. A woman in a beret and a peacoat walked toward me. She'd probably never dry heaved in a public space in her life. I felt sweaty. She was getting closer. I was beside a hedge. Maybe if I just stuck my head in, she'd assume I was looking for something. I retched.

I stopped puking just long enough to hear her walk by me, say "Ew," and keep going. I dry heaved one more time before my stomach finally calmed. I took a swig from my water bottle, swished it around, and spit it out. There was no point in feigning decorum right now.

I dragged my feet the rest of the way home.

"I just threw up in someone's hedge on Allan Street," I said as I walked into the kitchen, dropping my backpack on the floor.

Fiona sat at the table surrounded by textbooks. "Ew, do you have the flu?" She took a sip of her coffee, grimaced, and got up to reheat it in the microwave.

"I don't think so." I fell into the chair opposite hers and pressed a hand to my forehead. "I've thrown up, like, five times this week. I don't know what's wrong with me. Yesterday I dry heaved into a toilet at the library for like five minutes." It had been even more depressing than it sounded.

"Maybe you're pregnant," Fiona said, tapping her nails on the countertop while her coffee spun in the microwave.

The entire world came to a screeching halt. I almost told Fiona I couldn't possibly be pregnant because it wasn't part of the five-year plan. My body wouldn't betray me like that. Would it? Maybe if I didn't move, everything would be fine. I'd just sit like this forever and never deal with the potential consequences. Then an ambulance drove by, its siren blaring, and there was Adam above me: his hands on my body, the gentle release, a quiet crescendo that felt like sunlight and honey, every moment from that night playing in rapid succession.

She laughed when she saw the look on my face. "I was joking Charlie, relax."

I ignored her. The nausea crept back in. "Fiona, did you already have your period?"

"I finished it like a week ago. Why?"

"Because you pulled me into your cycle when we first moved in together." In that moment I was sincerely offended that she wasn't aware of the synchronicity of our moon cycles. My throat clogged with bile and panic. "Shit. Fiona, am I pregnant?"

She stood still, her eyes wide. "There's a test in the medicine cabinet."

I pushed back my chair and ran to the bathroom. I slammed the door. Opened the cabinet and searched for the test. Painkillers and Band-Aids fell into the sink.

It wasn't there.

I crouched and searched the cupboard underneath the sink. Toilet paper, pads, and random bottles spilled onto the floor. I found the box at the very back. I fumbled with the packaging, ripped it open, and dumped the contents onto my lap.

I read the instructions twice. I didn't understand any of it. Was sudden illiteracy a pregnancy symptom?

I just had to pee on it, right?

Sitting on the toilet, I held the unwrapped stick in front of me. The part that absorbed the pee was so small—how was I supposed to make sure I actually peed on it?

Without getting off the toilet I leaned over and opened the door. "I need a cup!" I called out.

"Got it!" Fiona yelled back.

A minute later she stuck a cup through the door, one I'd bought around Halloween. It said *I'm just here for the boos*. If I needed a reminder I wasn't ready to be a mother, this was it.

I took a breath and willed myself to relax.

Seconds felt like hours. Eventually, I peed in the cup.

I stuck the end of the test in the cup and stirred it around.

I placed the test back on the sink and waited, my fingernails making indents in my thighs.

Two lines appeared in under a minute.

I grabbed the box off the floor and scanned the instructions; it said it could take upwards of three minutes to show results. Did that mean I was *very* pregnant as opposed to *just* pregnant? Did that mean there was more than one in there?

"Shit!" I sobbed.

"What?" Fiona asked. "Can I come in?"

Pants around my ankles, I leaned over and turned the door handle. Fiona burst inside and wrenched the test from my fingers.

Her eyes widened as she stared down at the two pink lines. "Shit!"

She sat down on the edge of the bathtub with a hard thud, tapping the stick against her thigh while I hiccupped and sputtered. Fiona muttered, "Okay, okay, okay" in time with the whacking of the cheap plastic against her thigh. She looked around our tiny, mould-covered bathroom like maybe she could find a plan of action tucked somewhere between the ratty towels and empty bottles of conditioner we kept forgetting to throw out.

Fiona wrapped her arms around me and planted a kiss on my hairline. "Right. Give me twenty minutes." She tossed the stick into the sink before she stormed out of the bathroom, down the stairs, and out the front door.

I'd always wanted to be a mother. But that was a ten-year-plan kind of thing. Not a right-now thing. Not a right-after-you-graduate-undergrad kind of thing. It was something I was going to do when I was in a stable relationship. This past summer Nan had told me I should find a nice Mi'kmaw boy to have a kid with, keep the Indian status in the family, she'd said. God. I was supposed to pee on the damn stick while my loving partner, Mr. Status and Stability, was there holding my hand. It was supposed to be a moment so fucking tender and perfect.

Not this. Not by accident, and not in my shitty bathroom in my shitty apartment. I wasn't supposed to be alone with two out of three functioning vanity lights and an inordinate number of empty conditioner bottles. How did we have so many? Why hadn't I noticed before? I couldn't be a mother.

And Adam. God, Adam.

I stuck my head between my legs so I wouldn't pass out. What was I supposed to do?

By the time Fiona made it home, I'd hidden under a blanket on the couch.

"How're you doing, babe?"

"I've, um, decided that I'm just going to live under this blanket until I die."

"Okay. That might eventually get boring."

"Anything is better than having to deal with the hell I've brought upon myself."

"Sure."

Fiona put something down. Maybe on the table. Maybe on the floor. I refused to look.

"Want to take the blanket off your head?"

"Is my life over?" I whispered.

"Not if you don't keep it. You have plenty of time to be a mom, just not now."

How could I explain that even though none of this had gone the way it was supposed to, even though I was scared shitless, and my knees felt funny, the same way they did when Johnny broke his arm and it was bent at a really weird angle, keeping the baby seemed like the only option. "If I do?"

Fiona sighed. "I don't know. If I was in your situation I would think so. But that doesn't seem like the can-do spirit I should approach this with."

"Where's your supportive attitude?" It was getting hot under the blanket.

"I got some ice cream."

"With chunky bits?"

"No duh."

I lowered the blanket to just under my nose.

"Want to come out and have some?" Fiona cooed, like a mother. "We don't have to talk about anything. We can watch all six episodes of *Pride and Prejudice*." She held the ice cream out and shook it.

"You can even tell me all the annoying facts and interpretations you have about it," she promised as I sat up.

eighteen

I COULDN'T SLEEP. EMOTIONALLY, MY SHIT NEEDED TO BE SORTED out ASAP.

My five-year plan didn't involve dependents; it tentatively involved a cat in two to four years. My plan was good. It was linear. It made sense. It had evolved slightly but was the same path I'd decided on in second year. I'd always been the smart kid. The driven kid. The kid who, when every other classmate was picking their nose and holding books upside down, was reading chapter books. University was the natural next step after high school. And then, in second year university, a professor I'd really liked, Dr. Ross, had suggested I should think about grad school. So, I decided I would go.

I was weighed down by panic and the crocheted blanket Nan made me for my eighteenth birthday. I tried to draw breath all the way down to my toes, but it couldn't seem to make it past my throat.

Billy's near-decade-old words bashed around in my head.

Don't get stuck.

Don't get stuck.

Don't get stuck.

I didn't know how to move forward.

But then I saw Adam's face, the way his eyes lit up as he smiled. I heard the quiet, near reverent breath he took as we unknowingly made the baby growing inside me, and I knew that if I was going to rewrite my five-year plan, recalibrate the life I thought I'd have, I had to tell him.

nineteen

WELL ON MY WAY TO RUIN, I DECIDED TO DITCH CLASS THE NEXT day. I packed a book, my wallet, and a barf bag and headed home.

Even though I'd rather pluck my eyeballs out, I knew telling Adam was the next logical step. And right now, I was clinging to logic like it was a life raft in the middle of the ocean.

The leaves had all been ripped from the trees, which now stood bare along the old highway. Halifax had seen a smattering of snow the week before. The flurries had disappeared before they even touched the ground, but out here a light dusting clung to the frigid stalks of grass and leftover sprigs of wheat. In summer and autumn, I would pass gardeners tending their flowers, tractors ploughing the land, cows gathered in clusters, their tails swatting away flies. I hadn't seen a living thing out in the open since I'd left the gas station in Millbrook.

When I reached Adam's road, I kept driving. My whole "no point in delaying the inevitable" stance seemed wildly rash now that I had to go through with it.

I stopped at Billy's grave first.

I held on to things like a hoarder: buttons I might need, never mind I didn't know how to sew, old receipts, and, apparently, anger I wished I didn't feel. Since leaving Billy's grave in November, I'd kept the bitter feelings of resentment in my pocket, turning them over like nasty little treasures. As I stood on top of what I guessed were Billy's feet, I wanted to rage and scream and throw them until I broke his gravestone in half.

I crouched down, hidden amongst the graves blocking out the cold sunlight. A few years ago, someone broke a gravestone into giant chunks and left them scattered in the grass. Everyone had blamed teenagers. "Ne'er-do-wells who don't respect the dead." But maybe it wasn't dumb kids. The grief I felt was so heavy. Maybe the gravestone couldn't hold the weight of unsaid words, the grief of being left behind, or the complicated mix of feelings that come with sudden loss. I could still hear my mom crying on the porch, and I thought of the dizzying confusion I felt after the funeral, standing with the chickens in my parents' backyard, realizing everything would always be different. Even if my grief didn't crack Billy's gravestone, I just might give it a kick for good measure. Instead of committing a criminal offence, I stood up and whispered, "I hate you." The words got caught in the wind and I wasn't sure they had made it to the grave.

I turned my back. Stomping through the last row of graves I lost whatever righteous fervour I'd built up. My shoulders sagged. I hadn't talked to Billy since the funeral. Was I really okay with leaving it like this? I was angry, but I wasn't a monster. I hurried back to the grave, stopping somewhere on top of his stomach.

"That's not true. I'm sorry. I don't know what kind of psycho says that to a grave." I realized I was holding my belly, my hands pressed into its softness, and quickly whipped my hands back into my pockets. "It's just, there's been a lot of upheaval in my life...and I don't like it. You went and died on me. I...you know...with Adam and now I'm pregnant." I found myself whispering this part. "I don't know what to do." I swallowed. "I don't know where I go from here."

I paced, trying not to imagine walking over his body. "You would tell me what to do. You'd tell me so confidently I'd probably believe you." I sniffed. "You were supposed to be there when I had kids. You were supposed to be their eccentric uncle... You weren't supposed to die."

I felt the tears come, and I let them. "You were supposed to be at my graduation. You were supposed to tell some stupid story and I would pretend to be embarrassed but secretly I would love it. But none of that is going to happen anymore because you killed yourself. You killed yourself," I repeated. "And I don't know why. Why didn't you leave a note?" I took a deep breath and exhaled sharply.

"And how the hell am I supposed to know what to do about this baby. A baby, Billy. I'm in this constant state of panic and I'm also really, really mad at you and I can't imagine I won't ever be, and I guess...we'll both just have to be okay with that." I took another deep breath and wiped my eyes. I wasn't sure that was much better than "I hate you," but I decided to leave it at that. I didn't know how long I had until I would need to throw up again, and the only way I could make this day worse was if I threw up on Billy's grave.

twenty

ADAM WASN'T HOME. SINCE I'D BEEN GONE, HE'D HUNG Christmas lights across his porch railings and a wreath on the front door.

I took the key from under the front mat and went inside, settling on the couch with my jacket, scarf, and hat still on. And I waited, literally twiddling my thumbs.

"Adam, I'm pregnant." The admission was loud in the empty room. "*Preg*nant. Preg*nant*." I tilted my head at different angles as if the word were suspended in the air in front of me and to look at it differently would somehow make it make sense. "I'm with child. I'm carrying your child. You are the father." Each attempt sounded more awkward than the last, stirring up a nausea that reminded me why I was here.

Adam had a stack of books on the coffee table, a well-read volume called *The Encyclopedia of Country Living* on top of a book on homesteading. I shrugged off my jacket, got up, and rifled through Adam's CDs until I found a mixtape of angsty music from our adolescence. I began to clean. I did the dishes, watered plants, swept, and cleaned underneath the couch before I changed the music and laid down on the floor.

Adam found me listening to Jackson C. Frank with my eyes closed. If he was surprised to find me like this, he didn't say so.

He lay down beside me. "What's up, Charlie?"

I opened my eyes. "Hi."

Jackson C. Frank sang about the blues.

"Is everything okay?" Adam asked.

No. "What do you want from life, Adam? What's your five-year plan?" I turned to look at him.

He chuckled. "You and your five-year plans. Uh, I don't know. I haven't thought it out like you have. I think I'd like to get a cow. Maybe some goats. I want a family, kids, a wife, a dog." He thought for a moment. "Pretty normal stuff."

I didn't say anything. My eyes traced the outline of his profile. I could imagine him as a father. He would be kind. He would smile a lot. I could see him in thirty years, the hair by his temples grey. Tenderness clogged my throat and made it hard to breathe.

This was it. This was the moment to tell him. I opened my mouth. I closed it. I opened it again. I felt like a goldfish. A pregnant guppie. I sat up. Adam followed suit.

"Are you home for the weekend?" He took his baseball hat off and ran his fingers through his hair.

"No," I breathed out. "Just thought I'd stop by. I wanted to tell you..." My mouth felt like it had never tasted saliva. I sucked on my teeth. Looking around the room, I couldn't seem to swallow. "I'm... um."

"Are you feeling okay? You look a little pale."

What was I doing here? I couldn't tell him. We wanted different things, didn't we? The books on homesteading sat on the coffee table, just behind Adam's shoulder. He wanted a cow for god's sake and I had a life in the city; my shitty apartment and grad school dreams were the antithesis of everything Adam wanted. I couldn't upend both of our lives. I was a coward, and Billy's voice was ringing in my ears. "I'm actually feeling a bit feverish. Thanks for noticing. I should probably go."

"What?"

"I should probably leave. Go home. To the city."

"Are you sure you should drive? You could stay here. You seem—"

"No. No. Fiona wants me to do this thing with her. Like, a special thing that she needs me to be there for. Right now. I should go. Thanks for telling me about your five-year plan. I think it's really great."

"Yeah, no problem." Adam looked at me like I was deranged.

I stopped halfway out the door. I willed myself to tell him. We could figure it out together. But what if he was mad? I'd told him I was on the pill. Would he think I'd lied? My stomach churned. I wasn't sure I could face his reaction.

I opened my mouth. Nothing came out.

"Okay. Bye." I shut the door.

"Stupid stupid stupid," I muttered to myself as I trudged down the driveway to my car.

I had never been more disappointed in myself.

twenty-one

"DOES ANYONE HAVE ANY QUESTIONS?" DR. ROSS TURNED AWAY from the chalkboard which was a scribbled mess of dates and words all centred around *The Peace and Friendship Treaties*. She looked around the room. "No one? Charlotte, do you have anything you'd like to add?"

I looked up. I'd barely paid attention. I couldn't help but shut down when my professors lectured on Mi'kmaw history. When someone asked my opinion, they rarely wanted to hear the real one. They wanted me to say something that validated their own world-view. Right now, Dr. Ross wanted me to be thankful about the treaties. She wanted me to act like they were a gift from God, instead of a binding agreement between nations that one side repeatedly tried to ignore and refute. I felt a little betrayed that Dr. Ross would single me out. I liked her.

"Was I supposed to...I'm sorry, I wasn't aware—" Maybe if I stammered for long enough everyone would move on.

"No, no," Dr. Ross interjected. "I just thought, well, because, you know."

I blinked. I did know. But I wanted her to say it.

"You're a...well...because you benefit from these treaties. I thought you might have something to contribute. An interesting perspective, that's all."

"Don't you also benefit?" I asked.

"But I'm not a—"

"I mean, you live here. That's your treaty benefit, right?" I'd never been this blunt toward an authority figure. It was both thrilling and terrifying. I wanted to throw up and run a mile.

The person next to me shifted in their seat.

Dr. Ross looked stunned.

I probably did too.

I didn't talk back. I barely talked in class, period. Was it pregnancy hormones? Had I finally snapped?

"Well," Dr. Ross looked at her watch then clapped her hands. "I think we're at time for today. Next class we'll do some exam prep. Have a good weekend, everyone." She practically ran out of the classroom.

twenty-two

"DO YOU WANT TO TALK ABOUT IT?" FIONA CROSSED HER LEGS and leaned back on the arm of the couch.

I looked up from the book I was reading. "Talk about what?"

She looked pointedly at my stomach.

"No. I don't." If I put as much effort into studying as I did studiously ignoring my pregnancy I'd get A+'s on all of my exams.

She held up her hands.

"Do you know what I *do* want to talk about?"

Fiona looked mildly intrigued. I'd already told her I didn't have the guts to tell Adam, or my parents, about the baby.

"Robert Starritt." I showed her the cover of my book.

"Who?" Fiona scrunched up her face.

"Okay, get this. He was this guy from Ireland who wanted to move to Nova Scotia." Starritt wasn't on any of my exams. I'd only stumbled across his story, a small paragraph in a five-hundred-paged book, when reading about Irish immigration in the 1800s. I couldn't stop thinking about him.

"Okay...and when was this?" She turned the book over; it wasn't clear what she was looking for. A headshot?

"The 1800s. At that point there would've been a lot of 'farmland' up for grabs." I used air quotes. "An alternate phrase would be 'unceded Mi'kmaw territory,' but we don't need to follow that particular tangent right now."

"Okay." Fiona nodded, handing the book back to me.

"So Starritt hopped on a boat, but the boat he was on went to Quebec instead of Nova Scotia."

"That's a huge error."

"I know, right?"

"What did he do?"

I showed her the map on the endpapers. "He walked all the way from the St. Lawrence River to Cobequid Bay. Imagine how long that would take—all to essentially end up at my parents' house." I made a face.

"Yeah, but he got 'farmland,' right?" Fiona used air quotes too.

"No, he didn't."

"What?"

"It had all been parcelled off by the time he got there."

"What did he do?" Fiona seemed genuinely interested; it was the first time she hadn't been bored to tears by one of my history rants. A few times she'd even fake cried.

"He and his family moved up into these mountains behind my parents' and were part of this really vibrant community called Castlereagh. There was a train that went up the mountain for a while. A dance hall."

"Ooh, is it still there?"

"No, everyone either died or moved away: the story of rural Nova Scotia."

Fiona stretched her legs out across the couch. "It's very easy for me to picture you nerding out with other nerds over stories like this for the rest of your life."

"I mean, not if..." I gestured to my stomach.

"You could totally still do it. You don't have to, there are obviously other options, but you could. Realistically, if you keep this baby, our Toronto plans are kaput—but why would you go to Toronto to study obscure Nova Scotian history anyway?"

She was right, but I didn't want to consider that this could be our last year together.

I remembered our first conversation about where we'd apply for grad school. How Fiona's parents would only pay her tuition if she went back to Toronto.

"My mom has a cautionary tale about her friend Deb who came to Halifax for arts school and then never left," she'd explained. "So by only offering to pay for my master's and rent if it's in Toronto, she thinks she's saving me from Deb's terrible fate of marrying a hot East Coaster and living far away from my mother's tender embrace."

My first thought was that being hugged by Fiona's mom would feel a lot like being crushed by the Terminator. My second was that my plans for my own future were the result of my roommate's parents' helicopter tendencies. Was my whole plan chalked up to some fluke of friendship? I thought about my professor's offhand comment. Billy's advice.

Had any plans I'd made for myself ever been my own?

twenty-three

I FINISHED THE SEMESTER ON AN ANTI-CLIMACTIC NOTE. I dropped off my last paper at the History Department office without a single witness, just jammed it in my prof's mailbox and left. There was no one around to congratulate me, no one to applaud and say, "you did it, you wrote two thousand words of adequate bullshit, way to go!"

When I got home, I took my prenatal vitamin. I stood in front of the sink and gagged while I tried to swallow it. It ended up in the sink. I struggled to keep the pill down every day.

I'd picked up a bottle last week. The shelf stocked with vitamins had loomed in front of me. There were five different types. Did we really need that many options? Was I a bad mother if I chose the cheapest one?

I'd just gotten a phone call from my doctor, confirming what the pregnancy test had already told me. It hadn't been a false positive; I was due in August. I'd left the apartment as soon as I'd hung up and walked to the store.

I was alone in the aisle, but I felt like the entire store was waiting with bated breath. The teen at the cash probably thought I was an idiot who didn't know how to use birth control. Could everyone tell this was an accident? That I was ill-equipped for whatever came next?

It was just a bottle of chalky vitamins. The doctor told me to buy them. It was no big deal. I was just doing what I was told. I apparently loved to do that.

But, if I was being honest with myself, I'd already decided to have the baby before the doctor confirmed it. By the time I'd crawled under the blanket on the couch, near paralyzed with fear, it felt like the baby and I were in it together. Partners in this absolute shit show. It was a decision I'd made entirely on my own. One I would tell Adam about as soon as I went home for Christmas...or maybe the day after. Definitely before the New Year.

I took two bottles off the shelf. A cheap option and the expensive one. The contents were the exact same. I put the expensive ones back. I silently promised the baby I'd put the extra five dollars toward some pregnancy superfood that would make them really smart. "But it's also okay if you're a little dumb," I told them as I walked toward the checkout.

"Okay: one...two...three." I popped a second pill into my mouth and took a large gulp of water only for my throat to reject it. I coughed and spit into the sink. For every pill I managed to swallow, at least two were wasted. Once I'd finally swallowed a pill, I went to sit down. If I laid down, or moved around too much, I would throw up. My only option was to sit on the couch and sulk.

I didn't want to go home. I didn't want to face a house without Billy. I didn't want to tell everyone I was pregnant. I didn't want to not tell them. Not telling was the same as lying. I felt so tired. But I had to go. Johnny was coming home, possibly the only saving grace of this Christmas. And you knew things were bad when Johnny was the saving grace.

twenty-four

I DIDN'T REMEMBER MY CHILDHOOD BED BEING THIS UNCOMfortable. The mattress was rock hard, the pillow too soft. Mom had stuck some knit blanket underneath the duvet, the yarn felt bad, my legs were itchy. I needed to pee. Despite all of this, I refused to get out of bed.

Telling people shouldn't feel like this big a deal. I was just changing the course of my life and adding a new member to the family. Maybe I didn't even have to tell them in person. I could just leave a Post-it Note on the table. Tack the announcement onto the end of the grocery list on the fridge. *We need more toilet paper—oh, by the way I'm pregnant.*

But maybe I should wait until after Christmas. It was our first holiday without Billy. What if I upset everyone and ruined the holidays? I could wait till the New Year. Maybe Y2K would screw everything up and everyone would be too distracted to notice I was pregnant. Or we'd all die and all my worrying would be for naught. Except, I didn't want the Y2K to mess everything up. Terrifying as it was, I wanted whatever future was coming for me. I wanted to meet my baby.

I had to tell Adam. At least him. The rest of my family could find out on their own. I could award a prize to whoever figured it out first.

I forced myself to get up because I had serious concerns I would pee the bed if I waited any longer.

Mom stood in front of Billy's closed door. She'd lost weight in the past month and a half, her tiny stature now skin and bones.

"Are you okay?"

"Dad's gone to get Johnny. They should be back soon."

Mom stared at Billy's door.

"Have you been in there since—"

She shook her head.

"Do you want me to make breakfast?"

"Yeah, okay. I'll be down in a second."

I went to the bathroom then downstairs to start a pot of coffee. Making pancakes was a bit like a choreographed dance I had memorized years ago. I would gather all the ingredients and beat and whisk and mix without having to think about it. I grabbed the flour from the cupboard by the stove. Got the baking soda and baking powder from the cupboard by the sink. Grabbed the sugar from the—the sugar wasn't where it was supposed to be. I looked in two more spots before I gave up. I huffed. I stomped to the bottom of the stairs.

"Mom, where'd you put the sugar?"

She stuck her head down the stairwell. "I don't know."

I went back to the kitchen and searched through every cupboard. I eventually found it next to a pile of casserole dishes.

"Who," I asked the sugar, "would put you here?"

Johnny came into the kitchen with a burst of cold air. I paused, peanut butter–dipped pickle halfway to my mouth. He wore black Doc Martens, tight black jeans, and a loose red-and-black-plaid flannel. His hair was shaved close to his scalp and I thought he looked skinnier than he had in the summer, but maybe I was misremembering.

"What's up with Dad's hair?" he asked.

"He's growing it out."

"It looks terrible."

I shrugged. "He wants to be able to braid it."

Johnny ran a hand over his scalp and scrunched up his nose.

"Let's go see Billy," he said.

"Nice to see you too." I stood up and forced him to hug me. As I squeezed him, his foot tapped a staccato on the kitchen floor.

"Let's go," he said again. He grabbed a pancake off the stack and stuffed it in his mouth.

"Do you want to sit down and eat? Maybe enjoy it a little?"

"No." The word came out garbled. He grabbed my keys and handed them to me. He took another five pancakes and walked past his suitcases out the front door. It seemed like an awful lot of luggage for someone home for just the holidays.

I looked over my shoulder as I backed down the driveway. "Johnny, are you moving home?"

He shoved half a pancake in his mouth.

"It's just, that's a lot of luggage for a quick trip."

Johnny shrugged. He ate the other half of the pancake. We turned off my parents' road and onto the main street.

"I've been having a hard time," he said after finishing his short stack. "That's all. I'm on a new medication and I feel a little messed up. I just didn't want to be by myself anymore." His legs bounced up and down.

"I didn't realize you were on medication."

"That's 'cause it was working."

"Is it—"

"No. Just good ol'-fashioned depression."

We pulled into the parking lot of the church. I'd always thought our family was a sturdy bunch. We didn't have heart conditions, or inheritable defects. *Good genes* was what I'd thought.

"Do you think one of our ancestors pissed off the wrong person and got us all cursed?" I turned the engine off. "Like, what if our great-great grandmother pissed off the wrong auntie and now we're all screwed."

"What the fuck are you talking about?"

"It kind of seems like we're all doomed to be unhappy."

"That's a little dramatic, don't you think? I just have a chemical imbalance."

I wanted to wrap Johnny in bubble wrap and protect him from the world. Instead, I leaned towards him, with the intent to kiss his forehead because it felt like the appropriate thing to do. As I made contact, Johnny flinched.

"What're you doing?" He held his forearm up, as if to block an attack.

"I was trying to be comforting. It felt like a moment where comfort was in order."

Johnny grimaced. "Did we start kissing each other in this family? Is that something I missed while I was away? We're suddenly all touchy-feely now?"

"No, I was just feeling maternal." I climbed out of the car.

Johnny did the same. "I'm older than you."

"So? I can't—never mind." I waved my hand, slammed the door, and turned towards the graveyard.

"No, it's okay, do it."

"Do what?"

"Kiss my forehead. It'll make me feel better." Johnny's forehead was furrowed. He looked like he was fortifying himself for an unmedicated root canal.

He leaned down and let me place a quick kiss on his forehead. He flinched.

"Do you feel comforted now?"

"Yes," he replied curtly.

"All right, let's go see Billy."

The light was stark, the air cold, and the graveyard empty. The snowfall the night before was a long and deep exhalation. It had quieted everything to a gentle hush, dampening our footsteps while the slush muted the cars that passed by. We didn't talk as we picked our way through the snow and tombstones towards Billy's grave. A wreath had been placed at the base of the grave marker. I pictured Mom visiting Billy alone, the new and probably overpriced wreath clutched in her hands, and it made me want to cry. I shook the snow off the wreath before leaning it back against the stone.

"This is messed up," Johnny muttered.

He stamped his feet to ward off the chill and shoved his hands in his coat pockets. "Was it a good funeral?" he asked.

"Not really, unless you consider 'deranged' a positive adjective." I drew a line in the snow with my boot. "I keep thinking about it and I can't tell if it would've made him laugh or cry."

"I feel like everything could either make him laugh or cry," Johnny said, "and that made everything really magical and really fucking depressing at the same time. It'd be a lot to deal with."

We stood there for a bit longer and just stared at the ground. Snow had begun to collect on Johnny's shoulders; I dusted it off.

"You ready to go home?" I asked.

"Can I have a sec?"

"Sure." I made my way back through the gravestones toward the parking lot, leaving fresh tracks in the snow.

twenty-five

I SAT ON THE EDGE OF THE TUB. BILLY'S BODY WASH WAS IN THE same spot I'd left it. I opened the top and inhaled. If I closed my eyes, I could pretend Billy was sitting next to me. I wondered what he would say. What he'd think of the mess I'd gotten myself into.

Adam was coming over later and I knew I had to tell him. But I was afraid of how he'd react. Was this the end of both our lives? It kind of felt like it. Or, worse, would Adam see this as the life we were meant to live together?

I rubbed my stomach.

Adam was always joking about me moving home and marrying him. What if it wasn't some dumb joke? What if that was what he wanted when I told him? Would that be such a bad life?

What if I gave up everything to make it work? Or, what if he did? Would we resent each other in five years? Would one of us end up sitting on a porch, head in our hands, wishing we'd made different choices? I didn't want either of us to give up any parts of ourselves.

I thought of my nan, who, when she married my grampa, was told she couldn't be an Indian anymore. A huge part of her identity, taken away. Then I thought of Nan smiling and laughing as Grampa told a joke, how their wrinkled and weathered hands looked as they held each other and danced around their kitchen.

I played with the top of the body wash bottle, focused on putting it back in the exact same spot it was before, ignoring the long list of questions I didn't have answers to.

I jumped when someone knocked loudly.

"What're you doing in there? I need to take a dump," Johnny yelled.

I swung the door open, a forced smile on my face. "So good to have you home, big brother." I gave Johnny the middle finger as he barged past me and slammed the door.

"How is it," I asked Dad, who happened to be walking by, arms laden with decorations, "that he is so loud and obnoxious?"

He raised an eyebrow. "Have you met your mother?"

"Fair point."

"Speaking of your mother," he added, "you might want to check on her." He continued down the stairs, and I glanced down the hallway.

Mom stood by her bedroom window, a small package in her hand. I hovered in the doorway. I could tell her I was pregnant right now. She could tell me what to do.

She looked up at me and tried to smile before her face crumpled and she started to cry. She held her hand to her forehead, covering her eyes.

Maybe now wasn't the time.

"Do you want a hug?" I asked. Despite my earlier conversation with Johnny, we weren't a touchy family. We didn't hug freely.

Mom shook her head.

I straightened the duvet. Propped the pillows up on the headboard.

"I got this," she shook the box in her hands, "for Billy in September, at the yard sale. I kind of forgot about it but I was just going through Christmas stuff and found it."

I took the box from her and looked inside. There was a beat-up View-Master and a pile of reels.

"It was supposed to be a stupid gag gift."

I sat down on the bed and rifled through the reels. I put one in the slot and held it up to my eyes. I pressed the lever down, flipping the images until I'd made it full circle, then handed the toy to Mom. She wiped her eyes.

"He would've loved this."

"I know." She put the View-Master down on the bed. "I don't know what to do with—"

"What're you guys doing?" Johnny stuck his head through the door. "Whoa, cool!" He sat down next to us, held the View-Master up to his eyes, and pulled the lever in rapid succession just like I'd done. "Can you hand me another one?" He held out his hand.

We spent an hour going through all the reels, handing the View-Master back and forth. *Buck Rogers* comics. Claymation *Snow White*. Saturated scenes of Tallahassee and Miami. I swapped out a *Peanuts* reel and put in one called "Instructional Baseball." I clicked through.

Each image was a guy in a New York Mets jersey showcasing how to pose with the ball and bat. The last three pictures were the player throwing the ball from the pitcher's mound.

"Wow, I feel like I could really get out there and hit a home run," I said, handing the View-Master to Mom.

She laughed. It was short and soft, but it filled the room.

twenty-six

ADAM SHOWED UP ON CHRISTMAS EVE. IT TOOK EVERYTHING IN me not to close the door in his face.

"Hey," I managed. "Johnny's out getting last-minute presents, probably from the gas station so he shouldn't be long."

He held up his toolbox. "I'm here to fix your car." He said it hesitantly, like he was scared I'd snap at him. I didn't like it.

"You really don't have to," I said as I followed him outside.

"Beau Fielding told me your car nearly up and died outside Doug's yesterday. Said I was remiss in my mechanic duties if your car sounded like that."

"Beau Fielding is a no-good gossip."

Adam laughed, a little freer, and walked toward my car.

I sat down on the front porch. "In my defense, this is the worst it's ever sounded."

"If you'd have come home before Christmas, I would've fixed it then."

I bit my lip. "I was home."

"Those five minutes you were in my house, where I'm not sure you actually finished a full thought, don't count." Adam popped the hood.

This would be a great moment to tell him. We were on topic, even though Adam didn't know it. But I hadn't figured everything out yet. The logistics. What the next year would look like. Maybe it was better to wait till I knew. So that if Adam panicked, I could say *hey, don't worry, here's the plan.*

Adam opened his toolbox and rooted around. "Do you know what I heard the other day?"

"What?" My heart pounded. He couldn't possibly know, could he?

"Okay, so you know that ongoing feud between Karen Tagget and Ethel Meyers?"

I breathed out a puff of cold air. "Sure, Mom told me Ethel keeps calling Karen and hanging up even though she has a no-contact order."

"Hey, this is *my* piece of gossip."

"Sorry." I smiled.

"It's fine." Adam leaned against the hood and crossed his arms. "So apparently in the summer, like late August, Karen poured salt all over Ethel's garden and messed up her whole harvest. Isn't that insane?"

"Is that a crime?"

"I assume so."

"How much salt are we talking?"

"Probably buckets of it. Ethel's garden is huge."

"She's always on about her preserves." I rolled my eyes. "Like, we get it, you have a pressure canner."

"Would you like a pressure canner?" Adam asked.

I shrugged. "My birthday is within the next twelve months."

Adam turned around and tinkered with the engine.

"Did she do it in the dead of night?" I asked after a few minutes.

"I'm not sure. Possibly?" He paused. "Your engine is about to make me cry."

"It's fine, she's got character."

"Apparently," Adam continued, ignoring me. "She wasn't at church the week it happened, and Ethel was. And Callum Benoit swears he saw Karen out that way on his way home from church and there's really no reason for her to be out there."

"Yeah, but doesn't Callum have the hots for Ethel? He's biased."

"Gross." Adam pretended to gag. He grabbed a different tool from his box.

"Wait, is this like table salt or are we talking about like, road salt?" I asked.

"That, I don't know." Adam turned back to look at me, he smiled. "And you said this place was boring."

Okay, here we go, I thought.

And then Dad pulled into the driveway. Johnny hung out the passenger window, waving his arm wildly. He yelled for Adam. Adam waved back.

My stomach churned. I had to fight not to gag. "Thanks for this," I said quickly. "Bye."

I darted into the house to throw up.

"You're welcome," Adam called as the front door slammed shut.

twenty-seven

CHRISTMAS EVE WAS QUIET AND SLOW. *IT'S A WONDERFUL LIFE* played on TV like it did every year. Mom hated the movie, but Billy had loved it. Johnny and I were reading while Mom fiddled with the ornaments on the tree when Dad came in and put it on. Mom immediately started to cry.

I followed Dad into the kitchen and put a pot on the stove. Dad took four glasses out and put them on the counter.

"Do you think Billy thought about these things before he did it?" After searching, I found the jar of popcorn kernels in the fridge. Without meaning to, I'd kept a running tally since Billy's death of all the things I thought he'd have liked. All the things he might be sad to have missed. The first snowfall. Celine Dion's greatest hits album. The final book in the His Dark Materials series. My pregnancy.

"What do you mean?" Dad watched me pour oil into the pot and turn on the burner.

"Do you think he thought about the fact that he'd be giving up Christmas Eves and *It's a Wonderful Life*?"

Dad got the rum off the shelf.

"I'm having trouble wording this."

He poured more than a finger full of rum into three of the glasses, then went to pour some in the fourth.

"I'm okay." I smiled. "Just eggnog, please."

Dad put the lid on the bottle while I put a tester kernel in the pot. "There are just so many little things that make our lives feel worth living. That make moments special, or funny, or whatever. And Billy gave all those up."

Dad leaned against counter. "Maybe he didn't have as many of those moments. Or maybe he used to. Or maybe he still did, but they didn't add up to enough. I don't really know."

The kernel popped. I opened the lid and dumped the rest of the kernels in. Dad filled the cups with eggnog and stirred them with his finger.

"What if he regretted it while it happened?" There was an old photo of Billy resting on the window ledge above the sink. He was younger, smiling, the background a blur of foliage.

Dad wiped his hands on a dishtowel.

"That was morbid. Sorry."

"You don't have to be sorry." He pulled me into a hug, let his chin rest on the top of my head. "Okay?" He leaned back to look at me.

"Okay."

Dad stepped back from me. He picked up the bottle of rum and I shook the pot on the stove.

"You sure you don't want some?" He paused, the rum halfway to its spot on the shelf.

"No, I'm, well, I'm..." Should I tell my dad before my mom? Before Adam?

"Nick?" Mom called.

"Just a sec!" Dad called. He looked at me and raised an eyebrow.

"I'm fine. Thanks though."

I leaned against the counter and tried to will the nervous energy out of my body.

When I came back to the living room, Mom had joined Dad on his recliner. He had an arm wrapped around her. She fit her head into the nook of his neck and watched the scenes flick by in black and white. I sat down next to Johnny, who made a grabbing motion, never looking up from his book. I handed him the bowl of popcorn, picked up the copy of *Little Women* Johnny had gifted me earlier that day, and kept reading. I'd lost my copy years ago. I'd wanted to read it again but couldn't seem to find it in any second-hand bookstores. Johnny might've won Christmas with this gift. I wondered if he still read the way we used to.

We'd never had money to travel growing up. Mom had been a homemaker and a painter and Dad built furniture, usually custom orders; needless to say, the cash flow was slow. They tried to grow their own food in the summer and every fall we killed a pig to lessen the strain of having no money, but we were still poor. So Johnny and I used to read across the country. It was an idea introduced to us in elementary school: a certain number of pages equalled a certain number of kilometres. Long after our classmates had given it up, Johnny and I still tried to beat each other in reading races. Johnny would call out, "I'm in Manitoba, dipshit!" I'd respond with, "Who the hell wants to visit Manitoba anyways?" And then I'd stay up all night, just to get to Saskatchewan. It was the poor kids' vacation.

At some point that evening, I'd fallen asleep on the couch. I woke up as the sun rose over the trees, swathes of light pinks and purples spread across the sky. The front lawn glistened, an untouched expanse of snow. The house was still asleep.

I shuffled to the kitchen to start a pot of coffee. I yawned, resting my elbows on the counter. The furnace hummed. The old house creaked.

As soon as the coffee finished brewing, Johnny stomped down the stairs. He poured himself a cup and took a long sip.

He let out a sigh of contentment. "Merry Christmas, Charlie."

"Merry Christmas, Johnny."

Merry Christmas, Billy.

twenty-eight

I DECIDED TO SPEND NEW YEAR'S IN THE CITY. I'D LIED AND TOLD my parents I had plans with friends, but I really just wanted to sit in my bed, eat pickled beets, and cry, without judgement. Plus, the longer I stayed home, the harder it was to keep my pregnancy from my family. And from Adam.

New Year's Eve was always filled with so much expectation and promise that it was bound to be disappointing. There was a hopeful energy that things would be better, that we would be better. Last year, I had drunkenly stumbled my way into 1999 not asking too much of it.

This year I made a cake I didn't eat and fell asleep at ten. I'd spent a good chunk of the year trying, and failing, to not get worked up about Y2K. But now I truly couldn't care less.

Fiona returned to the apartment the next day. Her flight had been delayed and she got in well after midnight. She climbed into my bed, the frigid outdoor air clinging to her, crisp and clean.

"We didn't die," she mumbled.

"No, we didn't."

"Why is there a whole cake in the fridge?"

"I was too sad to eat it."

Fiona snuggled closer to me, worming her way under my blanket. "Happy New Year, Charlie."

"Holy hell, your feet are cold!" I jerked away.

Fiona laughed and pulled the blanket up. "Charlie, please," she whined, wiggling her feet until they found my legs under the quilt. I let her tuck them between my legs. "Did you tell them?" she asked.

"Hmm?"

"Charlie, you suck at lying, there's no way you can keep this up."

"It's not lying. No one asked me if I was pregnant. It's just withholding information. There's a difference." I was already lying to my family, why not lie to myself as well?

Fiona sighed. "Night, Charlie."

twenty-nine

DR. BISHOP UNWRAPPED THE BLOOD PRESSURE CUFF.

"Everything is looking great so far." She checked the file on her desk. "You're about eleven weeks, so we should be able to hear the heartbeat today." She smiled at me.

I tried to smile back.

"Hop up on the table and we'll get you set up." She rummaged through a drawer in her desk.

"It's a little cold," she warned before squirting blue gel onto my stomach. "This is the Doppler." She held up a small machine attached by a cord to a stick. "I'm going to rub this part on your belly and hopefully we'll hear something."

She rubbed the rounded edge of the Doppler in gel. The machine emitted loud static before it picked up what sounded like a horse's hooves on cobblestones.

"There we go." She smiled down at me.

"Is it supposed to be that fast?"

She nodded. "It's just where it should be. It sounds great."

We listened to it for a little longer. The heartbeat filled the room, loud and undeniable.

Dr. Bishop turned off the machine and wiped my stomach off.

I sat up, stared at my socked feet, and tried to memorize the sound of the baby's heart. Adam should've been here for this.

"Part of your prenatal care is making sure you feel adequately supported." She put the Doppler away and turned to me. "Is Dad part of the picture?"

I swung my sock feet back and forth. "It's complicated." I didn't want to explain to the doctor that I was too scared to tell anyone I was pregnant, let alone ask for their support.

Her smile was sympathetic. "It can be, for sure. Have you thought of all the different options?"

I told her I had.

"You have a few more weeks to consider an abortion, if that's what you want. Obviously, adoption is an option. If you do decide to keep the baby, there's a lot of great postpartum resources and support for single mothers, and also for, ah, Aboriginal mothers. Think on it. I'll see you in a month's time and if anything pops up before then, don't hesitate to call the office. Okay?" She smiled again.

"Sure, thanks." I slid off the table and slipped on my boots. Was she just being nice, or did she expect me to fail because I was young and Mi'kmaw? Was I reading too much into it?

The street was bustling with the energy of the new year. People rushed by. A bus stopped and let out a slew of people. A woman pushed a stroller into the building I'd just left. That could be me in six months, I thought to myself.

The wind whipped down North Street; flurries fell from the sky. I tightened the scarf around my neck and walked home.

thirty

I COULD STILL HEAR THE HEARTBEAT THAT NIGHT AS I TRIED TO fall asleep. The pulse thrummed in distinct opposition to Billy's warning, the words that had reverberated in my head for almost a decade.

Don't get stuck.

Thump thump.

Don't get stuck.

Thump thump

Don't get stuck.

Thump thump.

thirty-one

"ARE YOU COMING HOME FOR READING WEEK?" MOM ASKED.

"Probably not, sorry." I tried to reach the fridge with the phone to my ear. In the city I could pretend everything was fine. That didn't seem possible at home.

"Why not?" Johnny asked from the phone line in his room.

"It'd sure be nice if you did," Mom said almost at the same time.

"Charlie's coming home?" Dad asked in the background.

"I'm busy. I have a lot of schoolwork. My thesis..." My fingertips brushed the door handle. I needed another inch, but the cord was already taut.

Johnny scoffed. "Why don't you want to come home?" he asked. "What's wrong with home?"

I gave up on the fridge and sat down at the kitchen table.

"Yeah," Mom chimed in. "What's wrong with us?"

"Are you keeping something from us?" Johnny asked. "A face tattoo, perhaps?"

"Did you get a bad haircut? We won't make fun of you that much."

"What happened to Charlie's hair?" Dad asked in the background.

"I don't know, Nick, she won't tell us anything."

"How're those new meds working out, Johnny?" I asked.

"What new meds?" Mom asked.

"Oof," Johnny groaned. "Low blow."

"What new meds?" Mom asked again.

"Mom's still smoking," Johnny blurted.

"What? Mom! You said you were going to quit." I sat up straighter in the chair.

"I am quitting! I'm just not doing it all at once. I have a cigarette every Friday and that's it."

"Yesterday was Tuesday," Johnny pointed out.

Dad took the phone. "Don't worry, I'm working on a two-step program for her."

"What is it?" I asked.

"Throw 'em in the trash and stop smoking." Dad laughed so much he didn't notice when no one else did.

"I have to go to class."

"Bye." Dad hung up the kitchen extension.

"Just know, I see through your little distraction tactic and it's only reinforced my belief that you're hiding something. Adam said you've been acting weird. It's all adding up."

"To what?" I tried to sound casual.

"I don't know yet, but mark my words I'll—what?" Johnny yelled to someone in the house. "Mom, I'm fine. Goddammit, Charlie, now Mom wants to have a heart to heart—just a second!" Johnny yelled. "This is all your fault," he said before he hung up the phone.

thirty-two

DR. GAMBLE SAT ACROSS FROM ME. I LOOKED AT THE KNICK-knacks on his desk while he shuffled through my half-finished thesis, his thick glasses perched at the end of his nose. Framed photos faced him and I wondered who was in them. Next to them sat a rock with googly eyes glued to it, so at odds with his serious demeanour. His pens were in a cup shaped like a chicken.

"You're well ahead of schedule, Charlotte," Dr. Gamble said.

"That's good, right?" I looked up at him while the googly-eyed rock looked at me. I couldn't exactly tell him that because every other aspect of my life felt out of control I was treating my honours thesis like my own personal life raft. I trusted him, but I didn't think we were ready for that level of honesty.

"It is. But I also don't want you to overtax yourself. Academic burnout is very real."

I liked Dr. Gamble. At first, I wasn't sure. When I'd asked him to be my advisor, I'd been nervous. He came across as staid and rigid, but his research aligned with what I wanted to write about, so I'd mustered up the courage and stopped by his office hours. Since then, I'd realized that while I'd been right about him being staid and rigid, he was also incredibly invested in his students' academic careers. I genuinely felt that he wanted me to succeed.

"Have you heard about grad school yet?" he asked.

"Not yet."

"Have you given any more thought to whether you'll stay here or move to Toronto?"

"Here, I guess." Or my childhood bedroom if everything goes to shit. "If I get accepted, are you still okay to be my advisor?"

"If I didn't want to be your advisor, I wouldn't have agreed." Dr. Gamble raised his left eyebrow. He'd actively discouraged Toronto. "Leave these with me for the weekend," he said, straightening the papers on his desk. "I'll make some notes, and you can pick them up on Tuesday."

In the hallway, I fished my Discman and headphones out of my backpack. Would Dr. Gamble be so encouraging if he knew I was pregnant? Would he think I'd torpedoed whatever career I might've had?

I stuck my headphones on and turned up the volume. "Just a Girl," by No Doubt drowned out everything else. I trudged home, dreading the weekend to come.

thirty-three

BILLY WAS BORN ON THE IDES OF MARCH. HE LOVED THIS FACT; it gave him a sense of importance. Billy always made it a big deal, and this year was no different. It was like the day took on a pulse and as it drew nearer the pulse grew louder. We couldn't have ignored it if we'd tried.

Despite my refusal to come home two weeks before, I couldn't stay away for this. I skipped my afternoon class. I wore the baggiest sweater I could find. I wasn't sure if I had the start of a bump or if I was just bloated. It did not escape me that the sweater was one I had stolen from Adam.

Mom had made a cake that said *Beware the Ides of March* in icing. The writing was almost illegible; I only knew what it said because she made the same cake every year.

"Should we go see Billy?" I asked. "Is that weird?"

"I'll drive," said Adam.

"I'll bring a piece of cake." Mom clapped her hands and headed towards the kitchen.

"I'll bring a beer." Dad followed behind her. "Bring a cigarette," he told her.

"I quit, remember?" Mom said from the hallway.

"Not for you, for Billy. I know you have some in your purse. We'll do an offering."

We all stood in front of Billy's grave and stared at the stone in silence. Mom held a slice of cake on a paper plate in one hand and a beer in the other.

Johnny broke the silence. "You know how you're not supposed to speak ill of the dead? I think that's bullshit. We could all stand here and moan on about what an angel Billy was, or we could be honest. Which is what Billy would've wanted. I'll go first." Johnny cleared his throat. "One time, Billy borrowed my Blink 182 CD and scratched it."

"You've been holding on to that one for a long time, haven't you?" Adam said.

Johnny nodded. "I have."

"Billy told me he didn't even like Blink 182," I said to Johnny.

"Billy could be real careless, and obviously had terrible taste in music." Johnny stuffed his hands in the pockets of his coat.

Mom laughed. It came out abruptly, like she hadn't expected it. "His favourite record in high school was *Love Will Keep Us Together* by Captain & Tennille. He found it at the September yard sale."

"Now that's just depressing," Johnny said matter-of-factly, as if the title track hadn't been hugely successful.

"Billy either had too much empathy or not enough—like, so much empathy you ended up having to comfort him, or none at all," I said as I remembered all the times I'd had to comfort Billy through my own tears. "He was also a shit driver."

Everyone murmured their agreement.

Mom put the cake in front of the gravestone. "If Billy thought he said something clever he would say it over and over again until someone acknowledged him. It drove me crazy. I used to not respond on principle." She cracked open the beer.

"I never caught anything fishing with Billy because he couldn't stop moving around. He'd scare all the damn fish away. The man could never stay still." Dad sighed. "It was exhausting."

"You do love to sit."

"I do."

There was a moment of silence. We all looked towards Adam.

"Aren't you going to say something?" Mom asked him.

"I don't—I mean...It doesn't seem—"

"Now, Adam." Johnny turned to him. "You're like a brother to me. To Charlie."

I cringed.

"You are well and truly part of this family," Johnny continued, oblivious to mine and Adam's discomfort. "Which means you have to be as cold and callous as the rest of us. It's only right."

We all stared at Adam. He cleared his throat. "Billy sometimes smelled. Like, on occasion. Not all the time. It was like a BO smell. Or maybe like a bum smell?"

I placed my hand on Adam's arm to stop him, because I knew he'd keep going if we let him.

"Now that's just heartless," Dad said.

Mom brought her hand to her mouth and tried to hide her laugh. Her quiet snicker was contagious and I started to laugh too. If anyone else came into the graveyard they would've seen us losing our shit. They probably would've thought we were disturbed. I mean, maybe we were. What other family goes to their recently deceased family member's grave on their birthday with a piece of cake, beer, and a cigarette and tells them all the things that made them terrible?

Billy would've loved it.

Dad broke the cigarette and crumbled the innards in his left hand. He held out the offering and muttered something I couldn't quite hear. "Msit No'kmaq. All my Relations," he said a little louder than the rest as he sprinkled the tobacco.

Mom waited till he was done before she tipped the beer and emptied the bottle. "Happy birthday, asshole." The liquid stained the remaining snow, splattering messy lines of brown across my uncle's grave.

thirty-four

DAD RAN TO FIVE ISLANDS FOR FISH AND CHIPS. MOM FOUND Billy's copy of *Big Trouble in Little China* and cracked open a bottle of wine.

Johnny turned to me as Dad came through the back door with the takeout. He snapped his fingers. "Before I forget, do you have that book you were talking about."

"Yeah, it's in my backpack." I took one of the bags from Dad and put it on the table.

"Can I grab it?" Johnny asked.

"Here's some plates." Mom handed them to me.

"Where'd I put the keys?" Dad patted his pockets.

"Charlie?" Johnny asked again.

Adam pointed. "They're on the counter."

"What?" I asked Johnny as Mom handed me some cutlery.

"Can I?"

"Uh, sure." The forks and knives clattered as I set them down.

Dad opened one of the takeout containers and started to load his plate up.

"Save some for the rest of us, Nick." Mom nabbed a piece of fish as Dad reached for it. Adam opened a beer for himself and placed another by Johnny's empty seat. He offered me one but I shook my head. I took a pile of fries and my own personal container of tartar sauce. I tried to hide it behind my cup so no one would see it.

Mom searched the table. "Did you forget coleslaw?"

"Hey, Charlie?" Johnny stood in the doorway.

"No, it's right there."

"Where?" Mom searched.

"Right, there." I pointed.

"Charlie."

"What?" I looked up.

Johnny had a shit-eating grin on his face. He held my bottle of prenatal vitamins. I shook my head and silently willed him to put them back before anyone noticed.

"What's that?" Mom asked.

Fuck.

"It's, uh—" Johnny squinted at the bottle as if he hadn't already read the label. I was going to kill him. "Prenatal vitamins."

No one moved. Dad had a hunk of fish halfway to his mouth. Mom was looking at me like I had actually killed Johnny. I refused to look at Adam.

"What are those for?" Dad asked.

"They're for when you're pregnant." Mom didn't take her eyes off me. "Charlotte Francis, do you have something you want to tell us?"

"Charlie?" Adam shifted in my peripheral vision.

"The bottle"—Johnny shook it—"is almost empty."

I jumped out of my chair "I'm going to kill you."

"Are you pregnant?" Mom asked.

"Goddammit, Charlie, will you fucking look at me?"

Johnny turned to Adam. "Hey, don't talk to my sister like that."

I looked at Adam. "Is it..." He didn't finish his sentence.

I nodded, whispered, "yeah," then looked away again.

"Holy hell," Mom said.

"Wait, what?" Johnny looked between Adam and me, his little brain working to figure it out. "Ah, gross! What the hell?"

"How long have you known?" Adam asked.

"Why didn't you tell us?" Mom asked at the same time.

Dad was still holding the hunk of fish about an inch away from his mouth.

"What the hell is wrong with you?" Johnny asked Adam.

"How are you feeling?" Dad put down his fork. "I'm honestly surprised this didn't happen sooner. You've been dating for so long."

"Charlie—" Adam tried again.

"No, they haven't," Mom said.

"Well then why the hell was he staying the night so much?" Dad asked.

"Staying the night?" Johnny grabbed his beer off the table and opened it.

"Charlie—"

"I can't—" Johnny started.

"Can you all just shut up?" Adam yelled. It was the loudest I'd ever heard him speak. The table descended into silence. "Charlie," Adam spoke again, much quieter this time. I wished he'd kept yelling—this was worse. "Can I please talk to you outside?"

Adam pushed his chair back and waited for me to follow him.

"How long have you known?" he repeated as soon as the back door had closed.

"Since December." I hated how small my voice sounded.

"December? What the hell, Charlie?" He looked out over the back lawn. "Were you planning on telling me?"

"I tried—"

"Doesn't seem like something that should take four months to do." He looked exactly as angry as I'd pictured him these past four months.

"I just—"

"I don't know that there's anything you can say—"

"Will you stop interrupting me?" I yelled. "God, just shut up for a second." I scrubbed my face with both hands. "I wanted to. When I came home before Christmas, do you remember?"

Adam nodded.

"I tried to, but I couldn't. And then, I just...I don't know. I wanted to have a plan before I told you."

"That's not fair."

"I know." I couldn't look him in the eye.

"Do you? Like, what is wrong with you that you would think this was an okay thing to do?"

"I got overwhelmed! It was a lot. Billy's death and then this." I motioned to my stomach. "I just couldn't handle it." I grasped for something to make it better, or at least make sense.

"I would've helped you handle it."

"I know."

"Do you? Why the hell didn't you tell me then?" He was so angry. I couldn't blame him.

"I had a plan, okay?" I tried not to raise my voice. "A plan that did not involve getting knocked up, or moving back to this shitty town, and getting stuck here like all the sad little people who never left!" I was yelling by the time I finished.

Adam flinched as if I'd slapped him.

"I didn't mean—"

"I'm going to go."

"Adam, I don't—"

"Please stop talking." He walked down the porch steps and around the side of the house towards his truck. He got in and drove away without looking back.

The back door opened. Mom stuck her head outside.

I sniffed. "Did you hear all that?"

"Charlie, the whole damn neighbourhood heard that," Johnny piped up from behind Mom.

"This is all your fault." I willed myself not to cry.

"Ah." Mom held up her hand. "I will allow that Johnny was tactless and a huge asshole."

"Hey!" said Johnny from inside.

"But," Mom continued. She shut the back door, Johnny still in the house. She sat down on the porch step, and motioned for me to do the same. "You're the one who didn't tell anyone you were pregnant for four months. And a minute ago, *you* were a tactless asshole."

I sat down next to her.

"And I'm choosing to ignore the fact that you just called us all 'sad little people.'"

"It came out wrong." I slumped against the railing.

"You need to explain that to Adam." She pushed my hair back from my face.

"I know." I looked down at my nails. Pregnancy hormones had made them stronger. Could I blame my shitty decision-making on hormones too? "You called me Charlotte inside."

"That was a full-name moment if there ever was one."

thirty-five

"ADAM." I BANGED ON HIS FRONT DOOR FOR THE THIRD TIME. "Can you please open up?"

Nothing.

"I know you're in there. Your truck is in the driveway." I peeked through the door window. "I can see your shoes and keys. Come on." I rested my head against the cool glass. "I'm sorry, okay? I wanted to tell you…it just seemed big and scary, and I kept finding reasons not to. Which isn't a good excuse. I know that." I stepped back and cupped my hands around my mouth. "I didn't mean what I said yesterday. It came out wrong." I listened for a response. "It's kind of difficult to be articulate while yelling at a door."

Nothing.

"Shit," I muttered. I sat down on the top porch step and waited. I ran to my car to grab *Folklore of the Maritimes*, then sat back down on the step again. I read three chapters before I admitted to myself that he wasn't going to open the door.

I walked back to my car and sat in the driver's seat for a minute.

"I won't cry. I'll just fix this. I can fix this." I looked at myself in the rear-view mirror. When I turned on the car, the local radio station came on.

"This one's for my wife," Stan Rogers said before he started to play the opening chords of "Forty-Five Years."

"Goddammit, Stan."

I cried in Adam's driveway.

thirty-six

JOHNNY PULLED UP OUTSIDE THE HOSPITAL IN DAD'S TRUCK AND parked in front of me. Adam looked at me then turned away.

"How'd you get him to come?" I asked as Johnny bounded onto the sidewalk.

"I told him the Oxford was screening a documentary on small-scale farming." He balanced on the curb, rocking from heel to toe.

"And that worked?"

Johnny nodded. "Sadly."

I had tried calling Adam countless times over the past two weeks. I'd apologized until the voicemail stopped recording, then I'd called back and told him the date of the ultrasound. He never answered and he never called back.

I walked over to the car and tapped on the window. Adam didn't look over. I tapped again. I knocked. I tried to open the door; he'd locked it. I pressed my face against the glass so that my nose was squished upwards like a pig.

"Open the door, Adam." I stepped back.

Adam crossed his arms.

"Please. You don't want to miss this."

He rolled down the window. "If Johnny hadn't found those vitamins, I would have. And whose fault would that have been?"

I nodded. "I like to think I would've told you before now, but I might not have. I don't know. You can not like me, okay? I get it if you don't. Maybe just don't miss out on this because you're mad at me?"

The ultrasound technician rubbed the cool jelly over my lower stomach. Adam hadn't said a word. He had let me lead the way and he'd sat beside me in the waiting room. But the entire time he had been coolly indifferent. A couple sat across from us; he wouldn't stop touching her belly. She leaned toward him and whispered something. They both laughed. He kissed her forehead. I looked away and picked at the skin by my thumbnail.

The technician pressed the Doppler to my belly and Adam leaned forward. There was a screen across from us, the image all grey-and-white swirls on black, shapes I couldn't make sense of—and then, suddenly, the baby, our baby, came into view: a perfect profile shot. Hands curled into fists, knees tucked into a chest. One leg kicked out, and while I watched the movement on the screen, I felt the kick. Tiny, but there.

The technician captured the image and measured what she could before moving the Doppler to another part of my stomach. She clicked away, bringing our child a little more into the world each time.

"Do you want to know the sex?"

I looked at Adam, who looked at our baby on the screen. I nodded.

"I'll see what I can do." She moved the Doppler across my stomach. "Oop, do you see that?" The tech pointed to a small black shape. As we looked at it, the shape got smaller. "That's the bladder. He just peed."

"Inside me?" I looked from the screen to my stomach.

"Pretty amazing, huh?"

"Did you say he?" Adam asked.

"Yeah, you're having a boy."

Beside me, Adam started to cry.

"Aw." The tech looked between the two of us and smiled. "Happy Dad!"

I still wasn't sure whether I could fix my relationship with Adam, whether he would let me, but I knew that no matter what happened between us, this child would be loved.

Our baby moved on the screen and for maybe the first time it felt more exciting than it was terrifying. The baby stretched, and it felt like this was how it was always going to be. I was always going to be this child's mother. No matter what. It made me believe in the Creator a little bit more.

Beside me, Adam wiped his eyes. I wanted to reach out and squeeze his hand. Have him squeeze mine back. Instead, I kept my hand on the exam table and made a silent promise to myself and the child inside me, my son, that I would do everything in my power to give him a good life.

thirty-seven

"I JUST WANTED TO CALL AND REMIND YOU THAT YOU ARE A strong Mi'kmaw woman," Nan told me over the phone.

"I mean, I'm mixed, so—"

"Ah—" Nan cut me off. "You are a *strong Mi'kmaw woman*," she repeated. "Don't give me that colonial crap."

I was sitting on the counter in an oversized Led Zeppelin T-shirt and underwear eating a bowl of cereal. There were milk droplets on my stomach. I didn't feel like a strong Mi'kmaw woman. I felt like a slob with a gut and permanent back pain.

"What's with the pep talk?"

"I'm not allowed to call and uplift my kin?"

"You're allowed, you just don't usually take the opportunity."

Nan huffed.

I waited.

"Fine. We've all been talking and, quite frankly, we're concerned."

"Who's been talking?"

"The family."

"What part of the family?"

"All of it."

"Do you know how many cousins I've got?"

"I've made a lot of phone calls."

"They don't call you Nele'k Nan for nothing."

"Shut it, smart-ass."

"If I'm such a strong Mi'kmaw woman, why are you all so concerned about me?"

"I was trying to impart strength by calling you strong. Encourage you to live up to expectations, ya know?"

"I'm fine."

"You're depressed."

"I haven't talked to you in a month, how can you possibly know that?"

"I can sense it. And besides, what kind of granddaughter ignores her grandmother for a month? I might not last the year, you know."

"Nan, *you* are a strong Mi'kmaw woman and you'll outlive us all. Now"—I slid off the counter—"I have to put pants on before I go to class."

thirty-eight

FIONA SCREAMED MY NAME FROM THE BOTTOM OF THE STEPS.

"What?" I struggled to get off the couch as Fiona thundered up the stairs.

"They're here!" She waved a handful of envelopes in front of my face. I gave up trying to stand. Fiona tossed two into my lap and tore open her own. She screamed even louder.

"Jesus!" I flinched.

"I did it!"

"Which university?"

"Dalhousie!"

"What?" I sat up.

"I didn't want to tell you in case I didn't get in or didn't get funding, but I applied after you found out you were pregnant." Fiona took a deep breath. "Every morning, I listened to you gag trying to swallow your vitamins and I thought to myself, this girl is never giving this kid up. And I'm not ready to give you up, so I'm risking my parents' wrath to stay here."

I didn't know what to say.

"Bitch, open your letter."

I started to open the one from the University of Toronto.

"Not that one. I don't care about that one anymore."

I opened the envelope from Dalhousie, careful not to rip the letter inside.

"Hurry up." Fiona tapped her foot.

I read the letter. Then read it again.

Fiona plucked it out of my hand and scanned it.

"Holy shit, how'd you get a bigger scholarship than me?" she asked.

I took the letter back and read it once more. I knew I couldn't give it up. Just like I'd known I couldn't give the baby up when I'd hidden underneath a blanket on the couch, my carefully planned life crumbling around me.

"Do you seriously want to live here with me and a baby while we do our masters'? Like, you're okay with that?"

Fiona sat down next to me. "What about Adam?"

"I don't know." I thumbed the corner of the letter. Talking about Adam made me cry, so I tried not to do it too often. "We haven't spoken since the ultrasound. I've called so many times and he won't talk to me. I think I have to make decisions with the assumption Adam's out. I've messed things up so much...I have no idea how to fix it."

She took my hands. "Well, I'm in. I've been in since you found me hungover, half-naked, and wearing a sou'wester on the first day of university."

I laughed, squeezed her hands. "My dad will never recover from that."

"You've got this." Fiona squeezed back. "We've got this. And if Adam wants in, I'm perfectly happy to become sister wives."

thirty-nine

MY PARENTS HAD USED MY HIGH SCHOOL GRADUATION AS A reason to invite a whole herd of people over. I was fine with it, as long as everyone ignored me. I didn't want the attention. Everything had been going perfectly: my parents and their friends laughed as I sat inconspicuously in the corner by a bowl of chips, a veggie tray on my lap. I had a beer by the leg of my chair. No one was even speaking to me. It was perfect. But then Billy decided I needed to be front and centre. That everyone had to celebrate me.

He'd started with the story of my birth, and that's when I left the room. Billy had been a terrible, albeit very enthusiastic, storyteller. He would get excited, confused, and loud. The more confused he was, the louder he got. His stories involved tangents and asides and nonsensical anecdotes. The monologue that had started with my birth ended on Lorena Bobbitt with a brief interlude concerning Julia Roberts, her cancelled wedding, and subsequent dalliance in Ireland.

I could hear Billy screaming about Lorena Bobbitt and her husband's penis all the way in my room. I jimmied open the window and climbed out onto the roof.

I had just finished the beer, most of the carrots, and all of the dip when Adam crawled out my window and sat beside me.

"There's the graduate." He smiled and ruffled my hair.

I shoved his hand away. Adam looked down at the vegetable tray.

"You didn't ration the dip," he said. "What's wrong?"

"Just a little nervous, I guess." I felt better knowing there was one person in the world who could tell what kind of mood I was in based on how I ate dip.

"We have the whole summer."

I let out an unintelligible grumble.

"I'll tell you what, after you graduate from university as the top learner, you can come home and marry me. We'll have a bunch of babies. Problem solved. Life planned. You can even give them some of those weirdo hippie names you like." Adam pressed his shoulder harder against mine, leaning into me. That was the first time Adam made that joke.

I snorted. My eyes followed the smudgy trail of the Milky Way. I remember not wanting to look at Adam because my chest had ached a little when he said that. Inside, my parents and their friends laughed at something. A big uproarious thunderclap of joy.

I offered Adam half a beer and the cherry tomatoes. When he took the beer, I noticed his knuckles were bruised from when he'd punched a guy at a party a couple nights before. A guy who'd tried to feel me up and hadn't listened when I'd said no.

"Ouch." I winced, taking his hand to inspect it.

"It looks worse than it is." His fingers wrapped around mine.

My heart was in my throat. "How hard did you hit him?"

Adam shrugged. When I looked, our faces were closer than I'd expected. Adam smelled like smoke and beer, a hint of whiskey on his breath. He was so close and so still. We sat there for barely a moment but it felt like eons, our faces centimetres apart. And then Johnny stuck his head out his bedroom window and yelled, "There you are, fuckers!"

"You're almost out!" Johnny called as he climbed out and awkwardly crawled towards us, his sole mission to protect the joint and lighter in his hand. He sat down next to me and lit up.

I was still holding Adam's hand when Johnny passed me the joint.

Once it blazed out, we all scooched closer to the roof's edge. We let our legs dangle and tried to find constellations. We sucked at it. We hadn't even been able to find either of the dippers.

Now, four years later, I was graduating again. And this time, my family had all come into the city. Dad was beyond proud. He hadn't finished high school and now his daughter, *his daughter*, was a university graduate. He repeated it over and over again, loud enough for everyone and their uncles to hear.

My oversized graduation gown did little to cover my belly and all my shoes were too tight for my swollen feet. After a long and uncomfortable ceremony, we went out to eat, and Dad almost died when the bill came. He closed his eyes, leaned back in his chair, and prayed to the Creator for someone to step in and pay. No one did.

After a rowdy goodbye on the front porch of my apartment, my family left for home and I went upstairs. I yanked off my shoes, which was no easy task considering how tight they were, then I sat on the edge of my bed and folded up the final, unused ticket, and threw it in the trash.

forty

I HADN'T UNDERSTOOD HOW ADAM LOOKED AT ME UNTIL HE didn't look at me that way anymore. He used to look at me like I was special, like maybe he might love me. Now he just looked at me like I was a bigger dickhead than Gina Smith.

I'd spent the entire month since graduation studiously ignoring Adam while painfully aware of his existence. I thought about how his stupidly handsome face had looked when I yelled at him on my parents' back deck.

It was now mid-July and the heat was making me even grumpier. Adam and I stood outside my parents' house on Johnny's birthday, facing off on the porch. Sweat trickled down my back and I wondered if he could tell how close I was to screaming into the void and never stopping.

I wasn't going to say a word unless he did.

After a minute of painful silence, Adam muttered two words: "I'm in."

This was everything I'd been waiting for. But it all felt wrong.

"Are you?" What I really wanted to ask was what that meant. Lay it out for me, define *in*.

"I am."

"You're going to have to start answering my phone calls if that's the case."

"I needed time."

I nodded. I couldn't really fault him for that.

"I got into grad school."

"I knew you would."

"I'm going to go." I felt tense, my shoulders stiff.

"Okay."

"I'm not sure what that means for us."

Adam shrugged. "We'll figure it out. We don't have much choice."

"I'm sorry I handled this the way I did." I didn't like how stilted I sounded.

Adam said nothing so I kept talking. "I panicked. I didn't want to just move home and I don't know—" I rubbed my face.

"Live here like all the sad people who never left?"

I grimaced. "I didn't mean it like that. I don't think you're sad. I just..." I wet my lips. "I'm sorry about everything in the fall. I didn't—grad school is really important to me. I—"

"Did I ever ask you to give up grad school?"

"No, but—"

"Did I ever imply I wanted you to move back home and chain you to my bed?"

"A little," I said at the same time Adam said, "I just wanted to be with you."

"Give me some credit, Charlie."

"You were always making those comments about me moving back home!"

"They were jokes!" Adam took off his baseball cap and ran his fingers through his hair. "Sure, if you'd said Adam, I love you, I'm moving home, I probably would've revealed that maybe they weren't actually that jokey. But whatever. I would've compromised. You just never gave me the chance to. You never gave us a chance. And now this," Adam gestured between the two of us, "is where we're at."

I opened my mouth to reply but stopped when my stomach cramped. "Ow." I rubbed my stomach as the pain held on, then faded into nothing.

Adam moved toward me, arm outstretched. "Was that—are you?"

"I don't know. I've had a few cramps like this over the past couple hours."

"Why didn't you say anything?"

"Because the due date isn't for another two weeks. I thought I had to poop."

"We have to go." Adam took another step toward me.

"No, we don't." I took a step toward the door.

"Yes, we do."

"Even if I was in labour, which I don't think I am, according to the book I have time."

"Books don't have all the answers," he said.

I almost gasped. "Adam, this is a book written by people who've studied pregnancy and birth. It's based on *research*. It's accurate."

He rolled his eyes.

"We're going to go inside. We're going to enjoy the birthday party. Then, if things have progressed, we can go to the hospital."

Adam opened his mouth.

"I swear to god, Adam, you cannot change my mind." I opened the porch door.

"Okay, but for the record I think this is stupid."

"Thanks for the vote of confidence." I stomped down the hallway, leaving Adam in the foyer.

I took the cake out of the fridge. I may have been teetering on the precipice of parenthood, but the cake still needed to come to room temperature before we ate it. I placed it on the counter just as I had another contraction, much worse than the last one. I sagged against the counter.

"I've got to get the good napkins, Nick!" Mom yelled from the doorway. "Johnny's got a lady friend coming over."

I stood up and smiled wide. Maybe if I smiled through the contractions they wouldn't hurt so much.

"You okay?" Mom slowly reached for the pile of napkins.

"Yeah, why?"

"You look a little crazed."

"Just excited to celebrate Johnny." My stomach tightened and pain shot through my legs. "The good napkins, eh?"

Johnny's lady friend turned out to be none other than Sadie Butler, his high school girlfriend. Nan and Grampa also came by, armed with their comfy shoes and a bag of stale cheese puffs. Mom showed Sadie pictures of Johnny as a kid while he sulked like an embarrassed teenager. Dad and Grampa watched whatever sports were on. Adam and Nan stuffed their faces full of chips and appetizers. I hovered on the periphery, trying to pretend I wasn't in labour.

"Are you okay?" Adam asked for the thousandth time.

"If you ask me that again I'm going to murder you."

Adam sighed and went back to the snacks. I had a feeling he was using food as a distraction tactic.

I made it to the laundry room just as another contraction started. It began as such a small discomfort I thought I could banish it through sheer willpower, but it grew and grew until the only thing that existed was the pain. It was perhaps the first time in my life I was incapable of overthinking something. Though once it was over, I grabbed my copy of *What to Expect When You're Expecting* and combed through the labour section, trying to remember how far apart the contractions were supposed to be before we went to the hospital. I heard footsteps coming into the kitchen and stuck my head out the door.

"Pssst. Johnny." I pulled him aside, intercepting his beer run. "What is Sadie Butler doing here? Is she the lady friend?" I asked, momentarily distracted. I peered through the crack in the laundry room doors again.

"No, she just wandered in here. I don't know why she's here, it's kind of awkward really." He said it so matter-of-factly that I actually believed him.

"Really?"

"No, dumbass. Of course she's the lady friend!"

"I thought you only liked her because of her big boobs," I said, referencing a conversation we'd had years ago after they'd broken up. I looked past Johnny as if I could see her breasts from here.

"Yeah, and they're still big. It also turns out that she really does like Nirvana."

"I think you need to rethink your criteria for choosing lady friends. Nan's gonna die if you don't date a Native girl."

"Nan can go take a hike."

I gasped.

"Please don't tell her I said that," Johnny pleaded.

"What are you guys doing?" Adam stuck his head through the doors. As he did, I felt the beginnings of another contraction. They were still relatively far apart. Did this one feel worse than the last? No. Maybe? I pressed my hand to my back and stifled a groan.

"Are you okay?" Adam said, risking my wrath.

"I'm pregnant, my back is just sore." I cast a wide-eyed glance at Johnny. "Let's do cake!" I bared my teeth in what I hoped was a calm smile and shuffled into the kitchen.

I ordered everyone into the room, thinking I only sounded a little bossy, but the look Adam gave me as everyone came into the kitchen let me know I wasn't pulling off "calm pregnant woman." I jabbed the candles into the top of the cake and rifled through one of the junk drawers for a lighter. I lit the candles, picked up the cake, and just as I opened my mouth to sing happy birthday, Johnny interrupted me.

"Charlie, I think you peed your pants."

This didn't happen. Your water breaking when you're about to sing happy birthday to your brother was not a thing. Except there I was, in my parents' kitchen, Johnny's cake in my hands, candles lit, about to sing happy birthday, as amniotic fluid dripped down my leg and onto the floor. Seven pairs of eyes stared at me.

"I'm in labour."

"What? For how long?" Mom asked.

"Four hours, give or take."

"She wouldn't let me tell anyone," Adam whined behind me.

Johnny groaned. "Will the lies never end?"

"You can't be mad at me. I think I've been very stoic and I would like to be appreciated for that." I was still holding the cake, candles melting into goo.

"Should we wipe that up?" Sadie pointed towards the growing puddle of fluid at my feet. I had to admire her gumption. Dad, who was closest to the paper towel, had turned a chalky shade of white, presumably due to the painful reminder that his daughter was sexually active and had a vagina.

Sadie reached for the pile of good napkins.

"No, not those." Mom moved them out of reach.

The cake splattered onto the floor, all but one candle extinguished, as another contraction took hold and my hands went to my knees. Adam leaned over and blew the candle out.

"Fire hazard," he muttered, glancing at me.

I closed my eyes and tried to breathe through the pain; this contraction was much stronger than the ones before. As it ebbed, I felt hands rubbing my back. I looked down at the floor and saw a puddle of liquid, a smashed cake, and Adam's sock feet. One foot was completely in the amniotic fluid, but he didn't seem to care.

"Damn it, Charlie. Right in the womb juices," Johnny groaned.

"Can you not call it that?" I snapped.

"What else am I going to call it?"

"Do we have to do this right now?" Adam asked impatiently, his hands massaging my back.

Johnny held up his hands in surrender.

No one had made a move to clean up the mess at my feet.

Mom stuck out her hand. "Hand me the paper towel, Nick."

Dad was hiding in his chair with his eyes closed.

"Nick," Mom snapped.

Dad reached to his right, and without opening his eyes he fumbled for the paper towel and blindly tossed it across the room. He looked truly ill. The paper towel hit Grampa on the head. He'd been leaning over the chip bowl, shovelling food into his face. The paper towel bounced from his head, landed on the floor, and rolled towards me.

"Jesus Christ, Nick, now's not the time to get all weak in the knees." Mom bent down to pick up the paper towel.

"Yeah Dad, those womb juices aren't going to clean themselves."

"Johnny!" Mom gave Johnny the look I knew meant she'd reached the end of her rope.

Dad turned an even paler shade of white. I was about to tell them all to go to hell when I had another contraction.

"Honey, you gotta get straight to the hospital. This baby is coming now." Nan took a sip of her coffee.

"Check the book." I pointed to the laundry room.

My grandmother held a hand to her chest. "You're going to trust a book over your own kukumij?"

Mom darted into the laundry room, came back out, and started to flip through the book. She eventually stopped, silently scanned the page for a few seconds, and then agreed with Nan.

"She's right," she said. "You should probably just head straight there. We can follow behind. Adam, grab her hospital bag."

Everyone followed Adam and me out of the house, my family shuffling along like a herd of sheep. After two more contractions, I leaned against the car, wet from the vagina down, exhausted and annoyed.

I groaned. "Why are you all so close to me? Can everyone just stand on the other side of the property?" Adam rubbed my back; I wasn't sure he'd stopped.

Mom covered the front seat with a ginormous blanket to preserve the upholstery.

"I'll wash it." I awkwardly tried to climb into the car.

"Don't bother. Just burn it," Johnny said from somewhere behind me.

I climbed onto the blanket as another contraction started. They came like waves, a deep burning and clenching which turned into an all-out bodily panic that eventually faded away, leaving me panting and drained. Dad stuck his hand past Mom and handed me a braid of sweetgrass as Adam skirted the car and jumped into the driver's seat.

"What's that going to do?" Johnny eyed the braid.

"It's medicine, it'll help," Nan said.

"If you say so." Johnny didn't sound sure.

As Mom was about to close the car door I stopped her. I was suddenly very close to tears; everything was about to be so very different, and when the door shut, we would all be a little bit closer to a brand new world. A world where I was a mother.

Mom leaned down and kissed my forehead. "We'll be right behind you. I promise." She shut the door then banged on the roof.

Adam backed out and took off down the street. He white-knuckled the steering wheel as I groaned, clutching the handle of the door.

"It's okay, Charlie, everything is going to be all right."

Year Two

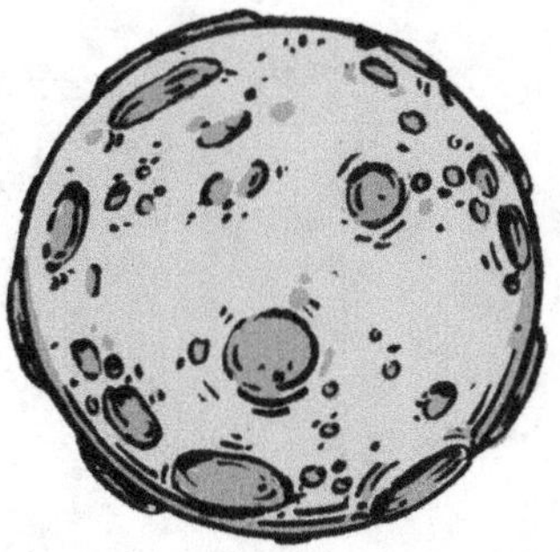

Wikumkewiku's

(We-goom-gay-we-goos)

Mate Calling Time

forty-one

IT WAS EVERYWHERE. UP ANGUS'S BACK. DOWN HIS LEG. ON MY shirt. In my hair. In his hair.

Three months ago, I would not have believed a baby could have this many blowouts. But here we were, again.

Three months of near daily poop catastrophes. Three months of perpetual exhaustion. But also: Three months of baby cuddles. Three months of loving someone so fervently I didn't care if he shit all over me. This kid could throw up in my mouth and I'd tell him I loved him with the vomit still in there.

Angus arched his back and the poop climbed even higher.

I held Angus away from my body, though it was too late to save either of us. "How?" I looked around. "Why?" I searched for a cloth. I was supposed to leave five minutes ago. I stuck my head out my bedroom door. "Fiona?"

She came running down the hallway. "What?"

"I'll buy you a bottle of wine if you deal with this." I held Angus toward her, his poopy orange back facing her.

She stopped mid-step.

"Please? I have to meet Dr. Gamble in fifteen minutes and I have baby shit everywhere."

She put a hand on her hip. "Throw in a pie and you have a deal."

I owed her a bakery and a vineyard at this point.

"You got it."

Fiona grabbed a towel from the bathroom and wrapped Angus in it. I darted back into my room.

"Your dad," Fiona said to Angus, "is real lucky to not have to deal with this on a daily basis."

"Trust me, he wishes he could." I took off my dirty shirt and rifled through the clothes on my bed for a clean one. "When he's not ignoring me, he loves to tell me how unfair the situation is."

Adam was right, it was unfair. Because I breastfed, Adam got stolen hours on the weekends while I struggled to balance the workload of a master's with keeping Angus and myself alive. When I was doing schoolwork, I felt terrible because I should be paying more attention to Angus; and when I was paying attention to Angus, I felt guilty for not doing schoolwork. And when I was trying to fall asleep at night, everything quiet and still after a day filled with guilt, poop, and an exorbitant amount of coffee, I would think of Billy and how life plowed on and he was still stuck in the ground, and I would feel like an asshole because I didn't think of him more. Visit him more. I felt like a failure because I wasn't doing more. Sometimes I wasn't even sure what I needed to do more of, I just knew I wasn't doing enough.

If it wasn't for Fiona, I would've lost my mind.

I put my hair in a bun to hide the shit and grabbed my backpack.

"This shouldn't take long," I told her as I slipped my shoes on. I kissed Angus's foot, peeking out from the towel. "No, it shouldn't," I said in an obnoxious baby voice. Angus smiled.

I jogged down the stairs and yelled, "Bye, baby!" as I threw open the door. Our new downstairs neighbour, Mac, was just unlocking his door.

"Hey, I hope Angus wasn't too loud last night, he was really having a moment."

"I sleep like a friggin' log. Don't worry about it."

"I probably still will," I admitted.

Mac laughed. "Take it easy," he called as I power-walked down the sidewalk.

Dr. Gamble absentmindedly clicked his pen while staring into space. His hair had grown out since I was in undergrad. Now I was a master's student with shit in my hair.

His skin was sun-kissed. If not for his dress shirt and sweater, I would've said he looked casual and carefree. It was unnerving. I tried not to shuffle too much. Eventually he cleared his throat. "As I've said before, the proposal in your application was strong, but it could be stronger. What we need to do is refine it."

I held in a groan. He'd been on about refining my research topic for a month. The second time he brought it up, clearly displeased with my first attempt, I made a joke about how every Thanksgiving my family shot off my dad's homemade potato gun and *refinement* wasn't really in my wheelhouse. He hadn't found it funny.

In fact, I would bet he didn't know what a potato gun was.

I didn't want to even entertain rethinking my thesis; that sounded a lot like starting over, and starting over sounded a lot like me starting a downward spiral.

"I don't get the sense that you've found the topic you could write a full thesis on. You need to be passionate about it."

"I just need a bit more time to do some more research. Gather resources." He was right. I didn't want to think about molasses and sugar and the hierarchy of sweeteners in 1800s versus present-day Halifax anymore. I'd written a five-page paper on the same topic in third year. The professor had said it was an interesting topic. And so, I'd run with it. Turns out, just because something is interesting for a few hundred words doesn't mean you should turn it into a full-blown grad school thesis. I didn't even care anymore. And I'd always cared about school. I wanted to spend all my time with Angus. I wanted to hole up in our apartment with him and never think about anything else. But I couldn't say any of that out loud.

Dr. Gamble had been surprisingly positive when he found out about my pregnancy. I hadn't told him, but when I dropped off a thank you gift after graduation, he'd taken one look at my stomach, deduced I wasn't smuggling a watermelon under my shirt, and bluntly asked if I was with child. Near tears, I'd told him I still wanted to go to grad school and he'd seemed surprised I assumed he'd tell me otherwise.

So no, I didn't want to write about sugar and molasses anymore. But I'd made my decision, and I didn't want to disappoint Dr. Gamble. I may have been floundering with my outline, but I'd figure it out. I wasn't going to backtrack now.

"Starting over isn't the end of the world, Charlotte."

I wanted to plug my ears and scream "la la la" until he stopped talking. I sat up straighter in the chair.

"I can do this," I told him.

I searched my backpack for a pen and paper. So far I'd found a pacifier, a diaper, and a stick of deodorant. I put a package of wipes on the table and all but stuck my head in the bag. At the very bottom I found a nub of a pencil and a notebook.

A girl smiled down at me as she thunked a bright blue backpack onto the table. She looked like she played volleyball.

"Hey, I'm Maddie." She sat down next to me, brushing her blond hair off her shoulder.

"Charlie." I smiled.

"I don't think we've actually met before."

I normally sat at the back so I could slip in late.

"God, I'm so jealous of your tan," Maddie said, not waiting for a response.

"Oh, uh, thanks."

"I just burn. Is it self-tanner?"

"No. I'm Mi'kmaw. Just good old-fashioned genetics."

"Oh."

That one syllable sounded loaded.

"Do you have, like, a really cool spirit animal?" Maddie smiled.

"I don't—not that I know of?" Why did that sound like a question?

"Oh." That sound again.

Thankfully, the professor walked in and Maddie turned to face her. There was that same feeling I'd had when the girl told me I should wear braids. Like I needed to apologize.

Like it was my fault I wasn't the Indian they had in mind.

forty-two

"I CAN DO THIS," I TOLD ANGUS AN HOUR LATER IN THE KITCHEN.

He looked up at me from his baby seat, his eyes such a similar green to Adam's, unblinking. I watched his stomach to make sure he was still breathing.

"You know, it'd be nice if you said something encouraging. Like, 'You've got this, Mom' or, I don't know, 'Your advisor is a nincompoop.'" I divided the bread dough in front of me into smaller portions. Angus said nothing. "I know he's not a nincompoop. I'm the nincompoop." I'd never said nincompoop so many times in my life. I was trying to cut back on my cursing. I picked up a portion of dough, brought the edges together, then rolled it on the counter into a smooth and perfect ball.

I'd been making bread for years. I understood dough. I knew how to tell when it was ready to move on to the next step. I got that sometimes bread needed a little more time than you thought. That, depending on the circumstances, it might require a different approach. I could adapt when baking because I understood how bread was supposed to feel and look. I wish I could say the same about my thesis. Up until this year I thought I'd understood academics in the same way.

But this year was hard. And not just because I was in the early days of motherhood. Grad school was a challenge I wasn't sure I was up for. I'd never anticipated feeling this stuck. Unlike with bread, I didn't know how to adapt. I wasn't sure I could.

Angus yawned, scrunching his nose. He smacked his lips. I put the dough ball into the greased baking tray and started on another.

Fiona bounded into the kitchen, red and sweaty from her run.

"Whoa. That's a lot of buns." She grabbed a glass from the cupboard.

"I'm not sure it's enough."

"Are you joking?"

I shook my head. "No."

"Hi, buddy." Fiona leaned down and kissed Angus and he squirmed in delight.

She filled her glass with water and took a sip. "So, you sure your family is cool with me coming for Thanksgiving? Isn't it, like, a classic colonizer holiday?"

"To be honest, I don't know that we've ever thought about it that hard. Dad is incredibly food-focused and there's no way he'd shun a holiday where overeating is expected."

"Hence the buns." Fiona nodded at the two baking trays filled with dough balls.

"Hence the buns."

I finally understood why people could do terrible things. I lay in bed, Angus sitting on my stomach, propped up by my knees. As my son stared down at me, I realized that I would lie, steal, and kill for him. I could picture him sitting alone on the playground in school, much the same way I had, lonely and sad and friendless. I hoped he'd inherited Adam's ability to connect with people.

Angus stared at me, his eyes big and round.

How vulnerable it was to have my heart outside my body.

"If anyone is ever mean to you, I'll drop kick them into next year," I told him. Angus smiled. "Is that funny?" He cooed. "Do you take joy in me committing a crime on your behalf?" Angus smiled even wider. "You'd probably only have to ask Uncle Johnny once and he'd happily do it. He's a menace to society." Angus cooed again. "Yes, he is."

My eyes stung, moved to tears by how many people we knew who would willingly throw-down on Angus's behalf.

"I'm going to make sure we have such a good life," I told Angus. "You're going to feel so loved and cared for. You'll be so loved you'll be annoyed about it." Angus stared at me blankly. "Not as into that as the drop kicking, eh?" He blinked.

I promised to play minigolf with him, even though I hated it. I told him I'd take him to powwows. I'd get one of my cousins to make him a drum. I'd learn how to make crepes because it seemed fancy. On Sundays we'd watch *Matilda* and I'd make luski with ginger ale.

I could see our future laid about before us and it was good and bright.

forty-three

FIONA LOOKED AROUND. "IS THIS ACTUALLY A TOWN? OR IS IT just a long road that happens to have a few stores on it?"

I'd said similar things in the past, but it rankled when it came from an outsider.

"Every town has a town centre, and this is ours." We had driven by the general store, liquor store, church, Legion, and a second church that was being converted into a museum.

"That was it?" She craned her neck to try and look back.

"It's a small town." We turned off the main street and onto my parents,' bumping over potholes and swerving to avoid a crumbled bit of asphalt by the shoulder.

Home felt distinct because I could picture myself at age twelve walking across the small bridge just before the general store to play in the river. We'd just driven by a tree Adam and Johnny had to rescue eight-year-old me from when I'd gotten stuck. At fourteen I'd driven Johnny's car into the ditch across from my parents' driveway when he insisted he could teach me to drive "no problem." At seventeen I'd graduated from high school and at a house party down an old dirt road Chris Lacombe felt me up and I punched him in the nose, and then, twenty minutes later, Adam also punched him.

The town I grew up in might've looked like nothing, but it felt like something. Sure, that might include a few potholed roads, an upsettingly long blackfly season, and a population that could recall my awkward high school years with disturbing accuracy, but the curve of the shoreline and the water lapping at my ankles lightened the heaviness in my bones. The sound of my family laughing made me wonder what the hell I was doing living away, though we didn't laugh quite as much as we used to.

Nan always talked about traditional territory and belonging and our ties to the land and I always thought it was bogus until I stood at the edge of the Cobequid Bay after being in the city for the first few months of undergrad. In that moment, I finally felt grounded. I remember wondering if I should come home.

And then, afterwards, the old woman who used to run the general store watched me a little bit closer than everyone else while I grabbed a bag of chips, was a little bit ruder while she rang up my purchases, and I remembered why I'd wanted to leave in the first place.

But Fiona didn't know that, and her criticism of my hometown, even if I agreed most of the time, bothered me.

"Leave while you can!" Johnny yelled from the open kitchen window. "They're fighting again!"

Fiona held three bottles of wine and the diaper bag while I balanced two trays of rolls and Angus in his car seat.

"We're not fighting," Nan yelled. "We're trying to decide what order we should cook the vegetables in."

Johnny opened the back door and yelled: "And they're fighting about it!" He stepped back to make space as we piled into the kitchen.

"Hello, hello." Mom breezed past us with a basting tube and a bag of potatoes.

"Hi." Sadie stuck her head through the kitchen door and smiled. "We're not allowed in the kitchen."

Adam squeezed past Sadie and took the car seat from me. He unbuckled it, lifted Angus out, and kissed him on the cheek. "Hi, buddy." He nabbed a green bean with his free hand as he left the kitchen with our son.

"Hi to you too," I grumbled after Adam disappeared.

I often felt overlooked by the people around me. I didn't make friends easily. But Adam had always seen me. No matter who else was in the room, I always had his attention. And now that was gone.

"Out." Nan pointed to the living room. "Hi, Fiona." She smiled.

"Hi, Agnes." Fiona passed her the wine.

Mom smacked Johnny's hand with a wooden spoon as he tried to grab a handful of green beans.

"Ow! Jesus Christ, Mom!" He rubbed his hand.

Mom and Nan had this weird unspoken rule that we were all meant to suffer in hunger the day of Thanksgiving. We had to fast until supper was served; it was the only thing they agreed on.

Sadie had set up a one thousand–piece puzzle on the living room table and declared we'd finish it before the day was out. I sat on the floor next to Fiona and started looking for edge pieces, grateful for the forced activity. It gave me something to do other than stare at Adam.

I rarely got to see him with Angus, but he'd taken to fatherhood with such ease. The first month I'd hovered, convinced something horrible would happen if Angus was out of my sight. He wouldn't take the bottle I'd painstakingly pumped and he'd be hungry. Adam would faint and there'd be no one to watch him. Adam had tolerated my presence, but Angus always took the bottle, and Adam had never fainted in his life. Eventually, I had to admit I wasn't needed. So I only saw Adam at drop-off and pick-up. I hadn't realized how starved I felt for his presence, how much seeing him with Angus would twist my insides.

The loss of experiencing parenthood alongside Adam was a grief I hadn't expected.

After a few hours, with half the puzzle done, we were all beckoned to the kitchen. We crammed around the table, elbows knocking, practically drooling over the food.

"Johnny, stop," Nan ordered. Johnny froze, a forkful of food in front of his open mouth.

"We have to go around and say what we're thankful for," she explained.

"Do we, though?" Johnny and Dad asked at the same time.

"Yes." Nan gave them both a wide-eyed stare.

"I can go first," Fiona offered. "I'm thankful for all of you letting me come and have Thanksgiving with you." She gave the table a big smile.

"That was sickeningly sincere. Can you leave?" Johnny asked, still holding the forkful of food to his mouth.

Fiona nudged him in the shoulder and his food fell back onto his plate.

"Your turn, Johnny," said Nan.

He groaned. "Fine. I'm thankful for Sadie."

"Awww." Sadie squished her cheek against his shoulder.

"Adam?" Nan prompted.

"Uh, I'm thankful for Angus."

"Dude, you can't steal my thing," said Johnny.

"What?"

"You can't also be thankful for a person. That was my thing."

"That's the stupidest thing I've ever heard."

"Jesus Christ." Mom slumped in her chair and stared up at the ceiling.

"Can we eat yet?" Dad asked from down the table.

"Fine," Nan snapped.

Everyone dug in. We scooped and ladled and passed food around the table. The only sound was silverware on porcelain and the occasional groan of pleasure.

There were moments in the past year where I could see, with startling clarity, how Billy would fit in. Right now, he'd clink his glass, stand up, and make a speech. I could almost hear his voice.

"Billy would've totally given a speech right now," I said. My family stopped eating. "I'm thankful for Billy." My voice rose in pitch. "And that he stayed with us as long as he could."

Mom sniffed. "Goddammit." She pressed her napkin to each eye, blew her nose. Fiona handed her a clean napkin.

"That was a good one," Nan commended.

"Yeah, but it was so good that no one else is gonna want to go because theirs can't possibly be as good, and they'll look like an asshole." Johnny paused. "So maybe that makes you the real asshole, hey Charlie?"

"I'm also thankful that Angus hasn't had a diaper blowout in three days. Is that better?"

Johnny nodded, his mouth full.

"Can I be preemptively thankful for the pie Johnny made?" Sadie asked.

"I'll allow it." Nan took a sip of wine.

"Nan, what are you thankful for?" Johnny asked.

"I'm thankful for you lot, and that I was allowed to cook the stuffing this year."

"They were out of onions!" Mom wailed. Last year, Mom hadn't put onions in the stuffing; Nan hadn't stopped talking about it since.

"Can someone pass the rolls?" Grampa asked.

Dad watched everyone finish their plates with eagle-eyed attention. As Nan forked the last piece of turkey into her mouth, he cleared this throat. "Is it time for pie?" he asked.

"How can you even think about eating again?" Mom asked, rubbing her stomach.

Dad shrugged, while Johnny was already at the counter, uncovering the pie.

He placed a pumpkin pie on the table. It didn't look quite right.

"This," he said with great fanfare, "is made from scratch. And I grew the pumpkin myself."

Sadie applauded.

Johnny cut it theatrically and passed the plated slices around.

Mom took a bite, then covered her mouth with her hand. "Oh, Johnny."

"What?"

"It's disgusting," she admitted as Johnny took a bite.

He spit the half-chewed pie onto his plate.

"How? I don't understand…I followed a recipe!" Johnny took a swig of water and swished it around in his mouth.

Adam handed me a plate. I handed it to Dad, who handed it to Mom, who handed it back to Johnny.

"What did I do wrong?"

Fiona leaned over to look at the pie. "It looks a bit lumpy. I don't think it's supposed to look like that."

I took a spoon and nudged some of the pie filling. "It kind of looks like scrambled eggs. I think you managed to make scrambled pumpkin pie. But I don't know how. It's actually kind of impressive."

Johnny was slumped at the table, his head the only thing stopping his body from sliding to the floor. "This is terrible. What a fucking tragedy."

Mom looked at the piece in front of her. "The bottom crust is almost cooked." She poked at it with her fork. "That's something to be proud of."

"Christ almighty," Grampa gagged at the end of the table. "This pie is terrible!"

Sadie reached over and rubbed Johnny's back.

"You guys can clear the table." Mom and Nan took the two open bottles of wine and disappeared into the living room. Dad ushered Grampa out the back door so he could show him something in his workshop.

Sadie started to collect dirty glasses. Angus stirred. Adam and I leaned over to pick him up at the same time.

Adam shot me a glance. "I've got it." He rocked Angus in his arms and soothed him back to sleep.

I cleared my throat and grabbed a stack of plates to bring to the counter.

"Holy shit, you were right." Fiona held up the two empty trays.

"The rolls are all gone."

"I told you." I tried to laugh off Adam's coldness, picked up a pile of plates and carried them to the sink.

Johnny put on The Cranberries and sang along obnoxiously.

I'm not sure if having four people clean the kitchen made the work faster or harder. We kept having to scoot around one another and at one point, Sadie almost dropped a stack of plates because Johnny had gotten too into "Zombie."

It could've just been Johnny who made it harder.

I couldn't take the crowded kitchen or Adam's refusal to acknowledge me for another second. "I have to take the compost out, want to see the pig?" I asked Fiona.

"Sure." She wrung out the dish cloth.

Johnny grabbed a bucket of scraps off the counter. "I'll bring his food."

"You coming?" Sadie asked Adam as she slipped on her clogs.

Adam grabbed a baby blanket off the back of a kitchen chair to drape over Angus and followed us outside.

"Here, Johnny Johnny Johnny. C'mere," Johnny whistled.

"Um, the pig's name is Johnny?" Fiona asked.

"Johnny Jr." Johnny dropped the scraps into the trough. Johnny Jr. trundled over and stuck his snout in.

Fiona looked back and forth. "And what was the name of the pig last year?"

"Henry. My cousin. He said it was a great honour," Adam answered.

"And the year before?"

"Barb. She works at the police station," I told Fiona. "We don't like her."

"Do you not think it's a little weird that you all name pigs after people you know and then kill them?"

We all thought for a minute.

"Not really," Johnny admitted.

"I think it's kind of sweet." Sadie hooked her arm through Johnny's.

"Jesus," Fiona muttered.

"That's a good one. There's always next year." Johnny swung the compost bucket back and forth and then, with Sadie by his side, walked back to the house.

Adam was showing Angus the pig, whispering things to him that were too quiet for me to hear. Like I wasn't there at all.

I gave Fiona a look and she and I walked back toward the house. I sat on the step.

"You really weren't exaggerating when you said things weren't great between you and Adam," she said, sitting down beside me. "You might've even been *underselling* it."

"I know. He barely acknowledges me. I get that I fucked up, but it still hurts my feelings. I mean, he cared about me once. Am I being stupid?"

"You're not. He legit flinched when you touched his arm. I've never seen a person look so disturbed."

Fiona had a real inability to make people feel better. Which was concerning given that she wanted to be a therapist.

When I was in labour, Adam had kissed my forehead. When Angus was finally in my arms, Adam had leaned in and whispered, "You did good," as he pushed the hair out of my face.

I clung to the memory of that, the feeling of his lips on my skin. It had been four months since he'd been anything but neutral to me. Four months of only discussing the details of Angus's life. Four months of that memory coming out of nowhere and punching me in the gut.

"But you know," Fiona said, "you should see how he looks at you when he thinks no one is watching. It's these quick glances filled with total want and yearning. And then, a moment later, he looks even more disturbed than when you touched. It's really fascinating." She paused. "He's clearly conflicted. I wonder if he'd let me do my thesis on him."

The door opened and Mom stuck her head out. "Your dad's got the potato gun out if you want to see a buzzed man do stupid things."

forty-four

I WAS LATE. AGAIN. THE PROFESSOR USHERED ME IN AND TOLD me to join the smallest group. I shuffled past a line of chairs, my foot catching on the last one. The hushed murmurs stopped as the chair leg scraped loudly across the floor.

"Sorry." I waved to the other group before dropping my bag and sitting down next to a guy whose name I thought might be Zack.

"Sorry I'm late. What'd I miss?"

"We were just complaining about student loans," Maddie told me.

"But we're supposed to be discussing the arrival of the first Loyalists to Canada," Zack added.

"Wow, that sounds..." I trailed off. I'd been bored to tears when I learned about this in undergrad. But much to my dismay, there wasn't huge variety for Canadian history courses. It was British colonialism or bust.

"Dull?" Zack supplied.

I threw up my hands. "You said it, not me."

Zack laughed. "Do you also think the amount of reading is nuts? Like, I've got an eye twitch from all the reading. My mom thinks I should get a second job so I don't graduate with a ton of debt, but I can barely handle the course load and TAing as is. Forget a job."

"Tell me about it." I tested my pen in my notebook; it was almost dead.

"But you don't have loans, do you?" Maddie asked. "Like, don't you get to go to school for free because you're Native?"

"Uh..." Did I answer this? Did I ignore her? "I mean yeah, I got funding from the university, but it doesn't have anything to do with me being Mi'kmaw." Why was I disclosing my financial information to her? What was wrong with me?

"Really?" She sounded skeptical. "It was probably really easy for you to get in though, right?"

What was happening? "No?"

"But I mean, you got in because you're Native, right?"

I couldn't tell if she knew she was being an asshole or not. She *had* to know, right?

Zack shifted uncomfortably.

"I got in on the strength of my application. Just like everyone else here."

"Yeah, but on that application, there was a box you could check if you were an Indian. And I bet you—" She drew a check mark in the air with her fingers and clicked her tongue.

My entire body was on fire.

Zack cleared his throat.

"What?" Maddie asked, looking between us. "I'm just saying, it's easier for you to get in and you don't have to pay."

"It wasn't easier." I could've laughed. Instead, I almost cried.

"Okay." She actually rolled her eyes.

She didn't believe me. I took a deep, rattling breath.

She didn't think that I deserved to be here.

My ancestors had survived centuries of colonization and genocide only for me to sit there and listen to some girl I didn't know accuse me of having it easy.

My ancestors are probably pissed at me right now.

That thought was enough to staunch the impending waterworks.

Our professor asked us to return to our seats, saving me from whatever blithering response I was about to mumble. I couldn't move.

"Ignore her." A girl with dark skin and long box braids sat next to me.

"You heard that?"

"It was hard not to." She chuckled. "Maddie's just mad she didn't get full funding."

I couldn't quite bring myself to laugh it off. I already felt stretched thin. It seemed like I struggled more than everyone else in my year. I was more chaotic, I barely made it on time. It felt like I was seconds away from a total implosion.

Maybe Maddie was right. Maybe I'd been let in to fill a quota and now it was becoming obvious I didn't belong.

forty-five

"MOM?" I CALLED OUT. THE HOUSE WAS QUIET.

It was the November long weekend, and I'd wanted to give Adam some time with Angus. Dad was trying to rope me into helping kill Johnny Jr. I was also contemplating asking Sadie if she knew anything about voodoo dolls. She was really into crystals; this seemed like a natural next step. This method of retaliation had been Fiona's suggestion.

"Nothing crazy," Fiona said when I told her what had happened with Maddie. "An ingrown toenail. A canker sore right in the corner, by her lips, so that every time she opens her big fat mouth it hurts."

I made a mental note never to piss Fiona off.

"Mom?" I called again.

"Up here," came her quiet reply.

She stood in the doorway of Billy's room, holding a garbage bag.

"Have you been in here since..." I stood next to her in the doorway.

"Not since the funeral. I thought maybe it was time to, I don't know, do something with it. It still kind of feels too soon. But it's also really hard to walk by his door every day. I don't know." She rubbed her eyes. "Maybe it'll be easier if it's not his anymore."

The bed was still made, still wrinkled in the spot where Mom sat when we picked out the clothes Billy would be buried in. While our lives ambled along, Billy's had stopped and his room had stood still, unchanged save for a layer of dust which had settled over everything.

Neither of us moved from the doorway. We didn't know how to alter something that stood as a relic of a person's life. If we tore down his posters, would we erase Billy from this earth a little bit more? If we moved his books, would we forget parts of him we never wanted to let go of?

The porch door slammed. Johnny called out, and I stepped over the threshold. I stripped the bedsheets because Billy had never touched them. The dust made me sneeze as I tossed them into the hallway. I pressed play on Billy's boombox and the first chords of Pearl Jam's "Black" came through the speakers. As if summoned by '90s grunge, Johnny appeared in the doorway.

"Want help?" He peered over Mom's shoulder.

"Finally decided to get out of bed, eh?" Mom asked, her voice sharp.

Johnny rolled his eyes.

"Throw those in the wash?" I pointed to the pile of sheets.

"What was that?" I asked after Johnny left.

"He just lays in bed all day. I don't know what to do," Mom whispered. "Any time I try to help I seem to make it worse. So I've resorted to biting comments, at least it riles him up."

"I'm not sure…is that smart?"

Mom shrugged. This was the same woman who'd gotten so fed up checking under my bed for monsters that she'd eventually said that, yes, there were monsters under there, but they were so tired of me asking about them they'd fallen asleep.

By the time Johnny had thrown the laundry on and come back with a snack, Mom stood by Billy's cluttered bookshelf. Johnny, cross-legged on the bare mattress, grabbed the baseball hat that had been hanging off the headboard and put it on.

"Can I have this?" he asked no one in particular. He took a bite from a whole carrot.

I shrugged, and Mom thumbed through a book she'd picked off the shelf.

I grabbed *Wuthering Heights* off the bedside table. A photograph was being used as a bookmark. It was of Mom and Billy. "Look at this!" I held out the wrinkled photo to show Johnny. He immediately lost it.

"Holy shit, Mom! You look like a real country bumpkin. Check out your hair!"

Mom shrugged. "It was the '60s."

Johnny gawked. "You mean, this isn't a costume?"

I tried to hide my laugh behind the book.

"Piss off." Mom snatched the photo out of Johnny's hand and grinned.

We cleaned out Billy's room while his mixtape played from the stereo. Pearl Jam switched to "The Old Apartment" by Barenaked Ladies and eventually the room didn't seem so stagnant and heavy.

We kept the posters up on the walls. We piled all of Billy's most precious possessions onto the bed. We dusted and threw out all the useless things Billy had hoarded—the last thing I tossed in the garbage bag was a decapitated Bob Ross bobblehead. A bobbletorso.

Johnny held a faded Black Sabbath shirt to his chest.

"You can't take all the shirts," I argued.

"You're a mom now. You have to wear, like, blouses and ankle-length skirts"

"That's the dumbest thing I've ever heard. I'm a mother, not a Mennonite. Give me that one."

"No. It won't fit."

"Rude!"

"Here," Mom interrupted us. "Take this." She held out the mustard yellow cardigan from the closet.

"Thanks." I rubbed the yarn between my fingers. I'd put it back after wearing it at Billy's funeral.

"Do you want the furniture out?" Johnny slipped the Black Sabbath shirt over his head. I would steal it from his room later.

Mom nodded. "I think we should just throw the bed out." She paused, thinking her decision through. "We should just get rid of it all."

"You sure?" Johnny asked.

She nodded her head decisively. "Yes."

We dragged the furniture to the end of the driveway and left it there. I made a sign that said *for free* and taped it to the dresser.

"Should we bet on how long it takes someone to nab these?" Johnny asked.

Exhausted, the three of us flopped down on the bed. We lay on our backs and looked up at the sky.

"I'm going to say a day," Mom said.

"I'm going to guess never and they fall apart and rot," I said. "They'll get covered by snow and we'll forget about them till the spring."

"Wow, negative much?" Johhny propped himself up on his elbows.

"Remember the bunkbeds? I'm pretty sure there's still a bedpost in the ditch." I twisted to try and look.

"Listen, we tried," Mom said, ever defensive about the forgotten bunkbeds of 1995.

The branches of the trees lining the road reached towards each other but didn't quite meet, leaving a breadth of untouched sky. In summer the leaves would obscure the sky completely, the road winding through a verdant canopy.

Someone drove by in a truck, then slowed down. They reversed and came to a full stop in front of us. The driver leaned over and rolled down the window.

"All that's going out?" he asked.

"Yup." Mom tapped the sign.

"Well, I'll take it off your hands." The man hopped out and came round back. He pulled down the tailgate. "Let's load 'er up!"

It took a few tries to fit it all, but once all the furniture was inside he closed the tailgate, thanked us, and drove off down the road.

Just like that, the furniture was gone and Billy's room was now just a room that used to be his.

But I knew the room couldn't be his any longer. I wasn't sure you should keep rooms for the dead.

forty-six

"I NEED YOUR HELP," I TOLD JOHNNY.

"What is it?" He slid his headphones off one ear and sat up in bed, his Doc Martens thunking on the hardwood floor.

"Do you sleep in those?" I asked.

"Focus, Charlie."

"Mom just told me I could move Angus's crib into Billy's room if I wanted to."

"Okay. Will the crib not fit through the doorway or something?"

"It's not that, it's just...do we not think it's bad"—I waved my arms in front of me—"juju to put a small child, a blank slate if you will, in a room last occupied by a man so unhappy he believed he was better off dead?"

Johnny scratched his non-existent facial hair. "I see your point."

"Right? Thank you. Mom told me I was being dramatic."

"Yeah," he added, "but Mom's got the emotional aptitude of a blade of grass."

"This is true." I don't know why I'd expected any different. "But seriously, Angus is not moving in there as is. I need you to help me cleanse the fuck out of the room."

Johnny took his headphones off completely and stood up. "Let's do it then."

Johnny and I sat cross-legged on the floor across from each other, the bundle of sage and a lighter between us. My grade three teacher had called it sitting "Indian-style." One day, when everyone was particularly rowdy, the teacher said, "Everyone sit Indian-style like Charlotte." A kid complained I had an unfair advantage because I was "an Indian."

"Now what?" Johnny asked.

I shrugged. "I thought you would know."

"Why the fuck would I know? Where'd you even get this?" He held up the bundle. The smell always made me think of Nan. I tried to picture her lighting it. I was sure I'd witnessed someone lighting sage at some point in my life, but I couldn't recall it now. Maddie would be so disappointed in me.

"Aunt Darlene," I told Johnny.

"Well, what'd she say?"

"Not to be a dumbass."

"Shockingly unhelpful." He flicked the lighter off and on.

We sat in silence for a moment, both looking at the bundle of sage.

"We just light it, right? Wave the smoke around," Johnny said. "That's what Nan does." Johnny stared into space for a moment. "God, are we bad L'nus?"

"But does she say anything beforehand?" I wasn't convinced that was all there was to it. I felt embarrassed that I didn't know.

"We're not casting a spell, it's not a fucking wand." He pointed the bundle at me.

"That's not what I meant." I forced myself to take a breath. We were seconds away from devolving into a full-blown fight. This wasn't the kind of energy I wanted to bring into my son's bedroom. Or Billy's.

"This," I gestured between the two of us, "is definitely not what we're supposed to be doing."

Johnny sighed and stood up.

"Wait—" I held out my hand.

"I'm not leaving." Johnny opened the bedroom window and stuck his head out.

"Dad?" he yelled.

"What?" His voice was muffled.

"How do we smudge a room so Angus doesn't grow up unhappy and maladaptive?"

I joined Johnny at the window.

Dad came out of his workshop. "You dummies don't know?" he yelled back.

"No, us dummies don't know, because you didn't raise us right!" Johnny yelled, leaning even farther out the window. "What kind of Native doesn't teach his kids to smudge?"

I could feel Dad's glare across the lawn. He turned around and went back into his shop. My shoulders slumped.

"Way to go dumb—" I started to say.

Dad came back out with a wooden bowl in his hand. He stalked across the lawn, muttering the entire time.

The back door creaked, then slammed shut. Dad stomped up the stairs. He appeared in the doorway, looked down at the sage and lighter, and turned right around.

"A lighter," he scoffed.

Johnny and I looked at one another. I shrugged.

We could hear Dad muttering to himself from his bedroom. Every drawer he opened and closed was a little louder than the last.

"Where are all the friggin' matches?" Dad asked.

"Is he talking to us?" I whispered to Johnny.

"I hope not because I used the last one to light a candle yesterday." Johnny looked worried.

"Oh, you're so screwed," I laughed.

"Okay, no matches," Dad said coming back into the room.

"Why do we need a match?" I pointed to the lighter between Johnny and me.

"Your nan told me you were supposed to use a match. She went to Saskatoon for a conference back in the '80s and an Elder there told her to never use a lighter. Said the butane fucks with the medicine."

"Did the Elder say *fucks*?" Johnny asked.

Dad shot him a look as he joined us on the floor, the bowl in front of him.

"Okay, well…a lighter is all we have. So, is it okay?" I asked.

"I'm sure Creator will understand," Johnny said. "A little butane never hurt anybody."

Dad looked seconds away from giving up on us entirely.

"I really can't move Angus into this room, Dad. We've been on the verge of a fight since we started. The vibes aren't good in here."

"You sound like Sadie," Johnny said.

"And Sadie is an angel." She had promised to look into the voodoo doll for me.

"Okay, okay. Enough." Dad held his hands out in front of him. "We use a lighter and we all promise not to tell your nan."

"Mutual assured destruction. I can get behind it," Johnny said.

Dad took a bracing breath. He brushed his hair out of his face and picked up the bundle, lit the sage, and laid the bundle in the bowl. He fanned the flame with his hands, the smoke growing stronger. He sat quietly for a moment, then held his hands over the smoke and rubbed them together, as if to wash them. Then he cupped the smoke and waved it over his head and arms. He brought his cupped hands to his eyes, his ears, his mouth, his heart.

He nudged the bowl toward me. "I think bringing good intentions into the room is enough, you don't have to do anything fancy. So, you want to cleanse yourself. Start with your hands. You want to do your eyes so you see good things, your ears so you hear good things, your mouth so you say good things, your heart so you feel good things, ya know?"

Johnny and I repeated Dad's actions, washing the smoke over our bodies. Sunlight stretched across the hardwood floor.

As Johnny finished with his heart, Dad sighed. He picked up the bowl, bringing the sage closer to his chest.

"You know, I have a lot of regrets about what I didn't teach you two growing up. I wasn't really sure how. We didn't grow up on the rez. And by the time you kids came along I wasn't really active in the community; I wasn't practicing the culture. I had to go through my own shit around my identity before I felt comfortable doing anything. I had a lot of conversations with your nan, but you guys were teenagers by then. When you were kids, I think I would've felt like too much of a phony trying to teach ya stuff. A bit of an apple if I'm being honest. I didn't think I had the right to smudge."

"An apple?" Johnny asked.

"Red on the outside, white on the inside," I said, not taking my eyes off the bowl.

Dad placed it back on the ground. The sage smouldered between us, its scent filling the room.

I thought about telling them about the girl in my class. I wanted to complain. I wanted Johnny to threaten to beat her up. I wanted Dad to tell me to ignore her, which, obviously I couldn't. But I didn't want to bring her into the room with us. I didn't want to ruin this moment.

The afternoon light caught the tendrils of smoke before it fell across our laps and the floor.

forty-seven

"I'M NOT DOING IT."

"I'm certainly not." Johnny gestured to his chest. "I have a redemption pie to make."

I gave him a look.

"You're childfree," Johnny said.

"Exactly," I said. "And I don't want to spend my childfree time killing a damn pig. Besides, he's your namesake."

"Who do you think is going to have to help Dad after the pig is unalived?"

Shit.

Johnny smiled.

"Smugness is unbecoming on you," I told him.

"Yes, well, I can live with being ugly for a day. Now go get 'em, tiger."

Why the hell were we still killing pigs anyway? There was a grocery store down the road, for god's sake.

I looked out the window. "Why do we keep doing this?"

In the yard, Dad was prepping the chute, his hair pulled into the world's tiniest bun.

"God, it looks even stupider than when it's down," Johnny said, ignoring me.

"He wants to—"

"Be able to braid it, I know, I know. It's just hard to look at, is all."

I left Johnny staring out the window and went out back to kill a pig.

The blood sprayed when I cut the throat. It splattered on my sleeves. It felt like it was on my face.

"That was the last time," I said, near tears. "I'm never doing this again."

"Uh." Dad blinked at me, the dead pig between us. "Okay."

I couldn't even wipe my eyes because I was covered in blood.

The kitchen smelled like pie as I came back inside; it mingled with the metallic tang of the blood covering me. Johnny was lying on the kitchen floor, tossing a hacky sack in the air and listening to The Relatives, a Mi'kmaw band from Eskasoni.

Mom came into the kitchen and leaned over me at the sink as I scrubbed myself raw.

"You okay?" she asked. "You look tired."

"Gee, thanks." I pumped more soap onto my hands.

"You're doing too much."

"I'm not sure how I could do less." The soap had foamed and turned a light pink from the blood.

"You could've postponed grad school. It'd be easier if you were closer to family."

"And then what? Have no career? I become a mother and suddenly I can't do anything else?"

"That's not what I'm saying."

"What are you saying?" I rinsed my hands and grabbed a kitchen towel.

"You're way too ornery to have this conversation."

Johnny got up and left the room.

"I already feel like I'm failing at everything. I don't need you to tell me I am too."

"When did I say that?"

"You don't get it."

"If I don't, it's because you won't tell me."

I threw the towel onto the counter, stomped upstairs, and closed my bedroom door. It took everything in me not to slam it. Why did I suddenly feel fifteen again? Except fifteen-year-old Charlie would be horrified by my shit show of a life. I was a mother with no partner, a student with no thesis, and a niece with no uncle.

Without Angus, I was completely and utterly alone.

forty-eight

I STOOD OUTSIDE MY CLASSROOM DOOR, ANGUS IN MY ARMS. I felt like a Dickensian orphan, standing on a stoop, waiting to be kicked. Dr. Driscoll rounded the corner. I took a big breath, bracing myself. I'd practiced this conversation at least ten times since Fiona had woken up sick this morning. Between puking into the toilet and trying not to poop herself, she'd repeatedly apologized for not being able to watch Angus.

Standing just outside the bathroom, Angus clutched to my chest, I told her it was fine. I'd considered asking our downstairs neighbour, Mac—who I only half-knew but was pretty sure wasn't a serial killer—but, standing in front of his door, I'd remembered he'd gone home to Cape Breton for the week.

I had no one else in this city I could turn to.

Dr. Driscoll smiled at Angus, then gave me a look that was decidedly less warm. Of course this had to happen during my historiography class. Dr. Driscoll was definitely the prof I felt the least comfortable with. He seemed like he'd never even met a child.

"And who is this?" he asked.

"This is Angus. My son." Sometimes I still shocked myself when I said it out loud.

"And why is he here?"

"Because my normal childcare"—I almost laughed out loud referring to Fiona in such a formal way—"is sick and I have no one else to watch him." I adjusted Angus on my hip. "You won't even notice he's here. He's so quiet." Angus chose that moment to blow a loud raspberry. We both looked at Angus and then one another. I was ready to cry human rights if he said I couldn't bring him. I'd practiced exactly how I would say it. Confidently and with conviction. Not a hint of the dithering desperation I felt.

"This cannot become the norm."

I opened my mouth, prepared to further argue my case. "Thank you," I said instead.

"I'm serious. Just this once. And if he disturbs the class, you'll leave immediately."

"Yes, I promise."

Dr. Driscoll held the door open for me. I dashed in before he could change his mind.

Ten minutes into class I realized I'd forgotten Angus's soother. Fifteen minutes in, I sacrificed my finger to the cause. Halfway through class, Dr. Driscoll divided us into groups, which should be illegal in university. As I joined my classmates, I was convinced Angus was about to chew my finger off. While his teeth were just beginning to peek through his gums, it was enough to hurt.

"Oh my god, he's so cute," the girl next to me cooed. "What's his name?"

I told her.

She looked surprised. "That's a great name. Scottish right? I kind of assumed he'd have, like, a cool Native name. But I guess if his name is kind of *out there*, he might find it hard when he got older, like, to get a job and stuff. Did you go with a Micmac middle name?"

Angus's middle name was Cedar, but I wasn't about to tell this girl that.

Angus bit my finger hard.

Dr. Driscoll dropped a stack of newspapers in front of us and moved to the next group to do the same.

"I've collected these over the last few months," he said. "I want you to look through them and, as a group, decipher which news stories you think will be notable historical events in fifty years. And which stories, while important now, might not matter as much decades from now." Dr. Driscoll looked at the clock on the wall. "Take the rest of the class. Make a list and we'll discuss next time."

I adjusted Angus on my lap; he whined when I tried to take my finger away. The girl beside me picked up the first newspaper, a large photo of Pierre Trudeau on the cover. He had died the month before and, according to the newspaper, a nation mourned. I wasn't sure any Indigenous nation did, but I wasn't about to say that.

The guy across from me picked up the second paper; the first page had a picture of a DFO boat ramming a Mi'kmaw fishing boat. The article was about the Burnt Church Crisis.

"You know," he said, shaking the paper stiffly, "I don't really understand what this is all about. Why can't they just fish like everyone else?"

I offered Angus another finger. He refused, arching his back and fussing until I gave him my battered finger back.

"Because we have a treaty right to fish like our ancestors did." I tried not to sound as cranky as I felt.

"Yeah, sure. But then shouldn't you be fishing in canoes or something? Pretty sure your ancestors didn't have modern boats." He laughed.

Angus chomped down on my finger and, at the same time, grabbed a fistful of my hair and yanked.

"Yeah, well I'm pretty sure your ancestors married their cousins. So, are you going to do the same?"

Oh god.

He glared at me. The newspaper in his hands folded over itself.

Angus gave up on my finger and tried to grab the newspapers off the table.

While the other group chatted amicably, our group sat in complete silence.

"Listen, all I'm saying is that we have a legal right to fish. And these people," I gestured toward the newspaper, "are exercising their right. They're not overharvesting. They're just trying to provide for their families. They're just trying to do what our people have always done. They can fish in a canoe or a boat—they could fish in a fucking inner tube if they wanted to. It doesn't change the fact that they have the right to do it." I picked up the next newspaper in the stack, desperate to move on.

"Are you going to apologize for calling my family incestuous?" he asked.

"I will after you do."

"Yeah, okay." He tossed the newspaper on the table. "I'm out." He stood up, pushing his chair back as he did. It made a loud, grating noise as it scraped across the floor. As he walked away, he mumbled something that sounded a lot like *fuckin' Natives*.

"I'll just write some stuff down so we have something for next class," the first girl said. "I'm sure it doesn't matter that much."

I shifted Angus on my lap and glanced at the other group. They were talking quietly and more than once someone glanced over at us. I was pretty sure the girl beside me was talking about the classwork, but I couldn't help but read into it. Was it worth it to lash out because of one stupid comment? In the awkward aftermath, I wasn't sure it was.

forty-nine

"HELLO?" MOM ANSWERED.

"Hi." I hadn't talked to my mom in over a week, maybe the longest we'd ever gone. I wanted to apologize for my adult temper tantrum, but I'd been hoping she'd apologize first.

"I'm sorry," I said.

"For what?"

I ran my hand down my face and asked Creator for patience.

Clearly, she hadn't been marinating in our conversation like I had. I wanted to throw the phone.

"The argument we had when I was home."

"Oh. Right." A pause. "Was that an argument?"

"I thought so."

"Okay."

Another pause.

"Are you going to apologize too?" I asked. This was going to turn into another fight. Or non-fight, depending who you asked.

"Uh...sorry?"

"I don't think it counts as an apology if it sounds like a question."

"I mean, I'm just not sure what I have to apologize about."

"Oh my god."

"All right, all right, I'm sorry. I'm real eaten up about it."

"Sure you are."

"I am!"

I rolled my eyes and wondered if she could hear it.

"Listen." Mom cleared her throat. "I'm trying to be better. After, when Billy died..." She paused. "I blame myself." Her voice cracked. "Maybe if I'd done more. If I'd said something when I knew he was struggling. I don't know. Maybe it would've helped."

She paused so long I thought she might've walked away.

"I know my parenting style hasn't always been *hold hands and talk about our feelings*. I'm not very good at that, but I'm trying to be better. I can see so much of Billy in Johnny. I always have. His humour. They have the same laugh. But since Johnny's been home, I see parts of Billy I wish I didn't. Johnny barely leaves his room. He's lost weight. He's this shell of himself. Just like Billy. And I can't let it happen again."

"I'll call him," I offered, more on edge than I was a moment ago. I leaned against the wall and watched Angus eat grated apple. "It wasn't your fault, you know."

"I just think I could've—"

"Mom. You were there for him all the time. I'm not going to pretend to know what Billy was thinking when he..." I cleared my throat. "But I guarantee he knew you loved him. That he was loved. How could he not?"

Angus took a handful of apple and threw it on the floor.

"Do you ever talk to him?" I asked.

"I mostly cuss him out." Mom laughed; it was blubbery.

"Oh my god." I started laughing. "I wanted to break his gravestone the first time I went to see him."

Mom laughed harder. "What is wrong with us?"

I laughed so hard there were tears in my eyes.

fifty

SNOW FELL, COVERING EVERYTHING IN A THICK BLANKET OF white. Giant flakes floated in the grey morning light. It was a new year, but everything felt the same. I'd spent the Christmas break alternating between stressing that things weren't magical enough for Angus, who truly had no idea what was happening, and trying to scrape together enough research to make my thesis work. Mom yelled at me on Christmas Day when she found me hunched over a stack of history periodicals during Angus's nap. She scoured my entire room for anything remotely related to school and hid it all. She told me I could have everything back after Boxing Day. I'd been adrift.

January had been much of the same so far. I had an eye twitch from reading so much. And a permanent gnawing in my chest that I wasn't doing enough for Angus.

I looked back out the window. The snow fell harder. It didn't seem like it was going to stop any time soon. I was supposed to drive home this morning so Adam could see Angus. I didn't want to tell him we weren't going to make it, but I knew I had to get it over with. Angus and I had gone home last weekend and Adam had spent every waking hour with him. I knew that wasn't enough. I would be distraught if I could only see Angus two days of the week. I picked up the phone, ready to apologize profusely.

Adam sighed. "You couldn't have left last night?"

His tone made whatever sympathy I'd felt wither. "I had plans last night." I adjusted Angus on my hip. He tried to grab at the phone cord and I craned my head to avoid his grubby hands. We'd just started solids. It was messy.

"Sorry, what was that?" I tried to focus on what Adam was saying.

"I just miss him."

"I know, I'm sorry." If I had a dollar for every time I apologized, I could buy name-brand groceries and wouldn't have to get my hair cut by Fiona with the kitchen scissors.

Angus waved his arms wildly, whacking me in the face.

"Do you want me to take him?" Mac asked from the kitchen doorway. He'd brought up a VHS of *Erin Brockovich* last night and, after realizing Fiona and I weren't in a relationship, he'd finally made his move. Fiona had told me to sleep with my white noise machine on. Thankfully I was so exhausted I passed out halfway through the movie and woke up on the couch. Mac was still here, so I assumed it had gone well.

"Thank you—watch his hands, there's banana on them." I handed Angus off to Mac.

"Who was that?" Adam snapped.

"Mac?"

"Who's Mac?"

"Our neighbour."

"How do you know him?"

"He's…our neighbour?"

Mac held Angus at arm's length as he attempted to grab Mac's shoulder-length hair.

"Why is he in your house?"

"We have lots of people in our house. We're very gregarious people."

"Charlie, you hate people."

It was embarrassing how undone I felt hearing Adam say my name.

"Listen." I wiped a chunk of banana off the phone cord. "Are we done playing twenty questions? Our street isn't plowed. I don't know when it will be plowed. I'm sorry I can't make it home this weekend."

Mac turned on the tap and attempted to wash the banana off Angus.

"He's strong," Mac grunted.

I nodded, hoping he'd shut the hell up so Adam wouldn't make any more comments.

Adam sighed again. "You've known the storm was coming for days."

"So did you. You could've come in. Listen, I have to go. Angus has Mac in a chokehold. You're welcome to come in whenever. Otherwise, see you next weekend."

Adam hung up without saying goodbye. I pressed my head against the wall. Mac was still fighting with Angus at the sink. I closed my eyes and tried to collect myself. Couldn't Adam tell that I was also disappointed we couldn't go home for the weekend? I'd planned to work on my thesis the entire time. Now I'd have to try to squeeze in an entire weekend's worth of work while Angus slept.

Was I a bad mom for wanting to hand off my kid? Was it even worse that I was upset it couldn't happen?

Mac shut the tap off.

I turned around. Angus and Mac were soaked, water dripping from their shirts onto the floor.

fifty-one

ANGUS AND I SAT IN A NEST OF BOOKS AND PAPER IN OUR LIVING room. Earlier I'd bundled him up in his snowsuit, taken him outside, and sat him down in the snow. He'd whacked at it with his gloved hands, laughing as they disappeared into the white fluff. I'd gone to grab the sled my parents had given him for Christmas from the back deck. When I turned back around Angus had face planted in the snow. When I picked him up he'd wailed, his cheeks and nose pink with cold. I'd given up on outside time after that.

"Here." I held up a rattle and shook it to show Angus, then put it out of reach in the hope he'd crawl to it.

Angus scooted on his bum toward the toy.

"This can't be good for your hips," I said, then turned to the next chapter in *Coast to Coast: A Detailed History of Rail Transport in Canada*. Angus ignored me as I read aloud; he didn't give a shit about the expansion of the railway, and I was struggling to care myself.

"It'd be more interesting," I said, "if they actually focused on who the railway most impacted."

Angus grabbed the toy and slobbered all over it.

"Like, we talk about the railway revolutionizing transportation, but what about the further subjugation of Indigenous peoples? This guy's main concern in this article is whether railways were worth the financial cost. But what about all the Chinese people who died so this railway could be built? What about all the Indigenous people who got shoved out of the way, who lost ancestral territory for this?" I pointed to the book's cover: a drab landscape, train tracks cutting through the wilderness, not a person in sight.

Angus looked at me. Drool leaked out of his mouth.

"You're right, I should probably bring this up in class."

I wouldn't, though. No one seemed to like it when I questioned the societal foundations they were raised on. They definitely didn't like when I snapped and implied they were the product of incest. My History of Canadian Industry professor, especially, was aggressively white. Dr. Smith was new this year. If I'd known how much he got off on colonialism, I probably wouldn't have taken his course. He seemed to tolerate me at best but was entirely in charge of my grade; I couldn't risk messing that up.

I looked at the page in front of me, which featured a large photograph of long-dead white politicians. I sighed.

I thought I belonged in academia. I thought school was my safe place, my home. But now I often felt at odds with everyone around me. I wondered if I'd made a mistake going to grad school. My perspective seemed to make people uncomfortable. If I bothered to challenge some colonial narrative, I was met with the argument that I was challenging fact. But I wasn't arguing against facts. I didn't contest, say, that the railway had been built. I was questioning the point of view from which we examined these facts.

Angus grabbed at my book. I handed him another toy.

I was so tired these days, I often didn't bother to question anything. I was just trying to make it to the finish line. Whatever that looked like.

Being Mi'kmaw, I'd always felt entirely separate from the other students. I knew becoming a mom would make grad school harder, but I hadn't thought it would render me totally incompatible with a scholarly life.

Angus scooted closer and shook his toy.

Yesterday a woman at the grocery store had smiled at me and Angus and told me to treasure every little thing because it all went by so fast.

I'd wanted to shriek. Instead, I smiled and went back to tallying my groceries so I didn't have to put anything back at the counter when I went over budget. It was always so embarrassing when I had to do that.

I was barely surviving, and it wasn't fair to either of us. Something had to give.

fifty-two

"HOOOOOLY SHIIIIT," JOHNNY SAID WHEN I PICKED UP THE PHONE.

"Johnny, what the hell? I was getting worried. Mom said you wouldn't get out of bed." I'd called at least twenty times this week.

"Well, I'm fine now. Adam cured my depression."

"Oh yeah, and how'd he do that?"

"He told Barb to fuck off." Johnny laughed on the other end of the line.

"What? Why?"

"Adam dragged me out of the house to go get food. Actually, it was more of a fireman's carry."

"Are you joking?"

"No, I was very depressed. Everyone was worried. I can't believe you didn't call."

"Johnny I—"

"Charlie, I'm joking. I can be funny. And I can be depressed. One at a time. Or maybe at the same time. You know how we love to laugh at terrible things."

It was true. We were a little fucked up.

"Anyways, Adam carried me to the car and drove us to Doug's. I walked into Doug's on my own because, despite what people think, I do have some dignity."

"Johnny."

"Sorry, Mom thinks I might have ADHD. So, Adam is forcing me to pick snacks when Barb shows up out of nowhere. Starts asking questions about the baby, sticking her big ole nose into everybody's business, as per usual. Adam is politely answering. I'm grabbing bag after bag of chips. My arms are so full. And then Barb says something very off-colour about you. I won't repeat it. Unless you want me to." Johnny paused. "All right," he said, barely giving me time to respond. "She said you should be settled down with that baby but instead you're an uppity Native and think you're smarter than everyone else, and then Adam told her to fuck off. I couldn't believe it. I dropped all the chips. Barb actually gasped. Doug told me I better pick all the chips up. Barb was so upset about the whole thing she left with unpaid merchandise. Doug ran after her yelling *shoplifter!* really loudly. It was glorious. And now I can see that life is worth living because moments like that exist."

"Back up a second. You're saying Adam stuck up for me?"

"It was the greatest thing I've ever witnessed." And then my brother hung up without saying goodbye and I stood in the kitchen, phone in my hand, the dial tone the only noise.

I wasn't sure how to feel. I was the mother of his child, of course Adam wouldn't let someone trash-talk me. That's all it meant, right? Adam was a kind person. I didn't need to overthink this. I shouldn't. I'd just put Angus down for his nap. I needed to study. My thesis wasn't going to write itself.

I had a few months until it was due, but I'd been stuck on the third chapter for over a week. I was starting to panic. I hadn't told Dr. Gamble yet. He'd probably say something logical like, "Let's rejig our timeline and postpone." The last time we met he was still wondering aloud whether or not this was the thesis for me. I'd almost passed out. It was February; this had to be the thesis for me. I would figure it all out on my own.

Johnny was probably exaggerating anyway. There was likely nothing to overthink. He'd probably embellished the story to the point that it was fiction.

And yet.

Whether or not the story was true, I felt like I could breathe a little easier. Johnny sounded okay. I was still worried, but I didn't have the impulse to drive home and drag him out of bed myself.

Angus cried out from his crib. I hung up the phone and sighed.

fifty-three

I LOOKED FOR THE GARBAGE BIN. "I THINK I'M GOING TO PUKE."

Dr. Gamble chuckled. Sadistic asshole.

I'd spent another two weeks slogging through my thesis before reaching out for advice. This is what asking for help got me.

I let out a moan and leaned over my chair. Why did fancy people never leave garbage cans out in the open?

"Having to do a second year is nothing to be ashamed of, Charlotte."

Sure, for other people. For me, it was something to be deeply ashamed of. It was mere millimetres away from failure. A second year was not in my five-year plan; my master's was supposed to be one and done. Wham. Bam. Thank you, ma'am. I didn't want to even think about what this meant for my funding.

"You've got a lot on your plate. We want to make sure your thesis is rock solid before you present it."

I took a bracing gulp. Where was the damn garbage can?

"Now, I'm going to suggest something you might not immediately love." Dr. Gamble was so calm. Did he know I was seconds away from vomiting all over his desk?

"I want you to take a break," he continued. "Finish your classes. Then, after the semester is done, go home. Take the summer. Read books you like. Spend time with your son. Just give yourself some time away. If you keep pushing, you're never going to figure out how to get around this wall you've encountered. You need to take a step back." He paused, thoughtful. "That's good," he said more to himself than to me, and began to scribble something down.

"This is—I don't—" I fumbled for words. I was going to cry. I hated crying in front of people. "I can do this." My eyes burned.

"I don't doubt your capabilities, Charlie. But my job is to help you produce something of value. Something you can be proud of. I'm also meant to guide you through the process of writing your thesis. And that can involve recognizing that we've been following the wrong thread."

We sat in silence for a moment while I focused on not sobbing like an idiot in front of him.

"I want to reiterate," he said eventually, "that you have nothing to be ashamed of. You'll see the wisdom in this sooner than you think, trust me."

Fat chance.

fifty-four

ADAM DROVE UP HIS DRIVEWAY, SOMEONE IN HIS PASSENGER seat. There was a car I didn't recognize parked in his normal spot. I'd finished the semester with little excitement. I'd read my textbooks, I'd written papers, and the whole time I'd tried to work up a modicum of enthusiasm; while I'd passed my classes, I'd failed at that. I'd had long and arduous conversations about my funding for next year. My tuition would be covered, but, because I was no longer full-time, I wouldn't receive any funding for my living expenses. Which meant I'd have to apply for TA positions so I could pay my rent and Angus and I could eat.

Since Angus's birth, Adam kept offering me money and I kept refusing. Last month he'd stuck fifty dollars in Angus's diaper bag. I'd stuck it in his mailbox when we'd left.

I hated that the first year of my master's had ended, not with a degree, but rather a staggering list of disappointments. So, taking Dr. Gamble's advice, I'd come home for the summer. I wanted to lick my wounds and eat my weight in chips. I felt turned upside down, and I hoped if I came home and stuck my feet in the ocean, I'd be able to reorient myself.

Adam hopped out of his truck. "Charlie, hey."

"Hey, I was banished from the Dalhousie campus by my advisor"—maybe if I joked about it I wouldn't cry again—"so I thought I'd come home. Give you more..."

I stopped talking when the passenger door opened and Gina Smith climbed out. I looked between her and Adam.

She walked over and stood awfully close to him. Weirdly close.

"Hey, how's it going?" She had the gall to smile at me.

I grimaced. "Swell."

Adam raised an eyebrow.

"Where's the little guy?" she asked.

"Asleep in the car." I pointed behind me, the two back doors open.

We lapsed into silence. I felt like Adam had just disembowelled me. Was it obvious I was breaking apart at the seams? I wanted to disintegrate. In the past, whenever I'd fallen apart, Adam had been the one to help put me back together. But now he was standing next to Gina Smith.

If he could forgive her, why couldn't he forgive me?

I wondered how long we could stand there in silence. I was more than willing to find out.

"Okay." Gina slapped her thighs, she hadn't stopped smiling. "I'm going to take off. You guys have fun. Bye, Adam." She squeezed his arm and waved at me. "Nice seeing you, Charlie."

Adam and I watched Gina drive away.

"Good thing she didn't hit your car this time." I couldn't resist myself.

"Charlie..."

"What was...um...so, Gina Smith?"

Adam shrugged. "She moved back home. Got in touch. We've hung out a few times."

He was stringing my intestines across the grass like grotesque lawn decorations.

"That's, um, okay...like, sexually?" I scratched behind my ear.

"I'm allowed to see people, Charlie."

"I know that. Why do you sound so defensive?"

"Because you look like you're about to throw a punch."

My face flushed. "I just don't want *our son* consorting with known criminals."

"*You* were the one who told me to forgive her."

"I meant, like, move on, live and let live, not like...get all up on her."

Adam threw his hands in the air. "You were the one who didn't want to date me, Charlie. Remember?"

"I had a—"

"Yeah, I know, a five-year plan. How's that going? Johnny told me you have to take another year to finish your master's."

All the air left my lungs. In that moment, I hated him.

Adam, of all people, knew what my degree meant to me. All the hopes and dreams I'd pinned on it. "You know what?" I pointed at him. "I hope she hits your fucking car again. Actually," I sputtered, "next time, I hope she runs you over."

Angus yelled from the car.

Adam and I glared at one another. I stomped over to our son. Once Angus was able to see me, I smiled.

"Hey, buddy." My voice was saccharine.

Adam stuck his head over my shoulder. "Hey, big guy."

Angus clapped and smiled. Adam picked him up, squeezed Angus to him, and carried him toward his house.

I rubbed my eyes and resisted the urge to make a face at the back of Adam's head.

This was going to be one long, painful summer.

fifty-five

IN THE DRAWER OF MY NIGHTSTAND WAS A DISCARDED magazine. I think I'd brought it home with me the week Billy died. The front cover was crumpled and a tiny rip ran through the word *orgasm*. I flopped back on my bed and thumbed through the pages. The pop star's expression was a little smug and I found her and her six-pack annoying. She'd had a good year but she didn't have to rub it in our faces.

How to have it all!

It seemed impossible. Futile. Maybe even selfish. Could I be enough for the people around me while also pursuing what I wanted? Was it possible for me to be a good mother and a dedicated student?

It didn't seem like it.

Was I wasting my time?

Dr. Gamble's time?

I'd promised Angus I would try my best to give us a good life—was I doing that?

Even if I did finish my thesis, would it really contribute anything to the world? To academia? I'd spent the last month and a half ignoring it but I could now see, with embarrassing clarity, how my thesis was never going to work. Dr. Gamble probably thought I was a stubborn idiot. He wouldn't be wrong.

What did I even want out of academia? When I first decided on grad school, I'd wanted to be a part of meaningful research. I liked how history could tug on your heartstrings. I was obsessed with facts and stories that made an impact on the present. I wasn't sure I was capable of the type of work ahead of me. Not now at least.

How to have it all!

Maybe it was time for me to face up to facts: having it all was impossible.

I was never going to have toned abs and I was never going to be a good mother and a good grad student. I put the magazine back in the desk drawer.

Maybe Maddie was right. Maybe I didn't deserve to be there at all, and now that I had to prove myself, I couldn't hack it.

Maybe it was time to admit defeat.

I stared at the ceiling and wondered how I would tell my supervisor I was dropping out.

Year Three

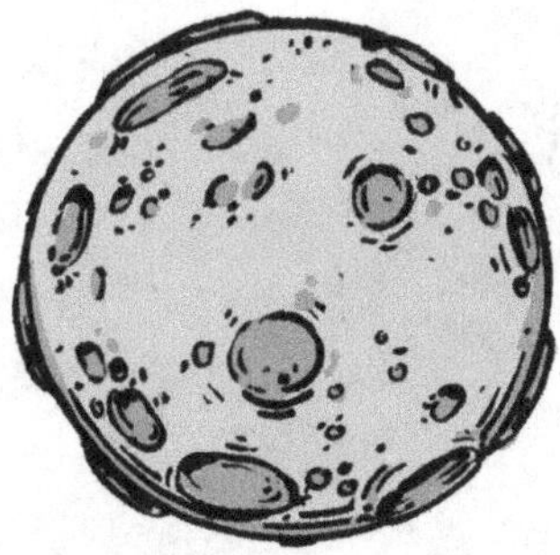

Nipniku's

(Nib-nee-goos)

Trees Fully Leafed Time

fifty-six

"CAN YOU CHILL OUT?" MOM ROLLED DOWN THE WINDOW AND stuck her arm out, waving a hand through the air.

"I'm as chill as I can be on this godforsaken road." My car lurched to the left. "We're going to bottom out."

"You're always like this after you see Adam."

"Not true." A branch scraped the right side of my car as I swerved to avoid a pothole.

"You get the most agitated I've ever seen you, and that's saying something. You can be real owly."

"Well, he's agitating." I steered around another pothole. "And you're distracting me. Quit prying." I leaned forward, focused on making it up Old Castlereagh Road. I wasn't about to call Adam and tell him I'd wrecked my car avoiding a heart-to-heart about him.

Mom ignored me. "I think you have feelings for him and it bothers you that things aren't how they used to be."

"Can we stop talking about this now?" My knuckles were white.

Mom shrugged and turned up the radio.

Some song about a truck in a field and a girl in tight jeans cut in and out as we drove higher up the mountain. Eventually the road ended. I parked and sat back, relaxing my shoulders.

I reached into the back of the car and grabbed a camera bag off the floor. I'd been home for a week when I'd run into Beau Fielding at Doug's General Store and he'd told me the historical society needed help. I thought he meant lifting heavy boxes or something because they were all too old to do it themselves. But now he had me half an hour into the mountains to take photographs for a museum display.

"Pictures of what?" Mom craned her neck to look around.

"A graveyard."

Mom whipped around. "In the middle of the damn woods?"

I shrugged. "I just followed the directions Beau gave me."

"If we die, I'm going to haunt that man."

"We're not going to die."

"Have you seen *The Blair Witch Project*?" Mom asked as she got out of the car.

I held the camera up and took a photo of my mom, then showed her the photo displayed on the screen. I'd never used a digital camera before, and I doubted Mom had ever seen one.

"What in the name of...," she breathed, staring at herself. "Where did you get this?"

"Beau lent it to me."

"Here, take one where my eyes aren't closed." Mom took a few steps back and posed, one hand on her hip, the other making a peace sign. After I took the picture, she hurried over to see it.

She stared at it. "This is nuts."

"Beau said there was a path to the graveyard." I scanned the woods surrounding us. "Clear as day, my ass," I muttered when I saw a wall of trees.

After searching for several minutes, we found the vaguest suggestion of a path and decided to follow it. Not far from the road we came across the first gravestone, tilted and partially sunk into the mossy undergrowth. The engraved name and dates were nothing more than illegible shallow grooves. I leaned closer and tried to make out the name. I couldn't come up with anything other than a possible C or O. Who was I standing on top of? Did anyone remember them? When had someone last told a story about them? It seemed like a second death, to have your name spoken for the last time.

I took a picture and moved on.

A handful of graves in varying states of disrepair were scattered in a small clearing the forest was trying its hardest to reclaim. I moved slowly, taking photos as my mom wandered about the clearing.

"Is this that guy you told me about?" She pointed at a grave, waving me over.

I crouched down to read the inscription.

In memory of

Robert Starritt

~1790–1870

and wife

Ann Fulton

1793–1855

"Yeah, it is." I took a photo, then moved behind the stone to get a different angle. It was hard to reconcile the man I'd read about, the full and vibrant life I'd made up for him, with this gravestone in the woods. Maybe by bringing him into the museum, by allowing him to exist outside of this forgotten place, I could give him a little bit of his life back. I took another picture.

On the back it said, *Arrived in Nova Scotia from Ireland in 1819. Walked to this site from the St. Lawrence River.*

Mom read it out loud. "Do they mean this very site?" She looked at her feet. "Or is it more of a vague site?" She gestured around us.

"It'd be pretty creepy if he walked to where they'd one day bury him."

"And depressing," Mom said. "Though it's already kind of depressing, considering this is how it ends."

I looked around the clearing. What did it look like when Starritt lived here? When he was buried, loved ones gathered around his grave, was the forest already encroaching? Did he suspect he'd end up reclaimed by the woods?

Did people say nice things about him when they stood around his coffin? Was he a good man? A kind one?

"Do you remember when Great-Uncle Irving died and it snowed at the funeral?" I asked. "It was the first snow of the year."

"Yeah, I remember."

"Do you remember what Billy said?" I asked.

Mom smiled. "He looked up at the sky and said it was a sign."

Everyone had turned to him, waiting with bated breath, for whatever he was about to say.

"He paused for so long." Mom started laughing. "And then said: 'It's a sign we all need to get our winter tires on.'"

"I've never heard Dad groan so loud in his life." My laughter joined my mother's. When it faded, birdsong trilled through the clearing. Was the bird laughing with us? I took another picture of the grave. Something rustled in the undergrowth.

"We didn't say anything when Billy was buried," I said after a moment. The only person who'd spoken was the priest. A man who didn't even know Billy.

"No. We didn't," Mom said, looking down at the grave in front of us. "I've finally moved past yelling at him."

"Me too."

"I talk about the most mundane shit. He's probably bored to death on the other side, if that's even possible."

At that point, Billy had heard enough of my drama to be entertained for the next century.

"When do you think was the last time someone talked to him?" I pointed at Starritt's grave.

Mom shrugged. "Hey, Bobby, sup?" she asked.

"Sup?" I scoffed. "He probably thinks you're speaking another language."

"Do you think he was a racist?" Mom whispered. "Hey, Bobby," she said a little louder, "have any Mi'kmaw friends?"

"Mom, you can't just ask—"

"What? We're just getting to know each other. I can't ask the guy some questions? I just want to know if he was down with the Natives, or if we're going to have a problem."

I rubbed my forehead.

"What do all your books say?" Mom asked.

"About what?"

"I don't know, all the stuff you read about him and this place." She gestured around. "What were the Mi'kmaq doing while Bobby was up here building dance halls?"

"I don't know, nothing." When I'd come home, Beau had given me a box filled with bits of local history. He said he needed help sorting and organizing everything, but as Beau placed the box in my arms, he'd admitted my dad had told him about my floundering academic career and he thought I could use a distraction. Bunch of small-town busybodies. I'd taken the box, convinced it was a pity gift, and spent the next week going through everything. Flyers. Diaries. Chapbooks written by local history buffs. Newspaper clippings. Nothing mentioned the Mi'kmaq.

"Nothing?" Mom raised an eyebrow. "Well, they had to be doing something."

"Astute as always, Mom." I shrugged. "Most of the books I'm reading are written by white people about other white people." I glanced at her. "No offence," I added, adjusting the camera strap. "I haven't gotten any shots of that corner." I tipped my chin towards a big tree at the end of the clearing.

"You look like your dad when you point with your lips," Mom said, swatting at a mosquito. "I'm going to hang out here with Ol' Bobby. Don't go too far."

I wandered around, stopping to snap photos of moss-covered gravestones. Mom was still talking about how she went to school with Fultons but never knew any Starritts. Or any Mi'kmaw people, for that matter, until she met Dad.

"And why was that?" Mom asked. I wasn't sure if she was talking to me or Bobby. I snapped her picture as she leaned over the grave.

The bottom of the car thunked against the edge of a giant pothole I'd tried my best to avoid. Mom winced. After fifty photos and just as many complaints from her about the mosquitos, we'd called it quits. Another pothole took up the entire road, impossible to avoid; I wasn't sure how I'd managed it on the way up. Mom and I both braced in anticipation. The car thunked again, and as we continued down the road, it sounded like something was dragging underneath us.

"Shit." Mom looked out the window behind us. "Think we lost anything?"

"What do we do?"

"Pull over and we'll take a look."

I stopped the car and got out. I muttered a string of curses as I went around to the back.

The muffler hung at an odd angle, centimetres from the ground.

"Oh, fuck me."

"What?" Mom got out of the car and crouched down beside me.

I gestured to my broken car. "It's going to fall off at the tiniest inconvenience."

"Do you have any string?" Mom asked.

"For what?"

"We can tie it." She was dead serious. This woman once tore her front bumper off while backing up in a field. She'd tied it back on with a rope and driven her car that way for three months until the string finally snapped, the bumper fell off, and she drove over it. Only then did she call Dad. And he'd had no idea what to do, so he'd called Adam.

I scratched my head. I had twine in the trunk.

fifty-seven

THE GRASS TICKLED MY BARE ARMS AND LEGS. ANGUS CLAMBERED around me as I watched the clouds drift across the sky. By early July, I was already yearning for autumn. As my skin soaked in the sun's warmth, I reminded myself to enjoy the moment.

Angus's tiny hands pushed into the softness of my stomach. He stood up, holding his arms in front of himself like a T.Rex as he fought to stay upright. He took a step, lilted to the left, saved himself, then fell on his bum in the grass.

"There's no rush," I told him. He was so close to walking. At almost a year old, he was ready for the next phase, but I wasn't sure I was.

He reached over again and squished my belly with his hands, pulling on the hem of my shirt.

"It's okay to stay still, just ask your papa." I closed my eyes. When I opened them, Angus was standing above me. He turned his head towards the driveway as Adam drove up.

Angus raised his arms as his dad got closer and Adam picked him up. Our son laughed as Adam tossed him in the air once before cradling him against his body. The sun shone behind them, catching on the curls of their hair, which were an identical shade of auburn.

"What's wrong with your muffler?" Adam asked by way of greeting. He kissed Angus's cheek.

"How the hell can you see it? The back of my car is practically in the woods." I'd parked it ridiculously close to the trees on purpose.

"Mechanic's intuition."

I waited.

"Your mom called me."

I sighed and shot a glance at the house. "She promised she wouldn't."

"She also said you were going to take it to someone tomorrow." He looked hurt.

Mom was almost as bad as Big Mouth Barb.

"I didn't want to bother you."

"What *bothers* me is that you were going to take it to Dan and let him charge you an arm and leg when I can do it in less than an hour for free."

"Well, considering our interactions for the last year have been entirely centred around Angus, I didn't want to ask you a favour."

"You can ask." Adam put Angus down on the ground. "I want you to ask."

Angus overbalanced and almost fell. Adam put out his arms to steady him, but our son righted himself. Angus took one tiny step. And then another.

"Oh my god," Adam said as Angus took one more step.

I was smiling by the time Angus staggered into my arms. "You did it!" I squeezed him so tight he grunted.

I laughed and looked up at Adam. He was laughing too.

For a second it felt like we were a team; like we were in this together, not just trudging along in close proximity.

Angus wiggled out of my arms and took four shaky steps toward his dad. Adam scooped him up and blew a raspberry on his belly. Angus giggled and then yawned.

"It's almost naptime, right? I can put him down." Adam kissed the top of Angus's head.

Our son looked up and pulled on his father's nose.

Adam's eyes crinkled as he smiled.

He looked at me, and his smile didn't fade like it normally did.

Something in my chest tightened, uncomfortable and thrilling at the same time. I told myself it was indigestion.

I clung to the fleeting feeling that the three of us were in this together.

We were a team. I just kept forgetting.

Maybe Adam did too.

I was taken aback by how deeply I wanted things to be different. My mom had been right during the drive up the mountain. But I could barely admit any feelings I had for Adam to myself, let alone someone who couldn't keep her mouth shut about my muffler.

fifty-eight

THE FRONT DOOR OF THE OLD CHURCH, SOON TO BE MUSEUM, was propped open with an empty milk crate. I slipped inside and walked toward the altar, my footsteps echoing in the half-empty space. After the building sat vacant for years, the town's historical society had purchased it for ten dollars last fall.

They'd sold half of the pews to an antique store in Great Village, and the remaining pews were pushed up against the walls. Over the past year, Beau and the rest of the society had been sourcing historical documents. Most of them pilfered from dead people's homes. Beau didn't like when I used the world *pilfered,* he said it made it sound illegal. The documents now sat in boxes piled on tables.

The arched ceilings and large stained-glass windows created an airy and spacious atmosphere. I could easily imagine the set-up. How they'd display the texts and photographs. Where larger items could hang on the walls. The museum had so much potential, I got excited just thinking about it. Beau stood at the base of the altar with Dorothy Mills and Meredith Fulton.

Despite being in his eighties, Beau still had a full head of hair. It stuck out at weird angles, and he often looked like he'd been shocked. He was wearing loafers, beige pants, a dark blue cardigan, and had a handkerchief tied around his neck. He wore the same outfit every day, like a cartoon character.

Dorothy, the youngest of the three by about twenty years, wore a pretty dress and heels. I'd only ever seen her in heels; she claimed she was too short for anything else. I didn't know Meredith as well as the others. She lived in Londonderry and always came across as a little grouchy. But once Beau roped me into helping them collect documents, I realized that while she was a little grouchy, she was also funny and made a mean corndog.

"Hey, Beau, I got the pictures." I waved the envelope in the air.

"Charlie, you're just in time!" he called.

"Just in time for what?" I asked, walking toward them.

"You heard that Frances Burns kicked the bucket a few weeks past? Well, I was just telling Dot and Meredith here that they finally got to clearing out her house. Christopher came home from out west to tidy up loose ends. He works in the oil fields out there, as you know. Anyway, Christopher gave me a call and said, Beau, you've gotta come up to the old homestead, Mom's got something you might want to see."

I leaned against the desk. Beau was nothing if not a long-winded storyteller.

"So, I got in the car and drove up. Christopher, he'd cleaned out most of the house and had a lot going to the shops in Great Village but had two containers for me, he said. Both labelled as *100-year-old stew* in Frances's handwriting. A poorer excuse for cursive I've yet to see. Chris and I think it's the frozen remnants of her family's perpetual stew."

Beau paused, smiling maniacally, waiting for my reaction.

"I don't know what that is, Beau."

He harrumphed, and Dorothy piped up. "Well, it's about time someone told you then. See, a generation or two ago a lot of farm families would have a pot on the stove, kind of pushed to the back." She held her hands in front of her chest as she explained. "The pot would just be there, simmering away, and you could just toss any old thing in. Leftovers. Whatever. Because it was always cooking it never went bad, and you could eat from it really whenever you wanted to. A lot of families liked to boast about how long their stews had been going, because the longer the stew had been on, the more flavourful it would be."

"And so, Frances Burns is claiming her stew is a hundred years old?"

"So it would seem," Meredith confirmed.

"Do we believe her?"

Beau harrumphed again. "The young are always so skeptical."

"I'm just saying, that's a long time."

"Your disbelief is taking away from my dramatic reveal, Charlotte."

"Sorry."

"It's fine." Beau reached into a bag on the desk. "I've defrosted one of the containers." He pulled out a Thermos. "And thought we could try it today." He twisted the top off, held the soup up to his nose, and took a loud sniff. "Smell the history, smell the umami."

He pulled four cups out of his bag, poured a healthy amount of soup into each, and pushed them toward us.

"This isn't going to kill us, is it?" I held the cup to my nose and sniffed. It smelled a bit like a barn, in the same way I thought chamomile did. I didn't want to drink it.

"Oh, come on Charlotte, live a little."

I sipped from the cup. Beside me, Meredith coughed. I don't know what I'd been expecting, but it wasn't this.

"That ain't good, Beau," I said.

Dorothy licked her lips and smacked them together. She took a second sip. "It tastes..." She paused, licking her lips again. "Freezer burnt."

Beau sighed. He put down his cup, braced his hands on the table, and looked to the rafters.

"Sorry the soup sucked, Beau."

Dorothy and Meredith had taken off. I'd helped Beau move a few tables and listened to him gossip. Despite letting him tell me, in great detail, about the infighting between his neighbours, he still seemed upset.

"Oh, that's all right. It's not really about how the soup tasted. Frances always was a shit cook." Beau put the Thermos in his bag. "Can't imagine the generations before her were geniuses in the kitchen either."

"If it really had been cooking for a hundred years, why stop it? She didn't throw it out, she kept it. It was obviously important to her."

"Well, you have to understand, Charlotte. Back in her time, people were having sixteen, seventeen kids. Not to mention extra hands on the homesteads helping out. Suffice to say, there were always mouths to feed. Frances had four kids and they all moved away. After her husband died, it was just her up there for a decade. What's the point in having a stew going when there's no one to feed but yourself?" Beau took off his hat and scratched his head. "People been leaving this place for years, and when they leave, things get left behind and forgotten. That's why we started this." Beau gestured around us.

I thought of Robert Starritt, who walked almost eight hundred kilometres to live in a place that one day wouldn't exist. What happened to Castlereagh? When did it stop being a place with a future?

"When do you think this place will be open, Beau?"

He replaced his hat on his head. "We're hoping for the spring."

"Should I expect a grand speech?"

He nodded. "If I make it that long."

I tried hard not to roll my eyes. Beau had been anticipating his death since I was in elementary school.

"Someone will have to take over eventually, you know." He gave me a look. "It can't be Dottie. No offence to her, but she's incapable. This could be your kingdom, Charlotte." He gestured grandly around the room at the half-empty display cases and piles of carefully wrapped and catalogued photographs.

While Billy's voice echoed from the recesses of my mind—*Don't get stuck!*—I felt a thrum of excitement, a moment of possibility. Could I have a future in this old church-turned-museum? I could easily picture myself here, preserving history, without all the tension and stress of academia. I looked around. Could I be happy here, or would I come to regret choosing this? I wasn't certain. And I wasn't sure how I ever would be. But it didn't matter, because I was leaving anyway. In two weeks.

"You remember I'm leaving, right?" I said. "Going back to school." Or not, depending on how much of a disaster my next thesis meeting was.

"Yes, yes. We all know you're determined to finish your master's. It's admirable, really. Your doggedness."

It didn't sound like a compliment.

"Admirable," Beau continued, "how determined you are to torpedo your personal life."

I looked up at the exposed beams of the church ceiling.

"Poor Adam," Beau muttered.

Poor Adam, my ass.

"I caught him crying next to the carrots at the farmers' market the other day," Beau added. Hopefully because Gina Smith ran over his foot.

"You did not."

Beau huffed. "I easily could've. That's how depressed that man is."

"Bullshit."

"Charlotte, we're in a *church*."

"It's almost a museum now."

Beau smiled, looking around at the chaos. "That it is."

fifty-nine

I'D THOUGHT THAT GOING INTO LABOUR AND DROPPING A birthday cake in a puddle of womb juices would been the most emotionally charged birthday I'd endure in my lifetime.

That was optimistic.

"Where should I put these?" Adam asked from the doorway.

I jumped, nearly falling off the chair I was standing on.

"You scared the shit out of me," I laughed, holding a hand to my chest.

Adam blinked, straight-faced. Helium-filled balloons bobbing in the air by his head.

"Uh, the living room? I don't know. Wherever you think is best."

Just as Adam was about to leave the kitchen, my grandparents came through the back door. Nan had been bugging me for a week to invite all our cousins. I'd wanted to; I wanted Angus to have a big, loud family, to feel connected to his community, his relations. Angus would never have Indian Status in the eyes of the government, but I wanted him to know that he belonged. The thought of calling people and inviting them, however, had seemed an insurmountable task.

Last year I'd gone to a party at Aunt Darlene's on the rez and people just showed up and brought food. Half of them hadn't been invited, but they were all welcome. It always seemed so effortless for her to nurture a sense of community.

I didn't grow up with that. But I wanted Angus to.

And so yesterday I'd called Aunt Darlene to invite her and asked her to bring some people with her. I'd jokingly told her it'd save me from Nan's wrath rather than admit the tender truth, that I felt disconnected and didn't know how to bridge the gap.

"Adam!" Nan yelled, throwing her arms in the air for a hug, nearly smacking Grampa in the face.

"Agnes." Adam smiled warmly. He let go of the balloons and embraced her.

"You're looking handsome as always." Nan patted his cheeks. "Doesn't he look handsome, Charlie?" She turned to me and smiled what you might describe as sweetly if you didn't know any better.

The silence was palpable. I tried not to wither where I stood. The balloons pressed against the ceiling, their shiny ribbons swaying in the air. Was it too late to cancel the party? Angus was only turning one. He wouldn't remember.

"Ah, leave her alone, Aggie." Grampa dropped their things by the door and kicked off his shoes. He pulled out moccasin slippers from one of the bags and slipped them on. "Where's the birthday boy?" He walked off, looking for Angus.

Johnny stuck his head in. "Yo, Adam. Is Gina coming?"

I almost dropped the bowl I had just grabbed.

"No," Adam said.

"Oh, thank god," Johnny said, giving an exaggerated sigh of relief.

The doorbell rang. I was going to have a heart attack.

"I got it." Adam sprinted to answer it.

"Wow, he couldn't wait to get out of here," Nan deadpanned.

Was she trying to make me cry? I grabbed a second bowl from the top of the cupboard and got off the chair.

"Did you know, Adam seriously thought you might throat-punch Gina when you saw her? I wonder if that's why she didn't come," Johnny mused.

"Feeling territorial, are we?" Nan asked me.

"Adam!" Fiona's voice danced down the hallway. "This is Mac."

"Mac, eh?" Adam sounded even less enthused at the prospect of having to spend time with our downstairs neighbour than he did with me.

I put the bowls on the counter and left Nan to scrutinize the food I was making. She picked up a piece of luski just as I was leaving the kitchen.

I wiped my hands on my apron and hugged Fiona.

"Here." Mac thrust flowers at me. A comically large bouquet of hyacinths, daffodils, pink roses, and daisies. "These are for you. I got a gift for Angus, but I figured you did most of the heavy lifting on his day of birth. So…flowers." Mac shot a glance at Adam.

"Thanks, Mac." I clutched the flowers. These were definitely not from the grocery store.

Beside me, Adam grunted.

We lapsed into silence. Adam looked at Mac. Mac shifted his weight from one foot to the other. Fiona looked between Adam and me, eyebrows raised, fighting a smile.

"Everyone is in the living room if you want to see the birthday boy. I'm just finishing up the food, and I'll go put these in water," I said, gesturing to the flowers.

"You cut the celery way too thick." Nan stuck her head out of the door to the kitchen. "No one wants that much celery in their mouth at once."

"Okay, Nan," I called back.

More silence.

"Living room!" Fiona practically yelled and ushered Mac out of the hallway.

"Nice guy, Mac," Adam said.

"Yup." Inches separated us. We were never this close without Angus. He reached up, and for the briefest moment I thought he was going to touch me, but instead he rubbed his neck. As my eyes met his, he quickly looked away and studied something just above my head.

"Well," I said. My mind was concerningly empty. My sentence fizzled out.

"Do you want help with the food?" he asked.

"Charlie!" Nan yelled from the kitchen.

I smiled. "No, it's okay. I won't submit you to the torture."

Adam didn't laugh. He stared at me for a few beats, long enough for Nan to call my name again. His eyes traced the contours of my face before making eye contact. I wanted to bury my face in his chest. I almost did, but then Adam walked away, leaving me alone.

I looked down at the flowers in my hand, their stems a little bent.

I searched the kitchen for a vase. I couldn't find a proper one and ended up using an old pasta sauce jar, the label half torn off. The fancy arrangement looked out of place in it, like it was trying to pretend it was something it wasn't.

Darlene showed up twenty minutes later with a group of cousins.

"Did you guys come in two cars?" I asked as I looked out the front door. There were too many people for the Honda Civic parked in the driveway.

"Shh." Darlene held a finger to her lips.

My cousin Ray stretched his back as he walked past. "Dibs on not sitting in the trunk on the way home," he said to the group. "Sup, Charlie."

"Hey, Ray, thanks for coming."

"Wouldn't miss it."

"Heard the little guy is walking now," my other cousin Norah said.

"My niece walked at ten months," Trevor said beside her.

"Well, according to the baby book it's totally normal to walk at twelve months." I followed them into the living room. Aside from Billy's funeral, I hadn't seen my cousins in well over a year. They all lived in the Valley. Whenever there were get-togethers, I always had a reason not to go: schoolwork, Angus, paralyzed by existential dread.

Dad was holding Angus at the far side of the room.

"Put him down!" Darlene squealed. "I want to see!" She walked over and squeezed Angus's thigh. "Look at the little legs," she groaned. "And the cheeks! I just want to eat you up." She pretended to eat Angus and he gave a hearty belly laugh.

"Let's see the little man do his thing." Ray came up beside me, his plate piled high with food.

Everyone in the room stopped talking and turned their attention toward Dad and Angus. Adam looked at me and grimaced. Our son hadn't walked since that day on the lawn.

Dad gently placed Angus on his feet. Angus looked up at him, tilted his head so far back he stumbled, took one step backwards, fell, and landed on his bum.

Dad picked Angus up and put him back on his feet.

Angus sat down on his bum.

Ray took an obnoxiously loud bite of celery. I shot him a look.

"Listen, I'm willing to believe anything," Fiona said, leaning against Mac on the couch. "I am an incredibly gullible and optimistic person. But I do not believe that child walks."

"He walked!" Adam said from the couch.

"He probably just doesn't like being the centre of attention." Angus was currently giving the room a goofy, two-toothed smile and clapping.

Fiona laughed. "No, that's you. Project much?"

I shot her a look.

"He's just feeling the pressure," Adam said.

Angus turned toward me. I crouched down and held out my hands.

"Hey, buddy," I said. "Wanna come over here?"

Angus turned to look at Adam, who walked over and crouched beside me.

"You made it sound like Angus was running track-and-field already," Mom said, laughing.

"I shouldn't have said anything," I mumbled, watching Angus grab at his socks.

"Come on, buddy," Adam waved Angus over. Angus smiled.

I thought he might crawl over, but instead he laid on his tummy and began to roll. We all watched as he rolled across the living room floor toward Adam and me. He stopped in front of us, sat up, and smiled.

"Wow," said Fiona. She placed her hand on Mac's thigh. "Maybe even more impressive than walking." Mac was trying not to smile.

Mom buried her head in her hands and laughed.

Ray took a bite of celery. "These celery sticks are the perfect size," he said. He finished chewing. "So, are you guys together or what?" He looked at Adam and then at me.

Somewhere behind me, Johnny laughed.

Johnny looked up from Beau's camera. "Can you guys get closer together? I can barely fit you both in the frame." Angus wriggled in my arms. We'd sung happy birthday and everyone else had gone home.

"You know you don't have to hold it so close to your face, right? You just look at the screen," I told Johnny.

"Stop trying to change the subject. Get closer to Adam." Johnny took his free hand and gestured for us to move closer.

"Why'd Beau even lend that to you?" I moved infinitesimally closer to Adam.

"When I told him I wanted to take pictures of you guys he practically threw the thing at me. Said he was *honoured to be a part of your love story*."

Was everyone hell-bent on making this the most awkward day ever, or was my family truly dense? I glanced at Adam. I'd been so worried after Billy's funeral that I would lose him. That he would move on with his life and some parts of him would become strange to me. And now, standing here, our child between us, I realized that because of me, that worry had come true.

"Sadie, babe. Please. Can you move them?"

Sadie pushed us closer together, gave my shoulder a pat in solidarity, and then slung Adam's arm around me.

I could feel Adam's arm hovering above me. The distance felt like being stabbed.

"There," Johnny sighed. "Now. Smile like you like each other." He held the camera up far too close to his face and took a picture.

I didn't need to look at the screen to know this photo wasn't getting hung on anyone's wall.

sixty

DOUG'S BOASTED AN ODD ASSORTMENT OF MERCHANDISE. One aisle had locally grown vegetables and homemade baked goods. The next had fireworks and potato chips. The way some shelves were organized made about as much sense as my parents' junk drawer. And at the back was the fridge, freezer, and a wall of VHS tapes for rent. The upstairs was filled with furniture and antiques. I bypassed the fireworks in favour of a bag of All Dressed, then pivoted to the period products. After a blissful nearly two years, Aunt Flo was back.

All of the packages looked really old. Could pads expire? Was I going to give myself some horrible infection? They all looked slightly off-brand. Where was Doug getting these from? I grabbed the package that looked the least mangled, squished between pickle jars, and went in search of chocolate.

"No baby today?" Barb appeared out of nowhere. I flinched.

"Uh, no," I said, recovering from the scare. "He's with his dad."

"It must be nice to have so much time away from your child." Barb raised her eyebrows. "I didn't leave my children until well after they were two."

Barb was the type of woman who would hold your hand, squeeze it, say 'it takes a village,' and then criticize you for allowing the village to help you.

"But I suppose it *is* nice for Adam to get some time with his son since he gets so little." Barb's smile didn't reach her eyes.

"We're making it work." I was seconds away from throwing the pads at her head.

"Not that it's any of my business." Barb held up her hands. "The city is just so far. And Adam is such a good father. Seems a shame."

"He's a great dad." At least that much I could say without screaming. What was happening? Was Adam campaigning for sympathy while I was away? Why had everyone in town decided to gang up on me? Barb, I could understand. But Beau too? This was starting to feel like a pattern.

Adam could glance in Angus's direction and people would applaud and praise him for being an active father. Meanwhile, I have the audacity to go to the grocery store for twenty minutes without my kid, and I'm in the running for worst mother ever.

Barb looked down at the pads in my hand. "No second child, that's probably for the best," she said before walking away.

sixty-one

HI, I MOUTHED, GENTLY SETTING ANGUS'S CAR SEAT DOWN. Angus stirred and I held my breath, hopeful he wouldn't wake up. His body slumped back into contented restfulness. "I'm going to go get the diaper bag," I whispered.

Adam followed me back outside, quietly closing the porch door.

"So, remember, next week Angus and I are heading back into the city. I have a meeting with my advisor and then school starts up again."

Adam stopped abruptly. "*Next* week? Don't you think you're kind of springing this on me?"

"I told you when we came home it was for the summer. The summer is almost over."

"It just seems—I don't..." Adam fumbled for words. "I don't like it."

"Okay." I tried to keep my face neutral. I didn't like it either. I didn't like a lot of things.

"There has to be something we can do."

I had to bite my tongue. If I started shrieking now, I might never stop.

He shook his head. "There has to be a better solution."

Fuck it. Between the period cramps, guilt over leaving home, and the stress of my impending academic revival, I snapped.

"What the actual fuck do you want from me? I've driven home almost every weekend even though gas is crazy expensive and I should be studying. My master's thesis is a dumpster fire. I'm doing my best and I get that it's not enough. At least I'm fully aware of my inadequacies. Can you say the same?"

"What does that mean?"

"God forbid you come into the city, right? Or that you put in some semblance of effort and stop making comments about how you think I'm doing a shit job. We can hack it right now, but soon that's not going to be enough. Angus is going to realize you can't stand me. I get that I'm being punished. That I fucked up." I waved my hands around. "That I'll probably fuck up in the future. But we are not setting a good example our son. I don't want Angus to grow up thinking 'wow, my parents really hate each other.'"

"Do you hate me?" He looked like I'd slapped him.

"No. But you hate me."

"Is that what you think?"

"It's pretty obvious." I was going to cry. I didn't want Adam to see me cry. "Here's his diaper bag." I shoved it into Adam's chest and stomped back to my car.

sixty-two

I DROVE TO THE GENERAL STORE FOR THE SECOND TIME IN AS many days.

Look at me now, Barb, I wanted to yell as I drove past her house.

I bought a chocolate bar and a bag of disgusting banana-flavoured candies and then drove down the road to the graveyard.

I slammed the car door, stomped across the grass, and sat cross-legged in front of Billy's grave. I placed the bag of gummies in front of the headstone.

"Sorry I don't have a plate." I broke a piece off the chocolate bar. "No tobacco offering either. I couldn't find any cigarettes. Maybe Mom truly quit. But I figured you'd prefer the sugar." I chewed the chocolate and then broke off another piece. "How's it been?"

I glanced at the fresh mound of dirt one grave over. "I see you have a new neighbour. Are they nice? Should I leave them a candy?" I waited. "They'd probably haunt me if I gave them a banana one." I took another bite of chocolate. The silence stretched between us. A bug whizzed by my ear and disappeared before I could wave it away.

"Things have been kind of terrible," I said. "Everything but Angus. I have to do a second year of my master's." I imagined the gasp. "I know.

"It's all gone to shit, Billy." I scratched my forehead and looked around. How fucking depressing could I get. Eating discount candy with my dead uncle in the hometown I promised him I'd get away from. The one he could never leave, now.

"I don't know what to do. You set me on this path and now you're not even here to help. Were you aware of how much I looked up to you? That *Don't get stuck* has been my life's motto for the past decade? It felt right for so long and now it doesn't. But I'm already here." Silence hung between us, heavy in the August heat. "And you're not."

A car pulled into the church parking lot and a family got out. They headed towards a plot a few graves down.

I took the final two pieces of chocolate out of the wrapper.

"So that sucks," I said quietly, more self-conscious about talking to a grave now that there was an audience.

I got up and walked to a nearby tree and pulled off the two largest leaves I could find. I laid one leaf down in front of the freshly dug grave beside Billy's and placed one of the squares of chocolate on top.

"Here you go. Who doesn't like chocolate, right?" I put the last piece in my mouth and let it melt as I sat back down in front of Billy's grave.

"I don't want to offend you, but right now I can't help but feel your advice was shit." I placed the second leaf in front of Billy's grave. "I wish you were here, so I could talk to you anyway."

I glanced over at the family; the husband kept looking over at me. Probably because I was talking to myself.

"All right, I should go." I dumped half the banana gummies onto the leaf. "We'll save the other half for another time, yeah?" I tied the bag up. "And next time I won't criticize your advice so much."

"Who are you talking to?" the little girl asked.

"Lillian!" her mother hissed.

I wiggled my fingers at the little girl. "Ghosts."

She smiled. The mom glared. Somewhere, Billy laughed.

sixty-three

A PLATE APPEARED ON THE ROOF BESIDE ME WITH A SANDWICH and a pile of chips on it. A cup of water placed beside it. Adam stuck his head out my bedroom window.

"Your mom said you've been up here for hours. Thought you might need to eat."

I sat up straight and stretched. My back hurt from hunching over a binder Beau had lent me the day before.

Adam was so close I could see the streaks of gold in his eyes. The same ones our son had.

"I lost track of time. Where's Angus?"

"With your mom."

"How was the beach?" Like the mature adult I was, I fully planned on ignoring our argument.

"Good. He tried to eat the sand." Adam climbed all the way onto the roof and sat beside me. "What're you reading?"

"A bunch of random stuff Beau's spent years hoarding." I thumbed through the pages. "Newspaper clippings. Transcribed stories. Obituaries. Some poor woman's journal. Seems invasive, but whatever."

Adam picked up the journal. "What'd she write about?"

I shrugged as he carefully flipped through it. "Everything. Recipes, town gossip, how much she loved her kids, how much they were pissing her off, finance stuff, her sex life—it was subpar."

Adam huffed out a laugh. He put down the journal and picked up a photo, one of the ones I'd taken with my mom.

"Is this up Castlereagh?" Adam asked.

"Yeah. It's Robert Starritt's grave."

Adam looked at the photo for a moment and then handed it to me.

"I can't stop thinking about him, ya know? Like, what do you think life was like for him? Do you think he was disappointed? Like, did he ever think 'I walked here for *this*?' Or was he constantly reassured that every step had been worth it? Do you think every year was a reaffirmation he'd been right to walk so far?" I looked out across the front yard toward the treeline and tapped the photo against my knee. "Like, how do you know? How was he so certain this was what he wanted that he took that first step and then every other one after that?"

Adam handed me half the sandwich he'd brought. "Eat."

I took a bite.

"How did you know?" I asked through a mouthful of sandwich. "Did you always know you wanted to stay?"

Adam took off his ball cap and scratched his head. "It never really seemed like I had a choice. Dad told me the shop was mine for the taking; the same week, my cousin's house came up for sale for cheap. It seemed too..." Adam waved his hand in the air.

"Serendipitous?" A few crumbs landed on my shirt but Adam didn't seem to notice.

"Yeah. It was kind of nice not to have to think. But I don't know... no one ever really asked me what I wanted from life until you did. It didn't really seem important until then. And then you didn't want the same things I did, and, well...you know." Adam readjusted his hat. He ate a chip off my plate. And then another.

"I'm sorry," he said.

"For what?"

"You were right."

"I mean, yes, always, but about what in particular?"

Adam smiled. Looking out over the lawn, he rubbed a hand through his beard. "I was mad and hurt and I didn't meet you halfway." He looked at me. "I didn't mean to make things harder for you... Though I guess maybe, subconsciously, I did. I didn't realize that's what I was doing until you pointed it out. I wasn't sure how to act when we weren't us. I'm sorry."

He picked up the other half of my sandwich and took a bite.

We ate in silence.

"What about you?" Adam eventually asked. "Did you always know you wanted to leave?"

I'd never mentioned the conversation I'd had with Billy to anyone. What if it sounded stupid when I said it out loud? What if I'd spent a decade of my life making decisions based on a conversation Billy had forgotten right after it happened?

I shrugged. "I don't know. Not always." That part was true. "I liked university. I wanted to keep going and I can't do that here." Also the truth, just not all of it.

Adam put his cap on my head. "I know you didn't put on SPF. Don't want you to burn."

"I don't burn—"

"You say that every year, and every year you burn. I'm going to go check on Angus." Adam climbed back through the window. I looked down at my tanned arms and hands and wanted to point out that I only burned at the start of the summer, but I liked wearing his hat so I kept my mouth shut. I picked up the journal and opened it to the page I'd bookmarked.

Adam stuck his head out the window.

"Did he have family here?"

"Starritt?"

Adam nodded.

"He did."

"Did they get here before him?"

"Yeah."

"Well, there you go. He wasn't walking to get to a place, he was walking to get to his family."

sixty-four

I LOOKED UP AT THE IMPOSING COLONIAL HOME IN FRONT OF me. "Thanks for coming with me," I said.

"I'm beginning to regret it," Johnny said.

The house did look a little haunted.

Sadie took a photo with her disposable camera, the click loud in the quiet afternoon.

Adam shuffled nervously, silent.

Beau had called that morning, breathless with excitement. "Cormac Bennet died!" he'd yelled.

"That's terrible," my dad said.

"Put on Charlie," Beau all but screamed.

After taking the phone from my dad, Beau repeated the news.

"That sucks. How's the family?" I asked.

"Yes, truly terrible. Charlotte, you have to get up there."

"Up where?"

"Cormac's house."

"Why?"

"Because Cormac's daughter called to offer the museum whatever they wanted. The caveat being that garbage removers are coming tomorrow. *Tomorrow*, Charlotte."

"Okay..."

"I have a colonoscopy appointment in two hours."

"Gross, Beau."

"Wait till you're old, Charlotte. You have to get up there," he repeated.

"Beau, I don't know what's what. How am I supposed to know what you want?"

"I have a list. Grab a pen and paper and I'll read it out to you."

"Did you write that list this morning or did you already have it? Do I want to know?"

"I have a list for almost everyone in town."

"Beau, that's so morbid."

"Your parents have a lovely antique axe."

"Oh my god, Beau."

"Charlotte, the pen and paper."

And now here we stood, armed with a list, gloves, and the hope this would be over quickly. Getting my parents to look after Angus was the easy part.

Adam unlocked the front door.

"Maybe these were his prized possessions and they'll all be neatly lined up in the entry—"

He pushed it open. The foyer was filled to the brim with piles: books, clothes, boxes of microwavable meals I really hoped were empty.

"My god," Johnny moaned.

I looked at the list again. "It's okay, we can do this. There are only four items."

A mirror supposedly from the 1700s, a vase made in Great Village in the 1800s, a pole from the railway to Castlereagh, which had been built in the late 1800s, and Cormac's grandfather's farm ledgers.

"A mirror. A vase. A pole. And a ledger," I read aloud.

"A pole?" Johnny asked. "What kind of pole?"

"A log-adjacent pole," I said, thinking of the pictures I'd seen of the railway. "Maybe."

"Oh, well that explains it then," said Johnny, exasperated.

Sadie was the first to go in. She turned around, snapped a picture of Johnny, Adam, and me, and then went deeper into the house.

"Does she have any sense of self-preservation?" Adam asked Johnny.

He shrugged. "Not really."

"It's the crystals." Adam and Johnny both looked at me. "She charged them last night. She told me on the drive up. You guys were too busy arguing about mad cow disease."

"I just wonder if it's that big of a deal," Johnny said. Adam opened his mouth to argue his point, again.

"I think I found the mirror!" Sadie yelled from somewhere in the house.

Johnny leaned against the railing on the front porch. "I say we just let her roam. See what she comes up with."

I gave Johnny a shove and walked through the front door, Adam behind me.

Cormac's house was a portrait of a life unexpectedly ended. The remote for the TV was on the arm of the couch, a half-empty glass of water on the side table, a well-loved blanket tossed to the side. I started opening kitchen cupboards. An opened box of crackers, multiple cans of Campbells soup. Coffee in the pot, dishes in the sink.

The house felt haunted, but not in the way I'd imagined when we stood outside. It felt like we were intruding. Like someone was still here.

Adam laughed in another room. I followed the sound to a bedroom. An inordinate number of pillows sat on the bed and bins of clothing against the far wall. Adam was bent over laughing. I stuck my head in and groaned. Leaning again the wall were at least twenty wooden poles of various sizes.

"Which one is it?" Adam asked, holding his stomach.

"You're not going to be laughing when we take all of them to the truck."

Adam straightened. "What?"

"Beau will know if it's the real one or not." He had a great bullshit metre, which he used for both good and evil.

"Found a vase. Looks old," Sadie shouted from upstairs.

I left the bedroom and walked across the hallway.

"Wow, those crystals are really something," Adam said, following me into the living room.

There was a bang upstairs. Silence. And then, "I swear it was already chipped," from Sadie.

I flinched.

"I'm sure Beau won't notice," Adam said.

I walked over to the bookshelf on the far wall. Adam went back to the bedroom and started taking the poles out to his truck. The shelves were full of Harlequin romance and murder mysteries. I quickly scanned the cracked spines, looking for anything that could be a farm ledger.

Had Cormac's family taken anything for themselves? The house appeared untouched, everything where it should be. It seemed sad to just throw out a life. When we cleaned out Billy's room, we'd looked at each item. Picked it up and considered what it meant to us and to Billy. I'd debated throwing the bobbletorso out for at least two minutes. It didn't look like Cormac or his belongings had been afforded the same care.

"This place is creepy as shit," Johnny called down the stairs. "Oh my god, this room is just entirely dolls." A door slammed shut.

Finished with the bookshelves, I moved on to the desk underneath a large bay window. I could see Adam loading the poles into the truck. I tested the drawers on the desk, all but one opened. It had a keyhole in the upper middle. With my luck, the ledger would be in there. I rifled through the contents of the unlocked drawers. Nothing. I tried the top drawer again. It jiggled but wouldn't open. I looked on the desk for something to unlock the drawer. There were several loose paper clips. I picked one up, straightened the wire out, and slid it into the keyhole. I didn't know how to pick a lock, but I figured if I poked around enough something might happen.

Adam made two more trips to the truck while I tried to unlock the drawer. When he came back in to grab more poles, I called out.

"Do you know how to pick locks?"

Adam came into the living room, looked at the lock, and held his hand out for the paper clip.

"I've been trying for like ten minutes," I said.

We both leaned closer to the drawer.

"I think you're supposed to make a loop at the end." Adam tried to bend the wire. "We need something to help me twist it, pliers or something." Adam leaned toward me, scanning the desk for anything useful. He then moved onto the drawers. He pulled open the drawer underneath the locked one.

He snorted, pulling out a skeleton key. "This might be helpful, eh?"

"Oh." I could feel myself blushing.

"You've always got to make things harder than they need to be, don't you?"

I looked up at Adam, we were closer than I'd thought. He was smiling, eyes bright with amusement.

There was a click in the hallway. Sadie stood in the entryway, disposable camera held to her face. She lowered it. "Cute," she said.

Johnny appeared beside Sadie, mirror and chipped vase in hand. "That doll room is one hundred percent haunted."

Adam slid the key into the lock and twisted until the lock clicked. I opened the drawer. Inside were a tattered black notebook and a stash of Werther's candies. I picked up the book and carefully looked through it. There were lists of produce and meat cuts with dollar amounts beside them, the occasional to-do list, a reminder of his wife's upcoming birthday. The writing was illegible in parts. One page was dated 1889.

"This must be it," I said, closing the drawer.

Upstairs a floorboard creaked, a door slammed. I looked at Johnny and Sadie, who stood in the hallway wide-eyed.

"The fucking dolls!" Johnny yelped, heading for the front door.

"We have good intentions," Sadie called as Adam gently pushed her toward the door.

I slammed the front door closed, quickly locked it, then dashed down the porch steps two at a time.

I climbed into the truck and tried to catch my breath. We all sat in the cab, our heavy breathing the only sound.

Sadie twisted around to look out the back window. "Wow, that's a lot of poles."

"I take back everything I've ever said about wanting to be a ghost hunter," Johnny gasped, still clutching the mirror and vase.

sixty-five

I TAPPED MY FEET ON DR. GAMBLE'S PERSIAN RUG, WORRYING the edge of the folded paper in my pocket. I'd spent the better part of Angus's nap rehearsing how to tell him I was dropping out. I'd contemplated bringing my own bag to throw up in but decided against it.

"How was your summer break?" He had a cup of tea. He'd offered me one but my mouth was so dry I imagined I'd choke on it.

"Good. Angus and I hung out at my parents' the whole time. He got to see his dad a lot, which was nice." I pinched the skin on my wrist. "Listen, Dr. Gamble. I've been—"

"What did you do while you were home?" he interrupted.

"Oh, I read a lot. I, um, volunteered with this historical society. They just bought an old church in the centre of town for, like, ten dollars."

Dr. Gamble tilted his head, narrowing his gaze. "What'd you do there?"

"Mostly moved heavy stuff for them." I shrugged. "They're all kind of old."

He chuckled, nodding.

"They asked me to take pictures of this old cemetery up in the mountains for a display. It was actually neat because I read a book in undergrad that mentioned one of the men buried there. And then I reread the book while I was home."

"Oh?" The steam from the tea was curling around him.

"Yeah, Robert Starritt. In 1819 he took the wrong boat from Ireland and ended up in Quebec City. He walked all the way to where my parents live to meet up with some of his family who'd already settled there."

Dr. Gamble didn't say anything. But he was listening.

"It's a little depressing though, isn't it? Like, he walked all this way. And now he's just buried in the backwoods up a mountain. The town is gone. I bet you most of his family doesn't live there anymore. Everyone moves away."

Dr. Gamble nodded, silently encouraging me to go on.

"When I was home, Beau, the head of the historical society, got this freezer-burnt 'perpetual stew' from this deceased woman's house," I said. "It's less suspect than it sounds. It's just...for lack of a better word, depressing? Because this woman chucked it in the back of her freezer after her husband died and her kids all moved away. And then I thought, why? When did it become unsustainable to live there? At some point it was inviting enough to walk almost a thousand kilometres to get there, and people thrived. Why did it change? I just...I can't stop thinking about it and I'm driving everyone around me nuts."

He was smiling. "You've found it, Charlotte." He hadn't touched his tea.

"Found what?"

"Your thesis topic."

"My thesis is about—"

"You're allowed to change your mind."

"But my application and proposal—"

"Is not a binding contract."

I thought for a minute. Professor Gamble waited.

"I'm allowed to start from scratch?" I asked.

"Yes, of course. Although I don't recommend doing it again, unless you want to be a master's student forever."

"I don't. No offence."

He smiled, and finally took a sip of tea before he spoke.

"When I was working on my master's, I was so obsessed with wartime propaganda in Nova Scotian newspapers it was all I talked about. My wife threatened to divorce me at least twice. When you find something you can't stop talking about, that's when you know you've found your topic." He paused. "I don't think you felt that way about your first thesis."

I found it almost physically impossible to admit when I'd been wrong. But the idea of finally admitting the truth to myself felt like a relief.

"You're right," I said. "The first thesis felt like I was fighting tooth and nail."

Dr. Gamble looked thoughtful for a moment. "Take a few days, do some research, and have an outline of a proposal to me by next

Friday. If it has merit, we'll aim for a full proposal to take to your thesis committee in six weeks. Does that sound manageable?"

It didn't. But he was tossing me a lifeline, and I wasn't going to turn it down it because it seemed too big to hold.

"Totally manageable."

sixty-six

FIONA PEERED OVER HER MUG AT ME. "I DON'T MEAN TO SOUND like a biatch, but you look like shit."

Angus spit out the sweet potato I was trying to give him. He grabbed his spoon and a handful of orange mush and tossed them both on the laminate flooring. I looked at the floor, then at Fiona. "Thanks."

"I'd be less worried if you told me to fuck off."

"Yeah, well." Angus threw another handful of potato.

My eyes stung. Some days it seemed like Angus survived on a solitary cracker. He wanted no part in what I put in front of him, no matter what it was. How did he have so much energy? He had started walking, then running, and there were moments I longed for the days he'd actually stayed where I put him. And then I felt racked with guilt because months ago all I'd wanted him to do was walk.

I'd just come back from what was probably the worst experience of my university career. I'd prepped the wrong material for the Intro to Canadian History class I was TAing, and none of the students had bothered to tell me they had no idea what I was talking about until the hour was nearly over. I felt sick when I realized I'd been unprepared. On top of that, Dr. Gamble had given the thumbs-up on my outline a month ago, but I was struggling to write my thesis proposal.

My thesis now focused on outmigration in Colchester County. I had pages and pages of notes devoted to reasons why people left the region I grew up in. I tried not to think about how I was one of those people.

I couldn't even properly complain to Fiona because she was so easy about everything. Didn't do a good job? There's always next time. Bombed a presentation? Consider it a learning opportunity.

It was such a healthy mindset, I couldn't accept it.

"Wow, this person did not understand the assignment," I told Angus later that night. I'd been reading a student's paper while Angus ate supper. Every night while we ate, I would either read from a textbook or a paper I needed to grade. Angus wasn't talking yet and we'd reached the point where he should be. A baby book I'd picked up at the library said to talk to him all the time and leave gaps where he could respond, giving him the space to do so. I would read a few sentences and ask him what he thought. We'd discuss what grade each paper should get. But still, his only words were *Mama* and *Dada*. I made a comment in the margin of the paper and continued reading aloud.

After supper we did bathtime, where Angus played to his heart's delight and I tried to control the splash zone. He got so much water on the floor I was convinced it was rotting and one day we'd just fall straight through into Mac's apartment.

Then, no matter how calming my voice, how dim the lights, how much lavender bedtime body wash I used, I would inevitably spend over an hour getting Angus to sleep. I tried to soak up the time spent lying in the dark room together. I never wanted to forget his quiet babbling, the way his small hand felt in mine, the sound of his breathing as he finally fell asleep. But as bedtime stretched on, I couldn't help but count how many minutes had passed, how little time I had to work on my thesis, grade papers, and clean up the food all over the floor in the kitchen.

Once Angus was asleep, it took every ounce of willpower to go back into the living room. All I wanted to do was curl up in the darkened bedroom and sleep for ten years. Occasionally, I would fall asleep next to Angus's crib and then wake with a start in the middle of the night.

Angus had started daycare the week before. He only went twice a week, but it was enough for me to feel like I had time to work without having to divide my attention between research and my son. It was great. I felt bad I thought it was great. Sometimes I wondered if I'd ever feel good about anything again or if, along with the twenty extra pounds I'd gained during pregnancy, I'd carry the weight of this guilt for the rest of my life.

Almost immediately after starting daycare Angus had gotten a cold. He was fine during the day. But when I put him to bed he'd cough and sniffle all night, keeping both of us up. Tonight, he fell asleep halfway through our first song; a pitchy version of Lightfoot's

"The Wreck of the Edmund Fitzgerald." I stood by his crib, afraid to move in case he woke up. I waited, barely breathing, and counted to one hundred.

I crept out of his room, quietly shut the door, and breathed out, my shoulders falling. I had to clean up the food on the floor. And then I had to finish grading the stack of papers on the coffee table. Fiona was downstairs at Mac's for the night. Maybe I could have a quick cry in the living room first. Maybe I'd take a break between papers and let myself sob for five minutes. I had options.

As I cleaned up the food, I marvelled at how far Angus was able to throw his pasta. Maybe he had a future in baseball. I chugged cold, day-old coffee straight from the pot and moved to the living room to mark. I made it through three papers. And then I woke up when the front door closed, bright morning light spilling in through half-closed blinds.

"Did you sleep on the couch?" Fiona asked, pausing in the doorway.

"I didn't mean to."

Fiona glanced at the papers strewn across the couch and table. She looked unhappy.

"I'll go start a fresh pot of coffee," she said, leaving me alone on the couch. I felt like I'd done something wrong. Like I'd been caught red-handed and had let her down in some way.

sixty-seven

I STOOD ON THE SIDEWALK OUTSIDE ANGUS'S DAYCARE TRYING not to feel offended. Angus had taken to daycare with such ease. I'm sure the parents whose children clung to them and screamed when they tried to leave were jealous, but I wished Angus would show a modicum of concern that I was leaving him with strangers.

I stared through the poppy-covered window. Angus was standing at a small kitchen, holding a spatula. Was I terrible for leaving him with literal strangers? Angus smiled up at a daycare worker who stood nearby. Or maybe I was an inadequate parent and that's why Angus was fine hanging out with random people all day?

A haggard-looking father dashed out the front door, his kid's screams following him.

The leaves had just begun to fall. A canopy of burnt orange, bright yellow, and deep red sheltered the sidewalk. The air was crisp. Walking past historic homes, a Chinese grocer, and a dog-walker handling three golden retrievers, a Great Dane, and a corgi, I was reminded of how the city felt when I'd first moved here. When I'd been enamoured instead of exhausted.

I was about to spend all day in the public archives. I looked up at the blue sky, bright through the leaves, and tried to soak it all in.

I spent hours combing through historical documents. It was slow going. Trying to decipher cursive from a hundred years ago felt like trying to decode an ancient language. I came across a letter from one British settler to another. They were discussing a person they called *Phillip the Old Indian*. Apparently, he had smallpox. His family lived in the backcountry, but he had come to town to ask for help. I found it half amusing, half sad that this man had been forever immortalized this way. I finished the letter and moved on to the next document, "Phillip the Old Indian" immediately forgotten.

I took a snack break three hours in and went to sit outside while I ate a peanut-butter-and-jelly sandwich I'd packed. I ran over the conversation I'd had with Johnny the day before.

He laid on the floor and let Angus climb all over him while telling me every detail I hadn't asked for but was desperate to know about Gina and Adam. Johnny didn't like Gina because she was annoyingly wholesome and a really good person (I agreed). He'd also told me there'd never really been anything between Gina and Adam. I said I didn't care and Johnny told me I was full of shit. He then told me I looked worse than I did when I'd had mono in high school. He said he was concerned. I'd told him I was fine.

I tossed the now empty sandwich bag in the garbage.

I was fine. I had to be fine.

I was not fine. Angus squirmed on my lap as we sat in the doctor's office. I was exhausted. My hair was greasy. I was about to cry for no good reason. The last four months had been hell. Christmas had passed in a flurry of last-minute shopping and studying. My gig as a TA brought in much-needed money, but grading papers was time-consuming and terrible. And all this while trying to make the holidays magical for Angus. I was miserable. But at least I was meeting my deadlines. I focused on that. I clung to it.

My proposal had been approved back in October with some notes on refinement: a symbol of my university career. But I had done it. The three months since then had been a blur of threading microfilm machines at the archives to pore over old newspapers and records, paired with mountains of readings, all while consuming a concerning amount of caffeine. Now I just needed to write an entire thesis in a few months while also taking care of an eighteen-month-old who had recently figured out how to open cupboards and throw their contents down the stairs of our apartment. I wasn't close to a breakdown at all.

Angus squirmed and tears pricked in my eyes.

"Here, let me take him." Adam plucked Angus off my lap and placed him on his own. "You look really tired."

"You're not supposed to tell people that," I snapped. "Between you and Fiona, I'm going to develop a complex."

Adam tried to distract Angus with his car keys. "I can take Angus for a walk after the appointment. You should nap."

I had more papers to grade. I couldn't nap.

The doctor arrived before I could respond.

"How's everyone doing?" she asked.

"Great," I lied.

"Because this is Angus's eighteen-month appointment I have a series of questions that I have to ask, just to make sure he's meeting his milestones."

"Sure." I nodded enthusiastically. I dreaded learning all the ways I was failing my son.

This new family doctor made me nervous. Since she'd taken over, a sign had popped up in the waiting room that read: *ATTN Native patients: Please don't ask for tranquilizers or pain meds*. It was a small sign, tacked just behind the reception desk, but I struggled to focus on anything else in the room. I always felt like it was screaming at me.

Her questions were fine, and she seemed happy with my answers until we got to the ones about speech.

"How many words does he have?" She looked between me and Adam.

"Uh." I glanced at Adam. "Two?"

"Yeah, just *Mama* and *Dada*," Adam answered.

"Okay." She paused. "We would expect a few more at eighteen months. Angus is obviously very engaged. I think we should do a follow-up around twenty-one months to see where he's at and go from there. You can book that on the way out."

"Okay, we will. Thanks so much." Was it my fault Angus wasn't talking yet? What more could I possibly be doing?

The doctor smiled and her teeth were too big and too white. "Everything else looks great though, so unless you have any questions, we're done for today."

Adam stood up and started to put Angus's jacket and boots back on.

The doctor leaned toward me. "I know that there can be a lot of intergenerational trauma with, you know, your people," she said, "and it's not that you're not a good mom. But I understand that it can be harder for you. I get it. So please, feel free to reach out if you need anything. There are great supports that are readily available."

I stared at her. My throat tightened and I willed myself not to cry. I tried to find a way to make her words harmless, but I came up empty. She kept smiling. She thought she was being kind. This was a moment she would marinate in later. One she'd pull out when she needed to feel good, to remember that time she was sympathetic and understanding to a poor Native mother.

I glanced at Adam. He was still struggling to get Angus's boots back on and hadn't heard.

If I called our doctor out on what she just said, I would be misconstruing something. I would be labelled as overly emotional. I would be in the wrong.

"I'll make the follow-up appointment," I said. I didn't want to. I didn't want to see her again. But I was lucky to have a family doctor. I could put up with her racism if it meant we had somewhere to go when Angus was sick.

I made the appointment at reception, the sign behind it stabbing my eyes like hot pokers, and walked in silence with Adam to the elevator.

"You okay?" he asked as we waited.

I nodded.

We took the elevator down and walked to his truck. I still hadn't said a word. I could feel my throat burning with the screams trapped inside. God, how many times had I felt like this? How many more times would this happen? Would everything always feel this heavy?

Adam buckled Angus into his car seat while I tried not to cry.

"I really don't think we have to worry about Angus," Adam said as he climbed in. "He'll talk."

I nodded again.

"Charlie? What's wrong?"

How could I describe this feeling of being less-than, of constantly being judged, of fighting against racist assumptions? He would never fully understand, no matter how well I explained it. And I knew I was too emotional right now to even try.

In the cab of Adam's truck, I wondered if I had imagined it all.

I took a deep breath, then let out this horrible sound, somewhere between a sob and a guttural sigh.

Adam rubbed my back while I wept. We sat there for so long I couldn't help but wonder if his arm was getting tired. I laughed and then loudly sucked back my snot. I coughed. And then sobbed again.

"Mama?" Angus called from the backseat.

"Yeah, buddy?" I tried to sound like I wasn't crying. My voice cracked and I laughed, wiping my eyes. I leaned back and squeezed his little hand.

"Angus," Adam said. "I am putting the key in the ignition. I am turning the key. I am starting the car."

"What're you doing?" I asked Adam.

"I'm describing in detail everything I'm doing. And then, because I've done this, Angus will start to talk. Right, buddy?"

"Dada," Angus said.

"Exactly. I am pulling out of the parking spot. I backed in. So that I may front out. Because that is the superior way to do it." Adam looked at me.

"Angus, I'm sitting here, listening to your father criticize how I park without actually criticizing it. I am no longer crying. We are going back to the apartment."

"Where your mother will take a nap." Adam pulled up to a red light and looked over at me again.

sixty-eight

THE DRIVE HOME WAS A BLUR OF EVERGREENS, BARREN FIELDS, yellowed grass, and farmhouses. Everything was cold and bleak and dead and we didn't even have any snow to mask it. As soon as I spotted Cobequid Bay I sat up, sighed, then slouched back in the seat. The tide was coming in, rushing toward the ruddy cliffs, swathes of rusted mud quickly disappearing.

After the doctor's appointment we'd gone back to my apartment. Adam took Angus for a walk and told me to nap. I pulled out my thesis research and made a cup of coffee.

Adam found me two hours later asleep in a nest of papers, books, and pens.

He looked annoyed.

"Pack your shit." He glanced at Angus, nestled in the crook of his arm. "Stuff," he corrected. "Bring whatever you need for the next few days. You're going to stay at my house and you're going to sleep."

"What about Gina?" I asked. I knew I sounded like a bratty teenager. Johnny had said nothing was happening between them, but I felt so insecure and vulnerable in that moment I couldn't help but lash out.

Adam rolled his eyes and walked away, not bothering to answer.

"I don't need help, it's okay, I can manage," I said as he started gathering Angus's stuff. I didn't want to be a burden.

"I know you can manage, Charlie. That doesn't mean you need to," Adam said as he stuffed board books into a bag.

I could've said no. I could've said I was staying in the city. But I didn't want to.

Instead, I packed up my thesis nest. Clothes. Everything Angus needed. And climbed in the truck without a word.

I felt like a failure in every aspect of my life, and it all felt worse because I could no longer deny that I needed help. I was supposed to be independent and capable. When I'd first gotten into university my dad had hugged me tight and said, “You’re going to move mountains, T’us.” Now, I couldn’t even sit up straight in the passenger’s seat of Adam’s truck.

This failure to thrive made me feel wrong and bad and unworthy. A deep self-loathing made its home in the very marrow of my bones.

I was so tired of letting everyone down.

I had never thought that this was how I would be in motherhood. When I first held Angus in my arms, I had been so full of love and hope and optimism about how our lives would be. Now, every day felt like a struggle and I didn’t know how to make it stop.

In Adam’s driveway, I leaned back against the hood of his truck. “I’m sorry, okay? I know I’m not doing a good job, and I feel like you’re annoyed with me.” I pressed my nails into my wrist.

“That’s stupid.” Adam picked Angus up. He sounded tired.

I angled my body towards his. “So, you’re not annoyed?”

“I am.” Adam scratched his beard with his free hand. “But not for the reasons you think. I’m annoyed with you because you’re not taking care of yourself.”

I pressed harder. I pinched my skin till it hurt.

“Stop doing that.” Adam’s eyes hadn’t left me, and when I glanced at them now, they were glassy and wide. Rebuttal died on my tongue. He shook his head and continued.

“You don’t ask for help. You try to do everything yourself. I always admired you for it. How you never really seemed to need anyone. But now it’s like you don’t know how to accept help. You don’t know when you need it. Fiona, your family, me. We’re all here, but we’re all worried if we offer to help, you’re going to snap at us.”

It was uncomfortable to hear myself described in such a way.

“I don’t know why you do it,” Adam continued. “But you don’t have to.” He readjusted Angus. “You’re not taking care of yourself. You keep hiding the money I try to give you in weird spots so I don’t find it until later. So, can you just let me do this? Let me take care of both of you.” We both glanced down at Angus and his ruddy cheeks, his breath making clouds in the air. “You do your thing: study, write, whatever, hang out with Angus. We can drive you in so you can teach your class, go to the library, the archives, whatever. But let me take care of everything else.”

I hadn't been expecting this. My body had been ready for a fight. Every sinew and tissue held so much stress and exhaustion I didn't know how to soften. But I could feel myself wanting to.

"Adam—"

"For the love of god, Charlie, do not try to argue with me."

"But—"

"Remember when you hid your pregnancy from me?"

That one hurt. But he'd said it without malice this time. Was there even a hint of wry humour, or was that wishful thinking?

"Um, yes..." I said tentatively.

"You can make up for it right now." His eyes held mine, unwavering. "Let me do this. I'm tired of watching you self-destruct."

I smirked in spite of myself. "This seems like a terrible deal."

"Not from where I'm standing."

He turned toward the house and I watched my son and his father walk away. This time, I followed them.

sixty-nine

AFTER ADAM MADE DINNER, WE'D CLEANED UP TOGETHER. The kitchen was quiet now, both of us subdued. Even Angus had been calm through the meal, and then I realized it was the first time we had ever eaten together, just us three.

Adam zipped up Angus's jacket, put a hat on his head, and turned to me. "I'm going to tire him out. You study and then it's bed by nine for everyone," he said.

I lifted an eyebrow. "Sure thing, Dad."

Adam grimaced. "Don't be gross."

He took Angus outside before I could respond.

I spent the next forty minutes writing my section on research methodologies and looking over the population data I'd painstakingly collected. I'd brought my gigantic desktop computer with me, and Adam had pulled what was possibly the world's smallest desk out of his basement and stuck it in the corner of the living room. The monitor took up almost the entirety of the desk, my stack of books and printed papers perched precariously on the edge.

Adam didn't have internet, but between dragging the desk up the basement steps and yelping when he found a spider on his arm, he'd promised to call about having it set up.

After typing and deleting the same sentence five times, I decided to call it quits. I slid the floppy disk into the hard drive to save my work and then placed it on a high shelf out of Angus's reach. Then I saved it on a second floppy disk and put that one on a different shelf.

I went outside and stood on the back porch as Angus and Adam walked around the property.

"And this is where we'll put the chickens," Adam told Angus. "I just have to build the coop and then we're all set. You can name 'em."

Angus looked up at Adam but said nothing.

If he'd just say one word, something other than *Mama* or *Dada*, I would feel better.

I cleared my throat and reached out for Angus. "Ready for bed, bud?"

He walked toward me as fast as his little legs could carry him. I met him on the bottom step and scooped him up. His nose was red from the cold. He brought his hand to my mouth and laughed when I pretended to bite it.

Adam held the back door open for us.

"Chickens, eh?" I said.

"Someday," he said as he followed us inside.

Angus was already snoring before his head hit the mattress. I closed the door, the snick of the latch sliding loudly into place in the quiet house. I froze and waited for him to start crying.

Nothing.

I breathed out and let go of the door handle.

Nan swore country air made people sleep better. I'd thought it was bullshit, but Angus did sleep better here. Always.

Adam was in the living room, writing in a notebook. I hovered in the doorway, feeling stuck in place. The ways in which our relationship was fractured made themselves apparent in the silence that stretched between us.

Whether heavy-handed or not, Adam had extended an olive branch today, and it felt like some tiny fissure of us had started to repair itself.

I walked across the room and sat at the other end of the couch, pulling my legs to my chest.

"What're you writing?" I asked him.

Adam handed me the notebook. He'd drawn a basic sketch of a chicken coop with measurements scribbled around it.

"This coop is going to be bigger than my apartment."

Adam shrugged. "Your apartment's a shithole."

He wasn't wrong.

I looked at the plans again. My relationship with Adam had always been easy. I'd never had to struggle with conversation, never had to overthink any of it. But now everything felt fraught and tenuous.

"Any new Karen and Ethel drama?" I asked, thinking of that conversation from years ago.

"You didn't hear?"

"No?"

"Ethel killed Karen in cold blood."

"What?" I all but gasped.

"Rumour has it, Karen told Ethel her potato salad tasted salty and Ethel went ballistic. Throttled her outside the September yard sale. Who knew Karen's last words would be about oversalted potatoes."

I blinked, my mouth agape.

Adam's shoulders shook, his mouth squeezed tight to hold in a laugh.

I shoved him and he burst out laughing.

"You're a moron," I said through my own laughter.

"*I'm* the moron? I totally got you. You should've seen your face."

seventy

"PLEASE TELL ME THERE'S ONLY ONE BED," FIONA WHISPERED over the phone.

"What? No, I'm in the third bedroom. He actually went out and bought me a bed, which was really nice of him."

Fiona gasped. "That's almost criminal," she said. "This is an ideal moment for the one-bed trope."

"I don't know what that means."

Fiona groaned. "Read a romance novel, would ya? It's when two people, the love interests, need a place to sleep and there's only one bed. I feel like it normally happens at an inn."

"An inn?"

"Reluctantly, the love interests agree to share the bed. They fall asleep on opposite sides of the bed but wake up entangled with one another all hot and bothered. Ready to bang."

"I don't know how to respond to that," I eventually said.

"Bought you a bed," Fiona muttered.

"I'm actually sleeping, Fi—like, a full eight hours. Though weirdly, I'm still very tired. Maybe my body is trying to play catch up."

"I was sure Adam would make a move," Fiona said, clearly disappointed.

"Adam is just trying to make sure I don't die from exhaustion."

"I saw how he looked at you the other day, full of longing and horniness. The boy is yearning."

I groaned. "Not this again. He is *not*. He just needs me healthy so he can keep holding a grudge against me. Especially since he forgave Gina Smith."

"Puh-lease. I bet my entire life savings he doesn't look at Gina Smith like *that*."

"Adam doesn't look at me like anything."

"You keep telling yourself that. Oh! I meant to tell you, Mac asked—ah, shit—" Fiona cut herself off mid-sentence.

"What?"

"Uh, I just realized I'm supposed to be at a meeting in fifteen minutes, I gotta jet."

"What were you going to say?" I asked.

"Nothing, I'll tell you later."

"Just tell me now."

A pause. "Fine, Mac asked to...borrow your"— another pause— "your whisk, and I said it was fine."

"Why do I feel like you're lying right now?"

"Charlie," Fiona sighed. "I'm not lying, I'm putting on lipstick. You know I can't multitask. Okay, bye!" She hung up.

I stared at the phone. There was definitely something she wasn't telling me.

seventy-one

"WE HAVEN'T TALKED ABOUT YOUR PHD APPLICATION YET. Do you need help with it?" Dr. Gamble leaned back in his office chair. He was wearing a new sweater and a floral tie. I'd been about to compliment the look but now I was contemplating what he would do if I just up and left his office.

"I honestly haven't thought about it." I admitted.

"*You* haven't thought about it?" Dr. Gamble looked gobsmacked.

"I was just trying to make it through my master's. I'm not sure a PhD is right for me." And thinking about a PhD would be a natural segue into thinking about the death of my five-year plan and current dumpster fire of a life. Which I already thought about enough.

Dr. Gamble scoffed. "I'm surprised, Charlotte. You've finally found what you're passionate about."

"I've had a rough go of it, if you haven't noticed." It turned out nearly failing out of grad school and being at my wits' end for the last year and a half killed whatever shyness I'd possessed when he first became my advisor.

"Please. Did your Starritt give up when he got his first blister?"

I wanted to point out that the last two years felt like more than a blister, but Dr. Gamble pushed his chair back from his desk and stood up.

"Wait here a minute." He left this office, shutting the door behind him.

I looked around. He'd added some new art to his walls. There was a second googly-eyed rock next to the first. There was now a box of peppermint tea next to his giant box of Red Rose.

The office door opened. Dr. Gamble placed a stack of papers on the desk in front of me and sat back down.

I picked up the papers. It was a PhD application package.

"I want you to take those home and seriously consider applying. I will help you in any way I can." He readjusted his glasses. "And yes, Charlotte, I will be your advisor."

"Wow, presumptuous much?"

Dr. Gamble smiled. "You know you were going to ask."

I would have. There was no one else in the department I trusted as much as him.

Back at Adam's I sat on the porch swing, legs tucked under me, while Adam and Angus ran around the front yard. The application was next to me on the swing. When I'd gotten home, I'd asked Adam what he thought. He'd been as surprised as Dr. Gamble that I hadn't already applied.

I wanted to make sure that a PhD was something I wanted to do, and not something I did because others expected it of me. I was done making decisions just to meet other people's expectations.

Parenting with Adam these last two months, I felt like I could finally think. Doing research, learning new things, was starting to feel exciting again. Writing my thesis, while still difficult, didn't feel like a slog.

I was also eating balanced meals again. I had vegetables and protein daily. Turns out all that talk of nutritional value and nourishing your body wasn't bogus. I was surprised I hadn't gotten scurvy.

A PhD now seemed like an actual possibility. But this, our life at Adam's, wasn't forever; it was a stopgap measure to ensure I didn't turn into a puddle. Adam deserved a full life, not one where he had to take care of me because I couldn't do it on my own.

I looked down at the application package beside me. Even knowing it would be messy and hard, I wanted this.

After the first two weeks of staying with Adam, I'd wondered out loud if I should go back to the city. I was well-rested and no longer felt unhinged. Adam had said I could stay for as long as I liked. So, Angus and I hadn't left. I knew we would go back to the city at some point. We had an apartment there; I couldn't play house with Adam forever. As much as we'd started to feel like a family, he and I weren't a couple. We didn't discuss the future any farther ahead than what was for supper.

But I couldn't make the life I'd promised Angus by avoiding the future.

I picked up the stack of papers.

seventy-two

JOHNNY DRUMMED HIS GLOVED FINGERS ON THE KITCHEN TABLE, his legs bouncing up and down. He wore a toque and a winter jacket.

"Can you go for a run or something? You're stressing me out with all that nervous energy," I said.

"I will literally die if I do that. I have zero stamina and the lung capacity of someone about to take their last breath." Johnny put half a grilled cheese sandwich on Angus's highchair tray. Angus picked it up and gnawed on it. I stuck his hat back on while he was distracted; he kept taking it off despite the chill in my parents' kitchen.

"Why are you here, anyways?" Johnny asked.

"Mom said she was worried Angus wouldn't remember what she looked like. By the way, where is she?" I asked.

Adam, Angus, and I had been living in an insular world over the past few months. Adam would wake early and go to work, I would spend the first part of the day with Angus, and Adam would take Angus when he got home so I could work on my thesis all afternoon. Then, after Angus was in bed, I'd either keep working or pass out. We usually went to my parents' for dinner on Sundays, but with my thesis deadline looming, I'd panicked and cancelled the last two. The last time we'd seen my parents was Billy's birthday.

"I don't understand how this happened," Adam interrupted. He stared at the broken windowpane above the sink: both the screen and the glass were gone.

"You do manual labour for a living," I told Johnny.

"Yeah, and I suck at it. The only reason Old Man MaCallum doesn't fire me is because he's frigging old. He thinks everything I do is impressive. Standing on two legs without any support is a superhuman feat in his eyes." Johnny bounced his legs so forcefully his knee hit the table and rattled the dishes on top.

"Jesus." I startled. "Just sit still."

"How did this happen?" Adam asked again, pointing at the window.

"Mom went all She-Hulk on it this morning. She tried to toss a spatula in the sink but threw it at the window and cracked it. Then, when she tried to cover the crack with duct tape she broke the whole pane and somehow popped out the window screen. And then left me to freeze to death. Dad'll fix it when he gets home." Johnny adjusted his hat and shivered.

Adam took a closer look. "It didn't occur to either of you to cover the window so you don't have freezing cold air blowing through the house?"

"That sounds high-tech," Johnny said.

"All right, well I'm going to go find some high-tech cardboard in the basement," Adam said.

"Suit yourself," said Johnny. "Maybe we like the cold. Ever think of that?"

Angus took his hat off and flung it across the table. Adam ruffled his hair and then walked out of the room.

I held an open milk carton while I searched for a sippy cup when a black behemoth swooped over me, its heavy body smacking into my head. I screamed as I threw the jug, sloshing milk onto my shirt and all over the floor. The creature swooped again. On pure instinct, I threw my hands up. My forearm hit the beast and my stomach roiled.

I screamed again, slipped in the milk and landed on my bum. I scooted backward until my back hit the fridge and looked around wildly for the creature.

Johnny scooped Angus out of his highchair and hightailed it out of the room. This might seem heroic, but it was most definitely a ploy to leave me to deal with whatever hell spawn had flown into the kitchen.

I looked up and saw a crow by the sink, pecking at a loaf of bread.

I got up as slowly as possible, careful not to make any sudden movements. Looking behind me, I turned my back on the crow, risking death to make sure my son was okay.

Johnny and Angus stood in the hallway wide-eyed, Angus clutched to Johnny's chest.

The crow made a hoarse cooing sound and I whipped back around. My feet slipped in the milk but I quickly righted myself. The crow hobbled across the stove, its talons clicking against the hard surface.

"Oh my god, what do I do?" I whispered to Johnny.

"The fuck if I know."

"Fug." A quiet word. Barely formed. But Angus had said it.

"Oh my god." I turned toward Johnny. "Did you just teach my kid the F word?"

"Fuck." This time Angus really hit the crisp K sound at the end.

"We can't tell Adam," I whispered.

"Tell me what?" Adam asked, holding a piece of cardboard and a roll of duct tape.

"Nothi—" I screamed and ducked as the bird flew to the top of the fridge. It cawed angrily and scattered unwanted flyers as it landed.

This was how I died.

"Is that a crow?" Adam stepped into the kitchen, either brave or incredibly stupid. "Is this what you were screaming about?"

"So sorry I'm not stoic in the face of—oh my god!" I squealed as the crow took off again, this time settling near the open window. It clicked at us.

"That's it, little birdy." I used the most saccharine voice I could muster. "Hop on out the window. Go back outside. It's nice out there."

We all held our breath.

"Fuck," Angus whispered.

"Christ almighty," I muttered.

"Was that?" Adam looked back and forth between me and Johnny and Angus. "Did he?"

"Listen. This isn't ideal. I know. But it *is* a word, so that's positive, right?" Adam didn't look convinced. "And besides, we have bigger fish to fr—" The word turned into a yelp as the bird hopped away from the window and spread its wings.

I was about to cry.

In a burst of feathers, the bird flew from the counter to the kitchen table. Lurching out of the way, I stumbled into Adam. Our feet slipped in the puddle of milk and, in a tangle of limbs, we hit the ground.

Adam let out a guttural *oof* that I will never forget (or forgive) as I landed on top of him.

The crow picked up Johnny's sandwich.

"My grilled cheese," Johnny groaned.

"Fuck," Angus said.

"You got that right, buddy," Johnny agreed.

The crow tried to swallow the sandwich but dropped it.

"Okay," Adam said from underneath me. "First we deal with this, then we talk about your foul language."

Maybe death was the best outcome in this situation.

Adam sat up, gently pushing me off him.

The bird dropped the sandwich, turned its head, looked me dead in the eye, and clicked its beak.

I scrambled back onto Adam's lap.

"Charlie, you have to let me up." Adam tried to pry my hands off of him.

"No." I clung even harder.

"You've had chickens your whole life. You can't be afraid of birds."

"I can and I am."

"I need to get this bird out of your house, and I can't do that if you won't let me stand up."

"Fine." I slowly detached myself.

We'd barely even stood up when the crow flew straight toward us. Adam let out the highest-pitched squeal I've ever heard and dove for the floor, taking me with him.

Johnny laughed from the hallway.

It was at this point, Adam sprawled on top of me, my entire body covered in milk, Johnny laughing in the hallway, that my dad opened the back door.

The crow swooped again, grabbed Johnny's grilled cheese off the table, and flew out the door, skimming the top of Dad's head.

"What the fuck?" Dad ducked, throwing a hand up in the air. He turned to watch the crow fly off.

"Waddafuck," Angus said from the hall.

I let my face rest against the floor and decided to give up completely.

"That was a whole sentence!" Johnny said.

Back at Adam's, once Angus was asleep for the night, I sat hunched at the makeshift computer desk and typed as furiously as I could while also being as quiet as possible. A few nights before, I'd been working on a particularly troublesome section of my thesis when Angus had woken up and started crying. Adam blamed me and my aggressive typing. Said he could hear me from the other end of the house.

I minimized the Word document and tried refreshing the online search I'd done for the fifteenth time. The internet had been installed but the connection sucked. I was going to have to go to the library in Truro the next day and print off an entire website's worth of information. Worst of all, I didn't have a single elastic and was using a chip clip to keep my hair out of my face, which was giving me a headache. I thought if a single strand touched my neck right now I'd scream. I could have sworn I had a whole pack but I had a sneaking suspicion Angus had been hiding them around the house.

Over the weekend I'd had taken a break from thesis work to finalize my PhD application. Then I'd lain on the floor in crisis for a half an hour. I spent the rest of the week obsessing over tiny details of my thesis while simultaneously wanting to hand it in so I could be one step closer to never having to look at it again.

The front door closed and I looked up from the computer.

"Here." Adam tossed something at me. I tried to catch it but fumbled and it landed on the floor. I picked up the sleeve of hair elastics and looked at Adam. He shrugged, kicked off his boots, and went to his bedroom.

"Night," he called.

I held the elastics to my chest in the blue glow of the computer screen, unable to help the grin that spread across my face. I tried to quash it, because really, what woman in her twenties reacts this way to hair elastics? My stupid heart certainly didn't flutter over things like this. But I was hopelessly, embarrassingly smitten at that moment. I saved my work and went to bed with a smile on my face and tried to hate it, I really did.

seventy-three

THE RAIN CAME DOWN IN HEAVY SHEETS, HITTING THE WINDOWS with an aggressive pattering. So far, April had been day after day of showers. When the rain wasn't likely to drown us Angus and I would go outside and jump in puddles. But today had been a constant downpour. Adam had said he would take care of supper, but filled with restless energy, I'd decided to make a pie. I sat on the floor next to the oven and waited for the filling to bubble. Angus drove a car into my foot. I'd laid his car mat out on the kitchen floor while I'd made the pie. I had to step over him as I moved about the kitchen. Angus sprawled on the mat, moving his dinkies back and forth, while I'd described in detail how I was making the pie. Adam and I were constantly narrating our lives in the hopes it would encourage Angus to talk more. I often found myself doing it when I was all alone.

Adam came through the back door, rain dripping off his jacket and onto the floor.

"Dada!"

Adam slipped off his jacket before he picked Angus up and hugged him tight. "Okay I went to the store and grabbed some things. I figured you needed to fuel up to finish your thesis." He'd been treating my thesis like the hockey playoffs. My unshaved legs were the equivalent of a playoff beard.

Adam set Angus back on the ground and put all the food in a line on the counter. "Do you think you'll finish tonight?" he asked.

"I hope so." My thesis was basically done. Now it was just a matter of going over it to make sure I'd cited everything and hadn't spelled anything incorrectly.

Adam pulled the last item out of the first bag and placed it by the others. It was a lot of my favourite foods from when I was a teenager. Bagel Bites, Kraft Dinner, and Dunkaroos.

"Wow, I really had a refined palate in high school."

"Charlie, I know for a fact you still eat all of these things."

"Among other things. There's nothing wrong with Bagel Bites."

Adam looked skeptical. "I genuinely have no idea how you and Johnny never got scurvy."

"There's tomato sauce on the bagels."

"You cannot be serious."

"Of course not." I was.

Adam reached for the second bag. "Because I know you *are* serious, I also got broccoli and oranges. Your body will probably go into shock, so maybe just have a small amount."

"Ha. Ha," I said, opening up a pack of Dunkaroos.

Angus walked over to me.

"Peas," he said, reaching for them.

"He really is your child," Adam said as he grabbed a baking tray from the cupboard.

After our totally balanced supper and two episodes of *Little Bear*, I gave Angus a bath while Adam cleaned the kitchen. Adam put Angus to bed so that I could start working. At some point, Adam went to bed. When I finally looked up, the only light in the house came from the glow of the computer screen.

My hands hovered above the keyboard, ready to continue typing, but I was done. I sat back. It was 1:30 in the morning. I looked around the living room like I was a stranger who'd appeared out of thin air. How did I exist in this space if I wasn't writing my thesis? There must be something else to do, something I'd forgotten. A typo. An awkwardly phrased sentence. I stared at the document on the blue-lit computer screen. Maybe I should read it one more time. But what would that really achieve?

"Are you done?" Adam asked from behind me.

"Jesus!" I yelped, jumping in my chair. "You scared the shit out of me."

"Well, are you?"

"Yeah, how'd you know?"

"The typing. It never stops." He paused. "It finally stopped."

I stretched in the chair.

"Come outside," Adam said, leaving the living room.

"Okay..." I got up, glancing back at the computer before following him.

Adam shuffled outside, something hidden behind his back. I quietly closed the porch door. The rain had stopped a few hours ago.

"Ta da!" Adam said, holding a bottle of champagne in front of him. "I worried we'd wake Angus up if we opened it in the house. Better safe than sorry, right?"

"Did you stay up for this?" I asked, my heart doing a weird thing I tried to ignore.

"No, it was the typing."

I rolled my eyes.

"I'm not kidding, it haunts me. I literally have dreams where it's just the sound of you typing," Adam fiddled with the wire on top, then held the bottle out. "Ready?"

I was.

The cork made a quiet popping sound and landed on the step, barely clearing the back porch. Adam and I stood there, staring at it.

"Well, that was a bit anti-climactic," he said.

I covered my mouth, trying not to laugh.

I did a bad job.

Adam grinned. "I was a little skeptical when I bought it. Who knew Doug's carried this stuff." He looked at the bottle. "It looked kind of old, and not in a good way."

I laughed harder.

"Maybe I should've sprung for a more expensive bottle." Adam took a sip and grimaced. "I definitely should've gotten a nicer bottle." He handed it to me.

"Stop, I can't breathe." I took the bottle from him and sat on the porch step next to the cork. Once I'd calmed down, I took a sip. It tasted like nail polish remover and dust. I gagged after forcing myself to swallow it. "This feels more like a punishment instead of a celebration."

Adam sat down beside me. "I tried my best," he said.

"Thank you. For this."

"I can't tell if you're being sarcastic or not."

"I'm serious. It's just my voice. You know how it gets when I'm trying to be sincere." I always sounded like a teen-soap actor when I tried to be genuine.

Adam hummed in agreement. He took the bottle from me and chugged. "Oh my god," he groaned when he was done. "If we chug it, it'll be over faster."

"We could just not drink it?"

"I spent twenty bucks on this, we have to drink it."

"Okay, just wait." I went back inside and got us two slices of pie.

Adam and I sat on his back porch steps for another half hour, the cork between us. Eating pie and drinking cheap champagne and laughing until our stomachs hurt.

seventy-four

I STOOD IN THE EMPTY HALLWAY OUTSIDE DR. GAMBLE'S CLOSED door. I had just handed in the final draft of my thesis. Before that, I'd submitted my application to the PhD program. I felt stalled, like all the momentum that had been carrying me forward for the last year had suddenly stopped. I didn't know how to exist without the pressure of my thesis hanging over me. But I had something new to stress about.

Actually defending my thesis.

I had carried a copy of it around for months. Scribbling, rewriting, reading aloud to myself. To have given it away, to not be able to change anything, put me on edge. What if I'd made a mistake? What if I hadn't noticed egregious typos? What if I'd blacked out and written something offensive? I couldn't even properly spiral; my brain was too tired. A door opened down the hall and snapped me out of my paralysis. I adjusted the straps of my backpack and left campus behind.

I stopped at Billy's grave on the way to Adam's. Despite spending most of my time in the last few months within ten minutes of the cemetery, I hadn't visited in a while. The loss of Billy still snuck up on me in unexpected ways—a commercial, a smell, a moment I wanted to share with him—and I'd be confronted with a harsh new wave of grief.

When I was a kid, I went swimming in the ocean and got pulled under by the tides. I was tossed about and I didn't know which way was up or if I would ever breathe again. My dad had yanked me out of the water by the back of my bathing suit. I hung suspended in the air, blinking against the bright sun. I sputtered and cried and tried to gulp air into my lungs.

These moments of grief felt a lot like that.

I weaved my way through the graves, trying not to step where I thought bodies might be.

"Hey," I said, stopping in front of Billy's grave. "Long time, no see."

I gave him time to reply. The wind gushed through the trees. A bird took off into the sky. The world moved around us.

"Sorry I haven't been for a while." I stayed quiet for a moment. "I don't have a lot to say right now. I just handed in my thesis and I kind of want to crawl into a dark hole and never leave." I looked down at the ground in front of me. "Maybe that was an insensitive thing to say, given your current resting place." It wasn't normally this awkward to talk to Billy. "You know what, I'm being weird. I'm just feeling bad because I don't come see you enough. Life just gets in the way. There's always so much to do and I don't want you to fall to the wayside but you do, and I feel real shitty about that. Adam tells me that I love to feel shitty about things. He says it's my natural state to feel bad about something."

A crow cawed from somewhere in the trees. I flinched.

"Yeah, I don't really know what's going on with Adam. I don't really want to talk about it, and since I'm the only one talking, we won't."

The sun came out from behind a cloud. I closed my eyes and tilted my head up. I tried to picture Billy as I wanted to remember him: laughing and full of life. Not the puffy shell of him I'd last seen at his funeral. Sometimes I couldn't help but think about how I'd stood on the edge of the Cobequid Bay and asked Creator to keep Billy safe and then Billy had ended up dead. Was already dead when I tipped that tobacco into the churning water. Maybe I should have defined what I meant by safe. Though I guess Billy could never hurt now.

"Okay," I said, opening my eyes, tears in the corners. "I'm going to go. I won't take as long to come back next time, promise."

seventy-five

MY THESIS DEFENSE WAS IN TWO DAYS, SO ANGUS AND I WENT back to the city. Adam had some things to finish up at work before he came to stay with us so I could panic and spiral and prepare without the added stress of parenting alone. I told him I'd be fine; he said he'd be there by six.

When I told Fiona, she'd smiled and whispered, "one bed," rather triumphantly. She looked crestfallen when I suggested she stay with Mac so Adam and I could sleep separately. As we had been doing for months.

That first day, I spent hours pacing the living room, going over any possible questions the thesis committee could throw at me.

"What of the decline of shipyards?" I muttered, only to pivot and begin walking in the other direction while expounding on the transition from wood to steel and the Long Depression beginning in 1873.

Fiona danced around the living room, Angus in her arms, chanting: "Mommy is brave. Mommy is good. Mommy's gonna kill it like we knew she would."

Angus giggled in her arms, his laugh a brief salve.

seventy-six

"YOU HAVE A CHICKEN FEATHER ON YOUR SWEATER."

Dr. Gamble sighed, plucked the feather off his sweater and put it on the desk between us. "You know, you agree to a couple of laying hens and before you know it you've got an entire flock, rooster and all."

"You have chickens?"

"I have an entire barnyard of animals. I knew there would be a commute to work when I agreed to a hobby farm, but I wasn't aware there'd be so many stray feathers."

"I assumed you lived in the city." I picked up the feather.

"No, no, my wife made it very clear early on in our relationship that she would live nowhere near a city."

I twirled the feather. "The commute must be terrible."

I thought of my own drives into the city. The scenery that flew by as I followed the old highway, tracing the dips and curves of Cobequid Bay. The drive into the city a few days ago with Adam at the wheel, his raspy, off-key voice as he sang along with the radio, Angus dozing in his car seat. Not so terrible.

"Sure," said Dr. Gamble, "but life without her would be even more terrible. And I'm lucky because I don't have to commute every day. Neither would you. You may find, depending on your schedule, that you don't have to be in the city as often as you think next year. But"—he slapped his thighs—"I am getting ahead of myself. How are you feeling about your defense?"

"Like I would rather keel over and die."

"Ah, you'll be fine. I would've told you if I thought otherwise. I know you're nervous now, and that that feeling will intensify once you're in the midst of your defense. But remember, Charlotte, you've been working toward this goal for years. You are here. You made it. Try to savour it, even just a little."

I brought it home with me. I didn't mean to, but as I unloaded my books and notepads from my backpack, the chicken feather floated onto my desk. I looked at it and thought of what Dr. Gamble had said about long-term stuff, about what I wanted and what I could have in my future.

There were things I didn't even want to hope for, dreams taking root that I wanted to plan for, but first I had to get through tomorrow.

seventy-seven

THE ENTIRETY OF THE LAST TWO YEARS CAME DOWN TO THIS. All the late nights and coffee you could stand your pen up in, the tear-stained notes and overdue library fees, poopy diapers and nursing while reading history books the size of my baby.

My hands shook as I moved the binder containing my thesis off to the side.

Three people sat across from me: Dr. Gamble, the history department chair, and a second prof, who I'd had in second year. I'd once had a ten-minute-long conversation with the chair where I'd had to use all my brain power to not stare at the spinach stuck in his teeth. The prof from my undergrad was incredibly smart and one time I saw her at the grocery store wearing an Alanis Morisette shirt. So I guess they cancelled each other out.

The room was silent. I could only hear my own breath.

"Should I—should I just begin?"

"Please," the chair gestured toward me.

"My research looks at socio-economic decline and subsequent out-migration in Colchester County." I tried to steady my voice. "Paying particular attention to the now near-obsolete community of Castlereagh. By the 1890s, Castlereagh boasted a schoolhouse, post office, and a church. In 1895 the Fossil Flour Co. Ltd was founded and a pole railway system covering a distance of ten miles was opened. The community was flourishing. By 1995, one hundred years later, Castlereagh was nothing more than a dirt road up a mountain, a handful of seasonal camps and sugar shacks, and an abandoned, derelict graveyard. What influences, both within and outside this community, caused such a drastic decline in this one-hundred-year period? When did Castlereagh become a place without a future, and can these findings serve as a projection for the rest of Colchester County in years to come?"

I took a breath and tried to savour the moment.

I sat on the floor across from the examining room. The hallway was quiet. I had nothing to distract me from reviewing every stumble or slip-up I might've made in the last hour and in my thesis paper. I started to pinch the skin at my wrists but stopped myself, shaking my hands out, then rubbing my eyes.

Each thesis committee member had asked a few questions which I was pretty sure I'd answered; I tried to recall what exactly I had said.

The door across the hall opened. Dr. Gamble poked his head out. "We're ready."

I stood up and tried to wipe the floor dust off my pants. I'd pass or I'd fail; either way, I didn't want a dusty bum. I followed Dr. Gamble back into the room.

"Congratulations, Charlotte," Dr. Gamble said, smiling. "While we have a few notes, we're happy to say you've passed. We were quite impressed with your research."

Two years of tension flooded out of my body. It was a miracle I remained upright.

"You're very articulate," Alanis T-shirt added. Did she seem surprised?

I plastered a smile on my face, but I wasn't sure how to take that as a compliment.

Spinach stepped forward. "Truly, congratulations. We understand you've applied for your PhD. Take some much-needed time off before you receive the results of your application."

"I will, thank you."

Dr. Gamble clapped me on the back as he left the room with Spinach.

"You know, apparently I have some Native ancestors," Alanis T-shirt said.

She smiled as I slipped my backpack on.

"Oh," I said, trying to sound enthused.

"Yes, my great-great-great-grandmother was Micmac. I did my genealogy last summer."

"Yeah, I guess that's something you..." I struggled for something to say. "...oughta know."

I walked into the glaring afternoon light. My knees were wobbly.

"There she is!" Adam said, waving.

"Mama! Mama!" Angus cheered from Adam's shoulders. He waved a bouquet of flowers so wildly petals fell to the sidewalk.

Steadying Angus with one arm, Adam pulled me in for a hug and planted a kiss on my temple. "Congratulations," he said.

"How do you know I didn't blow it?"

Adam rolled his eyes.

"Mama!" Angus shook the flowers from up high.

I smiled up at him. "Hey, buddy, I missed you."

"Snack?" he said, shaking the flowers. There'd be no petals left by the time we got back to Adam's.

"Want to get something to eat?" Adam asked me.

"I could eat."

Adam smiled at me, the corners of his eyes crinkling.

"You have flower petals in your hair," he said.

"So do you."

seventy-eight

I WALKED THROUGH THE NEAR-FINISHED MUSEUM, GLANCING AT each display, Angus on my hip. Beau fiddled with something at the front desk.

The museum detailed the history of Colchester Country from the time the first Europeans settled to modern day. A lot of the documents were materials I'd studied for my thesis; I recognized names and family trees. A copy of a Dutch settler's 1758 land grant. A black-and-white photo of a farmer and his cow circa 1912 (the cow's name was Eunice). A book of local recipes called *Country Cooks* that was part of a fundraiser for the women's church choir in 1986. By the time I'd looked at everything, I thought I'd have a permanent crease in my brow.

I went back to where I'd started and looked at everything again, this time with more care. Angus played with the buttons on my shirt.

"Hey, Beau," I called when I'd finished.

He looked up.

"Where's all the stuff about the Mi'kmaq?"

The silence echoed.

"Are there still boxes out back?" I looked around for an empty display case I might've missed.

"Uh. I wasn't—well, that is—I didn't—"

There was no stuff. Not a single thing about the original inhabitants of this land.

I tried to think of a joke I could make so I didn't have to acknowledge my hurt feelings, so I could lessen the sting of my accusation. I liked Beau, I didn't want to make him uncomfortable. But at the same time, he'd apparently left half my family out of the town's history. This land where they'd lived since time immemorial.

"The Salmon River and the Cobequid Bay were both important waterways for the Mi'kmaq. You mention both of those places, but don't bring Mi'kmaw people up at all."

I shifted my weight from one foot to the other and adjusted Angus. The historical society were the ones who'd forgotten, but I was the one who was bringing it up, and by doing so I was making it an issue rather than an omission.

"I'm sorry, Charlotte." Beau leaned against the desk. "It honestly didn't occur to me. The museum is meant to tell the history of the town, from when it was established. I didn't think that we'd forgotten anything." Beau looked around at the crowded tables and shelves. "I can make room if you'd like to put something together." He smiled. "Maybe over there? He pointed to a shelf in the corner. "I was going to put some books on the military there...but I can find room for them somewhere else."

I wanted to tell him it wasn't good enough. That he should've remembered even if I wasn't here to ask about it. That I shouldn't have to cobble together my own display as an afterthought. My ancestors deserved more than that.

But I already felt uncomfortable. So instead I said "sure," made an excuse about Angus needing to nap, and left.

The drive from the museum to my parents' house was just long enough for me to begin to spiral. Angus babbled in the back seat. He clapped his hands and asked for a snack.

"Snack? Snack?" He clapped his hands again. He had thankfully moved on from curse words to demanding food twenty-four-seven.

"We're almost home, buddy," I promised. I was on the verge of tears, and couldn't tell if they were angry or sad.

I thought again about the materials in the museum. What had been deemed important enough to display. I'd recognized nearly everything. I knew this information like it was my entire life story: dates of important events, what resources had been produced where and when and by whom.

What did that say about my research?

Once I'd fed Angus lunch, I brought him up to my bedroom to play. Dad had asked for my help with something and when I showed up, he wasn't ready. I'd been annoyed.

"Indian time," he said, shrugging his shoulders.

While Angus stacked blocks and drove dinkie cars around, I pulled out the box of documents I'd left here after I'd finished my thesis. I flipped through the pages and pages of research I had accumulated over the last several months. Personal accounts. Chapters from history books. Stacks of photocopied pictures. It was all white. The people being discussed. The people writing the books. The people in the photographs.

There were no Mi'kmaw people. No evidence, except in passing reference, that they existed.

I sat at the end of my bed and stared at a photo of the Bass River Imperial Brass Band. A line of sombre-faced white men stared back at me.

Sure, Beau had left Mi'kmaw people out of his display, which wasn't okay. But hadn't I done the same thing, by centring my thesis around people who'd "settled" the area? I bent the corner of the paper back and forth. Even the word *settled* erased the trauma my ancestors endured. It implied something calm and gentle and natural. The way dust settles.

I wasn't a full-blooded Mi'kmaw. I was mixed. Some of my ancestors were settlers. My mom's Irish family fled Britain's colonization and the potato famine in 1849. Dad's dad was Irish. I guess I could say I was Irish. But that wasn't how it worked. I didn't live in Ireland. I lived here, in Mi'kma'ki. I grew up with my Mi'kmaw family. Here, in Mi'kma'ki. I wasn't a fraction. Full, half, quarter. I wasn't a mixed-breed dog. I was L'nu. I didn't speak the language. Most of my cousins on the rez didn't either. I grew up Catholic like all good Mi'kmaw and Irish folks. I knew what the sacred medicines were but not always what to do with them or the cultural protocols to follow. Though I knew damn well to respect my Elders. My identity wasn't based on my status card or my brown hair and tan skin. I looked at Angus making *vroom* sounds with his dinkie. It was about my family. Past and future. I might not have the traditional knowledge when it came to ceremony, but that wasn't my skill set.

I was a historian. And I could research the shit out of stuff.

I'd centred my thesis around the people who colonized this part of Nova Scotia. But what about the people who were forcibly removed? I thought of "Phillip the Old Indian," and how I'd immediately discarded him, how little care I'd afforded his story. I'd been more concerned with the two British men discussing him as if he was a caricature. My body felt hot. I pinched the skin on my wrists before shoving my hands underneath myself. I'd been trying to stop.

I thought about the classes I'd taken, the mentors I'd been offered, the areas of study accessible to me: they all supported whiteness; they circled around the notion that white history and white perspective was what needed to be perpetuated.

And I'd readily gone along with it. I was so eager to please, so desperate to succeed, I'd forgotten to think critically about what I was learning. Especially in the last year; I had stopped speaking up in class because it was easier.

My ancestors would be so pissed.

Angus walked over and raised his arms high. "Uppie! Uppie!" He hopped in place.

My existential crisis would have to wait until after bedtime.

seventy-nine

AFTER THE FRIGID MONOTONY OF WINTER, SPRING FELT LIKE A blessing. The sun's tepid rays had melted the last of the snow; the yellowing grass, flattened and half mud, was now giving way to bursts of bright green. We were nearing the end of Penatmuiku's, Birds Laying Eggs Time. I could feel the promise of summer: warmth, life, and more than a few hours of sunlight a week.

Angus and I had been staying at Adam's ever since my thesis defense. Adam and I didn't discuss what it meant, but all kinds of questions gnawed at me. Where were we headed, and what would happen if I was accepted into the PhD program? I didn't know how to broach the subject; I didn't even know what I wanted. I had no real reason to stay with Adam anymore and we both knew it, but I didn't want whatever this was to end.

Angus stomped through a puddle, mud speckling his pants. I fought the urge to tell him to stop; he should be allowed to get dirty, even if I dreaded the cleanup later.

"Dad?" I called out.

He stuck his head out of his workshop. A new Mi'kmaw band called Forever was playing on his stereo. "What's up? I'm still not ready for your help yet."

"Can we talk for a second?"

"Sure." He brushed his hair, now past his shoulders, out of his face and walked over.

I told him about the museum, about my own research and how I'd let us down.

"Can you imagine what Nan would say if I told her I let some white guy talk shit about Mi'kmaw people and didn't say anything?"

Dad clicked his tongue. "Don't tell her then."

"I wasn't planning on it, I'm just saying." Angus handed me a rock. "Thanks, bud," I said, slipping it into my pocket. "I'm just disappointed in myself. But I'm also disappointed in everyone around me. Like, does no one care? It makes me not want to go back there."

Dad shrugged. "Institutions aren't made for us, Charlie. They're made to keep us out. Or, if they can't do that, they make us feel so unwelcome we can't help but leave."

Dad accepted the gift of a stick from Angus. "Thanks, kwis."

My dad wasn't one to complain. I'd never heard him speak like this before. It hit a nerve in me. "Is that why you dropped out of high school?" I asked.

He sighed, twirling the stick in his hand. "I left school for a number of reasons. But a lot of those reasons came from not feeling welcome in those rooms. People were pretty up front with their racism. They hide it better today. I think I even ended up believing a lot of it, you know? Like, I was lesser. Not as smart."

I thought of Maddie and her assumption that I wasn't good enough. That I'd been let in to grad school because of a singular checkmark and not years of effort. We were all just butting heads against the same barriers, the same assholes, the same fucked-up assumptions, generation after generation. I felt tired and enraged and like every part of me was stretched out beyond myself. I was smackdab in the middle of seven generations. I was holding hands with my ancestors while trying to push forward for those who'd come after me. I was standing in my parents' backyard feeling called in a hundred different directions when all I wanted to do was take off my shoes and sink my feet into the mud.

We both watched Angus totter towards the chicken coop. "Bock-bocks!" he said, pointing.

"You're never going to belong," Dad said. "But you're white enough they'll trust you." He scratched his jaw. "You can blend better than I could."

I knew he was right. My skin was lighter than my dad's. Lighter than Johnny's, even. And my proximity to whiteness made me more palatable. I thought back to the prof at my thesis defense trying to tell me she was Mi'kmaw too.

"You can speak the way they do," Dad continued, "but you'll never be one of them. You can't ever exist in that space without feeling outside it. But they'll let you in. And you gotta use that. You can make a difference by being there. Even if it's just telling people when they're being shitty."

"Is that what I should tell my profs when they're being obviously racist?"

Dad shrugged. "If it's true."

I watched Angus as he spoke to the chickens in their coop. God knows what he was saying to them. "I don't know that I want to be that person, though. It feels so daunting. And there's no one else like us there, Dad. No profs. No other grad students. It's like we don't even exist." I'd never tried to articulate my feeling of otherness to someone before. My dad seemed like the safest space to start.

"That's why it's so important you're there. You don't have anyone to guide you. You gotta bushwhack your way through all the crap. But you can help keep the path clear for others after you. You can be the person you don't have for someone else in the future."

I groaned. "Why do I have to be a trailblazer when every other person just gets to be a grad student?"

"Tough shit, kid." He started writing something in the ground with the stick.

"Whenever I say something the air changes, Dad. I hate it. No matter what I say it's like I challenge the ground that they stand on."

"That's because you do." He squeezed my shoulder before heading back into his workshop.

I looked down at the ground. With the stick he'd written one word.

Paniaq.

Spring begins.

I walked beside Angus down the road back to Adam's house. Angus loved this walk because we passed a pasture of cows he was obsessed with; he'd named them Nan, Doodoo, and Cow. I was a little worried how Angus would react come November when Dad killed the family pig. Maybe this year we'd put a stop to it. One could hope.

"Bye cows," Angus yelled for the tenth time.

A mail truck passed us as we walked at a snail's pace. The driver waved and we waved back. Done with school, I tried to make my days with Angus as slow as possible. I made the crepes I promised him I would. We read books on the porch swing. We lay on the grass and watched the clouds float by.

If I got into the PhD program, I would have to find a way to hold on to these slow and tender moments while reentering the world of academia. Walking down the road, the warm May wind brushing my skin, it felt possible. But I knew myself, and I didn't think I'd feel the same when I was elbow-deep in the archives.

We stopped and I opened the mailbox. I handed the flyers to Angus. There was an envelope from Dalhousie at the bottom of the pile. I opened it up and scanned the letter.

Angus skipped farther up the driveway, swinging his arms back and forth, the flyers still in his hands. He dropped one and then picked it up.

Standing at the foot of the driveway, I could see the next few years start to take shape. There were a lot of questions, but an equal number of promises. Beneath the thrum of excitement was the lingering discomfort I felt knowing all I'd done during my master's was conform to a colonial institution. I held the acceptance letter in one hand and the knowledge that I had to do better in the other.

eighty

"HOW DOES HE HAVE SO MUCH ENERGY? MY EYELIDS FEEL LIKE they're made of concrete." Adam and I sat on a large piece of driftwood and watched Angus totter along the shoreline.

"Is this a forever thing?" Adam leaned forward, elbows resting on his legs.

Angus had been waking up at 4:30 A.M. for the last week. It was horrible. Adam and I had tried to trade off sleeping in, but Angus was so loud it was impossible to go back to sleep.

"I really hope not," I said. "I got lulled into a false sense of security with those eight hours a night." The sun was just beginning to peek above the horizon. We'd come to the beach in the near dark, hoping the air off the bay would prove more effective than coffee.

Angus picked up a rock and flung it into the air.

"Angus, no!" Adam yelled, lurching forward, as if he could catch the rock from twenty feet away. The rock landed, missing Angus's head, but Adam was already halfway there. He put his hands on his knees and panted. "I feel like I just sprinted a kilometre. What is wrong with me? Am I dying?"

"You know they use sleep deprivation as a torture tactic, right?"

Adam flopped down on the beach and looked up at the sky, arms spread out. Angus picked up something from the shoreline and brought it to me.

"Wow, that's beautiful," I said, accepting a smooth piece of blue sea glass from him. "Can you find anything else?" I asked Angus. He looked up at me. The rising sun caught on his curls, making them look redder than they usually did. His hair had darkened since he was a baby. It was lighter than mine, though not by much, but when the sun hit his hair, it was a rich auburn. Angus went off in search of treasures.

Adam eventually gathered enough energy to get up, and we followed Angus down the beach. I didn't feel any less tired, but watching the sunrise over the bay made me feel okay. I didn't want to see the sunrise every day of my life, but I was glad to see this one.

Angus fell asleep as soon as we pulled away from the beach, Adam and I drove in silence. I fiddled with the radio until I found a station playing "These Days" by Nico. I sat back and watched the scenery roll by.

"Can you pull over?" I asked Adam when we neared the church.

Without asking why, he pulled into the church parking lot. I hopped out of the truck and made my way to Billy's grave, half of Angus's finds in my pocket. The sun rose behind the trees, warm light stretched through the trunks, falling on the headstones.

"Hey," I said, stopping at Billy's grave. The first year after Billy had been buried, the grass on top of him had looked different than the rest. Newer. More tentative. The blades struggling to break through the dirt. Now, his grave looked like all the rest.

"I brought you something." I fished a handful of rocks from my pocket. "Look at this one." I put the blue sea glass on top of the gravestone. "Pretty, eh?"

I put another one next to the blue sea glass. "I think this one has a little fossil. Maybe it's just a weird indent. I can never tell. Remember that time you thought you found dinosaur footprints and they were just weirdly shaped rocks?" I could hear the laugh in my voice. "Here's another one. It kind of looks like a heart." I placed it on the ground, and hoped the grass would still find a way to grow.

eighty-one

FIONA SIGHED ON THE OTHER END OF THE LINE. "I HAVE SOMEthing to tell you and you're not going to like it."

"What?" I sat down on one of Adam's kitchen chairs. He was outside with Angus and the house was quiet.

"Mac asked me to move in with him."

"Oh. Wow. That's...great. Do you want to?"

She laughed. "Charlie, you sound like I just gave you an unmedicated root canal."

"I do not. I'm serious, it's exciting."

"You suck at pretending to be enthusiastic."

"This is just my voice."

Adam came through the back door with Angus.

"I told him I would," she said quietly.

Why did I feel like dying? This was good. I was happy for her.

What's wrong? Adam mouthed.

Nothing, I mouthed back.

"Are *you* happy about it?" I asked.

"I am. And it seems like a natural step. You've been home so much and I've been spending all my time in his apartment. It feels like a good time to make it official. And I'll just be downstairs. Practically still in the apartment. You can just yell down when you need me! I'll come up all the time. I can watch Angus, same as before."

"Why do I feel like I'm being coddled?"

"Because you need to be coddled, Charlie. You hate change."

I thought about how different my life looked now compared to when Fiona and I first moved in together. "That's not true. I love change."

"No, you don't," Adam and Fiona said at the same time.

"Well, I'm happy for you," I said, ignoring both them and my sudden need to cry.

"Angus can have his own room!" Fiona said, eternally peppy.

Angus had a room at my parents', at Adam's, and now at my apartment. What child needed three rooms? Was this a sign of luxury or an unstable upbringing? Was Angus's constant crib-hopping creating problems that would only come to light years down the road?

"Charlie?" Fiona said loudly.

"Yes?" She could always tell when I was in my head.

"Call me tomorrow when you've had time to digest this and we can talk about it more then."

I grimaced. Not that she could see it.

"Love you," Fiona said before hanging up.

I really was happy for her, I told myself. I liked Mac. He was a good person and her boyfriend, not a homewrecker. Fiona and I couldn't live together forever. At some point we would outgrow our shitty apartment.

We already had, I just hadn't realized it.

eighty-two

"ARE WE READY TO PAAAAARTY?" JOHNNY YELLED AS HE CAME through Adam's front door.

I looked up from where I lay, half asleep on the couch. I had crumpled here after my conversation with Fiona. Adam had decided he would drop Angus off at my parents' and I would be forced to have fun for the rest of the day.

So here we were: childfree and, according to Johnny, ready to party.

Sadie came in behind Johnny, four pizza boxes in her arms. "Johnny went overboard," she said, loading the boxes onto the table.

Adam grabbed a slice and then disappeared down the hallway. Johnny brought four beers into the living room, a joint between his fingers.

"Aren't you driving tonight?" I asked.

"Calm down, I'll have one beer and then I'm done. And I will chauffeur whoever wherever whenever."

"And the joint?" I asked.

"For whoever wants it, Safety Sam." Johnny put the beers on the table.

Adam reemerged, Monopoly in his hands. I sat up so fast blood rushed to my head. This was a terrible idea. This damn game hacked away at our happy memories and tender feelings towards one another until someone ended up crying, yelling, or excommunicated from the family.

I tried to motion for Adam to put the game away before someone saw him. But it didn't work. Johnny caught sight of it and a competitive gleam overtook him. He clapped his hands together.

"Dibs on being banker!" he called before Adam had even made it to the living room.

About an hour in, Adam bought a property Johnny had been eyeing. On his next turn, Johnny landed on Adam's newly acquired property.

Adam leaned back in his chair. "You're looking a little strapped for cash there, bud."

"I'm fine." Johnny's shoulders were practically touching his ears.

"I can give you a grace period, but there'll be interest."

A vein in Johnny's neck throbbed.

I took a long sip of beer. I hadn't drunk since Billy's funeral and everything was feeling fuzzy. Johnny had bought some generic brand that tasted like water and I was on my third one. Was I being irresponsible? What if something happened to Angus and I was too buzzed to parent properly?

"Charlie?"

"Huh?" I looked up.

"It's your turn." Sadie was holding out the die.

"Oh. Um, I need to call Mom to check on Angus. Adam, can you roll for me?"

"Not allowed," Johnny said. "If you're not going to roll, you can't play."

"That's stupid, I just won't play then."

"Okay so your properties are fair game."

"No, I bequeath all of my *one* property to Adam."

Johnny crushed his beer can in one hand. "You can't do that."

"Yes, I can." I was halfway to the phone.

"Guys? I don't think it's a big deal if Adam rolls for Charlie."

At the sound of Sadie's voice, Johnny blinked and snapped out of some kind of trance borne from an innate desire to win. He rubbed his hands on his denim-clad thighs and took a bracing breath. "Sure, yeah, you're right."

What a marvel to witness the power of love.

Sadie handed Adam the dice and he rolled for me.

"How is he?" Adam asked as I hung up. He slouched against the entrance to the kitchen, his shoulder pressed against the doorframe.

"Sleeping. Mom told me to stop calling." It was only my fifth time.

Adam huffed. "She raised you and Johnny—don't you trust her?"

"That's exactly why I don't trust her. We were unhinged."

"You still are."

"Hey." We laughed as I gently shoved Adam's shoulder. He swayed more than he should have.

Adam watched me as I leaned against the counter, standing just a little closer than was proper, and then he reached out and cupped my face in his hands. His palms were warm against my cheeks, and I sank into his touch. I'd drunk just enough that this seemed like a natural response. Why wasn't he constantly cupping my face? I could probably achieve many a thing while being held like this.

I closed my eyes.

Why wasn't he always this tender?

But then again…I thought about the endless things he'd done for me: the rooftop chips and sandwich (it didn't matter that he'd eaten half of it), the study snacks and morning coffee, the regular oil checks he didn't know I knew about, the way he held Angus—a part of both of us that disturbingly existed outside our bodies—reverently and gently.

I thought about all the ways we tell people we care without saying it out loud. But what had I done? What did I ever do to deserve such tenderness?

I don't know who closed the gap first, but the feeling of his beard against my skin and the nip of his teeth against my lip felt like coming home. It was familiar and painful and comforting and I wanted to stay in this moment forever.

Adam hoisted me onto the counter and pressed into me. I wrapped my legs around his waist, heat pooling at my centre. He slipped his hand under my shirt, calloused fingers brushing against the soft skin of my stomach.

Johnny sang "We Are the Champions" loudly from the other room, and we jolted apart.

I sighed and rested my head against Adam's sternum. Eventually, I looked up at him. He pressed his lips to my forehead.

"Are we such emotionally stunted assholes that we can only be honest when we're drunk?" I asked.

"That was a fancy sentence for someone claiming drunkenness."

"I have a master's degree, I'm eternally fancy." I furrowed my brow. "*Inherently*. I meant inherently. Whatever. Next time you kiss me, we better be sober."

"Um, you kissed me."

"I did no such thing."

"Are you guys ever going to come back? I'm this close to beating Sadie!" Johnny yelled.

"If I didn't kiss you and you didn't kiss me, did we even kiss?" Adam asked, backing up a little. I leaned forward, the upper half of my body following him.

"It's probably easier if we didn't," I admitted.

"Is that what you really think?"

I wasn't sure. Adam went back to the living room and I stayed sitting on the counter.

I poured myself a glass of water, drank it all, and followed him.

Adam and I watched each other from across the table and I knew if I stayed the night, we'd end up having sex. There was a look in his eyes I hadn't noticed before.

Fiona was right.

Fucking yearning.

It reverberated through my body.

I wanted this. I wanted him. But not tonight. Not when we were drunk.

Johnny asked if I was ever going to take my turn, and I snapped out of whatever trance Adam and I were in.

Through all our bickering, Sadie quietly and consistently accrued more property and wealth. We didn't notice until the bitter end that she was ahead by a large margin.

"You're really doing well, babe," Johnny said, his eyes wide. The realization that his girlfriend was about to beat him ate Johnny alive. It killed him to smile and congratulate her while she stacked up all four railroads.

Eventually, and thankfully, we finished the game. I wasn't sure we'd ever actually finished a game before. Normally someone stomped off, cried at the table, or we all got bored.

"I won!" Sadie clapped her hands, blissfully unaware.

I believe something truly died in Johnny that night, or rather, maybe something new took root. It was a mark of newfound maturity that the table stayed upright, the evidence of Sadie's win neatly laid out in front of him.

"I'm going to go back to my parents' with Johnny," I told Adam. Johnny and Sadie were already outside. "I feel like if I stay here, we'll end up having sex and I don't want to do that right now. Not when we're drunk. Plus, I should be there in the morning. For Angus. You could come too." I blinked. "No—you shouldn't. Because of the sex."

Adam was a little slack-jawed and fuzzy. We stared at one another. Maybe I was drunker than I thought.

"Charlie?" Johnny called from the porch. "I'm leaving in two minutes, and I wait for no one."

"You don't want to have sex *right now*." Adam leaned closer to me. "But not never?"

This wasn't a conversation we should be having yet. We were a fresh wound, barely healed. But the nearness of him was intoxicating. I felt pulled to him by some gravitational force I didn't want to fight anymore.

"Charlie!" Johnny called again.

"Night, Adam," I said, stepping back.

I swayed a little on the way to the car, a reminder that we were both drunk and the kiss probably didn't mean anything.

Year Four

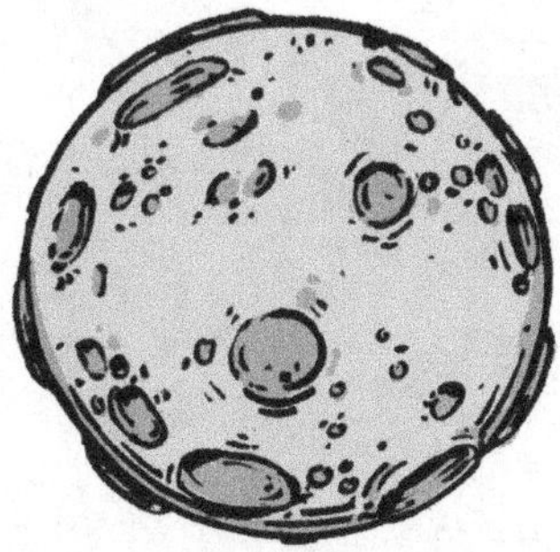

Peskewiku's

(Bes-gay-we-goos)

Birds Shedding Feathers Time

eighty-three

I RAN A KNIFE ACROSS THE TOP OF THE CAKE FOR THE THIRD TIME.

"I don't know how long she's been up," Johnny said from the hallway.

The recipe said to use an offset spatula, but what kind of asshole had one of those?

"But she won't stop baking. I don't know if she can." He was closer now.

The knife left tiny ridges in the icing.

"Shit." I was crouched in a half-squat, eye level with the cake.

Johnny walked into the kitchen backwards. "She seems a bit unhinged."

It had been twelve and a half hours since Adam and I kissed. And in another two weeks, I had a meeting scheduled with Dr. Gamble to discuss my research trajectory.

If I could just make the icing smooth everything would be okay. Dr. Gamble would help me figure out my new PhD path. Living without Fiona wouldn't feel like living without a limb. Angus would grow up to be a well-adjusted individual. And the kiss with Adam would either be forgotten or repeated; I wasn't sure which I wanted more. My hand slipped and the knife left a deep line in the icing.

Maybe smooth icing was outside the realm of possibility for me.

Adam followed behind Johnny. I stood up; my back screamed in protest. Adam smiled at me and my stomach dipped. Who was I kidding? Of course I wanted it repeated.

"Why are you making a wedding cake?" Adam asked.

"What? I'm not."

He pointed to my stress-baking project. "It's white and it's got tiers and everything."

"You guys getting married?" Johnny got an apple out of the fridge and bit into it.

"It's just a cake." I didn't even believe myself. My hungover brain had let me down.

Adam took in the mess behind me. The sink overflowed with dishes. On the counters sat a plethora of dough in various states of doneness.

"Are you…okay?" Adam asked slowly.

"Should someone get married?!" Johnny asked from behind.

"Well, um, I just—I started with a bread dough, but then I saw chocolate chips in the cupboard, so I started to make cookies. But then I forgot about the first bread dough and started to make a second. And then the cake—I don't know, I've just been thinking about cake." I brushed the icing-plastered hair out of my face.

"Are those pumpkin chocolate chip?" Adam reached for one.

"Yeah, I found an old can of pumpkin purée in the back of the pantry. It was only a little expired."

"They're my favourite." Adam took a bite.

"Oh, lucky for you." I knew they were.

"Do you need help?" he asked, finishing off the cookie.

"Like, mentally?" I asked.

"I meant cleaning the kitchen."

"Oh. No, it's fine."

"Hey Sadie," Johnny said into the phone. "Charlie made a wedding cake." There was a pause. "I don't know why. She's gone absolutely nuts." Another pause. "But I'm taking it as a sign that you and I should get married."

Before I could tell Johnny he was being an idiot, I heard a cry from upstairs. Adam started on the dishes as I left to get Angus.

"I can do those later," I said.

Adam waved me off and started to scrub a whisk.

Angus was trying his best to climb out of his crib, but stopped when he saw me. He raised his arms into the air.

"Morning, buddy."

"Mornin', Mama."

Once Angus started talking, the words hadn't stopped coming.

"You want some breakfast?" I asked.

Angus nodded his head. "Yeah. Hungy."

He wrapped his chubby little arms around my neck and rested his head on my shoulder. I held him a little tighter.

The timer on the oven went off as I came back into the kitchen. Still holding Angus, I took a second tray of cookies out of the oven.

Adam stopped what he was doing and kissed Angus on the head. He hovered for just long enough that I wondered if he was debating kissing my head as well.

Angus squirmed and reached out for his dad. I pointedly ignored the brief ache of disappointment in my chest as Adam took him from me.

Johnny had stretched the phone cord around the corner to finish his phone call. I tried to listen in, but he was talking too quietly.

I needed to figure out what I was going to say to Dr. Gamble. I should probably make a list. Head into the city early so I could fit some research in first.

Adam sat Angus in a chair at the kitchen table and as I fed him half a banana, I told Adam my plan.

Before he could respond, Johnny came back into the kitchen and hung up the phone.

"Don't eat the cake, 'kay? Sadie and I are getting married tomorrow."

"Ha. Ha." I peeled the rest of the banana for Angus.

Johnny leaned against the doorframe. "Who doesn't love an August wedding?"

I sat up straighter. "Are you serious? That's—you can't—don't you need a marriage license?"

Johnny shrugged. "We can legit get married some other time. Tomorrow, we party."

"Do you have food? Decorations?" I tried desperately to stop my mind from imploding.

"Nah. It'll all work out."

"How? How could it possibly work out?" I glanced at Adam, who had turned off the tap and was watching us. He didn't look at all concerned about the logistics.

"Will you guys be my groomsmen?"

I groaned. "Johnny, you can't have a wedding tomorrow."

"We can." He raised an eyebrow and I knew exactly how I would be spending the next twenty-four hours.

eighty-four

"THIS IS ABSOLUTELY NUTS," I SAID FOR WHAT HAD TO BE THE hundredth time since Adam and I had left my parents', Angus in tow. "Who does this?" I asked the wall of dollar-store decorations.

Adam sighed. "You did make a big white wedding cake, Charlie."

"I didn't mean to. It's only white because we didn't have any food colouring."

"Well, they probably took it as a sign. Sadie loves that shit. She's always trying to give me tarot readings."

"Seriously? What do they say?" I put a pile of decorative paper balls in the cart.

"The last one said I was going to live a long life, have a great love, and perfect health. The one before that said I was going to die tragically, there was something about a tower, and I was going to get a goat?"

The goat part seemed weirdly specific.

"I should get her to read my cards," I said, grabbing some streamers. "Maybe she could tell me what to do with my life."

"I thought you already knew what to do. Five-year plan and all."

"I think it's become painfully evident that while I may be able to craft a solid plan on paper, I have a horrible ability to follow through."

I took a dream catcher off the wall of poorly made trinkets. There was a photo of a wolf at its centre.

"Why is it that when I brought a dream catcher for show-and-tell in grade five, I got called a dumb Indian on the playground, but now everyone and their capitalist uncle are selling them?"

Angus reached for the dream catcher.

"I'm sorry, buddy, I cannot buy you this." I held it away from him. Angus whined. "Angus, this was probably made by a child not much older than you in a sweatshop somewhere. Your nan will make you one. A good one. Way better than this abhorrent monstrosity." I hung the dream catcher back up. Angus reached for it and whined even louder. Tears filled his eyes.

"Maybe we could buy it for him," Adam said.

I gaped at him. "We absolutely cannot."

Adam looked at the dream catcher and then at Angus, whose nose was now red, tears seconds away from spilling down his cheeks.

"But maybe..." Adam trailed off.

"No, no, no." I pushed the cart down the aisle. Angus reached toward the dream catcher like he was being forced to leave behind a beloved friend.

"But..."

"Angus, listen." I looked at Angus. "I will buy you anything else in this store. But I will not buy you that."

In the parking lot, Angus clutched the sweatshop dream catcher to his chest.

"As soon as he loses interest in that we are burning it," I told Adam.

Adam nodded. He hadn't even been the one to cave. Fiona would've called me a weak-ass bitch.

As we drove away, I watched Angus bring the dream catcher to his mouth and kiss it.

"Do you want help?" Adam asked from across the lawn.

"No, I'm fine." I was certain that if I tried hard enough, I could will my arm to stretch just a few more inches.

I chucked the strand of Christmas lights at the branch, hoping to clear the final gap, but the momentum from my throw caused the already unstable stepladder to tilt. I toppled to the ground and landed in a heap of limbs and lights. I rolled onto my back as all the air wheezed out of my lungs.

"Charlie! Are you okay?" Adam dashed across the lawn.

I scrunched up my nose. "I'm fine." The strand of lights hung haphazardly.

"You just fell off a damn ladder. For all I know you could be paralyzed."

I wiggled my body back and forth on the ground. "See? Fine. I can still do The Worm."

"You scared the shit out of me."

"Adam, I didn't exactly fall from a perilous height."

"I asked if you wanted help."

"Yeah, and I said I was fine."

Adam adjusted his baseball hat. "You don't have to be a damn martyr. You're allowed to let people help you."

He wasn't just talking about the lights. I sighed and closed my eyes. The moisture from the damp earth seeped through my sweater.

Adam lay down beside me.

"I want to help," he said, quieter this time. "I used to be the one you called when you needed help."

"I don't want to be a bother," I muttered. I thought of the past few months and how much I had relied on him. He'd told me repeatedly that I wasn't a burden. But I didn't really believe him. I needed to prove to myself that I could stand on my own two feet. Maybe just not on a stepladder.

"Charlie." Adam let my name hang in the air. "I thought we'd been through this."

The strand of lights slid off the branch and fell to the ground.

"Let me help you. Tell me what you want," Adam continued.

The list was long.

"I know you have a list."

I sighed. Sometimes having someone who knew you so well was a real nuisance.

"Okay, fine. I want to sleep past seven on a regular basis. I want to finish my coffee before it gets cold." I watched the clouds roll by. "I want to know I'm not wasting everyone's time with school; that it's not some stupid fucking venture. I want to do right by my ancestors. I want a pair of jeans that actually fits me. I read an article about the longevity of low-rise jeans the other day, and I'm scared, Adam. I need pants that go past my belly button. I want to wake up every day and know that I'm doing the right thing. Like I'm in the right moment and making the right choices for Angus."

I took a breath and focused on the solid ground beneath me, the way the earth supported my spine, how it held me. Not all that long ago it felt like my world had fallen apart, and now I was slowly building it back up again. "I want us to be the way we used to be, when I thought you might love me." Maybe I was concussed. "I want an endless supply of popcorn. I want Johnny to have a reasonable understanding of how much time it takes to plan and prepare for a wedding." Maybe if I kept talking, Adam wouldn't pick up on my most fragile and tender admission. I wet my lips and looked at the sky.

"You gonna look at me?"

"No. I'm paralyzed. Remember?"

"Charlie—"

The back door opened and Dad's voice carried across the lawn. "Charlie? What are you doing? Sadie is having a crisis in the bathroom and I need to use the commode."

I stood up.

Adam stayed lying down.

"I guess top of the list is these lights. Clearly, I am a squat troll who can't reach even the lowest-hanging branches. I'm going to deal with Sadie, and then I will come back to help."

I didn't give Adam a chance to respond before I hightailed it into the house.

eighty-five

ADAM AND MY DAD FINISHED HANGING UP THE CHRISTMAS lights while I helped Sadie with her hair. The store hadn't had enough of either type, so a canopy of mismatched lights, white and multicoloured, hung above us.

My cousin Ray fumbled with the stereo, trying to get the music to start. Static. Then loud bass. Then static again. He cursed and everyone laughed. I bounced Angus on my hip. He played with the beaded earrings Darlene had gotten me for my birthday.

"Careful." I gently redirected his hand. He reached for the earring again.

The opening chords of "Here Comes the Sun" by The Beatles played from the speaker. Ray clapped his hands and said, "Fuck yeah, let's get this party started." There was more laughter.

Then Dad opened the back door and Sadie all but floated out. She wore Nan's dress and had flowers in her hair. She looked past us all like we didn't exist and walked toward Johnny.

Oh my god, Johnny mouthed at her when she stopped in front of him. "You look like an angel," he whispered.

I blubbered, shocking both Angus and me.

The wedding was short. Another cousin, Trevor, fake-officiated it and took it way too seriously.

"Now, if you'll indulge me for one last thought about love."

This was his seventh such indulgence. They were all pretty asinine. But I was keeping that thought to myself until I could whisper it to Adam.

"Oh my god, dude," Johnny groaned.

Sadie giggled.

"Okay, fine, fine, have it your way," Trevor snapped. He took a breath. Cleared his throat. Adjusted the lapels of his jacket. "You may now kiss the bride," he said with the grandiosity of a Shakespearean actor, not an illegitimate officiant at a backyard wedding with a keg.

Sadie squealed, threw her arms around Johnny's neck, and kissed him.

Ray struggled with the speaker. Eventually, "From This Moment On" by Shania Twain started to play and Sadie and Johnny walked down the stretch of grass between their guests. The path was strewn with fake petals Johnny had insisted on and that I had insisted would need to be thoroughly cleaned up afterwards. So that's what I'd be doing the next day.

"Ladies and gentlemen, I present to you Mr. and Mrs. Francis!" Trevor yelled from behind them.

Sadie stopped and turned around.

"Oh, actually, I'm keeping my last name."

"Oh. Okay." Trevor cleared his throat again. "Ladies and gentlemen, I present to you Mr. Francis and Mrs. Butler."

Sadie turned back around and she and Johnny continued back toward the house.

"Doesn't quite have the same ring to it," Trevor muttered.

The music switched to some rap song I didn't know and two of Johnny's friends carried the keg down onto the lawn.

Mom laughed, loud and bright, as Dad pulled her into a hug and kissed the top of her head.

Hours later, "Forty-Five Years" by Stan Rogers played over a speaker Dad had set up on the deck. The sun was sinking below the trees, and swathes of pink and purple and orange spread across the sky. Adam's hand felt hot on my lower back. He'd taken my hand and gently dragged me from the periphery of the imaginary dance floor, and now we swayed back and forth to a song we both knew by heart.

"You look beautiful," Adam murmured.

I scoffed. Earlier, when I was locked in the bathroom with Sadie, she'd pulled out a mid-length black dress she'd thrifted for me and insisted I wear. I'd slipped it on, anticipating it would be too tight, cling to the exact spots I felt most self-conscious about. But the fabric had hugged my body in exactly the right way. I felt comfortable in it. Pretty, even. Then Sadie had grabbed mascara and red lipstick. I told her she was nuts. She told me I wasn't leaving the room until she'd done my makeup. And again, she'd been right. For the first time in years, I didn't look like I'd walked straight off a farm.

"What? It's true," Adam said.

I wanted to argue. To deny it. "Thanks," I said instead. I made eye contact with him for the first time since we'd started dancing. He leaned forward and kissed my forehead; it was so quick I might've imagined it.

Adam cleared his throat. "Where are Sadie's parents?" he asked.

"I guess they're not really keen on their daughter marrying a Native." I tried to make it sound lighthearted, so I could pretend it didn't hurt. "Their words, according to Johnny."

Adam pulled me closer. He held me, our bodies pressed against one another until the song ended, and for long enough after that I could tell he didn't want to let go.

I didn't want him to either.

"What's that Angus is holding?" Nan asked.

I tried to get Angus to eat a stick of cucumber. He'd eaten nothing but chips and candy since the party started.

"Nothing," I said a little too quickly.

Nan narrowed her eyes.

"You and Adam looked awfully cozy on the dance floor."

"It's a dollar-store dream catcher," I said. Nan loved to present you with two evils, to force you to talk about whatever she wanted to talk about. She was crafty.

"Why the hell would you buy that?"

"I'm sorry, have you never bought something under duress?"

Angus pushed the cucumber away. Nan held out her hand for the dream catcher and Angus handed it to her.

She'd made the exact same face when Mom left the onions out of the stuffing. "This is more likely to cause bad dreams than it is to stop them."

"I know, I know. I was waiting for him to lose interest so I could toss it."

Nan clicked her tongue. She handed Angus the dream catcher. "I will be back." I watched her walk to the house.

Sadie and Johnny danced, and Johnny tried to grab her bum. Sadie laughed and swatted his hand away.

Nan reappeared with a bag in her hands. She pulled a homemade dream catcher out.

"It's almost done," she said as she pulled a few loose feathers out of the bag.

"Do you always carry emergency dream catchers?" I asked.

"I like to have something to do while your grampa drives." She fastened the feathers to the bottom. Angus watched her intently as she finished it, while "Get Ur Freak On" by Missy Elliot played in the background. Was this what it meant to be Mi'kmaw in a modern world?

Angus readily accepted the new dream catcher but refused to give up the old one.

Nan tried to make him give it to her, but quickly gave up when he started to get upset.

She would not have been that indulgent when I was a kid.

"You're getting weak in your old age," I told her.

eighty-six

ANGUS WAS ALREADY ASLEEP AT MY PARENTS' WHEN ADAM LEFT for home. He had to work in the morning, so I'd stay here with Angus.

Mom opened the front door and sat down beside me on the porch steps.

"Do you love him?" she asked, not bothering to beat around the bush.

After dancing with Adam, I'd spent a lot of the night thinking about how I wanted more, and how, for that to happen, I needed to be honest. Now was as good a time as any to start.

"I think at some point I decided that I couldn't because it would make leaving hard," I said.

"But why were you always so hell-bent on leaving?" Mom asked.

"I didn't want to end up miserable."

"Why did you assume you would?"

I took a deep breath. Telling someone about the near-decade-old conversation with Billy felt tender. I'd always felt so sure about the decisions I'd made based off his advice. I didn't want to lay them out in front of myself and realize I'd been wrong.

"Because Billy told me I would," I said before I could talk myself out of it. "He said to make sure I didn't get stuck because one day I'd wake up and be sad like him. I've clung to it for so long. And then Billy died, and I felt like I couldn't second-guess it. Maybe if he'd left a note, I'd have felt differently."

I stared at the now empty driveway, ready to accept whatever advice my mom had to give. I took a sip of pop, feeling vulnerable.

"That's so fucking dumb."

I choked on my drink.

"What?" I turned to look at her.

"No offence to Billy, but I never listened to anything that man had to say. He gave the worst advice."

I shook my head. It wasn't that simple. "I thought he was dead and then I found him, and he looked so sad."

Mom looked at me with more than a little judgement.

"I was fifteen!"

"And now you're almost twenty-five. And you're still following his advice?" She raised her eyebrows.

"You didn't see him. He was sitting right here." I pointed at the step we were on. "He was so miserable. And he basically told me that I would be too if I stayed in this town."

"And are you happy?"

"Am I happy?"

"You just said you've spent a decade trying not to be miserable. Did it work?"

"Can't you give me advice without making me feel stupid?"

Mom shrugged. "If you weren't being stupid, sure."

I sighed, pinching the bridge of my nose.

"When I found out I was pregnant I was so scared. I didn't want to ruin Adam's life. Or my own. We wanted different things. Or I thought we did. Our lives just looked so different. I didn't think we could be together. It didn't seem easy." Little did I know how hard everything would be without him.

"Do you think it was easy for me and your dad?" Mom asked.

"Yes?" I said, unsure.

"Listen, Charlie, loving your dad is the easiest thing I've ever done. But the rest of it sucked. Do you think my parents wanted me marrying an 'Indian'? They had all these stupid preconceived notions and they couldn't see past them. They came around eventually, but it was painful. I felt like I had to choose between him and them. These two important parts of my life seemed so at odds with each other. Or I guess, one side felt very strongly about the other."

"What did you do?" It unnerved me to realize there were parts of my parents' lives that were a mystery to me.

"I told my parents they had to stop being racist a-holes, and I married your dad the next morning at the courthouse." Mom looked at me. "I think you and Adam are easy. It's always been easy. You just went and made it hard."

"There's a joke in there somewhere."

Mom shoved my shoulder. "Yeah, and as your mother, I don't want to hear it."

We both laughed.

"Okay, but seriously, stop laughing. I'm trying to impart wisdom." Mom was still smiling.

"Oh, sorry." I tried to make a sombre face.

"Yeah, you and Adam wanted different things. But what you really wanted, what you really *want*, is a life with each other. Just like your father and I did. That's all that matters. The rest of it is just noise."

"Wow, Mom, that was shockingly profound."

"It's not. Any idiot could see it."

I laughed.

"So," Mom looked at me, "I'm going to ask you again: do you love him?"

I sighed, defeated. "Yes."

"Well, maybe you should think about telling him that, yeah?"

eighty-seven

"I CAN'T LEARN ABOUT WHITE PEOPLE ANYMORE."

Dr. Gamble squinted at me through his thick glasses.

"That's not what I meant." I paused. "Well, actually, it is. I want to centre my PhD research around Mi'kmaw history. I understand that is incredibly vague and I will refine it, but I need to know if that's something I can do at this institution."

Dr. Gamble sat back in his chair. He looked to the corner of the room and absentmindedly clicked his pen. "My research is not particularly attuned to Native issues," he eventually said. "Or perhaps, I should say Aboriginal, as I believe that's a more suitable term now."

"I know. But no one's is." I sat straighter in my chair. "No one in the history department is studying Mi'kmaw history. Which, from an academic standpoint, is both great and terrible. Great, because I can carve out space for myself and do valuable research. Terrible, because I have so much space that I'm all alone with no one to guide me."

Dr. Gamble nodded tentatively.

"But I still need a supervisor."

"That you do."

"Would you still do it?" I asked. There was a lump in my throat. If he said no, I wasn't sure what I would do.

"Charlotte, I have little if any applicable research with which to help you. I would be an insufficient mentor."

"Anybody would be." I felt desperate.

Dr. Gamble raised an eyebrow.

"You're well published, you're constantly at conferences, you may have connections to people I could talk to, people who could help me, and if we cobble together enough of those people…" I spread my hands out in front of me. "I just need someone to support me rather than guide me."

"This is really what you want to do?" he asked.

"I've let myself down during my time in academia," I admitted.

"But you've done so well."

I nodded. "In perpetuating colonial narratives and normalizing the white perspective as the dominant lens through which we view history. I've let myself down, but I've also let my ancestors down."

He took a deep breath before he spoke. But he didn't disagree with me. "Think about yourself and what is best for you, Charlotte. You're not beholden to anyone else."

"I'm beholden to my ancestors, Dr. Gamble," I said. "The things they've endured. The lives they've led. I am here because my ancestors survived and persevered in the face of absolute horror. If I can tell their stories, their history, preserve them so they last beyond me, then I'm going to do that. I have to."

"You might be disappointed if you think you'll create change within this institution." Dr. Gamble leaned forward and placed his elbows on his desk. "But you're making me look at things a little differently, Charlotte. Maybe we can learn from each other."

eighty-eight

SUMMER TURNED TO AUTUMN AND LEAVES FELL IN A FLURRY OF reds and oranges. We had four pumpkins on our stoop. Angus and I had gone down to Mac and Fiona's apartment to carve them. I was still finding bits of pumpkin guts in Angus's hair.

I spent my days holed up in the archives and the Killam Library. My bank account and I were both grateful I was TAing again because it meant I could pay my bills without mooching off my parents, who I was pretty sure still occasionally mooched off my grandparents. Since I was now the only one paying rent, things were tight. I lived off ramen and potatoes while Angus got whatever fresh produce and protein I could afford.

I didn't have time to regret my decision, but I thought about it daily. That evening at the end of the summer, when I sat across the kitchen table from Adam and told him I should go back to the city.

"I still have the lease. I have to TA an early morning class. I don't know, what do you think?" I asked Adam.

I wanted him to say "don't." I wanted him to say "stay." I wanted him to say "what about marriage and spaghetti and kids with weird names?" I wanted him to tell me that the look in his eyes I thought might be love, was. But he didn't.

There was no longer a chasm between us, but whatever line we'd drawn felt just as hard to cross.

He said, "okay." And for the millionth time since we'd kissed I wondered if I'd made it all up. And yeah, I'd said I'd be more honest, but we were finally good now. I didn't want to ruin it. So when Adam said *okay*, I said it too. And now Angus and I were back in the city and it didn't feel okay.

Adam now came in on the weekends. We'd go to the museum, the playground at The Commons, Point Pleasant Park. But I was beginning to miss home. I wanted to stand on the edge of the Cobequid Bay and sink my feet into the mud. I wanted to sit on Adam's porch and watch the sun as it sunk below the trees.

I'd started to learn the Mi'kmaw language, and alone in the apartment all week, I would mutter to myself as I scribbled in a notebook; the pages filled with historical dates, anecdotes I'd collected from Elders, and Mi'kmaw words spelled both phonetically and accurately. I'd pick Angus up from daycare, we'd meander home, eat some semblance of a balanced meal, and he'd tell me about trains before bed.

"They go like this, Mama…HMMM, HMMM," he'd hum, a blanket pulled up to his chin, his head cushioned by a pillow with a train pattern. Clearly, my mini-lecture last year about the negative impacts of the railway hadn't made an impression. Angus would be asleep by eight.

And then our apartment would be quiet.

The saddest part of my day was when I would walk around and turn off all the lights. I would lay in my bed in the dark and try not to feel incredibly lonely.

But I was.

The first night home without Fiona I played "Nothing Compares 2 U" by Sinéad O'Connor and lay on the floor. I closed my eyes and let the music wash over me.

"Charlie?" Fiona called through the vents when the song ended. "Do you need me to come up?"

"No. I'm going to go to bed."

"Okay, I love you."

"Love you too."

One night, unable to take the next several hours of solitude, I called Adam. He picked up on the third ring.

"Everything okay?" he asked, a hint of panic in his voice.

"Yeah, everything is fine, sorry." Maybe it was stupid to call.

"What's up?"

"Nothing, I just thought I'd…never mind, you probably have things to—"

"How was your day?"

I slowly sat down on a kitchen chair and told Adam every mundane detail of my day, and when I was finished he told me about his.

We talked until almost ten, the only light the one above the kitchen stove.

"I feel like rigor mortis has set in." I tried to stretch but my back spasmed.

"I've just been pacing," Adam said.

"This whole time?"

"Johnny found these step counters and challenged me to a step-off."

"Why?" I asked after a long pause.

"Because he's bored now that the farm is slowing down for the season. And because he's way too competitive. If we do this every night, I'll really whoop his ass."

"Glad I could help."

"Night, Charlie."

"Night, Adam."

eighty-nine

"AND SO, YOU HAVE THE END OF THE SEVEN YEARS' WAR AND, specifically in our corner of the world, the French and Indian War. You have the signing of the 1760–61 treaty between the British and the Mi'kmaq." The professor stumbled over the last word. It came out sounding like *mickmah*. "My colleague at the University of New Brunswick has argued, in court and in academic papers, that these treaties were signed in light of British victory and connote *mickmah* submission."

I looked up from my scribbled notes. I was TAing this course. It wouldn't look good if I corrected the prof in front of the students. I kept writing so I could figure out quiz questions for next week.

"The question now is, in light of the Marshall decision, and in light of Burnt Church, do these treaties actually grant the *mickmah* special rights? Do they lift them above the law? Some experts, like my esteemed colleague, would argue: no, they do not. That, after their defeat at the hands of the British, *the mickmah*, now a conquered people, became British subjects and should be treated as such. I'm going to open the floor up to discussion, I'm interested to hear your thoughts." The professor leaned back against his desk.

A hand shot up beside me. "I agree that the Micmac people should be treated like everyone else. Isn't that what equality is? And besides, it doesn't really seem like that special treatment is doing them any favours. I mean, look at the quality of life on reserves. Look at the rates of alcohol and substance abuse."

I didn't want to say anything, but this was why I was here. I'd promised myself and I'd promised my dad.

I raised my hand, and the professor nodded in acknowledgement.

"Sorry to interrupt, I just wanted to make a note on pronunciation." I cleared my throat. "It's pronounced Mi'kmaq. *Meeg-emach*." I overexaggerated my pronunciation, dragging out the vowels, emphasizing the guttural *q* at the end. I hesitated, and then pictured having to tell Nan I let some white guy talk shit about Mi'kmaw people. "And secondly," I said, dread pooling in my stomach, "the British didn't beat the Mi'kmaq. We didn't lose a war."

Oops. I'd said "we." Was that bad?

"The signing of the treaties does not represent the subjugation of the Mi'kmaq," I continued, aware I was digging my own grave. "I would also argue that the government forcing Mi'kmaw people to live on reserves is not the same as us choosing to live there; it's not special treatment, it's oppression. I also wonder if alcohol and substance abuse is less a result of 'special treatment' and more likely a result of the Mi'kmaq having to endure centuries of attempted genocide."

Silence followed my argument.

"That's a bold word choice, Miss Francis. I understand that from your perspective, our shared history can be upsetting," the professor said, almost indulgently, "but let's not challenge fact based on emotion. And let's not—"

"But what you've said isn't factual," I insisted. Without a doubt, he was going to ask for a different TA.

"Care to elaborate?"

Could I elaborate? I didn't have decades of study behind me, I hadn't even taken a class on this topic because there wasn't one available. I knew the Mi'kmaq weren't a conquered people. We were still here. But how could I argue that when I couldn't cite papers and reference esteemed colleagues?

A student opened the door to the classroom and peeked in. "Sorry," she squeaked before closing it. The next class was starting to arrive.

The professor checked his watch. "Saved by the bell, so to speak." He glanced at me.

The student beside me chuckled.

I gathered up my belongings, my cheeks burning. I shoved my notebook in my backpack, determination taking root. I was not about to let this smug man in a tweed coat tell these students that the Mi'kmaq were a conquered people. He should spend an hour with Aunt Darlene and Nan and say the same shit, and see who was conquered after that.

ninety

I STARED AT THE PHONE ON THE WALL. I'D SPENT THE LAST WEEK perched on a kitchen chair talking to Adam after I'd put Angus to bed. My back was killing me. I had a phone jack by my bed. I could move the phone and avoid further injury. Today there'd been a twinge in my back that felt ominous.

I took the phone off the wall and plugged it in next to my bedside table. Then I sat on the edge of my bed and waited.

When the phone rang a minute later, I fumbled to pick it up.

"Hey." Why did I sound so breathy?

"Johnny accused me of cheating with the step-counter," Adam said by way of greeting.

"Seriously?"

"Yeah, he said there's no way I could've done double what he did. I told him it's not my fault he's a lazy arse. He said he wants a rematch."

"Of course he does."

At some point in the conversation, I decided it was fine to lie down. And then not long after, I fell asleep.

I woke up to light streaming through my bedroom windows, the phone practically suctioned to my face from a mixture of sweat and drool. I rolled onto my back and took the phone with me. On the end of the line, Adam snored. I smiled up at my cracked ceiling.

"Adam," I said softly.

He snored again.

"Adam." A little louder.

"Huh?" He mumbled, clearly confused.

"Why didn't you hang up?" I could hear the happiness in my voice, despite knowing that all these stupid smiles and the overactive butterflies in my stomach were for nothing. We'd never talked about the kiss. By now it was like some fever dream brought about by cheap beer and board games. I often wondered if whatever chance we'd had had fizzled out in that moment. Like, as our bodies had pressed together an entire realm of possibility had been born and had died in Adam's kitchen.

"I didn't want to."

"What'd you do, sleep on the kitchen floor?"

There was a pause.

"No," he said, "I moved the phone into my bedroom." My heart did stupid things.

Angus called out from his room before I could respond.

"Just a sec." I carried Angus back to my room and he snuggled into the second pillow, his eyes still soft and sleepy.

I picked up the phone and lay down beside him.

"Want to say hi to Daddy?" I asked.

Angus nodded and I handed him the phone.

"Hi, Daddy," he said into the wrong part of the phone. I adjusted it so his mouth was where it should be.

"Say it again."

"Hi, Daddy."

I couldn't hear Adam's reply, but Angus smiled.

ninety-one

I WAITED UNTIL THE LAST STUDENT SAT DOWN BEFORE THUNKING my backpack onto the table at the front of the classroom, and looked directly at the professor. He glared back at me. I ignored the part of me that wanted to apologize and sit down.

"Last class you asked me if I wanted to elaborate. I do." My voice didn't shake.

"We really can't dawdle, Miss Francis, we've got a lot to cover this class."

"Five minutes."

The professor checked his watch. "Fine." He gestured toward me with his hand.

I didn't have years of historical research behind me. I didn't have esteemed colleagues to back up my statements. But I had family history. I had lineage and ancestors and family memories that proved he was wrong; that proved the Mi'kmaq were not, and never would be, a conquered people.

I unzipped my backpack and pulled out family photo albums. I had stuck Post-it Notes on the photos I wanted to show because I knew the prof wouldn't wait while I flipped through page after page.

I opened the album to the first Post-it. "These are some of my cousins fishing lobster," I said as I lifted up the plastic covering and handed the photo to my professor.

The main focus of the photo was my cousin Brad, holding a lobster close to his face while he pretended to kiss it. In the background, my cousin Trish scowled while she leaned over the side of the boat, pulling up a net. You could tell she was trying really hard not to smile. Joy radiated from the photo. The sea in the background sparkled as the bright sun beat down.

I flipped to an older black-and-white photo of my nan, smiling at the camera, gripping her young son, my dad, in a side hug. In her other hand, Nan held a drum she made. Whoever took the photo caught my dad mid-strike, the leather end of the drumstick a blur.

As I removed them, I described each photo to the prof and the class. Tried to give them historical context.

"My dad was four in that photo," I said. "It was taken in 1958. It was only in 1956 that Canada decided Indigenous people were actual people, considered citizens of this country, though they wouldn't be able to vote in federal elections without losing their status as 'Indians' until 1960." I loved this photo of Dad, a wide smile on his young face, focusing all his attention on hitting the drum. "Thankfully, my dad wasn't sent to the Shubenacadie Indian Residential School. The institution was open from 1930 to 1967. Kids who had the misfortune of being sent there were forbidden from speaking their language or practicing their culture."

I picked up another photo of Nan and Grampa at their twentieth-anniversary celebration, sitting on a sofa, family squashed in beside them and on the floor at their feet.

"Maybe my dad didn't go to residential school because my nan and her kids lost Indian status when she married my grampa, who's white. See, the government discriminated against Native women for decades. Anyone heard of Bill C-31?" I was met with blank stares. "Well, it was a way for the government to correct gender discrimination in the Indian Act. Women who lost status could apply to have it reinstated, along with their kids'. My family did. I could spend an hour just talking about problems with the Indian Act and status." My professor shot me a look. "But not today, obviously."

The next photo was Nan standing with the Grand Chief at the annual St. Anne's Day Mi'kmaw celebration in the late '60s. I handed him a photo of Aunt Darlene in her deerskin regalia at one of the first powwows in the region in the mid-'80s. A photo of my cousin Andrew, holding up his band council election sign and grinning. There were photos of Johnny and me, and one where I'm wearing my first ribbon skirt. I'd made it myself and the rows of ribbons were all crooked. There was a recent photo of my dad, his hair nearly long enough to braid.

By the time I was done, the photos were circulating around the classroom. I'd handed out so many, everyone in the class was holding at least one.

"The Mi'kmaq aren't just some historical population the Europeans bested," I said while they looked at the pictures. "We are here. And we are existing in ways that honour our ancestors. And yeah, there's been a lot of harm done and a lot of trauma inflicted on the Mi'kmaq.

But we are still persevering and practicing our culture, despite so many attempts to stop us from doing so. That doesn't sound like a conquered people to me."

ninety-two

DESPERATE FOR SOCIAL INTERACTION THAT WASN'T WITH A toddler or a student, and in deference to Dr. Gamble's insistent pestering, I agreed to attend a History Department social. Normally they didn't work with my schedule, but this was a lunchtime affair and Angus would be at daycare, so I was running out of excuses. I was hopeful there would be snacks.

After bringing my photo albums to class I'd showed up at Dr. Gamble's office, out of breath and full of adrenaline. In a rush I'd told him what happened. He'd buried his face in his hands. At first, I thought he was crying or had given up on me completely. But he was laughing. His shoulders shook as he told me how much he disliked that professor and how proud of me he was.

Once he'd calmed down he'd told me, for the hundredth time, that though there were lots of professors like the one I'd just schooled, there were other potential allies out there. While he agreed with what I'd done, he was concerned I was burning more bridges than I was building. He'd said academia wasn't just about research but also connection and collaboration. I needed to network. I asked him how long he'd workshopped that speech. He said he'd liked me better when I was quiet and awkward.

I squeezed past the doorway where a group of students was arguing about obscure Russian history. I hoped I could get to the snacks uninterrupted, but as Dr. Gamble spotted me, he waved me over.

"You made it!" The way Dr. Gamble said it made it sound like I'd scaled Mount Everest.

"Here I am." I tried to sound peppy, but I had as much enthusiasm has someone headed for the gallows.

"Charlotte, this is Matthew, one of Dr. Driscoll's grad students. Matthew, this is Charlotte Francis, my PhD student."

"Oh," Matthew snapped his fingers. "You're the one doing Micmac history, right?"

Was it good networking to immediately correct someone?

"In broad terms, yes, I'm studying Mi'kmaw history." I made sure to make direct eye contact with him while pronouncing the word.

We lapsed into awkward silence.

"You're really leaning into it, eh?" He gestured to my braids and beaded earrings.

Good god. I hadn't even gotten close to the snack table yet; I wasn't equipped to deal with this.

Dr. Gamble took a sip of wine.

"What a weird thing to say," I told Matthew.

Dr. Gamble choked on his drink.

Matthew gaped at me.

"I'm going to go grab some cheese before it's all gone," I said, stepping away from the two men. I walked over to the snack table and filled a paper plate with food, grabbed a plastic cup of red wine, and stood awkwardly and, I hoped, unapproachably, near the alcohol.

I didn't know anyone here well enough to strike up a conversation, nor did I have the desire to. Looking around the room, this wasn't the case for the rest of the department. Small groups of mostly men talked to one another in the cramped department lounge. Almost everyone was holding a plate of food or a cup of wine. At least I wasn't the only food-focused grad student. I ate another cube of cheese. Standing alone by the warming deli spread, I realized how much I'd isolated myself in the last few years. Though if they were all like Matthew, that was probably for the best.

I took a sip of wine and grimaced. It was almost as bad as the champagne from Doug's. An inordinate number of men in the room were wearing sweaters with collared shirts peeking out. Curious, I started to count. I was pretty sure it was more than half.

"Wow. This is a real sausage fest, eh?" A girl I vaguely recognized appeared beside me. She brushed her box braids off her shoulder and took a sip of wine.

"Didn't we have a class together a few years ago?"

"You mean, the one where that really tall girl claimed you only got in because you met a quota?"

"That's the one." I finished my drink.

"I told my mom about that later," she said, laughing.

Her laugh was contagious. Plus, if I didn't laugh at things I'd probably just cry forever.

"I'm Izzie." She held out her hand.

"Charlie." We shook.

"What's your research on?"

"In vague terms, I want to look at the impact that colonization and the Indian Act had on Mi'kmaw women."

"Sick," Izzie said, nodding enthusiastically.

"You're in your second year, right?" Izzie nodded. "I saw the talk you did last year on farming conditions for Black Loyalists after the American Revolution. Really interesting."

"Thanks." Izzie smiled. "I still have nightmares about the hordes of mice." She ate a piece of cheese and made a face. "I feel like when the cheese starts to get warm it means it's time to leave." She threw her plate in the garbage. "Do you want to grab a coffee? I need a friend in this department who doesn't have wet dreams about Cornwallis and British imperialism."

I made a noise halfway between a laugh and a cough. A group of students standing near us looked over. I glanced at the clock. I had an hour and a half till I had to grab Angus.

"Sure, let's go," I said, following Izzie out of the room. I turned around once and made eye contact with Dr. Gamble. He smiled at me and raised his cup.

ninety-three

I DRAGGED THE GARBAGE CAN TO THE CURB. DUSK HAD TURNED to twilight and the street seemed empty. Angus had been rowdy and difficult to put down. After I sang what felt like a million songs and scratched his back for an hour, he'd finally fallen asleep. Across the road, light spilled from our neighbours' dining room window. They were a young family, three kids, two parents. I felt like a creep, standing on the curb in the dark, watching as the dad held Scrabble above his head and ceremoniously placed it on the table where the rest of them were gathered. They just seemed so happy it was hard to look away.

I thought I liked to be alone. I thought I enjoyed solitude. Turns out I wanted to be alone with another person. The only person I'd never wanted a break from was Adam. But because I was always so stuck in my head, I'd convinced myself that one day I might want a break from him too, and so I'd forced one.

Johnny had always told me I was shockingly stubborn. I hadn't agreed until now.

Aunt Darlene was a single parent. She was a total badass, and I'd never once gotten the impression that she felt like her life lacked anything. And maybe if it wasn't Adam I was missing, I'd feel the same way.

Change felt impossible and scary. To be anywhere but this tiny second-floor apartment with Angus. Just the two of us. Adam on the weekends. But this wasn't the good and full and happy life I'd promised my son. My first instinct was to dismiss the idea of change outright, to tell myself I wasn't brave enough. But, as night descended on the city with Siwkewiku's, the Spring Time moon, full in the sky, I thought of all the things I'd done lately that felt brave. The class I was TAing. The photo albums on my bedside table. Raising my son and going to school.

The street lights made tiny pools of light down the road. Wonky impressions of the moon in the sky. Standing under one, I forced myself to consider, for the first time, that I was capable of change. That I was already changing.

I pulled on the lid of the garbage can to make sure it was secure. Last time I'd left the bin open and birds had ripped the bags and spread my garbage across the street. Cleaning up my used pads while Angus watched from the sidewalk had been a low point. I looked back across the street at my neighbours' brightly lit dining room.

Adam and I had changed the course of our lives in less than half an hour one bitter, sad, November night.

Maybe I could change it again.

ninety-four

ANGUS KICKED OFF HIS SHOES AND RAN THROUGH A LINE OF graves. I kept my eye on him as I grabbed the Spirit Plate, a cup, and snacks I'd picked up on the way: Mello Yello and Spicy Nacho Doritos.

Halfway to Billy's grave I stopped to scoop up Angus's discarded shoes, my fingers contorting to hold on to everything. Angus squirmed and whined as he attempted to get his sweater off.

"Leave it on," I told him.

Angus pulled one arm from his sleeve and whined louder.

I put the myriad items down by Billy's grave and sighed. I put Angus's arm back in his sleeve and pulled down his hood, which he had yanked over his head in his fervent attempts at undressing himself.

I kissed his forehead. "I get it, April feels warm, but it's not that warm."

I placed the Spirit Plate in front of Billy's grave.

"Hi." I opened the Doritos and dumped a pile on the plate. "How's it going?" I ate a chip while Angus mumbled to himself a few graves over. He squatted in the grass and picked a newly sprung flower. Held it close to his face and breathed out through his nose. I couldn't figure out how to explain to him that wasn't how you smelled things.

I filled the cup with Mello Yello and placed it next to the plate, but it tipped over, fizzy neon sloshing onto the grass. "If that grass is dead next time, we'll finally have proof Mom was right to nag you every time you drank this." I used the stone to support the cup. "I figure it's probably fine if you drink highlighter-yellow liquid now. It's not like it could kill you." Silence. "Sorry, was that too morbid?" I ate another chip. The rocks from the beach were still on top of the gravestone.

"Remember when you told me to leave this town in the dust?" I paused, scratching my forehead. "How could you not? I bring it up every damn time I see you." Angus side-shuffled closer, flower in hand. "I've been pretty miserable lately. Which I feel I also keep you pretty well informed about. And while I'm not going to entirely blame you for my misery, I will reiterate that your advice was absolute shit. And if you were still alive, I would probably warn you away from doling out wisdom and life guidance to fifteen-year-olds. Or anyone, really."

"Mama, issa flower." Angus held it out for me to see.

"Whoa baby, it's so pretty. Are you going to keep it or do you want to give it to Uncle Billy?"

"I give to Billy." Angus tried to place the flower on top of Billy's grave but missed. The flower fell onto the grass. "Uh-oh." He bent over and picked the flower up by the petals, crushing it in his fist. "I be gentle, Mama. Issa nice flower."

"It's a beautiful flower, sweetie."

Angus readjusted the flower so that he held it by the stem, the crumbled petals drooping. He placed it on top of the grave again, this time moving so slowly I had to stop myself from laughing.

"Good job, buddy."

Angus stepped back, satisfied.

I focused on the grave. "Anyway, in summation: I'm sorry. I love you. But your advice was garbage and I'm not going to follow it anymore."

Angus squatted down next to the Spirit Plate.

"What's that, Mama?" He pointed at the food.

"Those are chips, but they're—"

Before I could warn him they were spicy, Angus popped a Dorito into his mouth. I watched in horror as he chewed, waiting for the inevitable tears. His face betrayed nothing. My shoulders relaxed. Maybe he had a high heat tolerance; maybe his taste buds sucked.

"Okay but don't have another—"

The corners of Angus's mouth turned downwards. He scrunched his face up.

"Mamaaa." His voice sounded raspy. He stuck his tongue out.

"Is it spicy?"

He nodded, his tongue still out. He stood up and hopped around.

"Okay, time to go." We had water in the car. I grabbed the bag of chips and the bottle of pop, scooped Angus up, and grabbed his shoes.

"I'll be back for the plate tomorrow," I told Billy. I wondered if maybe I shouldn't leave spicy chips that wild animals would inevitably eat. The squirrels probably wouldn't appreciate the zesty nacho flavour.

"'Picy," Angus panted.

I'd already fed the woodland creatures an entire bag of banana gummies. I'd choose something healthier next time, maybe nuts.

"Say goodbye to your uncle," I told Angus as I carried him like a football.

"Bye, Unkie," he repeated, his voice wobbly as he bounced up and down in my arms. "Is 'picy" he said again.

"I know, I know," I said as we shuffled along.

Angus chugged the whole bottle of water, half of it spilling onto the front of his sweater.

"I think we've figured out whose palate you've inherited. Your dad can barely eat black pepper."

Angus tipped the bottle too high and dumped the remaining half between us, wetting both our shirts and pants.

We both looked down at the wet patches.

"Uh-oh," Angus said after a long stretch of silence.

"Let's go home and change, yeah?"

Angus nodded.

"And then, do you remember where we're going?"

"Bock-bocks!" Angus cheered, throwing his hands and the bottle up into the air, spraying the last few drops of water in his hair.

ninety-five

ANGUS AND I STARED DOWN AT THE BOX OF CHICKS ON THE counter of Adam's kitchen. I may have been overzealous. The chicks pecked at the bedding Marvin had sprinkled on the bottom of the cardboard box. One fluffed its tiny wings. All ten chirped incessantly.

"Was this a mistake?" I asked Angus. I looked back at the brooder, bag of pine shavings, feed, and heat lamp I'd left by the door. The brooder took up more space than I'd anticipated. I'd told Angus this would be life-changing, but maybe it was just incredibly dumb.

"Soo many bock-bocks, Mama."

"Yeah, but is it *too* many?"

Angus squirmed in my arms and reached for the box of chicks. I set him on the counter, then cradled one of the chicks to my chest.

"Hold your hands like mine."

Angus cupped his hands together.

"Close to your chest."

He pulled his arms in tight.

"Good job, buddy. I'm going to put the chick in your hands, okay?"

Angus nodded. He hadn't taken his eyes off the chick since I'd picked it up.

"You gotta be careful, okay? Don't move, and you have to be gentle." I thought of the flower at Billy's grave.

I gingerly placed the chick in Angus's hands, ready to snatch it back if he started to squeeze or dropped it. But he kept his hands open and cupped. The chick pecked at his palm, and he flinched.

"Did it hurt?"

"No." He shook his head. The chick ruffled its feathers and Angus laughed.

When I put him down for a nap, Angus chattered nonstop about the chicks. "They're my friends, Mama," he said as he pulled the blanket up to his chin. "I wub them." He rolled over, nestling into his pillow and blankets. I brushed his auburn hair back from his face. His eyes went hazy and his eyelids drooped. When his mouth went slack, I stopped running my fingers through his hair and quietly left the room.

I set the heat lamp up over the box, and the chicks settled into a lump of downy fluff beneath its light.

Every time I talked to my mom, she asked me if I'd told Adam how I felt yet. She was relentless, but—and not that I'd ever tell her this—she was right. Adam and I had wasted so much time and there was no point wasting more. Except, faced with the prospect of laying everything out in front of him, I struggled to let go of the feelings I'd kept so close to my chest.

What if he said "Oh, that's nice." And left it at that.

What if he said "Well, too bad, you fucked up and now I'm actually in love with Gina Smith"?

What if he didn't believe me? What if I'd wrecked the trust we'd built over years?

So I'd panicked and bought baby chicks. Because ever since I ran into Marvin the chicken guy at Doug's, chicks seemed like the truest and best expression of love.

Which now, standing with a brood of chicks in Adam's kitchen, seemed ill-thought-out. And likely to fail. It also occurred to me that Marvin was probably just trying to get rid of ten chicks; he would've agreed with anything I'd said.

Did chickens scream *I love you, let's grow old together*?

I could take them back. But Angus was already in love with them. I'd have to live with the consequences.

When Adam walked in through the back door, whacking the end of the brooder, it took everything in me not to scream.

It was now clear to me that being a PhD candidate did not preclude someone from being a moron.

Adam looked up. "You okay?" he asked as he shuffled around the brooder.

"Yeah, I...um, I just." I tried to block the box with my body. As if he couldn't hear the chicks' constant chirping.

Adam toed off his shoes.

"Angus and I got chicks."

He looked at the pile of things near the door and then at me.

"From Marvin," I added.

"You...got chicks?" It sounded like he wanted to laugh.

"Yeah...You'd talked about it before and you mentioned the chicken coop to Angus and I thought it might be a good idea but now I'm not so sure and I have Marvin's number written down so I can call him and ask if I can bring them back. I got ten—which didn't seem like a lot, but now does seem like a lot. And if you hate this, I will remedy the situation as fast as humanly possible. Angus is napping and I can achieve a lot in that two-hour period. Though he's already been asleep for a while so we're probably down to like twenty minutes. But—"

"Charlie. Breathe." Adam took a deep breath, as if to show me how.

"Right." I relaxed my shoulders and breathed. Some of the tension left my body.

"You know, I called Marvin before I left work today and asked about chicks. He said he was all out. I thought he sounded weirdly smug about it. Now I know why." Adam's smile was big.

I shrugged. Heat bloomed on my cheeks. A rabble of butterflies took flight in my stomach.

Adam stuck his hand in the box and ran a finger along the back of one of the chicks. "Why'd you get chickens?"

"I've been thinking about moving back home. Permanently. Driving into the city when I have to. And I don't have enough on my plate. So, I thought, why not get chickens?"

Adam adjusted his baseball cap.

I could tell him I loved him now. It was there. On the tip of my tongue.

"I think it's better for us...for our family, if we live closer together."

"How close?"

Was he going to make me say it? I couldn't just move Angus and myself in without ever actually vocalizing that's what I was going to do?

"Uh, like under the same roof? But if that is not okay, I will take myself and the chickens and—" Was this what a heart attack felt like?

"It's okay." Adam's eyes were wide.

"It's okay?" This was what I wanted—why did it feel scary?

Adam nodded. "Is this part of the new five-year plan?" he asked.

"I think I'm done with five-year plans."

"You don't say." Adam looked amused.

We stood unnecessarily close in Adam's small kitchen. We watched each other and I think we both understood we were on the precipice of something, just like all those years ago in my bedroom after the funeral.

Adam took a step back and leaned over the counter, his hands braced on either side of the box of chicks. "You know, after my mom died, my dad wanted to move. He didn't want to live in a house where every room reminded him of her. So, he sold the house right before I started school and we moved here. My aunt was here and he thought it'd be easier. I was so nervous on the first day. I didn't talk to anyone. I remember just staring at the chalkboard. And then Johnny sat down beside me, practically fell on top of me he was so uncoordinated, and my entire life changed." Adam paused. "I feel stupid saying it, but I felt like I was meant to know you guys. That I was supposed to have your family in my life. And then you."

He glanced at me. Those green eyes with flecks of gold.

Our son's eyes.

"I don't know when it changed. But I know when I realized." Adam wet his lips. "Do you remember in high school when your dad took us to dig for clams and Johnny pushed you and you fell over?"

"Yes..." I'd been covered in mud.

"You were just lying in the mud, belly laughing up at the sky, and I remember thinking, *I am so in love with this person*, and then almost shitting myself because what a terrible thing to be in love with your best friend's sister. Especially when that best friend is as unhinged as Johnny."

That was the same summer I'd had that front-porch conversation with Billy.

"Didn't you go home almost immediately after that?" I asked.

"Yeah, 'cause I was in crisis." Adam adjusted his ball cap again. "When Angus was a baby—I don't know if I'll ever get over how I shut you out—I just didn't know how to act around you. I don't know how to act like you aren't the only person in the room that matters." He said it so bluntly, like it was a fact.

"You know, my dad never remarried, never dated anyone else until he met Mary a few years ago. And I never understood it. How someone could be so haunted by a person, so overwhelmed by their absence. And then you left, Charlie. And it isn't the same, I know it's not the same. But I get it now. When you're not here I'm miserable, and I don't ever want to be in a world where you don't exist. And if you let me, I will follow you anywhere. It doesn't have to be here. I'll move into your shithole apartment if you want me to."

My entire body rejected the idea of staying in the city. I wanted to be with Adam. But I also wanted this land. I wanted the bay and the trees and the sky. I wanted to look up and see the stars, maybe eventually figure out which constellations were which.

"I don't want that," I said.

Adam looked at me. "What do you want?"

Being honest made me want to crawl into a hole headfirst. But we both deserved more than what we'd made so far. And so, I told Adam the truth.

"I want to be happy. For both of us to be happy. I want you. I want this." I gestured between us. "I want us. Everything I thought would make me happy sucks without you. I feel like those mornings we woke up wrapped around each other changed something in my DNA and even though you're a blanket hog, I'm willing to put up with it. I want to be close to you always. I want to be so close to you that I'm inside your skin."

Adam wrinkled his nose and clicked his tongue. "Uh, you made it weird."

"I haven't made it weird enough." I leaned closer to him.

Adam pulled me toward him and kissed my forehead.

"I love you," he whispered into my skin.

"I love you too." I pulled at the edges of his flannel.

Adam pressed his body against my own. His lips a breath away from mine.

Angus cried out from his bedroom.

"I love him, but the kid has shit timing." Adam looked me in the eyes. "We'll finish this later," he said.

"Later," I agreed. I closed the gap between us, kissing Adam as bright daylight streamed through the kitchen windows. I could feel his smile against my own.

ninety-six

FIONA AND I STOOD IN THE NOW EMPTY LIVING ROOM OF OUR old apartment. Adam had just carried the last box to the truck. The flurry of packing and moving in an afternoon had lessened the emotional impact of my leaving. But now, faced with barren walls and dust-free corners, I had to acknowledge that a huge stage of my life was over. A part of me wanted to rush out the door, wave goodbye, act like this wasn't an ending.

"You know," Fiona said, breaking the silence, "I thought the Spice Girls breaking up was the saddest thing that could ever happen to me. But this is worse." Her voice sounded watery. I stared at the tack holes in the walls.

There were so many songs and movies and novels about romantic heartbreak. But what about platonic heartbreak? Where was the song about leaving the home you'd made with your best friend? Where was the poem about the ache in your chest and the funny feeling in your stomach because you knew things were never going to be quite the same as they were before? That even though you'd still be friends, you could never have the same ease and closeness you'd had when you lived together.

There were so many moments with Fiona I'd taken for granted, maybe had even been annoyed about at the time. I wished I could go back and revel in them, soak them in, pay closer attention while they were happening.

"I'll still be in the city a lot," I said.

"The spare bedroom is yours whenever you want it."

"I'm not going to cry," I told Fiona as tears obscured my vision.

"Neither am I," Fiona said, tears streaming down her face.

"Oh god, stop it," I blubbered.

"You stop it."

"I'm postpartum, my hormones are all over the place."

"You are not."

"I read somewhere that once you have a kid you're always post-partum, so I'm sticking with that, thanks."

"Even when your kid is, like, eighteen? You know what, never mind, this is not the conversation we should be having right now." Fiona wiped the tears from her cheeks, then pulled me into a hug.

"Bye, bitch," she said into my shoulder.

I cried even harder.

After a good five minutes of hugging and crying, Fiona and I walked down the carpeted steps of our apartment for the last time. The carpet was brown with three mustard yellow lines running down the middle. I thought it might be so ugly it was cute, like a hairless cat. This seemed like my last chance to decide, so I examined them one last time on my way down. I sighed. They were just ugly.

I was already mentally planning what order to unpack things in when we got home. I tilted my face to the sun and the budding trees, reminding myself not to think too far ahead, to enjoy the sun while it was here. The moon, Sqoljuiku's, Frogs Croaking Time, was also hanging in the sky, a faint white crescent in the bright blue.

I hugged Fiona one last time, squeezing extra tight.

"Adam," Fiona called out.

He looked up from the book he was reading beside the truck.

"Keep in mind, I know where you live, and I took a year of jujitsu when I was ten."

"Oh wow, did you make it to the Olympics?" Adam asked.

"Just know I was deadly while I did it. And I'm not afraid to tap into that reserve again."

"Stop threatening Adam," Mac said as he put his arms around her.

I waved Fiona off, laughing as I crossed the sidewalk, and tried to appreciate the bittersweet moment between endings and beginnings.

Year Five

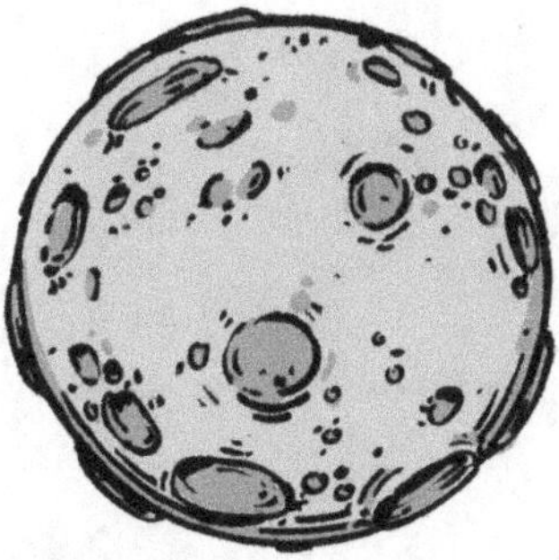

Kisikewiku's

(Gis-ig-ay-we-goos)

Berry Ripening Time

ninety-seven

NAN CALLED IN A TIZZY. "THE BLACKBERRY BUSHES," SHE SAID breathlessly. "It's too much." She lured my entire family to her house to pick berries one Sunday afternoon with the promise of seafood chowder and rolls. We all would've come for the berries alone, but no one bothered to tell her; we'd have been idiots to refuse her chowder.

The bushes hung heavy with fruit. Over the years they had grown wild and unmanageable—like Johnny's hair. He had started to grow it out and it had begun to flip at the nape of his neck. Sadie was beside him, quietly humming while she filled her bucket. She was completely obscured by the wild tangle of stalks. They hadn't gotten legally married yet. I'd printed off the forms for them, but they didn't seem overly concerned with the paperwork portion of "happily ever after."

"You know," I said to Johnny over a tangle of blackberry bushes, "your hair is getting awfully long for someone who made fun of Dad for growing out his hair."

"Yeah, but now that he can actually braid it, it does look pretty badass."

We both glanced at our dad, who was following his dad around the house with a tool kit, fixing everything Grampa perceived as wiggly or loose. Dad's hair was in a short braid that hung just below his shoulder blades. As soon as it was long enough to pull back, Mom spent a week teaching him how to braid it. It was a painful process that caused multiple arguments, but it seemed he'd finally gotten the hang of it.

I side-shuffled my way out of the bushes, thorns snagging on my sleeves and pants. I put down my bucket, which in a past life had stored corned beef.

After a morning of excitement—and peeing his pants multiple times because he refused to go to the potty lest he miss a moment of fun—Angus had passed out in my grandparents' bedroom. I quietly opened the door to peek in on him. At three years old, he was too big for the playpen my grandparents kept at their house. And most days, he was too big for naps, but running around and eating his weight in blackberries was a lot of work for a kid. I'd found him half asleep on a lawn chair before picking him up and bringing him to my grandparents' bed. Now, he snored softly, his little mouth slack, a hand tucked under his cheek. I wanted to pick him up and squeeze him. I froze, flinching at the snick of the door latch sliding into place, and listened for the ruffle of blankets and a sleepy whine, but Angus slept on.

I bounded down the back steps, now no longer wobbly after Dad's repairs, and squinted against the bright August sun, high in the sky. I was halfway across the lawn when Adam caught up to me and threw me over his shoulder. I squealed before clamping a hand over my mouth.

He twirled me across the field like I weighed nothing. Like I was light as air. I felt it. In the way he held me, the way the sun warmed my skin, the way the wind blew through my hair. I laughed until my stomach hurt as we spun across the yard. Adam carried me to the blackberry bushes and set me down gently. We held on to each other as the world tilted, trying to steady ourselves.

I walked backwards, pulling him with me, until we were amid the brambles. The thorns tugging at us. I wrapped my arms around his neck and kissed him. He leaned in and the weight of his body pressed against mine was heady and sweet. Tonight, Kisikewiku's moon would be nearly gone. Adam had gotten me a book of constellations and promised we would try to find them after Angus went to bed.

"Will you guys stop making out in the bushes?" Johnny grumbled.

"Shut up, Johnny. It's cute," Sadie whispered. "Feel free to keep making out," she added, a little louder.

Adam pulled away and smiled lazily. He went back and grabbed both of our buckets. He handed me mine and kissed me one more time on the forehead, then disappeared into the bushes.

Not long after, Fiona and Mac pulled into my grandparents' driveway.

Aunt Darlene showed up right before supper. We were all on our way to the house, our fingers stained purple and our buckets heavy and filled to the brim, when her car pulled in.

"Classic," Dad chided. "Shows up after all the work is done. What a lazy arse."

Darlene gave Dad the finger as she passed him on the porch steps.

Nan brought out her good cutlery. She and Darlene set the table and placed the spoons and knives on folded paper towels. Nan turned on some classical music and sat down at the head of the table.

"Is this enough work to deserve supper?" Darlene asked Dad as she placed the last of the cups on the table.

"I was just saying. Why's she get chowder if she didn't do anything?" Dad turned to Nan.

Angus clung to my arms with inhuman strength when I tried to put him in his own seat, so I settled him on my lap.

"All right," Nan said. She nodded and held her hands out, palms up. No one moved. "Albert, Nick, hold my damn hands. The rest of you hold hands too."

Nan closed her eyes once we all held hands. "Dear Father in heaven above and Kisu'lkw, thank you for blessing us with this wonderful food."

I always wondered how Nan was able to reconcile two disparate deities in her head.

Johnny crossed his eyes at me from across the table. I tried to kick his foot under the table but missed. He stuck out his tongue.

"Or rather," Nan continued, oblivious, "I should say thank you for blessing me with the ability to make such wonderful food. This chowder is particularly delicious, if I do say so myself. Thank you for the good weather. My tomatoes are really coming along wonderfully."

Dad had already finished one roll. Mom kept trying to hold his hand, but he evaded her attempts.

"Thank you for guiding Charlie. Though you really let her take her sweet fucking time, didn't you?"

I choked on air.

Adam put his head down on the table. His shoulders shook.

"I do have one question, dear God above and Kisu'lkw. Why the hell did you let the New Jersey Devils win the playoffs? Albert won't shut up about it. It's really trying my patience. Maybe next year the Penguins could win so I can have some peace and quiet."

Grampa nodded.

Sadie's eyes were half closed, like she was unsure just how much she wanted to commit to praying.

"Thank you, God, for the abundance of blackberries this year, but maybe next year you could be a little less generous. Amen."

"Amen," Johnny said, rather emphatically for someone who'd had his eyes crossed the entire time.

We all started to eat and Dad helped himself to his second portion. The only sound was Nan's classical music and cutlery clanking on porcelain.

ninety-eight

"HI EVERYONE, WELCOME TO ABORIGINAL PEOPLE IN ATLANTIC Canada. This is a new course and I'm really excited to be teaching it." Standing at the front of the classroom I still couldn't believe that I'd gotten the proposal passed to teach this as part of my graduate coursework. I owed Dr. Gamble a pie and a bottle of wine.

"I think it's appropriate to start with a land acknowledgement." I breathed deeply and tried not to pass out. "We are in Mi'kma'ki, the ancestral and unceded territory of the Mi'kmaw people. Can anyone tell me what *unceded* means?" I glanced at the faces in front of me and tried not to make a weird amount of eye contact with any one person.

Silence stretched. I was really hoping someone would answer. I'd sat in this exact classroom and watched many of my prof's questions be met with absolute silence.

"It means the government took it, but the Mi'kmaq didn't give it," someone piped up from the back. A girl who looked a lot like me but younger. She tilted her head so I could see her.

"That's a great summation," I told her. "That's exactly it. In the 1700s, a number of treaties were signed by First Nations and British colonizers in what we now call Atlantic Canada. We refer to those treaties as the Peace and Friendship Treaties. I won't get into the nitty-gritty details now, but of all the things promised and given, land was never one of them. That's not the case for all treaties across Canada, but here, land was never ceded. And it's important to acknowledge that." I was so focused on not letting my voice shake, I wasn't entirely sure what I was saying. I hoped it sounded smart. None of my professors ever looked like they were on the verge of passing out, hopefully I didn't either.

"I'm assuming not all of you are history majors," I continued, "but I think it's important, regardless of major, to understand that history is written by people in power. Yes, history can be uncontestable facts and dates. That's what initially drew me to the subject. Yet as you move through your degree and, to be even more dramatic, your life, I would urge you to consider the perspective and lenses through which these facts and dates are given. Who is deciding what makes it into your history textbook? Who is deciding which statues we erect? Who gets buildings named after them? It's important to think critically about the stories being told and who is telling them."

The rest of my lecture went by without any major issues. I didn't cry. I didn't throw up. No one said mean things to me. We went over the syllabus, a document I had probably spent too much time working on considering no one ever reads them. I encouraged my students to check the syllabus before asking questions about grades and assignments and due dates.

"It's very detailed," I'd said, knowing as they all nodded that they would just ask me anyway.

At the end of the class, as everyone filed out of the room, the girl who'd answered my question earlier stopped in front of me.

"I'm really excited about this class," she told me.

I smiled. "Me too."

ninety-nine

I PULLED INTO THE MUSEUM PARKING LOT AND TURNED OFF THE car. I sat there for a few minutes and stared at the front door. It was coming up on the one-year anniversary and there was a party planned for the weekend. I had taken a step back from helping with the historical society. I'd told Beau it was because I was busy, but really, I was hurt. I never ended up cobbling something together for the shelf; I couldn't bring myself to, knowing it was an afterthought. But last night Beau had called and asked me to stop by after-hours.

I knocked on the locked front door.

"One second," came Beau's muffled reply.

He opened the door wide and stepped aside. "Surprise," he said quietly.

At the far end of the museum, where the altar and pulpit used to be, a mural had been painted on the wall: Glooscap stood between two arched stained-glass windows, throwing clumps of mud and sticks at a giant beaver, creating the Five Islands.

I stopped walking, stunned by the large-scale mural. Beau stood beside me. I didn't look at him. If I did, I might cry. "Did Ray do that?" I asked. I recognized his brushstrokes immediately; his artwork always seemed so alive.

"He did indeed. I cornered your dad at Doug's and he gave me your cousin's number. Come, look." Beau ushered me farther into the museum.

Underneath the mural were display cases filled with pictures and letters and maps, all detailing the presence of the Mi'kmaq on this land for the last five hundred years.

"This should've been here from the beginning. I'm sorry," Beau said.

I looked over everything in the cases one more time. I noticed a typo on one of the placards, but I'd point it out another time; I didn't want Beau to accuse me of ruining the moment.

I turned around and stopped. On the opposite wall, surrounding the front door, was a painted archway of flowers and other plants native to our small part of the world. If I hadn't known better, I would've assumed the mural was watercolour, the plants and flowers delicate and soft. So unlike the artist.

"My mom?"

"And Ray. He asked her if she'd help."

I nodded. I didn't know how to explain to Beau that these murals and the display upon the altar made me feel like I belonged here; like I had a future here in this church-turned-museum.

Beau sighed. "Charlotte, I don't like the way things have been between us. I might not make it to winter, and I don't want to die with you giving me the cold shoulder."

I rolled my eyes. Depending on Beau's mood he might predict his imminent demise or challenge you to a foot race. Clearly, he was leaning toward the macabre today.

"What do you mean?" I asked.

"You didn't point out the typo."

I gasped. "That was on purpose?"

"It was a test, and you failed."

"How did I fail? I was trying to be nice! Not ruin a tender moment."

"You would let me have the one-year anniversary with a spelling mistake on display? The old Charlotte would never."

"What old Charlotte? I'm still the same person I've always been."

"No, you're not." Beau clapped his hands together before I could respond. "See you tomorrow at the party. Maybe come a little early. I have some things that need to be moved around. Now, if you'll excuse me, I have a placard to fix."

one hundred

SOMEWHERE IN THE HOUSE MY MOM WAS CRYING, HER SOBS muffled by the walls between us. I checked her bedroom—empty—and was about to check Angus's old room, now my mom's art studio, when I heard another sob and the shower curtain being flung open.

"Mom?" I knocked on the bathroom door. I gave her a second and then opened it.

She stood on the bathmat wrapped in a huge pink towel, her hair full of suds. Her hand was over her mouth as if she was trying to push the noise she'd just made back in.

"Mom, what is it?"

"That stupid soap."

"What?"

She pointed at Billy's generic body wash. "Every so often I use it instead of my own. Not a lot. Just when it feels too hard to handle."

It was moments like this when I was reminded that my mom was just a person figuring out the world for the first time. Why did we expect so much of mothers? It felt like we were never truly allowed to just be humans.

"And now it's empty. There's none left." She let out another involuntary noise and pressed her hand closer to her mouth.

"Do you remember, the day after we found out about Billy, you asked me if I'd even cried?"

Mom looked at me.

My eyes stung. "Earlier that morning, just after I woke up, I climbed in the bathtub and smelled that body wash. I cried so hard I thought I was going to puke."

Mom shook her head. "I never thought it'd be easy to move on. But I'm always surprised by just how much it hurts," she said. "This feels like his funeral all over again."

We both looked at the bottle of soap. Finding out it was gone seemed like another farewell; it'd been all used up and now we had to say goodbye a little more. My throat burned and I breathed through my nose.

"Wait," she said, "why are you here?"

"I just wanted to drop off some blackberry jelly."

Mom grabbed a piece of toilet paper and dabbed under her eyes. "Want a coffee?"

"Sure. Finish washing your hair. I'll make it."

Mom took a bracing breath and turned the shower back on. She picked up Billy's empty body wash bottle and placed it on the windowsill.

one hundred and one

"KEEP A LOOKOUT FOR SKIPPING ROCKS!" ADAM CALLED AS HE walked down the shoreline, Angus on his shoulders.

The tide was coming in. Tiny waves rushed toward me, broke as they washed over the beach, and fizzled out before they reached my feet. I slipped off my sandals. The week before, the waves had been huge, the bay angry and frothing as Hurricane Juan made its way toward our shores. Our driveway had been blocked by trees and we'd had a near miss with our new chicken coop. We'd just gotten power back after a few days. Fiona still didn't have power in Halifax, and classes had been cancelled all week.

Now, the bay was relatively calm. A handful of fishermen lined one of the lower cliffs. They waited in fold-out chairs, rods in hand, for the tide to reach its highest point. Someone had a radio on, but it was too quiet and too far away to recognize the song.

There was a sliver of mudflat left uncovered. I walked down the pebbled beach and sank my feet into the mud; it squished between my toes and stained my skin. The sole of my foot pressed down on a hidden snail shell.

Fiona had recently come into money of her own after one of her grandparents passed. Now that she wasn't tethered to her parents financially, she and Mac were talking about buying a house. I told her she should buy in Colchester County and she'd said *Over my dead body*. I'd tried not to take it personally.

Adam and I weren't much better off than my parents had been. Angus, and any other children we had, were never going to come into money. Maybe if I became a professor, but that seemed like a long way off.

I stepped farther from the pebbly beach and into the brown water of the bay. The Mi'kmaq called this We'kopekitk, which means "end of the flow."

It occurred to me that this was what we could give Angus. This was his inheritance: red mud between his toes, salty skin, and wind-tangled hair. I wanted him to know how it felt to stand ankle-deep in the water and feel the tide pull him toward the bay. I wanted him to take his first driving lessons on the Londonderry backroads, dust kicked up, clouding the rear-view mirror.

I wanted Angus to recognize the curved highway along the bay, low-lying blueberry fields, and bright, bleeding sunsets and call them home.

Adam skipped a rock. It hopped across the water, leaving ripples in its wake.

Maybe I was being overly romantic. Maybe it actually was all pig shit, bug bites, and nothing to do.

I stepped farther into the bay, the water now mid-calf. I walked till the waves lapped at the hem of my jean shorts. The ebb and flow of the water soothed my tired body, it calmed the tension that had made itself at home in the marrow of my bones. Academia was where I wanted to be, but it made everything so heavy. The material I was studying, the resistance I was met with. Sometimes it felt like the only things that kept me going were righteous indignation and the desperate knowledge that I was creating a path for those who came after me. I closed my eyes and let my body relax. Here, my feet in the water, I didn't have to push against anything. I felt held by the highest tides in the world.

Angus called out from the shoreline. I waved at him and he beamed. I laughed at his toothy smile. Earlier he'd had a temper tantrum when I cut his sandwich the wrong way. Motherhood was a gut punch and a warm hug; it was a cannonball into a frigid, rushing river, only to be warmed by the summer sun a minute later.

I turned back to the bay. Clear across was Noel Shore. Clouds hung low above the sloping green hills on the other side. At night, there would be a dozen twinkling lights from houses that rested along the land's edge. The water between the shores was calm today. If I hadn't been told all my life how dangerous it was, I might've thought I could swim straight across; it looked safe, like it wouldn't swallow me whole if I tried.

"What're you doing?" Adam called out.

The wind pushed my hair toward Adam and Angus and the cliffs that ran jagged along the edge of Highland Village.

I walked back toward the beach.

The water had reached my sandals where I'd left them. The tides moved quickly here. In an hour, the place where I stood would be just another part of the sea. The water lapped at the toe of one sandal, and as the waves receded, pulled the shoe a little closer to the bay. Soon, it would get whisked away. I slipped them on before the tide had a chance to take them.

I picked up sea glass, a long piece of driftwood, and a round rock on my way down the beach.

Adam leaned forward and kissed my forehead. I remembered the feeling of his lips on my hairline, the weight of Angus in my arms, just after I'd given birth. I'd remember it until the day I died. He'd kissed my forehead in his kitchen when we'd been drunk and confused and uncertain. He'd kissed my forehead the night before when I'd gotten my period again and cried because I wasn't pregnant; a hope I hadn't even admitted to myself until that moment.

From his dad's shoulders Angus threw his arms up, reaching toward the sky, and laughed.

"Ready to go home?" Adam asked.

I nodded. We were already there.

acknowledgements

WHEN I SAT DOWN TO WRITE THESE ACKNOWLEDGEMENTS, I realized that I never actually read them when I finish a book. I also learned that my partner always reads them. So, if you're here, if you're like him: thank you for sticking it out to the very end.

So much of writing this book was me in my bed talking to myself. Despite the solitude necessary to write, this story wouldn't exist if it wasn't for the community behind me.

I want to thank my mom for being my first reader, always. Thank you for starting all of your feedback with "it's good…don't cry, but…" To be understood is to be loved. And you understand that I'm always ready and willing to cry. You've read and supported and understood this novel through every iteration. You also understand punctuation in a way my brain won't let me. So thanks for that too. Thank you for showing up to every panel and event I've ever done. I appreciate the chauffeuring and the fact that you pay for parking.

Tim, thank you for reading my asinine poetry in university and deciding you still loved me. Thank you for scratching my back while I sat, hunched over my laptop, muttering to myself about imagined people and plotlines. Thank you for listening to me talk about the same imagined possibilities and problems over and over again (a dead horse hates to see me coming). Thank you for your patience and kindness and willingness to take all four of our kids on adventures away from the house when I desperately needed to write. At the risk of sounding corny (everyone else please look away), this life we've created together is more than I ever thought to hope for, and this book would not exist without your endless support.

I want to thank my kids for napping consistently over the past decade and going to bed at a reasonable hour so I could write this book. Thank you for accepting my paltry offering of boiled hot dogs after I found out my book was getting published because I was incapable of doing anything else and your dad was at the store buying aphid spray (I was truly your one and only hope). Thank you for accepting every mediocre supper I made during the editing process, though I have a sneaking suspicion you might like them more than my elaborate meals. And thank you for assuming that this book is going to make us wildly rich. Though I think that's mostly your attempt at manifesting wealth because I promised you Lego if it ever happened.

I grew up on stories. I ate books for breakfast and cut my teeth on the tales my grandparents would tell. I'm sad that I can't share this with them. Not in the ways I wanted to. They taught me there are lots of ways to tell a story. They handed me so many parts of themselves through stories. They passed down weird anecdotes and mispronounced words, and gave colour and life to ancestors I've never met and places I've never been. I would not be the storyteller I am becoming without them.

To the rest of my family, thank you for always assuming this is where we'd end up. I've wanted to be a writer since I was a little kid, and no one ever told me I couldn't. No one ever said, *that's an impossible dream*, or *maybe you shouldn't major in creative writing*, or *you know that writing is not a lucrative career choice, right?* I'm writing these acknowledgements because of a dream, a shared delusion, and blind support. I wouldn't have gotten here without you all.

Katharine and Emma, who have thrown me parties and celebrated every small success up until this point, thank you for listening to all my unhinged voice notes over the last however many months. Discovering voice notes was the greatest and worst thing that's ever happened to our group chat. I have quite literally forced you to live this entire experience with me, step by step, word by word, whether you wanted to or not. Despite how busy you've been with master's programs, pediatric residencies, cross-country moves, and babies, you have always been there to listen and respond to all of my incredibly mundane thoughts. Without you guys I might've started a podcast.

Erin, thank you for being a home for all my complaints and spirals. For standing on the sidewalk in the cold and listening to me dither and second-guess myself after school drop-off. Thank you for your reassurance that I could do this and that I am a good mom. You say that with such confidence I can't help but believe you.

Mercedes Peters, thank you for letting me pick your brain on what it means to be a young Mi'kmaw woman in academia.

Zeta Paul, thank you for creating a cover that is so beautiful and intricate. I cried when I saw it.

This book has been many things over the past decade. Stephanie Domet held this manuscript's hand when it was an awkward teenager that didn't know what it wanted to be. She did it with such kindness and thoughtfulness that it couldn't possibly do anything other than flourish. In a similar vein, I want to thank the Writers' Federation of Nova Scotia and all its crucial programming. Without the Alistair Macleod Mentorship Program, this book would still be a dream in a .docx file on my computer.

I want to thank Whitney Moran, my editor, for understanding the story I was trying to tell. You changed my life the day you called to tell me you wanted to publish my manuscript. I will be forever embarrassed that I let the call go to voicemail because I thought it was a roofing company I was trying to ghost. Thank you for immediately picking up when I called back. I don't know that my nervous system could've handled it if you hadn't.

And lastly, I want to thank you, the reader, again. When I was seven, I wrote a short story about a Beanie Baby world. My teacher loved it and I've been chasing that high ever since. I hope you love this story too.

Wela'lioq.